tate *of*

orr○w

—

Lar.
Cou
1st i.
Pres

Also by Melinda Salisbury

The Sin Eater's
Daughter

The Sleeping
Prince

The Scarecrow
Queen

The Heart
Collector
and other stories

state *of*

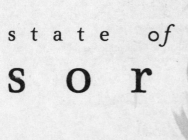

sorrow

MELINDA SALISBURY

■SCHOLASTIC

For my brother, Steven.
I'm so happy I'm in your tribe.

Scholastic Children's Books
An imprint of Scholastic Ltd
Euston House, 24 Eversholt Street, London, NW1 1DB, UK
Registered office: Westfield Road, Southam, Warwickshire, CV47 0RA
SCHOLASTIC and associated logos are trademarks and/or
registered trademarks of Scholastic Inc.

First published in the UK by Scholastic Ltd, 2018

Text copyright © Melinda Salisbury, 2018
Map illustration by Maxime Plasse

The right of Melinda Salisbury to be identified as the
author of this work has been asserted by her.

ISBN 978 1407 18027 4

A CIP catalogue record for this book
is available from the British Library.

Printed by CPI Group (UK) Ltd, Croydon, CR0 4YY
Papers used by Scholastic Children's Books are made
from wood grown in sustainable forests.

3 5 7 9 10 8 6 4 2

This is a work of fiction. Names, characters, places, incidents
and dialogues are products of the author's imagination or are used
fictitiously. Any resemblance to actual people, living or dead,
events or locales is entirely coincidental.

www.scholastic.co.uk

The Humpback Bridge

The Humpback Bridge had stood for almost a millennium, the sole link between the nations of Rhannon and Rhylla. It was an impressive sight; at the bridge's peak it curved over one hundred feet above the River Archior, spanning a vast body of water that flowed aquamarine in summer and gravestone grey in winter.

The bridge was made from starlight, so the stories had it, constructed in a single night by the legendary Rhyllian king Adavere Starwhisperer. They said that Adavere had fallen in love with a Rhannish woman the other side of the river, and sworn he would find a way to reach her. One night he took his Alvus wood violin to the banks of the river and began to play, until the very stars above were listening. Gradually they descended and gathered around him, bespelled by his skill, until the light spilled out of them like tears. And crafty Adavere had worked swiftly to gather up the light with his enchanted bow, fashioning a bridge from the illumination.

The stars had fled back to the heavens before he could finish, so the tale went, which was why the Humpback Bridge had no parapet. Ice-smooth and borderless, the bridge was both architectural marvel and certain death to all but the surest of feet.

And yet, it was the only possible place to sign the Peace Accords between Rhannon and Rhylla. The place the nations joined each other, entered each other, where neither side had the upper hand, or advantage of home territory.

But how could His Excellency, Harun Ventaxis, 104th chancellor of Rhannon, and First Warden of the Heart, be expected to climb it safely?

The Jedenvat – the Rhannish council – insisted that he could not cross it unless some way was found to temper the lethal stone. To which the new chancellor had coldly replied that they had better find a way, and fast. He had much to prove to his people. No bridge, no matter how deadly it was, would prevent that.

Until recently, the republic of Rhannon had been at war with the neighbouring kingdom of Rhylla, and the bridge barricaded and forgotten between them, for no general would even consider trying to send an army over it. Both countries were small, and ought to have been allies, but there were too many differences between the people that led to too many suspicions, fears and prejudices.

The people of Rhannon considered those of Rhylla to be immoral, hedonistic dreamers, while the citizens of Rhylla thought their southern counterparts were unromantic, bureaucratic and stiff. The Rhyllians pitied the Rhannish, and the Rhannish didn't trust the Rhyllians. And that was aside from their fears about the so-called Rhyllian "abilities", fabled to have arrived with the stars the same night the Humpback Bridge was formed.

In fact, war had simmered beneath their collective skins for so long it was almost a relief when it spilled out as blood on to cobbled streets and green fields.

But it kept spilling, and spilling, until fifty years had passed, with no sign of resolution. Citizens of both realms called it the Eternal War, with neither side believing there would ever be a winner.

Until the 103rd chancellor of Rhannon, Reuben "Windsword" Ventaxis, dropped dead during one of his numerous war councils. And just like that, change was, miraculously, in the air.

Well, as far as change ever went in Rhannon, for only the Ventaxis family were allowed to run for election. So the 104th chancellor would be Reuben's only child: his scholarly, sullen son, Harun.

His first act in his new lifetime role as chancellor was, at the recommendation of his mother – now styled the Dowager First Lady – to write to the Rhyllian queen to end the war.

To the relief of both countries, Queen Melisia – who had tried to broker peace with Reuben, and his father before him, no less than thirty times – agreed immediately, ordering her troops to withdraw at once.

That was three months ago; and now Harun was preparing to travel to the bridge. There, at the peak, the Peace Accords would be signed, and the war would be officially, finally over.

Assuming, of course, the problem of the bridge could be solved.

*

It was touch and go, right up until the week before the meeting. The Mason's Guild of Istevar, Rhannon's capital city, had been consulted, cajoled, and the head mason even threatened with imprisonment if he couldn't come up with some way to make their side of the bridge less treacherous. They'd tried scoring the stones with sandpaper, then with saws, but it had no effect; the lack of use and weathering had hardened the stone to a diamond-like state.

In the Summer Palace, on the bank of the Archior some five miles south-west of the bridge, Chancellor Harun paced up and down in his family's private quarters, muttering to himself. His wife, Cerena, rubbing her belly to try to soothe the frantic child within, was exhausted just watching him. Her pregnancy hadn't been easy, her ankles and fingers swollen constantly, the infant restless around the clock. It had been the same with her firstborn son, Mael, and he'd continued to be a hurricane child, never still for a moment.

Mael, who would turn three on the day of the Peace Accord signing, was currently sleeping, and Cerena had hoped for an hour or two of peace, to rest her legs and mind. Her husband, it seemed, had no such needs.

"Harun, you shall wear a hole in the carpet if you continue," Cerena finally snapped.

The chancellor looked down at thick red pile out of reflex, but his rebuke died on his lips. He rushed across the room and gave Cerena the kind of kiss that threatened a third son in her belly before the year was out.

Taken aback, the first lady blushed. "Whatever was that for?"

"Carpets," Harun beamed. "Carpets."

4

*

In Rhylla, on the morning of the meeting, the pewter-eyed prince consort, Caspar, smiled at his wife, Queen Melisia, over breakfast. He waited until the serving staff had left them to their privacy before he spoke, in a voice pitched low and loving.

"All well?"

Melisia's hands moved to her stomach, and she returned her husband's smile. Cerena was not the only one with child, though Melisia and Caspar's pregnancy was still a secret they alone shared. Melisia thought of the child inside her, and how good it was that there would be a peaceful world for her to grow up in.

Her half-brother, Vespus, had pushed her to press on, to defeat the Rhannish while they were in chaos after Reuben Windsword's death, but she'd been glad when the warlord had died and his son had reached out to offer peace. It wasn't cowardice that had made Melisia want peace — the queen herself was an excellent fighter – but the war had gone on for long enough. Now was the time to rebuild, and rejoice. To grow and nurture and create.

"All well, my love," she replied. "All well." She leant across the table, eyes fluttering closed as her lips parted. Caspar moved to meet her in the middle.

An hour before noon, the Rhannish and the Rhyllian leaders approached the Humpback Bridge. It was a midsummer day, the hazy sun already promising higher temperatures to come, the air thick with the scent of jasmine and sandalwood, masking the greenish smell of the water. On each side of the river, young men and women threw flowers into the paths of the nobles as they walked, pink moonstar blossoms on the

Rhyllian side, white windflowers on the Rhannish.

Both parties paused inside the fortified towers on their respective sides of the bridge. At the top of the Rhannish tower, in the stateroom, an aide handed Harun his copy of the treaty. As Cerena fussed with Mael, Harun smoothed his moustache again, blotted a bead of sweat from his temple with a silk handkerchief, and looked down at the scene. On his side the red carpet lay exactly halfway along the bridge. And on the Rhyllian side, it was bare, glittering in the sunlight. Queen Melisia was already in place at the foot, Caspar beside her. How small she looked, Harun thought, from so high up.

A tall Rhyllian man, his hair the same shade of blond as the queen's, dressed in shimmering robes of lilac and green, joined them. As Harun watched, the man stepped forward and raised his hands. From the road beside them vines moved, winding out over the stone, covering it, and when the man gestured earnestly to them the Rhyllian court laughed, loudly enough to reach where Harun stood. Melisia tried to look stern as she rebuked the man and he waved his hands again, commanding the carpet of vines to retreat, but her face was too full of mirth for the frown to take.

Harun, meanwhile, was burning as crimson as his own silken carpet. He looked again at the bridge, the one half carefully covered, and the other still bare and deadly. The Rhyllian queen needed no aid to climb it. . .

"Pull the carpet away," Harun snapped at his advisors.

"Your Excellency?"

"Do it."

With a worried glance Harun's advisors rushed from the room, and Harun watched as they conferred with the guards. Then the carpet was stripped away, to the shocked murmurs of the gathered Rhannish people.

"What is it?" Cerena asked.

"If they can climb with no carpet, I can too," Harun insisted.

"But—"

"I will not be made a fool of by that needle-eared baggage," Harun bellowed.

He stormed from the room, tearing down the stairs and out, the trumpeters stuttering the beginning of the fanfare, so fierce was his haste to get on to the bridge.

As the clocks in both towers simultaneously began to ring the hour, both leaders stepped on to the bridge. It took three steps before Harun's feet began to slide from under him, and he was barely able to right himself. A glance back at his wife showed her displeasure, and he dared not look up to see if Melisia already awaited him at the top. Slowly, bent at the waist to keep from tumbling, he mounted the bridge like a crab to greet his former enemy.

Queen Melisia made no indication she'd seen the carpet rolled away, nor his struggles, allowing Harun his dignity. The Peace Accords were signed, to the cheers of both crowds, and Queen Melisia and Harun clasped each other's forearms in respect, Harun clinging to Melisia as he lost his balance yet again. When Melisia nodded to Caspar to approach, he climbed the bridge, sure-footed as a goat, and waited.

It was clear to all that Cerena would not be able to do the same.

"It's all right," Melisia said in accented Rhannish.

Humiliated, Harun looked at his heavily pregnant wife and made another decision.

Begging Melisia's pardon, he slid and stumbled back down

the bridge and held his arms out for Mael.

"It's too dangerous." Cerena was pale and shrill. When her voice carried, Harun's olive skin flushed again and he snatched his son from his wife.

His face taut with determination, he began the climb back towards the Queen of Rhylla. Mael wriggled in his father's arms, his sobs turning to screeches, and Harun, beyond embarrassed, decided to return Mael to his mother and get as far from the bridge as possible. Harun inched his way down, and Cerena stepped forward, reaching for the child.

Harun slipped.

Cerena lunged for the boy, but Harun twisted, hoping to break Mael's fall with his own body. As Cerena crashed into her husband's back, Harun let go of his son.

Mael made no sound as he tumbled into the aventurine waters of the Archior.

Guard after guard vaulted over the sides after him; the first lady had to be restrained to prevent her from doing the same. Harun turned wide, disbelieving eyes on the retreating backs of Melisia and Caspar, hurrying away from him as though his calamity was contagious.

Harun hauled himself to his feet, stood like the eye of a storm as chaos exploded around him: Rhannish and Rhyllians moving and calling and crying. He was frozen, a statue, his gaze dull and unseeing.

"Your Excellency?" The blond Rhyllian man, the same one who'd summoned the vines, was there, watching him.

Harun turned slowly, as though every inch must be paid for, felt, and borne like a great weight.

"How?" Harun's voice was soft.

"I'm sorry?" The man spoke in lightly accented Rhannish.

"I don't think I understand you."

"How did they cross it? One of your so-called abilities, the ability to cleave to stone? Tell me."

The Rhyllian looked at the collapsed figure of the first lady, the wailing retinue on her side of the river. Below, in the Archior, men were drowning, begging for help that would not come.

Harun, though, was staring at him, his face slack, his hands spread wide.

"Gum," the man said finally. "Not an ability. Just tree sap, on their shoes. It makes them sticky. Gives traction."

Harun nodded. When he descended the bridge, he did so with no problem at all.

The first lady's scream when she was told the body of her son had not been recovered shattered the mirrors in the Great Hall of the Summer Palace, the glass cascading to the floor and lying there, reflecting sunlight all around the room. Harun killed the messenger himself, stabbing him in the throat and then cutting out the tongue that had carried the news.

The windows of the Summer Palace were covered, and the surviving mirrors turned to the wall. Through the palace's grief they all clung to one thought: Mael's baby brother. All hopes rested on the new child, a new Ventaxis son.

She was born a month too soon. And she was born a girl.

Cerena went into labour the night of Mael's disappearance, and it became obvious the baby wouldn't come easily. She laboured a whole day and night, before the midwife finally confirmed the baby was breech and needed to be turned. She tried, and then a nurse tried, but it was no good. The baby wouldn't turn.

9

Cerena was finally rushed by carriage to a small hospital in the North Marches, swearing she was being torn in two. The Dowager First Lady remained by her side, telling her to breathe, commanding her to live. Harun remained at the Summer Palace.

Despite the best efforts of the midwife and nurses at the hospital, the child came out feet first, the cord around her neck, grey-skinned from the lack of oxygen. As Cerena collapsed back against the bed, a battalion of nurses trying to comfort her, the midwife cut the cord but made no move to loosen its death grip on the child's throat, frozen by the terror of what it might mean for her if the baby died.

The lifeless infant was snatched by the Dowager First Lady and hurried away from the careless midwife and heartbroken mother. The midwife did her best to make Cerena comfortable, but the blood wouldn't stop coming, no matter what she did. It seemed that poor Harun was to lose his entire family in just a few short days.

Then the Dowager First Lady appeared in the doorway, holding the babe. Still a little grey, still scrawny, still small. But unmistakably fighting to survive, thin legs kicking frantically.

The same could not be said for the first lady. Too many heartbreaks, too many disappointments. As she lay there, the stink of death in the air, the Dowager First Lady asked her what she would name the baby.

"Sorrow," she'd said. "For that is all she brings us."

PART ONE

Yesterday, upon the stair,
I met a man who wasn't there.
He wasn't there again today,
I wish, I wish he'd go away...

—*William Hughes Mearns*, "Antigonish"

Sorrow

The headache blossomed like a flower inside Sorrow's skull, the agony unfurling petal by petal, until it was everything. She sucked in a deep breath and found the cause of the pain: the thick, sickly reek of Lamentia, creeping in through the open doors.

She turned from the man standing before her and scoured the dim room, watching for ribbons of telltale smoke drifting across it. But there was nothing, no sign of the drug, and a glance at the others there, all politely waiting for their turn to talk to her, showed no one else seemed to have noticed it. She gave a tentative sniff and instantly the skin along her shoulders prickled, her whole body flooding with heat as her head gave a violent throb.

"Miss Ventaxis?" The man, a steward from the West Marches, was staring at Sorrow. "Is everything all right?"

All Sorrow could do was blink, clenching her jaw tightly and praying the nausea died away before she disgraced herself.

"Miss Ventaxis? You really don't look well."

"Can't you...?" Sorrow spoke through gritted teeth. "Can you smell ... anything?"

The steward blinked, then sniffed. "No, Miss Ventaxis," he said slowly. "I don't think so. What kind of smell?"

Sorrow shook her head and took a deep breath, regretting it instantly. She gagged, and the steward gasped.

"Miss Ventaxis! Someone, please—"

"No." Sorrow spoke firmly, holding up a hand. "I just need..." The odour seemed to swell again, and Sorrow abandoned what she was going to say, moving to the doors in three uneasy strides.

She paused just outside her rooms, turning left and right, scanning the passage. There was no one in sight, save the two guards posted by the open doors at the end, and as Sorrow tentatively inhaled, steeling herself against fresh pain, she found the scent was gone. She gulped in lungfuls of clean air, her head falling back with relief as her headache retreated and the churning in her stomach eased.

As she straightened she found a presence at her shoulder, and turned to see Irris Day behind her, eyebrows arched in question.

Sorrow stepped closer. "I thought I could smell Lamentia," she whispered.

"Here?" Irris peered down the corridor, to where the guards were feigning disinterest in the two young women hovering outside Sorrow's parlour. "I can't smell it," she said finally. "Does your head hurt?"

"It did. And I can't smell it any more, either."

"It must be coming from the west wing. . ." Irris's tone was thoughtful.

Both girls turned again to the open doors, and Sorrow was struck by an idea. "I should go and see," she said, trying to conceal her eagerness. "The palace is full of guests. It would be a disaster if any of them came across something they shouldn't. I know your father would. . ." She trailed off as Irris gave her a long look, punctuated by a subtle nod of her head at the people waiting in Sorrow's rooms.

Sorrow's shoulders slumped as she understood her friend's silent message. She was going nowhere yet.

The emissaries and messengers had descended on Sorrow half an hour ago, surprising her and Rasmus Corrigan in the middle of an illegal game of Malice. Sorrow had answered the door and found the dignitaries begging for an audience, forcing Rasmus to hide the board and the pieces beneath the tatty cushions on a moth-eaten sofa, before making his escape.

Sorrow looked back and saw the steward from Prekara shift uncomfortably on the very same sofa, as though she could feel the marble figures concealed beneath her. A swift burst of vindictive glee thrilled Sorrow at the woman's discomfort, before shame doused it. It wasn't the steward's fault she and the other representatives had been sent to Sorrow's rooms. The blame for that lay squarely with Charon Day, the vice chancellor of Rhannon, and Irris's father.

"I'll go," Irris said, in that moment sounding and looking exactly like the vice chancellor. "You have other work to do." She gave Sorrow a consolatory pat on the shoulder and left her.

Envious of her friend's temporary freedom, Sorrow hesitated in the doorway, allowing herself one more moment away from the people waiting for her. She wasn't used to so many being in her rooms, and with the windows perpetually hung with the heavy black drapes, the air was dense and stifling. Even with the internal doors thrown open, the room now smelled of a thousand stale breaths, fresh sweat, and the sourness of despair.

Eau de Rhannon, Sorrow thought, before she could stop herself.

Then she sighed, steeling herself, and returned to the man she'd been speaking to.

"My apologies. What can I do for you?"

"I need to discuss the Decorum Ward in the West Marches—" He fell abruptly silent, hunching his shoulders, head hanging.

Taken aback by his posture, and certain he hadn't finished speaking, Sorrow waited, but the steward said nothing else. "What about them, Mr. . .?"

It was her turn to pause, as she realized she'd forgotten the steward's name. Charon would be furious if he were here. Hastily, she continued. "What about the Decorum Ward?"

He made no reply, and Sorrow noticed then that the silence in the room had changed, becoming thicker, fraught, and that the cause of it – and the reason for steward's sudden submissive state – was behind her.

She turned to find the massive form of Meeren Vine filling the doorway, and instinct made fear scuttle like insect legs over her skin. As though he knew, and he fed on it, Vine seemed to expand, standing taller, seeming broader, his cruel gaze fixed on the steward.

"And what is it you need to say about my men?" The captain of the Decorum Ward's voice was a roll of thunder, rumbling from deep inside his barrel chest.

The steward flinched, and something about the motion tugged at Sorrow, cutting through her own alarm. Vine had no business being in her rooms and she wouldn't have him bullying people. Not here, at least. Here, she was the law.

"Perhaps if you give him a chance to speak, we'll find out," Sorrow said, keeping her voice steady, locking her shaking knees beneath her mourning gown.

Vine stepped forward, using his bulk to crowd her, so she had to look up to see him properly. She forced herself to not lean away, but to stare directly into a face that might have been carved from granite. He had no hair, no beard, nothing to distract attention from his eyes, so dark they might have been black. Shark eyes, unreadable, and unforgiving.

When he remained silent, Sorrow turned back to the steward. "Please. Go on. What do you need to say about the Decorum Ward in the West Marches?"

The steward swallowed. "It's not a complaint," he said hurriedly, eyes flicking to Meeren Vine before returning to meet Sorrow's. "Just, there have been a few ... instances of disruption over recent weeks, and the Decorum Ward say they're already stretched too thin for what they earn. We've told them there is no more money, but it was made clear that wasn't acceptable to the Ward." He said the last in a rush of words, the syllables running together as he forced them out. "That's why I'm here," he said. "To ask for more funds. For them."

He looked again over her shoulder at where Vine still stood, before dropping his gaze to the floor. Sorrow hated having her back to the captain, hated having him in the palace at all. *He should be outside, with the other animals*, she thought. But she kept her expression neutral as she asked, "What kind of 'instances of disruption'?"

"Attacks against them," the steward mumbled.

"Them? You mean the Decorum Ward?" Sorrow wondered for a moment if she'd misunderstood him. "The Decorum Ward are being attacked?"

He confirmed it with a single nod. "It's graffiti . . . mostly. . . And a brick was thrown through the Ward's headquarters, with a note attached, calling them . . . well, nothing pleasant."

"I'm happy to be explicit if he won't, Miss Ventaxis." Behind her Vine leant down, bringing his mouth level with Sorrow's ear. His sharp breath stirred the hairs that had escaped from Sorrow's braid, and she fought to suppress a shudder.

She spoke through gritted teeth as her nails bit into her palms. "That won't be necessary, Captain Vine."

There was much in Rhannon she disliked, but nothing came close to the mixture of fear and hatred her father's Decorum Ward wrought in her. None more violently than their captain.

Only the most thuggish, vicious men and women – those who'd actually mourned the end of the war – had signed up to the newly minted Decorum Ward, following the death of Sorrow's mother, with Vine climbing the ranks fastest of all. Sorrow was too young to remember, but her grandmother had told her how the Ward lined up proudly to receive their work tools: badges showing iron fists over crude hearts, and thick leather batons they wore proudly at their waists, unless they were smacking them menacingly against their own hands, or using them on the people.

Since then they'd prowled the various districts of Rhannon, spying, policing, taxing, and – whenever they decided it was appropriate – doling out punishments. It was their job to make sure no one in Rhannon ever forgot the deaths of Mael and Cerena. That no one behaved as though their every moment wasn't soaked by the loss of the first lady and the Ventaxis heir. That everyone kept their heads bowed, and their mouths shut.

It was no surprise now that the people were rebelling against them. There were only so many times you could kick a dog before it would bite.

And apparently some of the Rhannish people were finally baring their teeth. Sorrow found she liked the thought of it. Good for them.

"It's not just the West Marches," Vine said, and Sorrow turned her head towards him. Happier he had her attention, he sauntered back to the doorway, folding his arms as he leant against the frame, blocking the exit. "There have been incidents in Prekara, and the North Marches too. Graffiti. They call themselves 'the Sons of Rhannon', these vigilantes. There's animal shit –" Sorrow winced at the outraged gasps of some of the others there "– being smeared on the doors of the Wards' homes. Stones thrown when our backs are turned. All them. We've tried appealing to the district senators, but they've done nothing. Say there's nothing they *can* do. That's why I'm here."

"Does Lord Day know about this?" she asked.

"I've sent him word."

"Then I expect he's dealing with it."

Meeren Vine's expression darkened. "That's not good enough, Miss Ventaxis. We're trying to do our job, the job your father told us to do. Collecting his taxes. Keeping his order. We've not had a pay rise in five years and now we're dealing with insubordination and attacks. Surely that counts as an attack against him? What does he have to say about all of this? I want to hear it from him."

"You can talk to me." Sorrow tried to inject some steel into her voice.

"I want the organ grinder, not the monkey."

"Remember to whom you speak," Sorrow snapped, not needing to pretend at steel any more, as she turned fully to face him. "I'm the daughter of the chancellor. I'll *be* the chancellor one day. Don't forget it." She paused, taking a deep breath, forcing herself to sound calm as she said, "Now, if you don't mind, these men and women are waiting to speak to me. Feel free to join them if you have anything else you want to say. In your turn."

His jaw was rigid with outrage, his midnight eyes boring into hers. Sorrow was too aware of the baton hanging from his belt, the size of his large hands, the corded veins that mapped his muscular arms. It felt as though an age passed, before finally he gave an obsequious nod and drew back.

Sorrow kept her shoulders straight, and her chin high, as she deliberately turned away from him to address the room.

"Does anyone wish to speak about something other than the Decorum Ward?"

To her surprise, a single hand rose, and she beckoned the small, neat-looking woman forward.

"Yes?"

"Senator Kaspira has concerns about the Rathbone family again."

Sorrow hadn't expected to ever feel grateful at the mention of the thieves and occasional pirates that plagued the district of Prekara, but right then she'd take them over the Decorum Ward. "I thought they'd gone to ground since Jeraphim Rathbone was jailed," Sorrow said.

"It's his eldest son, Arkady—"

"Oh, sorry, my lovely." Meeren's voice was a loud, oozing drawl as he interrupted. "Am I in your way?"

Sorrow whirled around to see Irris standing beyond the doorway, hidden behind Vine, her lips pressed together tightly. The captain of the Decorum Ward took a tiny step aside and held out an arm as though to welcome her, giving Irris no choice but to attempt slipping past him, or else remain outside. Irris appeared to consider her options, then pressed her body against the door frame and edged into the room. Meeren licked his lips as her arm brushed his stomach, meeting Sorrow's eyes as he did.

"You need to go to your father," Irris said on a breath once she'd reached Sorrow.

Her head gave a throb of agony that had nothing to do with Lamentia then, but everything to do with Harun. "Where's his valet?" she whispered back.

"I've sent him to get some rest. Sorrow, the man was exhausted. I don't think he's slept in days." There was a hint of reproval in her tone. "And Balthasar is with the chancellor."

"Then surely your father should—"

"I went to him first." Irris cut her off. "He told me to send you." She paused. "I'm sorry."

Sorrow had thought her spirits couldn't sink any lower. "It's fine. I'll go right away."

She didn't mean it. And from the look on Irris's face, her friend knew it. But she nodded, allowing Sorrow the lie.

"I'm afraid I have to ask you all to leave," Sorrow announced to the room. "I have some urgent business to attend to. If you write down your complaints, I'll do my best to get to them as soon as I can."

The people began to file out, their expressions a mixture of bewilderment and disappointment, but none protested, meekly doing as she'd asked. Vine remained in the doorway until last.

"Are you OK?" Irris asked her once he'd gone. "What did Vine want?"

"Mostly a good smack," Sorrow murmured, mindful he might be loitering to hear. "So, no, I'm not."

"Can I do anything?"

"Arrange to have me kidnapped by the Svartans and kept there in luxury as a political prisoner until I die?"

"I'll write to them now." Amusement laced Irris's whisper. "Do you want me to stay? Or come with you?"

"No; thank you, though." Sorrow turned to her oldest friend. "I need a few moments alone before I deal with my father, that's all. I'll see you at dinner."

"All right." Irris gave her hand a squeeze and was gone, closing the door behind her.

Sorrow pulled at a loose thread on the hem of her sleeve. She watched as the embroidery began to unravel, feeling a spark of pleasure at the destruction, until a soft sound behind her made her turn.

Despite her command, someone had stayed behind.

Rasmus Corrigan stood by the window, his violet eyes fixed on her.

2

A New Layer of Guilt

He pushed his long pale hair behind gently tapered ears, carefully avoiding the row of silver rings that pierced them lobe to top, and offered Sorrow a faint smile. Like every other person at the palace – in the country – he was dressed in mourning: a long black coat, tight at the waist, flaring over his hips down to his knees; wide legged black trousers beneath; black boots on his feet. The uniform of Rhannon.

But Rasmus was Rhyllian. Where the black brought out the yellow tones in Rhannish skin, it complemented his paler complexion: shadow to moonlight, ink to paper. Even lovely Irris, with her wide eyes and heart-shaped face, could not make the mourning black look as good as Rasmus did.

He watched her, looking as cool and crisp as ever, despite the layers of clothing, and the heat, and Sorrow was painfully aware that by comparison she looked wilted, and more than a little frazzled.

Still, she returned his smile with the ghost of her own, and that was all it took to bring him across the room, moving with impossible grace, to pull her into his arms. She relaxed against him, pressing her face into his chest, instantly feeling calmer.

"I didn't know you'd come back," she said.

"Of course I did."

"You don't think my orders apply to you, then?" she murmured into his shirt.

"You're not my queen."

"I'm not anyone's queen," Sorrow replied.

"As near as, if the line of subjects here petitioning you is anything to go by. And as you said yourself, you will be the chancellor one day. . ." Rasmus said, an edge to his voice.

Sorrow looked up at him. But before she could reply, the pain in her head pulsed, threatening to return, and she grimaced.

"Headache?" he guessed.

Sorrow nodded. "I thought I could smell Lamentia earlier."

He lifted his head, and inhaled. "I can't smell anything."

"No. It's gone now. Or it was never there, and I'm losing my mind."

"We can't have that." He pressed his fingertips lightly against her temples, and the pain faded. "Is that better?"

His touch made her feel lighter, less substantial. "You're good to me," she said quietly.

He traced along her brow bone to the top of her nose, then across her cheek, until his index finger brushed her ear. "What's the point in being able to take away pain if I don't use it?"

She'd joked once that if she'd had an ability it would be

the opposite of his – destroying things, causing pain – and he'd grown quiet, brows drawn together.

"That's not how it works, and you know it," he'd said.

She'd tried to explain it was a joke, of sorts, but he'd shaken his head.

"You shouldn't say things like that." He'd been upset; he wouldn't let her touch him, keeping her at arm's length while he spoke. "You know that's part of how the war began. Because there were stories that my people could use their abilities to hurt."

"Ras, I know—"

"Then don't say it, not even in jest. They're a good thing. They're only used for good. Besides –" his voice had softened then "– you could never hurt anyone."

She'd been too ashamed to argue.

Sorrow was shaken from the memory as his hand moved into her hair, pushing it back, stroking gently. "So, why the need to clear the room? What news did Irris bring?"

"My father. . ." she said, not needing to explain further. Though Charon would have been furious if he'd known just how informed Rasmus was about the chancellor's problems, Sorrow couldn't keep it from him. "And Senator Balthasar has joined the party."

Rasmus gave her a sympathetic look. "Does Lord Day know?"

Sorrow nodded. "Charon thinks I should deal with them. Like Charon thought I should be the one to speak to the people here, despite the fact I have no power, or authority." She leant back and then forward again, resting her forehead on his chest. "Stars, I miss Grandmama. She'd know what to do."

Rasmus reached for her hand, lacing his fingers with hers

and bringing her palm to his lips. "I know. Everyone misses her."

Not quite everyone, Sorrow suspected. In the months before the dowager had died, Sorrow had realized the vice chancellor would never quite meet her grandmother's gaze, and his mouth would pucker sourly when he looked over at her in the dining room. Charon never said a bad word about her, as far as Sorrow knew, but once she saw it, it was clear he didn't like her. Not that it mattered; Sorrow had loved her enough for the whole country.

Absently, Sorrow pressed a hand to her chest. It was the only pain Rasmus had never been able to heal, in a place she hadn't known existed until she lost the only mother figure she'd ever known. And now, she realized, she'd lost so much more than that. She'd lost a teacher and a guide too – someone who both knew what had gone before, and how to govern. If only they'd had more time... More time for everything.

"It should be her here, doing this. No, actually, it should be my father," Sorrow corrected herself. "He should be the one listening to the stewards, and dealing with Meeren Vine. He should be the one making decisions. Not me. I don't know what I'm supposed to do." She leant into his chest, and sighed.

"Right now, you should take a break. Let's run away." Rasmus rested his chin against her forehead as he murmured into her hair. "Irris will help cover for us, I'm sure. We'll pretend your headache has forced you to your sickbed, then we'll sneak out. Dress as servants and steal down to the lake. No one will be around; they'll all be preparing for the memorial tomorrow. We'll avoid the Decorum Ward and relax. We could talk. We *should* talk, Row. You've been avoiding me."

"I have not."

"Don't lie," he said gently. "You're not as subtle as you think. So, make it up to me. Let's escape for a while. We could spend the rest of the afternoon swimming, or fishing. And we can finally talk." He slipped his arms around her.

Stars, it was tempting. To be outside would be such a luxury. Yes, it would be hot there too, but the dry, natural heat of the summer sun. Not the fetid heat of grief and madness, incubated in a palace that hadn't changed at all in almost eighteen years. She imagined sinking into a pool of clear water, pushing her head beneath it and watching her hair float around her. She shivered despite herself, so vivid was the thought of it.

But then he'd talk, and she'd have to listen. Have to hear his futile arguments, have to watch his face fall when she told him he was wrong. Have to hurt him. It was inevitable they'd both get hurt, but there was a difference between her finally telling him they would never, could never be properly together, and circumstances forcing them apart. One was a kinder sort of cruelty.

She shook the thought away.

"I can't, Ras," Sorrow said finally. "You know I can't."

She allowed herself the luxury of his embrace for a moment longer before she freed herself from his arms. He sighed softly as she did, but she ignored it, walking to the window and sweeping the curtains aside, pushing the frame open, relishing the small act of defiance.

She was surprised to find it was raining, for the first time in at least a month. The air that rushed in was crisp, and smelled fresh and earthy, and droplets lashed her face. It made her think again of sinking into a lake or river, and she opened the window as wide as it could go, raising her face to the sky. Lightning flashed, and seconds later thunder followed, the pressure low across her forehead. Perhaps that explained the true reason for the headaches. Not because she'd thought she smelled Lamentia, but the storm.

She let the water run down her face, not bothering to wipe it away, and it scored her cheeks. As she watched her reflection she realized it looked as though she was crying, and it reminded her of something Rasmus had once said about the Winter Palace. The Court of Tears, he'd called it. An entire palace locked in grief and sadness. But it wasn't just the Winter Palace that slumbered like a fairy-tale princess.

Beyond the palace walls the country existed on a knife edge. Artists were not permitted to create art, save for government-sanctioned homages to Mael. Merchants could not stock fripperies – no ribbons, no trinkets, no vases, no flowers. The universities were prohibited from teaching arts subjects. There was no music. No performance. No games.

It was treason to wear anything lighter than dark grey or brown, treason to read books for pleasure, treason to laugh. Pregnant couples were treated with suspicion, and had to take great pains to assure anyone who'd listen that their union was made out of duty, and not in happiness. No one held hands, nor kissed. No one smiled, or at least not where they could be seen. Make-up and perfume were banned; even haircuts were seen as frivolous and vain, sometimes enough to warrant a visit from the Decorum Ward.

Children silently haunted the streets like drab little wraiths, never laughing, never smiling. They were taught from infanthood not to, for fear they'd be caught in a moment of joy when Mael had no more moments.

The Land of Tears would be more apt. All of Rhannon was forced to weep for what was lost.

Rasmus moved behind her and placed a hand on her shoulder, thumb rubbing her collarbone. His skin was cool, pale against her bronzed tone. Each of his elegant fingers had multiple silver rings on it, some at the base of his fingers, some just above the knuckles, the small green and blue stones in them the only colour in the whole room. They lit up when lightning flashed above them, glowing like lights, and spontaneously she kissed the back of his hand, feeling his chest swell against her spine as he smiled, thrilled that she'd done it. He leant down to kiss her neck, and her eyes closed for one delicious moment before she broke the spell.

"I suppose I should go now." She let the drape fall back into place, shutting out the storm, and raised a sleeve to dry her face as she turned to him.

"I suppose you should."

But she didn't move.

"I hate this," she said, so softly she might not have spoken. "I hate all of this. It isn't right. Grandmama told me – even during the Eternal War there was still life. Hope. Art. Music. Growth. People went on holiday to Meridea, and sailed out to the Skae Islands on pleasure cruises. People studied, and started businesses, and invented. Nothing has changed in almost eighteen years, Ras. It's like Rhannon is trapped under glass. Something has to change. Someone has to do something."

"Who? You?" When she didn't reply he asked again. "Who, Row? Your father is a mess, granted, but he's still alive. Right now the only way things will change is if he dies, or you overthrow him. Is that what you want?"

"No. Of course not."

Rasmus watched her carefully. "You know they want you

to," he said slowly. "Why do you think Lord Day sent everyone to you?"

"To help prepare me. To teach me, so when the time comes—"

"He wants it to be now, Row. You'd have his full support if you did choose to depose your father. Sometimes I get the feeling he's waiting for it. Waiting for you to suggest it. Which is why we need to talk, because things are changing, and fast. And it will have an impact on us. We need to be ready—"

"Rasmus." Sorrow moved her hands to his chest and pushed him gently back. "Not now. I have to go."

"Wait. Please, Row."

She paused. He didn't often say please. Rhyllians never did. Nor sorry, nor thank you. Rhylla didn't have a single word that translated to mean the same thing, and in Rhylla the phrases they used instead were potent, Ras had told her. Powerful words that were only spoken when they were truly needed. He said the Rhannish versions were used too freely to fill holes, after goodwill had been dug up, too easily tossed around so that they were all but meaningless. So for him to say "please"...

Her brown eyes met his violet ones. "We will talk. I promise. Just let me get through the next two days. After the memorial ceremony, we'll talk properly."

After a moment he released her wrist, his mouth a line of grudging acceptance.

"I'll see you later?" she asked.

"Ever your servant, Row." He bowed low, taking her hand once more and turning it over to kiss her palm.

She slipped her hand from his, leaving him there, a new layer of guilt coating her old ones like varnish.

3

Lamentia

Sorrow walked through lantern-lit corridors, her footsteps silent on the threadbare carpet, in no hurry to get to her father's apartments. The palace, as always, felt still, as though in the midst of a great sleep, and when she trailed her fingers along the decorative stucco on the wall, thick dust coated the tips, leaving a glaring smear of white in the grey.

As she crossed the landing between the wings, something brushed her cheek, and she lifted a hand to gently catch it. A small spider, ink-black and gleaming, scurried across her palm, and she carefully placed it on the banister, watching it skitter away out of sight.

Sorrow had grown up unafraid of spiders, simply because there would have been no end to her terror if she had been. The neglected Winter Palace was a haven for them.

While her grandmother had been alive she'd tried to keep a

grip on things, fighting dirt and decay in a palace determined to atrophy. But Sorrow hadn't bothered since she'd died, allowing dust and cobwebs to accumulate. What was the point? They did their best to discourage visitors; the guests who'd come to Rhannon for the memorial dinner would be smuggled into the palace via the east wing, straight to the state dining room, and they'd leave the same way the moment the feast was over. The stewards who'd visited her earlier were herded in and out the same way. Though there was room for them all, the suites simply weren't in a fit state for guests. And neither was the chancellor.

Sorrow tried not to leave the east wing, using the rooms there to dine, sleep and work. There, at least, she could make things comfortable; sew up the holes in her hand-me-down furnishings, scavenge cushions from the cavernous storerooms to cover the damage she couldn't mend. She'd found other treasures too, like the Malice board, storybooks and even some old jewellery, though she assumed it was paste, and not real gems. Sometimes at night she'd take them out, trying to imagine where she might wear a ruby the size of a duck egg, or emerald earrings that were so heavy they made her lobes hurt when she tried them on.

In her room she could push back the drapes, and open the windows when there was no one to tell on her. She could smile illegal smiles with Irris and Rasmus, play games, talk about dreams and hopes.

The rest of the Winter Palace felt too big: a mausoleum for the living, where sunlight was banished and the oil lamps were always lit. Where every moment, no matter the hour, felt like the dead of night: those quiet hours when it felt unnatural and strange, dangerous even, to be awake. Sorrow hated to walk the palace, because it made her feel like a ghost, too.

As for her father's quarters, in the west wing, Sorrow avoided them as much as she could, avoided thinking about them if she could help it, unwilling to deal with the tangled mix of guilt and fury that rose whenever she thought of the chancellor. And with good reason.

The moment she crossed the balcony along the central complex of the palace and opened the doors to the west, the sweet reek of Lamentia smoke – real this time – assaulted her nose.

Sorrow raised her sleeve to her face to breathe through the fabric, her headache rallying once more, her mood souring even further.

Almost as soon as she passed through the double doors to her father's reception rooms, she found Balthasar, and the source of the Lamentia reek.

Disappointment flooded her as she looked at the senator for the South Marches. He was a relatively young man, barely in his thirties, handsome, and recently married; Sorrow and her grandmother had attended the subdued ceremony a month before she died. And now here he was, slumped in a chair beside the covered window, a small bone pipe, still smouldering, between his fingers. He'd clearly wasted no time heading here once the meeting of the Jedenvat had finished.

"Senator Balthasar," Sorrow barked.

One bloodshot eye peeled open, looked at her, and then rolled back into his skull. A single tear fell as the lid shut once more. Sorrow closed her own eyes, breathing through her sleeve as she counted slowly to ten, trying to decide what to do with him.

She'd thought him too driven to be so foolish; after all, he'd been shrewd enough to talk his way on to the Jedenvat eighteen months ago after Harun fired his predecessor. He'd done it despite his age, despite having no family ties to the council, and despite being a descendant, albeit distantly, of the royal family the Ventaxises had deposed centuries before. It was no small thing he'd achieved, and Sorrow knew he must have wanted it very badly.

But perhaps that's what led him here – his ambition, right to the inner circle of the chancellor, and his addiction.

For a while, Sorrow hadn't known Lamentia existed, shielded by her grandmother and Charon, for once working together to keep it from her, and the rest of the country. While she'd secreted herself away with Rasmus, they'd been dismissing servants and guards, silencing the Jedenvat, and locking down the palace. Already in the habit of avoiding her father, Sorrow had no idea the headaches she suffered from were triggered by the drug's smoke. She'd been only too happy to stay away from her father's rooms when they'd asked her to.

The truth had been revealed when her father offered her a pipe in the early hours of the morning after his mother had died. At breakfast the dowager had been fine, signing papers and smiling at Sorrow. But by dinner she was bedridden, writhing and sweating, an anxious Sorrow forced to keep away in case her fever was contagious. It wasn't, but it was mortal, and by dawn the dowager was cold, and still, and gone. Sorrow and her father stood beside her bed, alone together for the first time Sorrow could ever recall.

She didn't know what to do, how to be, around this stranger she called "Father", so she'd kept her eyes on the body of the woman who'd been both parents to her. Movement had caught her eye, and she'd looked up to see Harun reaching into a pocket of his robe, pulling out a small ivory pipe, the bowl already packed with something. She watched as he lit it and sucked the mouthpiece greedily, finally exhaling a cloud of smoke that instantly caused a familiar pain to bloom across Sorrow's forehead.

"It's Lamentia. It'll help," Harun had said, tears welling in his eyes as he held the pipe out to her.

"What does it do?" Sorrow watched her father's pupils widen, then contract. "What is Lamentia?"

"It'll help you grieve," he said.

Fear twisted her innards. "Where did you get it?"

Harun had brought the pipe to his lips again, and smoke whispered out of his mouth, drifting towards her.

Sorrow had backed away from him, clutching her head. "I don't want it."

"You need it." The tears spilled down his cheeks. "We all need it. Or we'll forget to miss them." He'd reached out towards his daughter with trembling, stained fingers.

Sorrow had fled straight to Charon, the only adult left she trusted. And he confessed he already knew, and that he and her grandmother had been working to keep Harun's use of it contained. But the insidious grip of Lamentia had tightened on the chancellor, despite Charon and the dowager's efforts to halt it.

And now one of the senators, a man who sat on the Jedenvat council, had taken the pipe Harun must have offered. Fear inched an icy path down Sorrow's spine, obliterating the incessant warmth of the palace, as she realized if he had, then others might follow. And sooner or later, the secret would be out.

*

35

Balthasar moaned as a trickle of blood leaked from his nose, and Sorrow's rage spiked, burning away her revulsion.

Sleeve still covering her nose and mouth, she passed the incapacitated councillor and headed towards her father's private suite. When she saw the guards on the door, she beckoned one of them to follow, leading him back to Balthasar.

"Take him to the cells to sober up. Give him food, water, make him comfortable – not too comfortable," she amended. "He's not to leave until I, or Lord Day, say so."

The guard nodded, and bent to lift the prone man, but Balthasar was too far gone to stand, let alone walk. The guard looked at Sorrow, gave a shrug, and hauled the young senator over his shoulder. Sorrow watched him go, waiting until he was out of sight, before she turned back towards Harun's private rooms, dread squatting like a toad inside her stomach. What state would she find Harun in this time?

Her foot nudged something and she looked down. Balthasar's pipe had fallen to the floor and Sorrow picked it up, examining it. It was beautifully crafted, a mermaid curved around the stem and shank, holding the bowl in her arms, peering coquettishly over the top, back towards the lip. An antique, she realized, something from the days past when artists could create beautiful things for the sake of it. And look what Balthasar had used it for. . .

She dropped it to the floor and stood on it, grinding it under her heel and leaving the pieces on the floor, as she strode towards her father's quarters.

The remaining guard opened the door for her, and she entered the inner sanctum of the chancellor of Rhannon.

The chancellor was alone, prostrate in front of a candle-strewn altar, sprawled beneath a large portrait of a boy with impossibly curled hair curving against tawny cheeks, brown eyes staring soulfully out, a birthmark on the left-hand side of his neck shaped like a moon. Her mother had been born with a mark too, though Sorrow hadn't known it until Charon had told her. In the few portraits that existed of her, the first lady's neck had been covered, as the fashions of the time dictated. As they had remained. Sorrow pulled at her own high collar, before approaching Harun.

"Father," she said softly, kneeling beside him. "I'm here, Father."

The chancellor looked up slowly, dazed, his eyes raking over her. His pupils were pinprick small, and his nose ... his nose was red, and weeping clear fluid. Lamentia frosted his thick beard. Her stomach dropped as understanding knocked her back two full paces. He wasn't smoking it any more. He was inhaling it.

"You stupid, stupid... Father!" Sorrow barked.

At the sound of her voice, his eyes came momentarily into focus, and he looked past her into the room.

"Mael's gone," he said, his voice hoarse.

Sorrow's hands became fists at her sides.

"My son. My heir. Mael. Born and died on the same date. What unkindness is that, to be so exact? How can we bear it?"

Sorrow shook her head and reached for her father's arm, roughly lifting him and half dragging, half guiding him to a chair by the bed. She poured him a glass of water and held it to his lips. "My boy," he murmured, pushing the glass away.

"Drink," Sorrow barked at him.

"I have no desire. Everything tastes of ash. How can I drink, or eat, when my only son is dead?"

Sorrow's mouth tightened. It wasn't grief killing the

chancellor's appetite. "Mael wouldn't want you to starve for him." She tried to soften her voice.

"What would you know of Mael's wants?" The chancellor's glassy eyes were sharp briefly, blazing at her. Then they filmed over with fresh tears and he began to weep once more.

She should be moved by it. Her father's weeping should move her. But she'd seen him weep too often for it to muster any emotion in her, save for resignation, and a low, simmering anger that she did her best to ignore. He was supposed to be their leader. Thanks to Lamentia, the only place he seemed willing to lead them was down a path so dark Sorrow didn't know if Rhannon could ever recover.

Sorrow knew what had happened at the bridge – everyone knew – how Harun had inadvertently saved himself, but damned his son in the process. Sometimes she felt guilty that her life had heralded her mother's death, but Sorrow's guilt was nothing to Harun's. Nothing at all.

His need to atone became a lash of contrition on the back of the kingdom. He'd worked night and day to remain grief-stricken, to punish himself, turning the entire realm into a monument for his lost family.

In the Hall of Remembrance at the Summer Palace, Mael's possessions were on show behind glass cases: the birthday presents he never got to unwrap, his first pair of boots, the blanket he'd been swaddled in as a newborn. His miniature riding whip, a book of stories he'd never learned to read. Pride of place was a tiny coronet, as though he'd been born a prince, and not merely the son of the chancellor. It was so small that Sorrow could wear it like a bangle if she liberated it. One day she might, she thought spitefully. One day she might raze the Hall of Remembrance to the ground.

Sorrow hated her brother sometimes.

But sometimes she envied him too.

Sorrow watched her father give in to weeping, waiting until he was bent double and his body was consumed with sobs before taking the chance to slip a vial from beneath her dress. It was a sleeping potion, nothing more, but necessary to keep him from the powder that controlled him. It was supposed to be for her – she'd never been a good sleeper – but she saved it instead for these occasions, when she had to deal with Harun. She added a few drops to the water glass and held it out to her father again.

"Just a little," she said, taking his shoulder and pulling him up. "A toast, for him."

"He was the best of us," the chancellor said. "It was my fault. My pride... My fault."

"Drink," she said again, ignoring his words. She'd heard them too many times before.

Finally, he opened his mouth and allowed her to drip the water on to his tongue.

With his stomach empty and his body weakened, the sedative acted quickly; his eyelids began to flutter and she lifted him to his feet, her arms around him as he stumbled to the bed. She lowered him down, rolling him on to his back.

He looked up at her, once again a flash of lucidity brightening his eyes. "Why don't you cry for him?" he asked.

Then his eyes closed, his breathing softened, and he was unconscious.

Sorrow straightened and looked around the room, lined with portraits of her brother. Mael aged one, two, and finally three, all painted from his living image. Then afterwards, four, five, six, seven, all the way up to twenty. Mael as a golden child, a gilded youth. Mael as a shining young man, strong-jawed, haughty-eyed.

Unlike his sister, the painted Mael never had an awkward phase; he never had spots, and his hair was never greasy. Each year, a new one was commissioned, imagining how he would look if he still lived, and he was always glorious. The chancellor was supposed to unveil the latest one the following day, after they'd returned from the bridge, and Sorrow was dreading it.

With a start she realized that with Harun unconscious, albeit by her hand, Charon would expect her to lead the mourning feast that very evening. That the people who'd come from across Rhannon, the Jedenvat, the stewards, wardens, landlords, they'd all turn to her to lead them.

Something inside her lurched, as though she was looking down from a great height. If Harun was still incapable tomorrow, she'd have to lead the mourning then too; she'd have to stand on the bridge and face the people, enact the ceremony, and say the words. Because there was no one else. Not any more.

Despite the heat, she shivered, and looked again at the portrait of Mael from last year. He was wearing a high-collared shirt, covering the crescent-shaped birthmark on his neck, hair a shade lighter than hers falling loosely to his shoulders. Sorrow touched her own messy braid, and the painted Mael stared back at her with accusing eyes.

Sorrow had never had her portrait taken. As far as she knew, no one had ever so much as sketched her likeness.

"Why don't I cry? Because I never knew him," Sorrow said quietly as she left the chancellor to his slumber. "Because to me he's always been dead. And I'm alive. I want to live. Not mourn, or wallow. Or even rule. I want a life."

4

Only Rhannon Matters

Six hours later, dressed in a heavy silk mourning gown that stuck to her skin, a pair of small onyx studs in her ears, and her hair newly braided into a crown atop her head, Sorrow sat alone on the platform in the banqueting hall. Though the places beside her were set, the cutlery and plates polished to a dull sheen, the chairs were empty.

Sitting at the head of the room always made her feel vulnerable, too aware that everyone could see her, too aware of the swathe of space to her right and left, leaving her a target in the centre. Soon, all eyes would turn to her and she would have to lead the prayers for Mael, a prospect that made her skin feel too tight, stretched thin over anxious bones. She knew the words she had to say; stars, everyone in the room knew the words. But it was the first time she'd have to say them. Take that role. It was enough to send her hand reaching for her glass.

The heat in the banqueting hall was a living thing, a hundred candles sucking the air from the room while adding to the summer heat searing the palace outside, and sweat pooled beneath her breasts and trickled down her spine from beneath her hair. When she tried to raise her glass to sip the bitter wine, the dress clung to her, making it almost impossible to move and sending her into palpitations at the feeling of confinement. She fought the fabric, and the seam in her armpit gave way as she forced the cup to her mouth. For a moment she was grimly satisfied she'd managed to ruin another of the hated gowns, until she remembered she'd have to mend it later.

It was horrible, unnatural, to have a feast in almost-silence. Although it was how it had always been for her, she knew from books, and Rasmus, but mostly from some instinct, that it wasn't right. There ought to be talking to counter the bone-shuddering scrape of knives and forks against plates. There should be music to mask the sounds of chewing and slurping. Laughter. Flirting. Debating. Even fighting. Instead the dining room was embarrassing: a hundred people, all in black, who must surely want to be somewhere – anywhere – else, instead of sitting playing audience to a concert of each other eating.

Across the room Rasmus sat at the consulate's table, nodding over the bones of the feast with the Rhyllian ambassador, Lincel: the woman Rasmus was officially in Rhannon to aid.

Once, the table had been full of delegates from other lands: representatives from the desert republic of Astria to the east, vast Nyrssea neighbouring Rhylla, Skae with its one thousand islands, and polar Svarta. Sorrow remembered, back when she was a child, when the tall, pale-skinned envoy from the top of the world had given her a sweet that looked like bark, but tasted like salt. She, Irris and Rasmus had taken turns to lick it until it had made them sick and then they'd hidden it in an old vase and forgotten it.

They were long gone now, the other ambassadors, all claiming illness or family problems, returning quietly to their own lands, no replacements ever arriving. With hindsight, Sorrow was glad of it – she couldn't imagine how they'd have kept the world from knowing about Lamentia had Rhannon been full of foreign diplomats. But at the time she'd missed them: their accents, their customs, and their stories. Just the Rhyllian envoys had remained, bound by the Peace Accords to maintain a diplomatic presence in Rhannon, come what may.

She tried to catch Rasmus's eye, but he was absorbed in whatever he and Lincel were discussing. A frown drew his brows together, and Sorrow's expression darkened in response. Rasmus wasn't made for misery, it didn't suit him, and she wanted to go over and rub his forehead until the frown vanished and he was himself again. The moment she had the thought she pushed it away. She shouldn't think like that.

Instead she glanced around, and saw Meeren Vine, sitting on the furthest table with some of his brutes, looking directly at her. Her stomach knotted as she realized he'd been watching her. Waiting, it seemed, because the moment their eyes met he lifted a hunk of meat to his mouth and tore into it, peeling the dry flesh from the bone with his teeth. Sorrow's stomach turned as she forced her gaze away, reaching for her wine glass. She drained it, not protesting when a server appeared and refilled it.

An odd, deliberate cough drew her attention to the table directly below hers on the dais, where it became apparent Irris had been trying to get her attention. When Sorrow finally looked down, Irris tipped her a swift wink before saying something to her father. Then Charon turned to Sorrow, though his expression was the opposite of his daughter's: his brown eyes questioning, his mouth turned down at the corners. Worry, she recognized, as guilt tickled her.

She should have gone to him after seeing her father, instead of seething in her rooms. He'd want to know what happened with Harun, and she ought to have told him what she'd done with Balthasar.

Lord Charon Day was in his late fifties, a decade older than her father, though Harun's drug use had aged him far beyond what nature had done to Charon. He had risen to his role during Reuben's time, succeeding his own uncle as vice chancellor in the last years of the warlord's office. Rumour had it Harun had once intended to replace Charon with his own man. But then Charon had jumped into the Archior after Mael, and when he'd been fished out, alive, but with the bones in his legs smashed beyond repair, Harun had told him his position would await him when he'd recovered. For once, he'd kept his word.

She resolved to talk to him after the meal, tell him everything then. Perhaps he could be persuaded to lead the memorial tomorrow. . .

Almost as soon as she'd thought it, she realized there was more chance of Harun cartwheeling into the hall wearing rainbow-coloured clothes. Charon would insist she took up the mantle. He'd been doing it more and more since her grandmother had died – he'd even handed over the majority of the funeral plans to her. The past four months had been a ceaseless parade of things she had to deal with now – papers to be signed, meetings to attend, protocols to learn – at Charon's insistence. She hadn't realized how much her grandmother had protected her from it all. "Irresponsible", Charon had called it, in a singular show of open criticism when Sorrow revealed she didn't know how the Rhannish tax system worked. And that was only the tip of the iceberg...

As the feast went on, Sorrow eyelids began to droop, the heat, the quiet and the wine lulling her into a daze, and twice her head fell forward, jerking her back into awareness. She picked at the remains of her food, the meat overcooked and chewy, the bread blackened, designed to bring nothing but base sustenance to the eater. Graces forbid she accidentally enjoyed a meal. Rasmus had told her about the bread at his aunt's court, fluffy and steaming, the smell alone enough to draw you to kitchens to beg for a little. Stars, what she wouldn't give just to try it...

The people began to stir, lowering their knives and looking to the dais. Sorrow didn't notice, lost in her thoughts. It was wrong to wish her father dead, though she'd heard him beg for Death to restore his golden son and take his dark daughter instead. Even so, like her hatred for Mael, sometimes the desire to be rid of her father rose like a snake inside her. But she always tamed it, locking it back in a box inside her mind. She'd have to govern if he was gone. Submit her name, and be elected. Take control of Rhannon... Try somehow to repair the shattered land, and people... Be responsible for it all. The people, the land... All on her.

Suddenly even the thought of Rhyllian bread wasn't enough to whet her appetite.

"Sorrow?" She was so lost in her thoughts she hadn't heard Charon approach. He sat in his wheeled chair, looking up at her, the worried expression returned to his face. "I think it's time, Sorrow. It's getting late."

Sorrow dipped her head guiltily, the motion buying her a second to recall herself. From the corner of her eye she saw Charon shake his head as he turned his chair abruptly and wheeled back to his table. When she looked up Rasmus's eyes were gleaming, not with tears but amusement at her distraction. She looked away, rising to her feet, her hands clasped before her.

"My father wanted very much to be with you tonight," she lied, her voice deadened by the endless drapes. "But this night, of all nights, is hard for him. To remember that eighteen years ago, Mael still walked among us, is unbearable for him. For us all. This land has lost much, and is poorer for it. If you would pray with me now."

She paused to allow them time to push away from their tables, for those who were able to kneel on the stone floor, heads bent, hands clasped before them. "Our beloved Grace of Death and Rebirth, we beseech you today to care for Mael, our dearest son."

The speech was a modified version of the one her father, and later her grandmother, used to give, and the words were scored across her brain, and that of everyone there, she could see them now, their lips moving as they mouthed along with her. A woman sitting at the Jedenvat table had covered her face with gloved hands, her chin lowered to her chest, praying.

". . . and we pray that one day soon we will be reunited with him in the kingdom of—"

Before Sorrow could finish a scream rent the air, and everyone turned to the sound.

It was the praying woman, head still bent, clutching at

the hematite beads around her neck, as though they were the cause of her malady.

Everyone around the woman recoiled suddenly, scrambling over benches to get away from her. She turned towards Sorrow, her hands outstretched as though pleading. Her hands were covered in blood. And her eyes ... her eyes...

The woman's eyes were sliding down her face, like the albumen of an egg, blood and pinkish fluid coating her cheeks. Her screams were now silent, her mouth gaping as she continued to tear at her necklace.

Fear wrapped icy fingers around Sorrow's heart as she vaulted over the table, running towards the woman. What was this? Some disease?

But no, as Sorrow got closer she saw the redness around the woman's nose, like it had been around her father's. She saw the small vial that she must have dropped. She hadn't been praying. She'd been taking Lamentia. Inhaling it, as Harun had. And it had done this...

The necklace broke, sending dozens of small, shining dark beads to the ground, the sound like hailstones against the tiles.

"Call a physician." Sorrow's voice was shrill with fear. "Someone do something!" For a moment, no one moved, then two of the guard stepped forward, their faces grey as they edged towards her.

The woman saved them the need to aid her. She took a great gasp that sent those who'd been nearest her tumbling even further back and then she slumped to the floor, spasming briefly before falling unnaturally still.

Immediately everyone in the room froze too, their eyes on the body. Irris stepped forward then, removing the cape from

47

around her shoulders and placing it tenderly over the woman's head. Her movement broke the spell, and Sorrow heard someone begin to sob.

"Return to your lodgings." Charon took charge as Sorrow stared at the now-covered body. "Add your prayers for –" Charon paused, searching for the woman's name "– Alyssa's soul to those for Mael's. Pray for them both."

Alyssa. Charon's words penetrated Sorrow's stunned horror. Balthasar's new wife. So he'd dragged her into his addiction with him. And now she was dead.

The court began to leave, but Sorrow couldn't take her eyes from the covered mound on the floor. She kept seeing Alyssa's empty eye sockets, the remains of them glistening on her cheeks as she collapsed. Irris moved to her side as the room emptied, leaving the two of them and Charon behind. When Irris slipped an arm around her shoulder, Sorrow leant into her friend's touch.

Behind her Charon was now giving orders to the guards. "Remove the body to the infirmary. Find her husband."

"He's in the cells," Sorrow said in a low voice, and Charon turned to her sharply. "I found him earlier when I went to see my father." She paused then, watching the guards lift Alyssa's ruined body and leave with it, waiting until they were out of earshot before she continued. "He'd ... he was under the influence of Lamentia."

"Balthasar? Or the chancellor?"

"Both. I had Balthasar sent to the cells. I didn't know what to do with Father." She immediately imagined Harun as Alyssa had been, tearing at himself, the empty sockets of his eyes as he lay dying in front of his paintings.

Charon took a deep breath, and spoke quietly, mindful of

the people still hovering ghoulishly at the door. "Sorrow, this drug is a disease, and we are losing the fraction of control we have on it. We can't contain this any more, not if people like Balthasar and Alyssa are using it. The Graces know who else might be secretly under its influence."

"I know..."

"Do you? Sorrow, if the people heard about this, if they knew your father – our chancellor – was in the grip of it... If our neighbours found out how weak we are... Astria and Nyrssea particularly might be inclined to try taking advantage of it. You know that. We can't coast on your grandfather's reputation for much longer. Harun is not Reuben Windsword, and frankly we're lucky we've been able to hide it thus far. I fear those days are over. We must act."

Sorrow couldn't speak, managing only to nod her head. She couldn't stop seeing Alyssa... Her hands clawing at her chest, trying to rip her clothes away... Her eyes...

"Father, I don't think now—" Irris began, but Charon silenced her with a look.

"It has to be now."

"What has to be now?" Sorrow asked, her voice colourless as glass.

"It's time to have the chancellor declared unfit to govern and for you to be sworn in, officially, as chancellor presumpt until we can arrange a formal election."

It was enough to shock her from her torpor. "I can't. I can't be the chancellor."

"We can have the Jedenvat pass an emergency addendum that waives the law in light of extreme circumstances and you being the only heir. We'll pass something that says you'll co-preside with the Jedenvat until your twenty-first birthday.

You're eighteen in three days, so the part about residency will be fulfilled."

"That's not what I meant. I didn't mean legally. I meant. . . I can't. . ." Sorrow pleaded with Charon. "Charon, I can't. . ."

"You have to. Sorrow, you must have known this was coming."

She shook her head. Despite what Rasmus had said, she hadn't believed it. Hadn't wanted to.

Charon continued, his tone deliberately soft. "If it had been your father who died tonight, you'd have to take his place. Sooner or later it will be you anyway. This way, we have a fighting chance at helping him. We can find doctors to treat him – maybe it's not too late to save his life. If we act now, we have the advantage. Better that than waiting for the chips to fall and then scrambling to pick them up."

Irris's arm tightened around Sorrow's waist.

"I don't want this," Sorrow murmured.

"It doesn't matter what you want; there is no one else," Charon snapped, before taking a breath. "A woman died before your very eyes tonight. Before the eyes of two Rhyllian representatives and Meeren Vine. If something isn't done, not only will it keep happening, but it will make the entire country vulnerable. I'll call the Jedenvat to order. Tomorrow morning, before we leave for the bridge. We'll vote on it."

Irris's arm tightened around Sorrow, and she was grateful for it. The bones in her legs had turned to liquid, her stomach aching with fear. It was happening too fast . . . she needed a moment to think, to plan. To breathe.

"It should be you," Sorrow looked at Charon. "You should be the chancellor."

"Sorrow, you know the laws. Only a member of the Ventaxis

line can become chancellor."

"I'm not ready," she said finally. "I'm not ready for this."

"Sorrow." Charon's voice was tender then, his dark eyes full of pity. "It doesn't matter. Only Rhannon matters, and there is no one else. It's you, or it's no one."

5

Bad Blood

Irris kept pace with Sorrow as they made their way back to Sorrow's rooms, though neither spoke. The palace, always quiet, now seemed eerily so in the aftermath of Alyssa's death; the only sound was the fluttering of the curtains as the two girls moved past them, the oil lamps guttering in the breeze they created. It was all Sorrow could do not to break into a run, and to keep running, out of the palace, out of Rhannon. Away from this place, and the legacy she didn't want. Not yet. Maybe not ever.

But what choice did she have? Charon was right – there was no one else. Her family had seen to that, centuries ago. They were clever, her ancestors. Manipulative and canny. They'd paid off the nobles who'd survived the initial purge of the royal family – the Mizils, the Blues, the Marchants and others – buying their support with land and titles, and together they'd disposed of, or discredited, those who wouldn't join them.

The time had been ripe for revolution, the nation starving while the royals feasted and feted. When the Ventaxis family and their supporters had risen up and overthrown the king, they'd become heroes. And they'd insisted they wouldn't govern unless legally elected to the post; they didn't want to repeat the mistakes of the monarchy.

They told the people they would get to choose their new leader. Somewhat like the kings, the chosen family would hold office for life, an enduring and stable authority, free from the uncertainties of other countries who changed leaders every five or so years. But – and the Ventaxis family insisted this was the crucial difference – their presence would a democratic one. One the people elected themselves, at the death of each chancellor.

Even though there was only ever one name on the ballot, and it was always a Ventaxis.

The choice, the people were told, was always theirs. And the people lapped it up.

Ironically, Sorrow was the only person who was aware she had no choice in it.

Her chambermaid was in the middle of turning down her bed when she and Irris strode into her apartments. They passed through the sitting room, and into Sorrow's wardrobe and dressing room. The maid followed hurriedly, but Sorrow dismissed her.

When the door closed behind them, she turned to Irris and took a deep breath.

"What happens next?" Sorrow said.

Irris didn't hesitate. "My father will summon the Jedenvat

to a meeting tomorrow, announce there is a Ventaxis successor willing to take over the chancellorship, and then they'll vote on whether the present chancellor is unfit to govern. After that, they'll call you in, give the verdict, and invest you."

Sorrow swallowed. "What if the vote doesn't pass?"

"It will pass," Irris said, offering Sorrow a small, sad smile.

"I don't think I can do this." But even as she spoke, Sorrow knew it was useless. From the moment she'd found her father earlier, she'd known, even if she didn't want to admit it, that she was out of time. That whatever hopes – however pointless, however insubstantial – she'd had for her future, they were over. "I don't *want* to do this," she said instead. "Not yet. It isn't fair. What about what I want? What about. . ." She didn't finish.

Irris gave her a curious look. "What do you want?"

"I don't know, necessarily." Sorrow rubbed her forehead. "But my father was thirty-two when he became chancellor. He was married with a child, he was educated, he'd travelled – he'd been to Meridea, Skae and Nyrssea. I'm seventeen," she said. "There are parts of my own country I've never even *seen*, for the Graces' sake, let alone anywhere else. I don't know the people. How can I be chancellor? I barely know Rhannon."

"So you want to travel?" Irris asked, clearly confused.

"Yes. No. It's not about that." Sorrow paused, trying to find a way to explain the maelstrom of anxiety, anger and sheer terror inside her. "It's one thing to know the storm is coming, but it's another to be caught in it. And now I'm caught in it. For ever."

"Row, I know you're scared. . ."

"I'm not scared. I'm. . ." She paused. "I've been locked up in this . . . this dungeon of a palace my whole life. As of tomorrow, that's all I'll ever have. This palace. This life. At seventeen, that's it. My future decided."

"Sorrow, I know——"

"No, you don't know." Sorrow threw her arms wide, as though gesturing to all of Rhannon. "I've only ever known Rhannon as it is. This *is* Rhannon, for me. No one in their right mind would want to be in charge of this. No one in their right mind would want me in charge of it."

The truth slipped from her before she could stop it, and she turned away, trying to unbutton her gown, her shaking fingers making the task more difficult than it ought to be. "Rhannon is too broken to survive another useless leader." In her haste to get the wretched dress off she pulled one of the buttons free, sending it flying across the room. And in temper she pulled off a second, flinging it after the other. "Damn this dress. Damn everything."

It was too much. The weight of a whole country, on Sorrow's shoulders — a broken, dark country at that. What if Rhannon couldn't heal from what her father had done to it? Some sicknesses went too deep — Harun was the living proof.

Irris reached for her hand. "Sorrow, you have an opportunity anyone else would die for. People have, in the past. You can remake the world how you want it to be. You can make all your dreams come true. You can make everyone's dreams come true. You have that power, it's right there — take it."

"What if I can't?" She couldn't meet Irris's eye as she pulled her hand away. "What if I'm not enough?"

She hadn't been enough for her mother to live for. She hadn't been enough to keep Harun away from Lamentia. How could she do anything except make it worse?

She'd heard the legend of how she'd been named, what her mother had used her dying words to proclaim. It wasn't a name at all, but a threat. *Sorrow is all she brings us.* Wasn't that a sufficient warning to Charon? She was cursed. She *was* a curse.

There were days that she was so full of darkness she couldn't speak in case it spilled from her, coating, ruining, drowning everything she loved. It was inside her sometimes, the same need her father had to destroy, and to self-destruct. The way she had destroyed her mother, and any final hopes that Harun might have recovered. The way she ran to Rasmus, even as she knew she could never give him what he wanted and it would break him. What if she unleashed that on Rhannon? There was no one to depose her. No one to stop her.

"What if I make it worse?" Sorrow said aloud, without meaning to.

"You can't talk like that," Irris warned her. "People will see it as a sign of weakness—"

"I *am* weak," Sorrow bit back at her. "That's what I keep trying to tell you. I'm not strong enough to do this. You're all backing the wrong horse."

"You're the only horse, don't you get it?" Irris finally lost her temper. "Fine. So be it. Let your father carry on as he is. Until he dies, and there's no one to take his place. And then sit back and watch as civil war breaks out, with people like Lord Samad or Balthasar trying to take over. Or when Nyrssea decide to invade, because they've figured out we don't have the money or troops to stop them. Or when Meeren Vine stages a coup and kills us all, before turning the country into a prison state. Is that what you want? Is it?"

"You know I don't," Sorrow said in a low voice.

"And do you think you are the only young woman who's had to step into a role she didn't expect to, and make the best of it?" Irris's eyes blazed. "Put aside her own plans and make do, because it was for the greater good? Remember, Sorrow, I had a life before I came back here. I had plans of my own."

Sorrow hung her head, ashamed. Lost in her own anguish, she had forgotten.

Eighteen months earlier, Irris had been enrolled at the university in Istevar to study conservation. She'd spoken about it as long as Sorrow could remember: her dream of becoming an archivist at the state library, specializing in the old scrolls, the ancient history of Rhannon, before the Ventaxis family and their allies had overthrown the king and taken the country.

She was three weeks into her studies when Harun had dismissed her brother, Arran, and another councillor, Coram Mellwood, from their places on the Jedenvat, due to some imagined slight. Balthasar had taken over from Coram, and Charon had immediately proposed Irris as Arran's replacement. Luckily Harun had accepted.

Irris had stepped into her brother's shoes easily, and Sorrow had been so wrapped up in the new situation with Rasmus that she'd never thought to ask if she regretted what she'd lost.

"I'm sorry," she said. "Irris, I'm so sorry. . ."

"It doesn't matter," Irris said stiffly. "But I get it, Row. I know what you mean. And I agree, it's not fair. A seventeen-year-old should not be shouldering this burden. But . . . what choice do we have? You can fight it, or you can lean into it and make it work. Trust me."

Sorrow nodded sheepishly, and Irris continued. "Your grandmother would want you to do this, you know."

Sorrow almost laughed then, shaking her head. "Would

she? Then why didn't she teach me any of it? She taught me about the old festivals and rites, showed me colours and books and told me tales, but she never taught me about taxes, or office, or anything that would help if this day came. Doesn't that tell you anything?"

Irris sighed. "She was trying to give you a childhood. Didn't you know?" Sorrow looked at her blankly. "She and my father argued about it all the time. He wanted you to start attending meetings and she told him not before you were eighteen. She said she owed you that, at least, and it was worth pawning her retirement if it meant you had some kind of youth. But she had planned, after your birthday, to teach you. And..." Irris paused, taking a deep breath before meeting Sorrow's eye. "She promised my father that if yours hadn't pulled himself together by the time you were twenty-one, she'd have you depose him. I think she'd agree that after tonight, none of us have a choice."

Sorrow was stunned. Was it true? She'd always assumed her grandmother had kept her away from the council because of her mother's dying words. Sorrow hadn't minded, because it's what she believed too – in fact there had been a relief to her beloved grandmother agreeing with her, however unspoken the agreement was. But it wasn't true, according to Irris. Though it explained why the vice chancellor and the dowager disliked each other.

Irris smiled sadly. "Besides, as I keep saying, no one is asking you to do this alone. I'm behind you, my father's behind you. Bayrum Mizil and Tuva Marchant will back you. That's more than half of the Jedenvat. And the rest will fall in line when they realize they stand to profit from it. So, one last time... You can do this. You *will* do this. And you will excel at it."

Sorrow was silent as she finished unbuttoning the gown

and shivered as it fell to the floor, the air temporarily cooling her skin. "Do you really think they'll accept me as the chancellor?" she said, the question declaring a truce.

"Are you joking?" Irris paused. "They'll be delighted. Well, Lord Samad might not be thrilled. Nor Kaspira. And Balthasar won't easily forgive you for locking him up, although losing poor Alyssa will hopefully make him realize how damaging Lamentia is. But what they all value most are their lands and their money. If they think opposing you might ultimately lead to them not being appointed to your Jedenvat, they'll bend over backwards to support you, whether they like you or not."

"I meant the people," Sorrow said. "Not the Jedenvat. I know who my friends are there. Will the people accept it?"

Irris picked up Sorrow's dress and handed it to her. "It will be odd for them, to begin with. Your age, even your sex will concern some, I suppose. But the bright side is anything you do after the last eighteen years is going to be a relief to the vast majority. I think once they realize that you don't mean to govern like your father, they'll be happy."

Sorrow looked down at the garment in her hands.

Back when she was twelve, Sorrow had burst into her grandmother's bedroom unannounced, and found her standing before an uncovered mirror, a sapphire dress held against her body. In fright she'd shouted at Sorrow, then ushered her into the room.

"You can't ever tell anyone," she made her granddaughter promise. "Your father would be very, very angry."

"I won't." Sorrow had reached for the fabric. "It's pretty."

The Dowager First Lady had bundled both Sorrow and the dress into her arms. "One day there will be colours again," she'd said. "This isn't for ever."

Sorrow wanted colours again. Since that day, there had been nights when she had lain sweltering in bed, unable to sleep, and her mind had wandered into the future, a future where she had more control. She'd be lying if she said she hadn't fantasized about having power, even as the reality of it terrified her. She'd imagined a future where she might not have to lie inside a curtained room at the height of summer. A future where sun was allowed to shine through windows. A future where there might be joy in the land once more. As her grandmother had promised.

Sorrow left her friend and entered her wardrobe, crossing to the short railing of formal dresses, all black and austere, and began to thumb through them.

Irris came to stand by her side, her own gaze falling on the clothes before them.

"It would be nice to wear something a little more colourful," Sorrow said.

Irris rubbed her arm gently. "Something really garish, like, I don't know. A dark grey? Maybe even a navy blue. You'd look good in sapphire blue." Irris echoed Sorrow's earlier thoughts. "It'd work well with your skin. I quite fancy pink. Hot pink."

Sorrow tried to imagine what her friend would look like in hot pink. Irris was lovely, with her heart-shaped face, deep brown eyes ringed with masses of dark lashes, a strong nose, a generous mouth. In hot pink she'd be devastating.

"Why are you staring at me? Do I have something in my teeth?" Irris asked, snapping Sorrow out of her imaginings.

"I was thinking how very beautiful you are."

Irris opened her mouth, then closed it, her cheeks flushing a little darker. "Well," she said, smoothing down her own dress to cover her surprise. "You don't have to flirt with me, you know you have my vote."

Despite her mood, Sorrow smiled. "You're right. I'll save it for Samad, then."

Irris gave an unladylike snort. "Indeed. Well. . ." She began to rifle through Sorrow's wardrobe. "For tomorrow. . . Might I recommend something in . . . black?"

"What else?" Sorrow reached for a tunic and matching trousers.

"Why don't I send for some wine, and I'll help you draft some ideas on what we want the new Rhannon to look like?" Irris said.

"We?"

"I said you didn't have to do it alone. I meant it," Irris replied. "Besides, the sooner you're all settled, the sooner I can get back to university."

"You'll leave, once I'm chancellor?" A new surge of panic gripped Sorrow's heart.

Irris's eyes sparkled as she replied. "Well, that all depends on my pay rise."

Sorrow jostled her friend out of the way. "Perhaps I'll make a law that means all students have to wear salmon pink and lemon yellow," she said slyly. "Salmon-pink and lemon-yellow wool."

"You wouldn't dare," Irris said.

"Watch me. If you thought my father was bad, you just wait for the hundred and fifth chancellor."

Hoping her words weren't tempting fate, Sorrow sashayed out of the wardrobe, leaving Irris laughing softly behind her.

But Sorrow couldn't help wishing that Mael had lived. That he was standing where she stood now, facing what she faced.

6

Wants and Needs

The lamps had burned low, and the wine was all gone by the time Irris rose to leave, some two hours later. They'd started out well, talking about disbanding the Decorum Ward, redistributing money back to the universities so they could teach art and literature courses again. Reopening libraries, theatres, dance halls. But they abandoned writing their plans when the ideas got increasingly silly, and Sorrow declared there would be a national cake day, where everyone had to send her cakes.

"You've never even had cake," Irris said.

"It doesn't matter. I already know I love it."

"It is lovely," Irris admitted.

"How do you – oh, of course."

"I'm older than you." Irris smirked. "I had three whole years of cake. And you would love it. *Will* love it."

The clock on the wall gave a soft chime, and Irris

looked up. "I should go. We'll both need to be up very early tomorrow."

The two girls embraced, and Irris left Sorrow humming tunelessly to herself as she prepared for bed. She washed her face and hands, pulled her nightgown over her head and slipped under the sheet.

As soon as she did, the glow from laughing with Irris faded, and fear took its place. This time tomorrow she'd be chancellor presumpt. . . Preparing for an election. . . Responsible for all of Rhannon. . .

Adrenaline forced her out of bed, and into her dressing room. She shoved the endless hangers of black clothes aside, until she found what she was looking for.

There was a hole in the wall the size of a coin, and Sorrow pushed a finger into it, pressing until the hidden mechanism inside released and a section of the wood panelling detached from the rest, revealing a door. The same door Rasmus had used to sneak from her rooms when the stewards had arrived earlier, and the way he'd crept back in after they'd left.

She returned to her bed, picking up the small lamp from beside it, and lit it. Then, in silence, she entered the passageway.

She and Rasmus had found it by accident years ago, before they became more than friends. They'd been messing around in the corridor of the diplomatic wing, mocking a bureau of old artefacts that seemed to have been hidden down there, out of sight of the rest of the palace. Sorrow had reached for a particularly ugly vase, fashioned like a kind of dolphin, but as she'd tried to lift it the bureau shifted instead, revealing a passageway behind it.

They had slipped into it and, holding hands, followed it all the way along until they'd found themselves, to their surprise, in her wardrobe. They'd never discovered the real reason for it, hadn't wanted to ask in case someone blocked it off, though Sorrow fancied it was for some ancient ancestral chancellor to sneak out to see his mistresses. It had made for great fun when they were children, and become even more useful as they'd grown, and things had changed. Not even Irris knew about it.

Moments later she had reached the end, stepping into the corridor where Rasmus's room was.

He was lying on his bed, still fully dressed, reading, when she entered the room without knocking, and he looked up in surprise.

"Row?"

She tugged her nightgown over her head and dropped it, releasing her hair from its crown. Rasmus put down his book and stood.

"Row, what's—" he said, but she gave him no time to talk, tugging at his shirt, unlacing it and yanking it over his head. She pressed into his body, warm and living, and felt a peace begin to spread through her, beneath the wildness of fear and need. She pushed him back on the bed, silencing every word he tried to say, and soon he stopped trying, responding in the way she needed him to. Somewhere beneath the wanting, she knew she wasn't being fair, that she had to tell him what had been decided, and what it meant for them, but she couldn't think of that then.

She reached across to the drawer beside the bed and pulled out a small bag, and he took it from her, emptying the contents into his mouth and chewing, his hands stroking at her the whole while, his rings cold against her rapidly warming skin. When he bent to kiss her, his lips tasted bitter and green,

64

and she licked the flavour away. He made a sound deep in the back of his throat, and she closed her eyes, pulling him against her, into her.

Her hair was damp when they separated, her mouth sore from kissing. He'd curled himself around her, one hand stroking her spine.

"Are you all right?" he asked, and she nodded against his chest.

"Are you?" she murmured.

Above her head he gave a soft snort. "Well ... I suppose so." She could hear the smile in his voice and it made her ache.

The first time she'd seen Rasmus smile, it had terrified her. It wasn't the first smile she'd seen, but it was the first one that was wide, and full, with no guilt or fear behind it. It was so open she hadn't known it for a smile at first.

She was eight years old, as was he, newly arrived there to live with his father, Vespus, the then Rhyllian ambassador, after the death of his mother back home. When he'd found her in the nursery, his face had changed, widening, his eyes narrowing as his lips had parted and he'd bared his teeth at her. She'd punched him in the nose and run from him, her short legs pumping down the corridor as she tried to put as much distance between them as she could. But his legs were longer, he'd grown up on milk and honey and fresh air, and he easily caught up to her in the old ballroom.

"Why did you hit me? Why do you run from me?" he'd asked in halting Rhannish, tucking his fair hair behind pointed ears. She'd remained mute and staring, balled fists ready to hit him again if she needed to. "I only want to be your friend."

He'd raised a hand, long slim fingers pointing towards

the ceiling, and eventually she'd uncurled her own, her pudgy fingers spread like a starfish as she mimicked his stance. He'd pressed his palm to hers, and the feeling sent a spark of something new through her body. Joy, she would realize later, when he gave her the word for it. Peace.

"Now we are friends," the Rhyllian boy said solemnly.

"You won't growl at me any more, then?" she'd asked.

"I never did growl at you."

"You did. Like a dog. But silent."

"I smiled at you. Not growled."

Sorrow shook her head. "You mustn't smile here. It's forbidden."

As though she'd said something funny, the boy smiled again, then clapped his hand over his mouth, violet eyes wide.

Sorrow frowned, chewing her lip, as she came to a decision. "Show me," she'd demanded.

And Rasmus had smiled for her on command.

7

The Jedenvat

Sorrow slipped out once he'd fallen asleep. In the dim light, he looked almost Rhannish. With his ears hidden by his hair, there was no sign of his Rhyllian heritage.

They'd first kissed a little over a year ago. One moment they'd been playing a Rhyllian card game Ras had smuggled to her rooms – she'd complained he was cheating, he'd tried to explain the overly complex rules – and then her mouth was on his, their lips the only parts of them touching in a frozen kiss.

They separated, and laughed, not quite meeting each other's eyes, and continued with the game as though it hadn't happened. And three nights later, Sorrow had found herself kissing him once more, but this time with confidence, curiosity, his hands on her shoulders, hers at his waist. It happened again the next night. Then again. And again, until sliding her arms around his neck and pulling him close when they were alone was almost a reflex. Things might have been different if Lincel hadn't made it clear she didn't need the aid of a fifteen-year-old boy who now spoke Rhannish better than he spoke Rhyllian. And if Irris hadn't been occupied taking over from her brother on the Jedenvat, leaving Sorrow and Rasmus alone more and more.

They had no future – they'd known that all along. Laws had been passed centuries ago forbidding Rhyllian and Rhannish relationships, the price death in both countries. But it wasn't enough to stop them. The fact it was forbidden made it sweeter, another secret, another rebellion, along with laughter, and games, and open windows.

As their relationship deepened, as kisses became much more, Sorrow wanted to know what happened when Adavere Starwhisperer crossed the bridge to Rhannon.

"He married her? The woman he built the bridge for? So Rhannish and Rhyllians could marry once?" Sorrow was shocked when her grandmother told her.

"Well, yes," her grandmother said, rubbing the bridge of her nose. "Quite literally once. Before Adavere built the bridge there were no relations between our people and theirs. It was impossible because of the river. So Adavere and Namyra – the Rhannish woman – were the first. And also the last."

"Why?"

"Adavere had a gift," the dowager continued. "An ability. He claimed it must have come with the stars when he charmed them down. Because after that, his very presence would soothe and calm. Just to be near him would bring a feeling of bliss. But the gift was a double-edged blade, and while it eased away the bad, it also numbed the good. Adavere's gift was especially strong, and it drove Namyra mad in the end. Every emotion she had was taken from her by him, leaving her a shell. She stopped sleeping in their rooms, stopped dining with him, even began hurting herself – anything to feel something. It broke her heart to withdraw from him, but it was the only way she could feel at all. Eventually she packed her things and fled in the night.

"She came back here, to Rhannon, and of course, Adavere came after her. It almost caused a war – in fact, some believe it was this that first created the bad blood between our countries – the abilities, and the power it might give them over us. Finally, after realizing the misery he'd left his bride in, Adavere returned to Rhylla, and passed a law saying relationships between his people and the Rhannish were forbidden, on pain of death. And the then-king of Rhannon made it law here too."

All Sorrow knew of what the Rhyllians called their "abilities", she'd learned from Rasmus. Neither Charon nor her grandmother had ever mentioned that the Rhyllian ambassador and his son could do things she couldn't. He, of course, was able to soothe away pain – a skill she later took advantage of when her monthly courses harassed her. And his father was gifted with plants, able to coax them into growing faster than they might, in places they might not naturally, or to yield more fruit than they would normally.

But this gift of Adavere's sounded different to what Rasmus had told her about his own ability. Dangerous, even. The law made sense to her, in light of that.

Just not sense enough for her to stop kissing Rasmus Corrigan when he lowered his mouth to hers.

Sorrow remembered the story of Adavere and Namyra as she climbed back into her own bed. She'd meant to talk to him after they'd finally sated themselves, to tell him that she was stepping up as chancellor presumpt, and that night had to be the last between them. That from tomorrow she could be his friend, but nothing more.

She tossed and turned for the rest of the night, too many thoughts in her mind to allow her rest. The tentative knocks of her maids at her door were a relief, when they finally came.

"Pardon, Miss Ventaxis, but it'll be dawn in an hour. Your bath is ready."

Sorrow shed the skin of her night-time self and became Miss Ventaxis, daughter of a drug addict and a dead woman, sister to a ghost that would not stop haunting her. And soon, the leader of the land.

Sorrow was bathed and dressed within half an hour, refusing breakfast, her stomach churning too much to contemplate food. Unable to settle to anything, she paced her room, marking the minutes in circuits, until word came from the Round Chamber at precisely seven bells, summoning her to them.

When Sorrow entered the Round Chamber on shaking legs, the Jedenvat were seated at the table in the centre of the room. Someone had brought wine, despite the hour, and they replenished their glasses now, pouring one for her. No servants were permitted inside the Round Chamber, no ambassadors or visitors.

Named for its shape, the Round Chamber had once been a jewel in the Rhannish crown, the walls painted with painstakingly detailed maps of every country on Laethea: Rhannon, Rhylla, Astria, Meridea, Svarta, Nyrssea. The Skae Isles to the north of Nyrssea were rendered so finely that even the fierce water women could be seen frolicking in the grey seas that surrounded them. Whales and sea beasts were painted into the oceans; albino bears dotted the Svartan landscape. Once, a team of five painters had been retained by Sorrow's grandfather, endlessly painting, erasing, then repainting borders as his battles played tug o'war across the lands, claiming then losing ground so fast the landscape of Rhannon changed almost daily.

The paint hadn't dimmed, thanks to the curtained windows. The sea-maids' teeth still glittered in the candlelight; the desert of Astria was still gleaming gold. The only thing that had changed was the scar where the bridge between Rhannon and Rhylla was. Sorrow didn't know who'd done it, but someone had come into the room and hacked at the wall until the bridge was gone, leaving flaking plaster and paint chips in its place. A lifetime of seeing it never dampened the shock whenever she looked at it. Though she knew the reason for the bridge's scouring away, and even understood it, it seemed to her to bode ill – that the only land link between their lands had been destroyed on the map, and no one had thought to repair it. Not even her.

"Welcome, Miss Ventaxis. Please, sit," Charon said.

It chilled her to be addressed so formally by him, and she found herself standing straighter, her shoulders back, in response. When he bade her sit, she moved to the chancellor's seat, her back to the defaced bridge, her empty stomach churning. When she rested her hands on the tabletop she saw they were trembling, and so she folded them into her lap instead.

Charon was sitting to her right, appearing taller than the rest of them thanks to his wheeled chair; beside him was Bayrum Mizil, merchant councilman and warden of the North Marches, the province that held the Humpback Bridge. Bayrum's family had defended the bridge for four generations, and next to Charon and Irris there was no one she trusted more.

To his right sat the sea-grizzled Senator Kaspira of Prekara, allegedly descended from pirates and thieves, and round as the pearls that were harvested from the seas beside her archipelago to the north-east; then Lord Samad, minister of Asha, who looked hewn from the sands of the wild desert county to the south. Then Irris, taking the place of her brother, Arran Day, former senator of the East Marches. After being fired by Harun, Arran had returned to his family seat, keeping a low profile, and Irris had represented their family ever since. Finally Tuva Marchant, senator of the West Marches, bordering Meridea, who'd stepped into power when her husband was killed during the war.

Balthasar's empty seat was like a punched-out tooth between the occupied ones. Sorrow averted her gaze from the gap and took a deep breath as Charon turned to her.

"Miss Ventaxis. This morning the Jedenvat held an emergency meeting to discuss the situation with the chancellor, Harun Ventaxis, 104th chancellor of Rhannon, and First Warden of the Heart. In light of numerous recent events, I, as vice chancellor, moved to pass a motion declaring no confidence in the chancellor, due to his current mental and physical difficulties. The motion passed, with five votes to one, and one in absentia."

Sorrow wondered who'd voted against. Samad, she decided, from the sour look on his face.

Charon continued. "Following this, I moved to pass a motion to invest you as chancellor presumpt, until such time as an election can be held and you can legally be voted into office. This motion was denied by four votes to two, and one in absentia."

Sorrow reeled from the announcement, her emotions changing so fast she didn't know what to feel. Denied? So she wouldn't be chancellor. . . Irris had been wrong. . .

Charon cleared his throat, drawing her attention back to him. "Finally, I moved to pass a motion to invest you as chancellor presumpt, with a codicil granting the Jedenvat the power to preside with you, until such time as you turn twenty-one and can govern alone. The motion passed with a majority of six. The Jedenvat of Rhannon move to depose your father, and invest you as chancellor presumpt."

Sorrow's ears were ringing, and she blinked, hard, trying to collect her thoughts.

Opposite her, Bayrum Mizil and Tuva Marchant were beaming, and beside them Irris was smiling too, and nodding. When Sorrow turned to Charon, he raised his eyebrows expectantly.

She realized they were waiting for her to speak, but her tongue was useless, her brain empty of words.

"So now. . ." she finally managed.

"Now we go to your father, inform him of our decision. Depending on his . . . state, and reaction, we'll decide how to proceed, but the most important thing is that we invest you. Then we can make our way to the bridge."

"Wait," Sorrow said. "I'd like to propose waiting to invest me until tomorrow."

The look of impatience that crossed Charon's face told her he'd expected her to do something like this.

"Sorrow—"

"Today is the eighteenth anniversary of Mael's death," Sorrow said to the room. "It would have been his twenty-first birthday. To do it today would be the height of cruelty. We can surely afford to wait one more day, now the decision is made and we're all agreed?" Then she turned to Charon and spoke in a low voice. "I'm not playing for time; I'll do this. But

I don't want history to remember me as the girl who deposed her father on the anniversary of her brother's death. I want... I want to be better than he is."

Charon gave her a long look, then nodded. "Very well. Tomorrow."

Sorrow pushed back her chair. "Thank you. We should get ready to go to the bridge. I'll go and see if my father is ready." She lifted her glass and drained it in one, leaving the room while she still could.

As she walked to the west wing, climbing the great stair that split the foyer, she tried to sort through her feelings. Oblivious to the guards who opened doors to her, murmuring their sympathies, she saw and heard nothing, save for her own thrumming heart, and the faces of the Jedenvat as Charon had announced that final, vital motion.

No matter what Irris had said, no matter how much fun it had seemed last night, it still felt to her as though the trapdoor had opened, the axe had fallen. Her old life, pathetic as it had been, was over.

Unless...

There was always a chance, she told herself as she approached the west wing, that the spell had broken. Perhaps now, eighteen years later, on the day he would have turned twenty-one, Harun would finally be able to let Mael go. He might be waiting, weak, but determined to see this through. Maybe he could finally heal, and take his place.

The hope died a swift, cruel death when she saw her father's valet outside his doors, wringing his hands as he waited for her.

"Miss Ventaxis..." He paused and looked at her. "I don't

think the chancellor is going to make the ceremony this year. I don't know where it came from, I thought. . ."

She didn't reply, and moved past him, opening the doors herself.

Sorrow found Harun face down in a pile of Lamentia powder. He'd sniffed so much of it he was in a stupor, incoherent and drooping, his eyes streaming tears that were tinged red. Sorrow stared at him, at the mess, and then swept the Lamentia to the floor, creating a toxic cloud that she had to back away from.

The chancellor protested feebly as she destroyed the pile, and she turned on him, her jumble of emotions honing itself into one clear, bright feeling.

"Your son would have been twenty-one today," she leant over and hissed at Harun. "And I'm glad he's dead, because it means he doesn't have to see you like this."

Harun didn't look at her. Instead he laid his head back on the table and closed his eyes.

"Enjoy today, Father. Tomorrow, things will be different."

Without another word she left him there.

"My father won't be joining us," Sorrow said to Charon as she levelled with him in the hall. "And I've changed my mind. Find a clerk now, and have the papers drawn up ready for when we return later. Let's get this over with."

She left him and Irris staring after her as she marched through the doors to the palace, to where her carriage was waiting.

8

The Bridge Again

The journey, from the capital city of Istevar to the bridge in the North Marches, took around four hours, so Sorrow settled in to seethe her way through it. Irris read beside her; Charon sat opposite, going through papers, a rug over his legs, despite the heat.

Sorrow didn't say a word throughout, not even when they changed carriages, her mouth set in a line, her fingers tapping at her thigh until she could climb back into her seat and stew over her father some more. The temperature wasn't helping her mood, either; by midday, under the high sun, the bridge would be unbearable. All traces of yesterday's rain had vanished, sucked down by the greedy earth, leaving the world exactly as it had been before.

Sorrow shuffled to the window and pushed the curtain aside, hoping to entice a breeze into the stuffy carriage. When she couldn't find one, she shot a look at Charon, and, when sure he was absorbed by his work, looked out of the window. The homes they passed appeared abandoned, though she knew they weren't. They all had an air of neglect, evident in the scuffed paintwork, the missing tiles on roofs. Weeds grew in gardens, strangling pathways; fragments of old plant pots jutted out of the soil, and vines crept untempered along the sides of the houses.

The temples were sadder still, the gold paint that once gilded them faded and peeled away, columns crumbling to dust under the relentless sun. Though never overly religious since the fall of the monarchy, the Rhannish had always attended the Graces' temples at holidays, and for personal celebrations, her grandmother had said. But now, of course, there was nothing to be thankful for. Nothing to celebrate. Weddings and funerals took place quietly in homes and were dealt with swiftly and efficiently.

As for the Rhannish themselves...

Her grandmother had told her that once the crowds had thronged these roads during the midwinter and midsummer festivals, even during the war. There had been music and singing, hot wine and cold beer. People had kissed openly, laughed loudly.

The crowd today was thin, and silent. The people were reedy and spare, bones jutting above necklines and in cheeks. They stood stock-still under the sun as though it couldn't burn them, couldn't warm them, watching the procession of carriages with blank faces. Their clothes were shabby and faded, the blacks paled to charcoal, and Sorrow looked down at her own dress, newly dyed and midnight dark. There was no embroidery on the tunics of the people, no onyx and hematite in their ears or at their throats. When Sorrow made eye contact, they held it steadily, offering no sign of greeting, or even acknowledgement. It made her uneasy. She tried to remember the year before; had it been like this then?

Last year her grandmother had led the mourning when Harun had been incapable, though she'd told Sorrow her father was simply ill. Sorrow had stood with Irris and Charon throughout the ceremony. She couldn't remember the people. She realized then she'd never thought of them, at least as anything other than a distant mass. Behind the walls of the Winter Palace, they hadn't felt real to her. Here, today, they felt very real.

She looked back at them, watching the Decorum Ward pacing up and down the streets. And as the crowd turned their eyes on them, the hatred obvious, Sorrow's worries grew. How on Laethea could she fix this?

Charon cleared his throat, and Sorrow leant back, allowing the curtain to fall into place, ashamed of how relieved she was to be hidden from view once more.

"You know what you need to do? At the bridge?" he asked.

"I think so. Step in the gum, take the doll, and climb halfway up. Address the people; Irris will come and remove my veil, so I don't fall off the side. Then I go to the apex, say a final prayer, and throw the doll in."

She hadn't meant to sound flippant, but Irris snorted, and Charon's expression darkened. "Don't toss it in, for the Graces' sake, Sorrow. You need to show some respect."

"I wasn't going to fling it over my shoulder." Charon made to reply, but Sorrow headed him off. "Is everything arranged for when we get back?" she asked, before he could chastise her again.

He nodded. "I sent a bird from the coach stop. The papers will be ready by the time we return. You'll need to sign them, and we shall sign them too. Then they will be sealed, and you will be chancellor presumpt of Rhannon. We'll also prepare the papers to announce your intention to formally run for the chancellorship, and to call for an election three months from now."

Sorrow took a deep breath. "I suppose we'd better send word to Mira in Rhylla, and the other ambassadors in Nyrssea, Astria and so on, to warn them of the change. I'm sure the other rulers and leaders will have questions."

"The falconer has been briefed to select his swiftest birds and make them ready. But, while we're speaking of ambassadors..." Charon began, then frowned, uncharacteristically awkward. "You will need to do something about attaché Corrigan."

Beside Sorrow, Irris stiffened. Sorrow had been unable to keep her relationship with Rasmus a secret from her best friend, despite the danger it put all three of them in. And while Irris didn't approve, she would never have given them away. Irris kept her attention on her book as Sorrow frowned and said, "Why? What has he done?"

"His devotion to you is starting to raise some eyebrows."

"His devotion to me?" Sorrow could feel her skin heating and prayed the vice chancellor wouldn't notice. "I don't think I understand."

"We – that is to say myself and some of the Jedenvat – are concerned that his feelings towards you are no longer platonic. Surely you've noticed the way he looks at you?"

"He's my friend, he cares for me." Sorrow tried, and failed, to sound nonchalant.

"Sorrow, I think there may be more to it than that. He

spends far too much time in your company, in your rooms, neglecting his duties as attaché to the Rhyllian ambassador. It's dangerous. Especially for you, and especially right now. You're about to be sworn in as the chancellor presumpt of Rhannon. There will be scrutiny because of it; people will want to know why. We'll have our work cut out hiding Harun's defects, if we even can; there must be no question of any scandal attached to you too. The law of both Rhannon and Rhylla states clearly that citizens may not become involved with each other. It's treason."

Sorrow shifted in her seat, moving the curtain and peering out of the window once more, pretending to examine the low white cottages they passed. "I know," she said. "But there's nothing like that between us."

It wasn't even really a lie, she told herself, as her mood plummeted further. Once they were back in Istevar later that night, she was going to tell him about the Jedenvat's – her – decision.

"I think you both need reminding he's in Rhannon to do a job on behalf of his queen." Charon looked out of the window too. "He's not ours. He's theirs. You cannot forget that." The carriage slowed to a halt, and Charon sighed. "We're here. It's almost time. Let's talk about it later."

Irris, who'd finally looked up, gripped Sorrow's hand and squeezed. "Are you ready?"

Sorrow nodded.

Irris reached into her bag and pulled out the lace headscarves, draping the first over Sorrow's head and a second over her own. Sorrow knew in every carriage in their train, women would be doing the same. Outside in the streets, the women would be covering their faces, and men would be bowing their heads.

The carriage door opened, and Charon lifted himself across the banquet, closer to it, waiting for an attendant to lift him out and place him in his chair. Once he was settled, he gave his daughter a nod, and Irris reached into her bag one more time to pull out a bundle wrapped in black satin, passing it to Sorrow. And Sorrow unwrapped the glass doll that she would carry to the top of the Humpback Bridge and throw into the river, reenacting how her brother had fallen from her father's arms eighteen years ago.

When Charon gave the signal, she stepped down, cradling the doll, and began the walk to the bridge.

The crowd's attention turned to her in an instant, as they realized it was she, not her father, who would lead the mourning today. The faint hum of restlessness like a wave at the understanding Harun wasn't there at all. She faltered then, almost tripping over her gown. She paused, and cradled the doll in one arm, using her other hand to lift her skirt. The people turned to watch her pass, heads bowing, hands rising to press against chests, over their hearts. In front of them stood a row of the Decorum Ward, each of them holding a weapon. They watched her too, with flat, cold eyes, and beneath her veil her face burned.

Ahead of her, the bridge loomed, tall and blinding in the sunlight, and Sorrow's mouth turned dry as she realized she'd actually have to climb it. Somehow she'd not really focused on this key part of the ceremony, too mired in thoughts of her father, and Rasmus, and Rhannon. Now, with the Humpback Bridge dominating her vision, she could think of nothing else, save how terrifying a task it was. This was where Mael had died, on this bridge, as their father made this same ascent.

It would be so easy to fall.

At the base of the bridge, a tray of gum, donated every year by the Rhyllians, waited, and again Sorrow stiffened, wondering how she'd manage to step in the gum in her long skirts and keep hold of the doll. But then Irris was there, helping her move her skirts so she could take them in one hand before stepping into the tray. Keeping them aloft in one hand and clutching the doll in the other, Sorrow took a deep breath and began to climb.

There was a fleeting moment where, for the first time in her life, she sympathized with Harun. The bridge was so much steeper than she'd thought possible, and even with the gum anchoring her, every step felt treacherous, her body straining forward to try to steady itself. She was all too aware of the lack of barrier on both sides, and her insides turned to liquid, her bones brittle as kindling, as she tried to tamp down the wild fear that she would trip, and hurtle into the water just as her brother had.

She stopped midway to the apex, sweat soaking the back of her gown, and turned slowly to face the crowd.

"I stand here before you on behalf of my father." She raised her voice so it would carry, fixing her gaze on the solid ground behind them. "Eighteen years ago we gathered here to celebrate the end of a war. It should have been the brightest day in our history, and yet, it became our darkest. Not one day has gone by where we haven't felt the loss of our beloved Mael. Today, on the anniversary of his death, we remember him. We—"

A murmur went through the crowd and she lost focus at the unexpected interruption, stumbling over her words.

"We honour—"

The murmuring grew louder.

Peering through the lace to see what disturbed them,

Sorrow saw the crowd looking beyond her, looking up at the bridge. A few were even pointing, pushing their veils back from their eyes. Her gaze lit on Rasmus, further back in the crowd, frowning at something behind her, his expression both joyous and fearful.

Sorrow turned. And froze.

Behind her, a small group of Rhyllians had appeared at the peak of the bridge, right where she would stand to release the doll.

She knew some Rhyllians came to watch the ceremony – that was expected; they were a curious folk – but they never actually climbed the bridge. Never looked down into Rhannon. Now she could see three of them up there, spanning the bridge with none of the fear that gripped her. She didn't recognize the two on the outer edges, so alike they had to be twins: both slender, tall and dark-skinned, their hair braided into neat rows that fell to their shoulders, the female wearing a voluminous dress the same shade of ochre as her brother's tunic and trousers.

But she did know Lord Vespus, Rasmus's father, who stood between them, shining in his green coat. He looked like his son: their hair the same shade of buttery moonlight, violet eyes, bladed cheekbones. Rhyllians aged slowly, the gradual whitening of their hair the only real way to tell they were aging, and Vespus could have been anywhere between thirty and eighty. It was only the hardness of his eyes that made him look old enough to be Rasmus's father.

He'd been kind enough to her when he'd been in Rhannon, always generous when packages arrived from Rhylla, saving some kind of sweet or treat for her, delivered with a sly wink and never mentioned again. But today his mouth was a grim line as he searched the crowd behind her, his eyes clearly seeking someone. It took every ounce of self-control to not turn, but she didn't. She kept her focus on Vespus, so she saw when his gaze stilled and a smirk played about his lips, saw the small nod he gave to the Rhyllian woman beside him. Then she did look around, following the line of his sight until she saw Rasmus, somehow paler than usual as he watched his father.

Panic flooded her, as Charon's words about the obviousness of Rasmus's feelings rushed to the front of her mind. Was that why they were here? Had someone told them they thought Rasmus's behaviour was questionable? Had they come to take him away?

No. It wasn't fair. It was all about to end anyway. It was over, last night was the last time...

She looked at Charon, silently begging for help, and he gripped the wheels of his chair as though to go to her. But he couldn't, and he gazed back helplessly, his eyes imploring her, to do what, she didn't know.

Sorrow was on the verge of descending when she noticed a young woman with an infant in her arms, standing at the front of the crowd. The woman was watching her carefully, though her gaze kept flickering back to the Rhyllians on the bridge. She pulled the child she held a little closer, and looked again at Sorrow. Waiting to see what she'd do, Sorrow realized. They were all watching her, waiting for her response. She wanted to run. Every instinct inside was insisting she run. But she couldn't. Not if she was going to become their chancellor.

She turned her back fully on the Rhyllians, her heart ricocheting inside her chest, and took a deep breath.

"We honour him," Sorrow said. Movement near the carriages caught her attention and her fear grew as Rasmus excused himself, edging closer. With the veil over her eyes she couldn't make it clear to him that he should go. "And we remember him, today, and always," Sorrow finished.

On cue, Irris stepped forward, spilling a little of the gum over the sides of the tray in her haste to climb up to Sorrow. She moved with much more surety than Sorrow had.

She fussed around, lifting the veil from Sorrow's face, buying herself time to whisper. "Are you all right? What should we do?"

"Keep Ras back," Sorrow breathed. "I'm going on."

Irris gave the faintest of nods, and then Sorrow turned and began to climb the bridge.

Vespus and the two other Rhyllians watched her progress, slow but sure-footed as their own people, thanks to the imported gum. She gripped the doll tightly to her chest, where her heart thudded against it, her damp palms threatening to end the ceremony much earlier than planned. Each step felt as though it took a lifetime, until finally she was at the top.

Vespus was mere feet away, watching her, his companions standing sentry either side of him. He smiled at her, the sight familiar and startling as she caught a fleeting glimpse of Rasmus in his face. Then he turned, looking back towards Rhylla, and as Sorrow followed his gaze, her fear exploded into horror.

Hundreds of Rhyllians had come out today, far more than the few she'd seen at the top of the bridge. They crowded the road leading up to the bridge, and it knocked Sorrow dizzy to see so many of them, so many colours, so many faces, smiling, laughing, quietly talking to each other. They turned as one to her, the motion rippling through them like silk in a breeze, until every eye there was on her.

Sorrow gripped the doll as though it was a real child and looked back at Vespus.

"Hello, Miss Ventaxis," he said in Rhannish, his accent more pronounced than it had been when he'd lived in Rhannon. His eyes flickered over her, as though assessing her for market.

"Lord Vespus," Sorrow replied, fighting to keep her voice from shaking. "It's good to see you again."

"And you. It's been – how long – two years since I left Rhannon? You've become a young woman."

"It happens to the best of us."

Vespus laughed and the sound was obscene to Sorrow, given where they stood, and why.

"Is the chancellor not with you?" He craned to see past her, the exaggerated motion causing her to grit her teeth.

"He's unwell."

Vespus's expression was serene. "How terrible. Today of all days. . ."

"Is Ambassador Mira here?" Sorrow asked.

"She too is unwell. Hopefully not suffering the same ailment as the chancellor," Vespus said.

The hairs on the back of her neck rose, as though her body was warning her. She looked at the former ambassador, a man she'd thought of as, if not a friend, then certainly not an enemy. But in that moment, he felt like a threat. Sorrow swallowed her worry. "I think not. My father's ailment has much to do with grief, I feel. After all, he lost his mother four months ago."

Vespus nodded. "Of course. My condolences again to you and yours. I'm sure the chancellor will be back on his feet in no time. And it seems you have plenty of support." He nodded behind her.

Sorrow turned to see Rasmus, now standing with Charon

and Irris. Irris looked furious, trying her best to shoulder Rasmus behind her, though Rasmus's attention was fixed on Sorrow. As she watched, Lincel joined them, saying something to Rasmus that made him try harder to move past Irris.

"I see my son still insists on being by your side, like a faithful puppy."

Sorrow turned back to Vespus. "He's been a good friend to me," she said carefully.

"A good friend," Vespus repeated. "A friend? Surely more to you, after all this time?"

"Of course. Better than a brother." Fear forced the words from Sorrow, as if that lie might save him.

Vespus's mouth twitched, and she knew then that it was too late. Vespus knew about her and Rasmus. Somehow he knew it all. "Better than a brother?" he echoed. "How interesting."

As though he had timed it, the clocks in the towers began to ring out the hour, but Sorrow was frozen, rooted to the spot. She wanted to turn, to race from the bridge, away from Lord Vespus and the rising fear inside her. His sly gaze held her in place even as his two companions descended the bridge, returning to head the throng of Rhyllians on their side. Each toll of the bells felt like a blow, and Sorrow could do nothing but take it, trying to keep her spine from bending.

Then, at the tenth bell, Vespus turned to look down at his companions, nodding, and at some synchronized word from them the rest of the Rhyllians parted down the middle. They moved as one, their brightly coloured clothes flashing, swirling together and confusing Sorrow. The eleventh chime sounded, and she caught sight of movement at the bottom of the bridge. Something not as bright as the Rhyllians but that drew the eye anyway.

As the final peal rang across the river, Sorrow dropped the doll.

It smashed against the diamond-hard surface of the Humpback Bridge and shattered, showering pieces everywhere.

Behind her she heard Rasmus shout her name, heard screams from the crowd, as the echoing ring faded away.

But they couldn't see what she saw.

A boy, standing there, dressed like a Rhyllian in a long coat of kingfisher blue. But bronze-skinned as she was, brown-eyed as she was. Tall. Lean. Smiling.

She knew that face so well. Had seen it staring down at her that morning, as she'd dealt with Harun. Sorrow had watched him grow up on canvas. The whole country had. No one could mistake him for anyone else. Here he was, no longer paint but flesh, and blood, and bone.

"Not better than your real brother, though, surely?" Vespus said, his smile all teeth.

9

An Unwanted Miracle

The fragments of the doll glittered at her feet, crunching beneath her shoes as she took a step back. At the sight of the shattered relic, and the now-motionless Sorrow atop the bridge, the Rhannish people moved like a tide, first surging forward, then ebbing away, crying out, the cries becoming fearful and pained as the Decorum Ward pushed against them with force, barking at them to stay back.

But Sorrow only had eyes for the young man looking up at her from the Rhyllian side of the bridge.

In that moment there was no one else in the world but them. She couldn't tear her gaze from him: his wide lips, slender shoulders, long, lean body. His build was more Rhyllian than Rhannish, more delicate than he'd been painted.

She flinched when he took a step towards her and tried to tell him to stop, to wait, but she still couldn't speak, shock paralysing her. Behind her she heard movement, heard the wet sound of gummed footsteps mounting the bridge, voices calling her name, muted calls and shouts, the orders of guards for people to step back, but still she remained frozen, eyes fixed on the boy before her.

Mael.

For one wild, terrible moment, she smiled, her back to the crowd. He'd returned. Finally everything would be as it should have been all along. She wouldn't have to depose Harun; he'd be fine now his son was home. And Mael was the heir, he'd be the next chancellor, and his return would be what healed Rhannon, and made things change... She wouldn't have to do it any more...

Her smile faded, the feeling of elation vanishing as quickly as it had come.

She had no time to think about why, as the boy took another step up the bridge and the crowd behind her surged again. Sorrow realized if she didn't do something, they'd see him. And if that happened, all hell would break loose. If they tried to climb the bridge... There was no parapet. People would die. Dozens of them.

"You stay back," she said, finding her voice. "Stay there."

He recoiled as though she'd struck him, stilling at once. Sorrow turned away, facing Irris and the guards who were slowly trying to reach her.

"Stop," she commanded. "I'm fine."

Irris looked stunned but did as Sorrow said. The soldiers, however, kept moving.

"Miss Ventaxis—"

"I said I'm fine," she snapped. "Go back down. That's an order."

"Sorrow?" the boy called. His accent was Rhyllian, his voice clear as it rang out. "Are you her?"

Irris and the guards looked beyond her, seeking the source of the voice. They'd heard him.

Sorrow turned, head spinning, hands shaking with fear, and spoke to Irris.

"Keep everyone away from the bridge. No one is allowed anywhere near the bridge. Irris, give orders to Vine to keep his people calm, but make everyone go home. Now."

"Go home? But that's. . ."

"Irris, please?" Sorrow begged.

Irris paused, glancing at Vespus and the two other Rhyllians, who'd been watching the exchange in silence. Finally, she nodded, and motioned the guards to follow. Sorrow waited until they'd reached the bottom before she looked back to where the boy remained, watching her with hungry eyes.

"You don't think you can stop them from seeing him, do you?" Vespus asked softly.

"Lord Vespus, you have to understand. It's too dangerous—"

Before Sorrow could finish she heard Charon command someone to stay back, followed by Rasmus snapping, "She needs me."

"Let him come," Sorrow called suddenly. Maybe Vespus would listen to his son.

He was at her side within a heartbeat, standing so close his shoulder pressed into Sorrow's. He swore vehemently when his gaze found the seemingly Rhannish young man surrounded by Rhyllians below.

"Rasmus," Vespus said, drawing his son's attention from the boy.

"What is this?" he snapped at his father in Rhannish.

"How good to see you too, son," Vespus said. "I trust you're well?"

"I asked you a question, Father. What is the meaning of this? Who is that?"

This time Vespus replied in Rhyllian, too fast for Sorrow to catch the words.

"Impossible," Rasmus said.

Vespus held out a hand and gestured at the boy. "And yet. . ." He returned to Rhannish, looking to Sorrow as he did. "Won't you acknowledge your true brother, Sorrow?"

Sorrow's heart felt as though it was fighting its way out of her chest as she locked eyes with the boy, and a single thought lit up her mind.

This will change everything.

"Come here, Mael," Vespus said.

"No, he stays there." Sorrow snapped out of her trance. "You have to stay there."

The boy hesitated, but at a nod from Vespus continued, climbing the bridge with the ease of a Rhyllian.

"Stop," she pleaded. "You don't understand."

He paused, his expression full of regret, but shook his head and kept walking.

Behind her Sorrow could hear the crowd getting louder, the people of Rhannon dormant and downtrodden for so long now awake and desperate. They were ignoring Charon and Irris, pushing back against the guards, demanding to know what was going on, their need to know greater than their fear.

The Decorum Ward did not like being ignored, and at Meeren's order they began to lash out with their clubs and the hilts of their knives, slamming into the heads and bodies of the citizens closest to them, regardless of sex or age. Sorrow screamed at them to stop, torn between trying to keep Mael back and helping her people. She watched as one of the Ward smashed his club into the face of an old man, blood cascading from his nose, as the crowd roared and pressed against them, their own makeshift weapons in hand. The woman who'd been holding the child was struck and went down, swallowed by the crowd.

"No!" Sorrow screamed again. "I command you to stop."

At first she thought the silence that fell over the crowd was because of her cry, that the people had finally heard and obeyed. Stillness rippled through them as though a spell had been cast; one by one they stopped pushing and shouting, Decorum Ward and citizens alike, staring. But their eyes were fixed on something behind her, and she knew that the boy Vespus claimed was her brother had reached the top of the bridge and was standing there, visible to all.

The sun was behind him, picking out the lighter strands of his hair, creating a halo around him as he held his hands out towards Rhannon. He looked down at the people who were motionless, unable to believe their eyes.

Sorrow was as transfixed as they were, even as horror curdled in her stomach. It was too late. She'd failed. There was a rushing sound as they gasped as one, and then one thousand voices whispered, "Mael?"

The volume rose, and it became a chant, half of the Decorum Ward joining in, the Jedenvat and the nobles climbing back out of their carriages, all turned towards the boy like flowers to the sun.

Sorrow sought Charon, desperate for his help. But the vice chancellor was staring at the boy too, his face ashen. Irris was standing at the base of the bridge, her mouth open.

Beside the boy, Vespus was smiling.

Sorrow turned to Vespus. "Lord Vespus, you have to get him out of here."

"Father..." Rasmus began, but Vespus snapped something at him in Rhyllian, and he closed his mouth mutinously.

"Miss Ventaxis, we need to take him to the chancellor." Vespus's voice softened once more.

Bright white fear gripped Sorrow again as she remembered the state she'd left her father in. The state the Winter Palace was in...

Then she realized it was an unnecessary worry, because they couldn't go there, they'd never make it. She had a vision of them trying to travel through Rhannon towards Istevar, the crowd following them, growing and swelling, engulfing the carriage. The Decorum Ward trying to keep order...

They'd all be torn to pieces by a people desperate for the miracle of Mael.

"Please," she begged Vespus. "It's too dangerous. The crowd... Surely you can see how it will go?"

She turned to where the people were screaming once more. So many hands reaching forward, towards where the boy stood, his wonder now turned to alarm at the sight of the straining crowd.

"She's right," he said, eyes wide. "People will get hurt. Look at them... I didn't know..." He looked at Sorrow. "I didn't think... I'm sorry."

Sorrow shook her head tersely, and looked to Vespus.

"There is an inn, on our side of the bridge, with a garden that overlooks the river." Vespus gestured to his left. "It's called Melisia's, for my half-sister. We can go there for an hour or two to give the crowd time to disperse. Bring Lincel, if you'd be so kind," he added.

Sorrow nodded. "Thank you."

Vespus looked thoughtfully at the crowd. "I'll position a guard on the Rhyllian side of the bridge too," he said. "Deal with your people. We'll wait out of sight. Come." Vespus turned from her, cupping Mael's elbow in his hand.

Halfway down the bridge the boy looked back at Sorrow, apology written across his features.

Sorrow turned away.

Rhylla

As a child, Sorrow had spent hours hiding in some corner of the palace with Rasmus, asking questions about Rhylla, building it in her mind. She'd filed every single word and description away: where the castle was, the roads to get there, where his family's estate was, where the meeting places were. She'd memorized the colours, the scents, the flavours, until his memories of his home were almost her own.

She'd never imagined her first time crossing the border would be like this: her head bowed, heart beating a frantic tattoo against her ribs, hysteria scratching at the edges of her mind like a monster, demanding to be let in, as she fled a crowd that was in serious danger of becoming a mob. The Rhyllians had followed Vespus after he'd left, and she didn't know where they were now; the road was empty of everyone, save her, Charon, Rasmus, Lincel, and the guard Vespus had

96

promised to leave by the bridge. She could hear the Archior rushing somewhere to her right, drowning out the noise from the people, but she saw only the ground as they moved swiftly towards the place Vespus had chosen for their meeting.

In the end, she'd left a pale but determined Irris and the rest of the Jedenvat in charge of keeping the Decorum Ward in order and making sure the crowd were cleared.

"And send a bird to my father's valet to bring him to the Summer Palace," Sorrow said. "The Jedenvat and you need to go there too, as soon as it's safe."

"The Summer Palace?" Irris was confused.

"We can't go to Istevar. Word would spread along the way, and the crowds would be too much, we'd never get there. Besides, the Winter Palace isn't exactly ready for guests."

Irris nodded grimly.

"Tell the steward they're to travel in a plain carriage and keep the curtains drawn. They're not to speak to anyone and no one must know who's inside. I want to be the one to tell my father."

"What about guards with you?"

"I don't want any."

"Sorrow—"

"We'll be fine," Sorrow said firmly, nodding to the crowd down in Rhannon. "It's not the Rhyllian side of the bridge I'm worried about. You need all of them here. Trust me, Rasmus will be there."

She turned to go, but Irris gripped her wrist.

"Is it... It's not him, is it?" Irris stared at Sorrow. "It can't be."

Sorrow was numb. She didn't know if he was the lost boy. Her thoughts from the night before came back to haunt her;

she'd wished he was alive. That he'd stood where she stood, to take her place.

It was as though her wish had brought him back, at the exact moment she needed him. And the thought sent a chill down her spine that she didn't understand. All she knew was that now she wished she could undo the thought, have never had it.

The only practical thing she could think of was getting him away from the bridge, away from the people.

Sorrow stared at her friend. "I expect we'll find out," she said blankly.

They hugged briefly, and Sorrow left her, descending the bridge into Rhylla with Charon's wheeled chair on her back, Charon himself being carried by Rasmus. Sorrow didn't know which of them looked more uncomfortable with the arrangement. Lincel followed behind, appearing to Sorrow as though she wished she were anywhere else.

To Sorrow's surprise, Vespus really had waited for her, standing with the boy and the two Rhyllians who'd first been with him on the bridge, at the beginning of a track that led away from the main road.

"Did you think we'd go back on our word, Lord Vespus?" Sorrow spoke slowly, careful to keep the anxiety from her voice.

"Of course not. I told you we'd wait. We didn't want you to miss the track and follow a wrong path."

"How considerate of you."

Vespus gave a swift, shallow bow and took Mael by the elbow once more, guiding him down the track, the two dark-skinned Rhyllians fanned out behind them in a way that suggested to Sorrow they were Vespus's guard.

This close to the border there was no difference in the

landscapes of Rhylla and Rhannon; the plants were the same, the temperature was the same. So instead of looking around, Sorrow kept her eyes fixed on the boy claiming to be her brother.

As he walked at Vespus's side, Sorrow noticed he walked like a Rhyllian, his arms held still, his back perfectly straight. She looked at the others with them. All of the Rhyllians moved with a grace she found unbearably lovely, despite everything else that was happening. She wondered briefly if any of them had abilities – Lincel didn't, Rasmus had said. But the other two, the twins. . . They might. She knew little of Vespus, but she imagined he'd prefer to surround himself with people he considered special. She was so busy watching them all she didn't see the inn until they were right outside it.

Vespus stopped, and turned to Sorrow. "I assume you'd prefer this conversation happened without an audience?"

Taken aback by the consideration, she nodded.

"Then we'll move out any patrons who might be in there, and tell you when it's clear."

Still herding the boy, he vanished around a corner, the other two Rhyllians following him. Lincel hesitated, as though unsure of whether to stay or follow her people. As she chose, moving decisively after Vespus, a thought struck Sorrow.

"Wait," she called. Lincel halted and half turned towards her. "Did you know?" Sorrow asked her.

"No," Rasmus said at once. "Of course she didn't."

Lincel said nothing and Rasmus's jaw dropped.

Sorrow asked again. "Did you know?"

"I'm not permitted to reveal the confidences of my court," Lincel said finally.

"You knew about this?" Rasmus whirled on Lincel. "How long?"

"I'm not permitted to reveal the confidences of my court," Lincel repeated.

"I am of *your* court. Our queen is my father's half-sister. My aunt," Rasmus exploded.

Lincel didn't reply. She didn't look away from Sorrow, but there was no malice or challenge in her expression. Lincel might have been commenting on the weather. Sorrow made her decision.

"I don't want you in my country any more," she said to the Rhyllian woman. "You won't return with us today. You'll remain in Rhylla. Your belongings will be sent on to you."

Sorrow turned to Rasmus.

"I'm staying in Rhannon," he said before she could speak. "I'll act as interim ambassador until you or my aunt decide otherwise. I'll write to her tonight."

For a moment Sorrow was dumb. It was no small thing he was offering, she knew that, and it wasn't done for the sake of duty. He was doing it for her, declaring where his loyalties lay, and Sorrow's throat tightened as gratitude choked her. A beat too long passed as they locked eyes with each other, until Charon coughed pointedly.

"I'm grateful, Ambassador Corrigan," Sorrow said, her voice deeper than usual. Lincel shrugged, and Sorrow didn't know if it was meant as an apology or not. Not, she decided, as Lincel followed Vespus, leaving the rest of them waiting.

Charon looked at Sorrow. "We need to find out if Mira knew," he said quietly, and Sorrow nodded. If the Rhannish ambassador to Rhylla had known, and not told them, it was treason.

While they waited for Vespus to summon them, Sorrow examined the outside of the inn, trying to focus on that, instead of what might happen within. Like a Rhannish building, it was low to the ground – if she stood beside it on tiptoes she could reach up to touch the edge of the flat roof – though she'd expected that. Ras had said buildings in south Rhylla were very like those in Rhannon; because the weather was largely the same, the south Rhyllians had adopted a lot of their neighbour's architecture and customs. But unlike a Rhannish building, it was *alive*.

The walls were curtained by a thick, flowering plant with star-shaped leaves; only the gold glass windows studding the walls gave Sorrow an occasional glimpse of white plaster around them. Fat, fuzzy bumblebees drifted lazily between ruby-coloured blossoms, their hum low and steady, so different to the vicious, lean insects she freed from her rooms to stop them stinging her. She caught a flash of bright blue – *were the bees here blue?* she wondered – and stepped cautiously closer to see what it was.

"It's a bird!" she said in shock, rearing back as the tiny thing hovered in the air, before it vanished around the same corner Vespus and his cohorts had moved beyond. She turned to Rasmus for confirmation; he nodded.

His eyes were soft as he watched her taking it all in, his mouth fighting a losing battle with a smile.

"All clear," a female voice called, and Sorrow dropped her gaze from Rasmus's, catching the pinched look of anger on Charon's face as she turned to follow Vespus.

She rounded the corner of the building to find the Rhyllian twins waiting outside a round, honey-coloured door, three of the blue birds flitting around the woman as though she were a flower. She offered a friendly smile, which Sorrow was too anxious to return, nodding instead. After a pause, Charon wheeled forward to enter first, Sorrow behind him, helping him tilt the chair to mount the doorstep, and Rasmus at the rear.

All three stopped as the door closed firmly behind them and the Rhyllian woman passed them, heading towards the back of the inn, then disappearing around a corner. When Sorrow turned, she realized the male twin must have remained outside.

It was dark in the inn, compared to the summer brightness, and much cooler. The skin across Sorrow's shoulders prickled, and her senses sharpened. She fisted her hands, relishing the press of her nails against her palms, the pain somehow reassuring.

"This way," Vespus called in Rhannish, from somewhere deeper in the building. Sorrow took a moment more for her eyes to adjust to the softer light, and then began to move towards where Vespus, and the boy, waited.

They weaved around benches and tables made of the same golden wood as the door, polished to a buttery shine; in the centre of each one was a small vase with a red flower, like those on the walls, inside. There were curtains at the windows, red and white check, and the floor beneath Sorrow's feet was a red too, tiled, clicking in a friendly manner under her heel, whispering beneath Charon's wheels. Again her focus wandered, and despite where they were, and why, she wanted to stop and stare, to savour this moment, this place that was like nothing she'd seen before. It looked so *cosy*. So welcoming, as though it existed only to be inviting. And the colours everywhere. Sorrow was dizzy imagining what it might be like further inside the country.

Gentle fingers brushed the base of her spine, and she reached a hand behind her, squeezing Rasmus's hand guiltily, before pulling away as they turned the corner to where Vespus waited.

Shadowed by the sunlight beaming through the window behind him, Vespus sat with his elbows on the table before him, fingers steepled beneath his chin. Lincel was on one side of him, her expression remorseless, the boy on his other. And beside the boy sat the unnamed Rhyllian woman.

"Please, sit." Vespus gestured to the chairs opposite him, and immediately Sorrow's heart began to beat rapidly. Trying to mask her strain with a show of confidence, she reached for a chair, only for Charon to stop her.

"Miss Ventaxis cannot sit with her back exposed to a room," Charon said.

Vespus's reply was smooth and immediate. Too smooth. "Forgive me, I thought it would be easier for you, Lord Day, to not have to navigate a small space with your chair."

Sorrow was familiar enough with politics to know it for what it really was – another power play – and it seemed Charon agreed, for his jaw twitched and he replied, "Very thoughtful of you, but it remains that Miss Ventaxis cannot sit here, and that is my main concern. I assure you I'm more than capable of navigating any space before me." His words were measured but loaded, and a silence bloomed between the men as they considered each other.

"Wait," the boy said, breaking the stalemate. "Let me out?"

Vespus nodded, and the Rhyllian woman stood to allow the boy to step past her. Without warning he lifted the table and swung it around, moving it ninety degrees, leaving Vespus and Lincel now sitting at the head of the table.

"There," he said, smiling at Sorrow. "Now no one has to have their back exposed, and Lord Day can easily fit his chair at the end of the table."

It was a neat and swift solution. Without raising his voice the boy had taken command and, gently and easily, arranged things for everyone. He gestured to her to choose a side, and Charon chose for them, heading to the left. Sorrow followed, slipping behind his chair, to sit in the middle, Rasmus taking his place at her left. All of them placed their hands on the table, keeping them in sight. On the other side, Lincel, Vespus and the boy positioned their chairs opposite the Rhannish. The third Rhyllian slid her chair back beside the boy.

The moment they were all seated, a man appeared carrying a tray full of glasses and a carafe. They all remained silent as he filled each glass with a golden liquid, before melting away as quietly as he'd appeared.

The boy looked at his glass, then at Sorrow, and raised it towards her, a question in it.

Sorrow ignored the toast. "What can I call you?" she asked him.

"Mael," Vespus said. "That's his name."

Sorrow bit her tongue to stop from snapping at him, though her narrowed eyes advertised her annoyance.

The boy – Mael, she supposed she'd better think of him as, at least for now – smiled apologetically at her and pushed his hair behind his ears.

She saw the mark on his neck, a darker patch of skin the shape of a crescent moon, and gasped without meaning to. He paused, his fingers twitching as though he'd tug his hair back over it. But then he gave a slight shake of his head and left it pinned back, leaving the mark on show.

Sorrow had to fight to not look at Charon, though she was sure his attention was on the boy's neck too. On the birthmark everyone knew Mael had.

"And this is Aphora," Vespus continued, drawing her attention back to him, as the Rhyllian woman bowed her head, folding her hands on the table before her.

"Why is she here?" Charon asked.

"I was the one who discovered Mael." She spoke directly to Sorrow, in clear, though heavily accented, Rhannish. "Lord Vespus asked me to come so I could give account direct to your father. My brother, Melakis, was there too. He's outside, watching the door for us."

Sorrow nodded. But before she could tell Aphora to begin, Vespus clapped his hands together.

"If no one objects, I'd like to order some food. We had an early start today and no time for breakfast, and it seems to me we can talk and eat at the same time. I assume you have time?" he asked Sorrow.

She didn't think she could eat. Her stomach felt too small and too stone-like for food. Besides, she didn't want to delay, needing to get to back to Rhannon and see what damage Vespus's actions had caused. "I'm afraid not. I need to be at the Summer Palace to greet my father," Sorrow said.

"So we are not to go to Istevar?" Vespus said.

"The Summer Palace is closer, and it's less dangerous to get there, both for us and my father, given what happened at the bridge. I've already sent word asking him to leave Istevar at once. I expect he's travelling now." She hoped that was true.

"Then by my reckoning we have time for at least two courses." Vespus smiled easily. "Don't worry, Miss Ventaxis, we'll be there in good order. I shouldn't think the chancellor will arrive much before nightfall, whereas we are just a couple of hours away. What do you say?"

The boy – Mael – spoke. "We'd be honoured if you would."

There was nothing to be gained from refusing, she realized. Vespus was right: Harun wouldn't get to the Summer Palace until much later, and if they stayed it would give them more time to hear Mael's story. And examine it. She gave a small nod, ignoring the way his face lit up at the gesture.

Vespus beckoned, and the same server as before, silent-footed and lithe, glided to the table. Sorrow tried to listen without looking interested as Vespus ordered.

"Do you want me to translate?" Rasmus leant over and asked.

Sorrow shook her head.

"Are you all right?" His voice was barely above a whisper, impossible for anyone but her to hear. She nodded, but kept her eyes on Vespus, trying to follow the lilting of his words, trying to avoid the stare of the boy beside him.

The weight of his gaze was like a collar around her neck, choking her. He watched her, and her skin burned in response. Her pulse raced, she felt it in her fingertips where they pressed into the smooth wood of the table. Too fast.

When he finally looked away, she studied him from the corner of her eye. He looked so healthy. She'd never seen a Rhannish person look so well. Most everyone she knew had a pale cast to their bronze skin; very few people went out into the sun, unless they worked under it. This boy looked as though he bathed in it, his skin gleaming, like his neat white teeth.

"He's ordering everything on the menu," Mael said abruptly, startling her from her thoughts. "I don't suppose you've eaten anything Rhyllian before?"

"Of course she has." Rasmus answered for her, his tone challenging. "I used to share the food I was sent with her."

"I was just asking."

"And now you know."

"Rasmus. . ." Vespus broke off from ordering to glare at his son, and Rasmus folded his arms, staring back at him.

"What?"

"Try to show a little courtesy."

"I was civil. He was the one patronizing her."

Vespus spat something at his son, something that caused Rasmus's skin to flush, and even the boy and Aphora looked taken aback. Rasmus abruptly closed his mouth, as the whole table lapsed into strained silence.

Rasmus had taught her Rhyllian, but it had always been conversational – greeting and parting phrases, talking about the weather, food, family members. Rhyllian was less straightforward than Rhannish, no one-word translation for most things – *goodbye* was "when next we meet I will be blessed", and *mother* was "she who grew me beneath her heart". Sorrow had loved the romance of it, but it made following a conversation between native Rhyllians impossible to anyone who hadn't been born to it, or spent a lifetime studying it. It reminded her that she and Charon were at every disadvantage at this table.

The mood was broken by the arrival of the food. And Mael had not lied; Vespus really had ordered everything. The surface of the table was covered: bowls of olives, glistening with oil. Spiky leaves from unknown plants were dotted with bright blossoms and drizzled with something dark and sticky-looking, golden bread woven into knots and braids and sprinkled with seeds. She could smell almonds – mazarine, she realized, the sugar-almond paste Rhylla made for celebrations – and a cheese oozing from its rind, pungent and almost-sour. There were pears, tomatoes, plums, figs, dates, flaking pastries dotted with green nuts and dripping syrup.

"Eat," Vespus insisted, and began to serve himself, Lincel and Aphora following immediately.

Sorrow didn't know where to begin, staring helplessly at the food.

"The summer pears are especially good," Mael said, holding one out to her.

Sorrow shook her head, grabbing a plum and a handful of dates before he could say anything else. Aware his eyes – all eyes – were on her, she pushed a date between her lips and bit down.

The flavour exploded in her mouth, impossibly sweet, chewy and soft, and she raised her hands to her face, convinced she'd have to spit it out because it was too much.

"Tasty, aren't they?" Vespus said, holding the apple like an orb.

She nodded, and forced the mouthful down her throat. Without allowing herself time to think she took a bite of her plum. It was the opposite of the date; tartly sour and succulent, the antidote to the sweetness that she needed. She took a second bite, a third, a fourth. Soon she was gnawing at the stone in the centre; there was plum-flesh caught between her teeth, juice sticky on her chin.

She wanted more. Suddenly ravenous, she reached for one of the loaves and tore some off, using it to scoop up some of the cheese, taking her knife and smearing it across the bread. She followed that with a handful of olives, the stone at the centre a surprise that temporarily made her think she'd cracked a tooth. She devoured handfuls of the tiny, succulent tomatoes;

plucked more dates from the pile, ready for their sweetness now; sliced a fig into quarters and ate it, skin and all, then another with more of the cheese. She ate with her hands, they all did, reaching out to take and grasp, using their plates for discarded stones and seeds and pits, using knives only when fingers wouldn't suffice.

Rasmus alone didn't touch the food, but Sorrow was barely aware of it, barely aware of anything except the feast before her, her worries and fears buried by the food. As Rasmus sat back in his chair, upright and stiff, sipping water from a tumbler, she and the others filled their bellies, drinking deep draughts of a sharp wine that tasted like sunshine.

"Shall I bring more, my lord?" The server had reappeared and addressed Vespus, and Sorrow realized they'd almost finished the food.

She sat back, dazed, looking at the remains of the feast. Only some of the fruit and the sleek slab of mazarine remained. They'd devoured it all.

Vespus glanced around the table, then shook his head. "No. Leave what remains, and bring coffee. That will do."

The server nodded, and began to stack the empty platters before taking them away.

"How did you enjoy your meal?" Vespus licked his fingers as he looked at Sorrow.

"It was delicious," Sorrow said honestly. It *was* delicious. Even now, with a painfully full stomach, she itched to reach for the golden peach that still remained. She wanted to split it open, eat half as it was and the other half piled high with mazarine. Everything here tasted extraordinary, she didn't think she could ever tire of such food, hadn't known it could be this good.

She sat back, frightened by the strength of her need, reaching instead for her water tumbler and taking a long drink. Even the water tasted better here, crisp and light and somehow *cleaner* than Rhannish water. She'd never known before that water had a flavour.

"There's something ancient and honourable about breaking bread with friends," said Vespus. "And your country showed me hospitality for a time. It is good that I've been able to repay that. To your health." He raised his wine glass. "To you both." He tilted the glass to Mael, then drank deeply.

The server returned with an odd silver pot and seven tiny cups, pouring a thick dark liquid into each one. The drink smelled warm, rich and faintly bitter, and Sorrow's mouth watered once more. As the server placed a jug of cream and a bowl of sugar cubes in the centre of the table, Vespus held up a finger to stop him.

"Open the window, would you?" he asked, and the server bowed, edging behind the Rhyllians and unlatching the hexagonal window, pushing it open, the scent of the blossoms on the wall mingling with the coffee aroma.

As the server vanished back into the recesses of the inn, Vespus added a single lump of sugar to his coffee. "To business, then?" he said. "Mael, are you ready to tell your sister what happened to you?"

At his words the good feelings from the meal, and the companionship that came from eating together, evaporated, leaving Sorrow on edge once more. Her jaw tightened, but she said nothing, watching as the boy nodded, reaching for the cream and adding a good amount to his own cup, turning the liquid a pale brown. He added two lumps of sugar and stirred the drink. He looked up at Sorrow, smiling briefly.

"Lord Vespus tells me the Rhannish drink their coffee black, but I never did develop a taste for it without cream," he said.

Sorrow said nothing, raising her brows pointedly. No more chit-chat. She was there for a reason.

"All right." He cleared his throat. "I don't remember falling from the bridge," he began, eyes fixed on the whirlpool he'd made in his cup. "But sometimes I dream; it's cold, and dark, and I can't see. I can't breathe. I think it must be some memory of the river, but I don't remember it truly. I don't remember my mother, or my – our – father." He looked at Sorrow and she lowered her gaze to the inky darkness of the coffee. "I can only tell you what I was told of that day, second-hand. But first-hand, I can tell you what I lived after."

The hairs on her arms and the back of her neck stood on end, despite the heat of the day, and without realizing it, Sorrow leant forward.

"Tell me," she said.

11

The Imposter's Tale

The old Rhyllian woman found him in the water, half a mile from her home, caught in the rushes there. Her cottage was downriver, miles from the bridge, miles away from most things. She'd lived alone for a long, long time and she liked it that way.

The war had made life by the water dangerous, as in Rhannon, most Rhyllians had abandoned their riverside homes during the war, fearing foreign marauders, but no one bothered the old woman in her tiny tumbledown cottage. Fat brown chickens safely pecked at worms in her walled garden, offering eggs up in gratitude for their sanctuary. She grew her own leaves and greens, knew where to harvest berries in the small woods a little further inland. She had the river for her water, and for fish, and in her garden she had goats and fowl.

She'd been on her own for so long she was out of the habit

of speaking aloud, and she made no sound when she saw the small figure bobbing in a shallow pond branching off the main river. It was a place she often sat, allowing tiny fish to nibble the calluses on her toes as she gathered the algae that liked to grow there for soup. But today there was a boy there.

She could see he was dead; his eyes were closed, his rosebud mouth open, his body still. A Rhannish child, she realized as she saw his bronze skin and rounded ears. He was dressed in white and green, the fabric torn where the water had tried to steal it away. She stepped into the pond and saw the birthmark on his neck, like a moon. She bent, the bones in her back clicking as she did, her knees creaking. There was a moment where she thought about leaving him there for nature to attend to, but then chided herself. If it were her little one in the water, wouldn't she want someone to fetch him out?

She closed her hands around his pudgy arms and lifted him, grunting at the weight. He was bigger than he'd looked, heavier too. She hauled him up, pressing him to her shoulder, and waded out of the water. On the bank, she lowered herself to the ground and set the boy beside her.

His eyes were open.

For a moment the two stared at each other, the old woman and the boy. Then he began to cry. And so did she.

"She took me to her cottage," Mael continued. "She said that I was ill for days, that I lapsed into a deep sleep almost as soon as we got there, and for a while she thought I wouldn't survive. Despite it, she kept feeding me broth, cleaning me, tending me, and finally, after almost a fortnight, I woke up properly. According to her, I ate some toast, and an egg, and began babbling to her. Of course, she couldn't understand a word I was saying, and I had no idea what she said either. But we muddled along."

"Why did she tell no one she'd found you?" Charon asked.

Sorrow looked at him gratefully. She had questions, at least a thousand of them, but they crowded her throat and her mouth, leaving her unable to speak, as though she'd been the one half drowned.

"There was no one to tell. We lived in the middle of nowhere. She had no visitors that I ever saw, until Aphora and her brother, Melakis, came. She never left the little world she'd created for herself. She didn't need to."

"But surely she must have realized you had a home, and a family. Did you not tell her who you were?"

"I expect I did. But in Rhannish. Which she didn't speak. And by the time I'd mastered enough Rhyllian I'd mostly forgotten everything that came before. It was only when Lord Vespus questioned me that I found I remembered some Rhannish, and even that was limited, given how young I was when I fell. Before that, I only knew her, and the chickens, and the moon and the trees and the river. I never questioned it. Not until..." He looked to Aphora. "This is where Aphora comes into it."

The Rhyllian nodded, topping up her water tumbler before she began to speak.

"My brother and I were out riding," she began, and Sorrow sat up as something occurred to her.

"Wait, when was this? How old were you then?" she asked Mael.

Both he and Aphora looked to Vespus.

"How long ago?" Sorrow repeated to Vespus.

"Two years," the Rhyllian lord supplied slowly.

Sorrow and Charon reacted at the same time.

"You've been keeping this a secret for two years?"

"You found him two years ago and said nothing?"

Even Rasmus had slammed his tumbler down and was staring open-mouthed at his father.

"If you'll allow him to explain. . ." Vespus began.

But Sorrow had realized something else and turned her attention to Lincel. "You sat in my home, under my roof, for two years and you said nothing." Her voice was cold. "You knew everything that was happening and you said nothing. You spied, and lied—"

"I never lied."

"Don't you dare defend yourself to me," Sorrow spat. "Traitor."

"Miss Ventaxis, I must ask you to calm yourself," Vespus said softly.

Sorrow's skin flamed with both anger and embarrassment at being corrected like a child. Rage gathered in her chest, but before she could release it a warning hand squeezed her knee. Rasmus, staring straight ahead, was gently gripping her leg.

It was enough to bring her back to herself, and she took a deep breath.

She folded her arms, turning to Aphora. "Fine. Continue."

Aphora's mouth thinned at the command, but she inclined her head and began to speak once more.

"My horse threw a shoe, so we decided to cut across the land, hoping to reach somewhere before nightfall to attend to the horse. And the first cottage we came to was Beliss's—"

"My . . . guardian," Mael interrupted. "Her name is Beliss."

Aphora nodded. "We approached, knocked on the door and were surprised to find it answered by a Rhannish youth."

She nodded to Mael. "At first we assumed he was there with a Rhyllian lover –" Sorrow kept her expression carefully blank "– hiding from the authorities. But then Beliss herself came in, and it was obvious that they weren't what I'd believed. We didn't know what else to do, so we sent for Lord Vespus. We waited three days, asking the boy the same questions, over and over. 'Who are you? Why are you here?' But his answers were always the same; he was Beliss's child, it was his home. The old woman herself refused to be drawn, until Lord Vespus arrived. But he got her to speak, and finally confirmed what we'd begun to hope. That we'd found the lost Ventaxis heir. Alive, and well."

There was something odd about the way she was talking. It sounded rehearsed. The pauses, the inflections, even the way she raised her brows as though unable to believe it herself, had the air of performance.

Charon's flat tone when he replied "How incredible" told Sorrow he felt the same.

"It was the first I knew of it." Mael leant forward earnestly. "I'd never questioned that I was supposed to be there, or that she was my mother."

"But you don't look Rhyllian," Sorrow said. "Not at all."

"I didn't know what Rhyllian or Rhannish was." His eyes lifted to hers. "I knew me, and I knew Beliss. That the only two people in my world didn't look alike meant nothing to me. I looked nothing like the goats or the chickens either. For all I knew, everyone in the world was a different colour, and a different shape."

"You must have been surprised," Charon said. "When they told you."

He shrugged. "Of course. Of course I was. You see, I liked

116

my life. I liked – loved – Beliss. She'd been everything to me, taught me everything I knew. It was my home. I didn't want to be someone else and I didn't want to leave."

"So you were taken to the capital?" Sorrow didn't care what Mael had or hadn't wanted; all *she* wanted was to hear the rest of the story. She let her impatience seep into her voice. "And then?"

He sat back, slumping in the chair. "Yes. And I could still remember nothing, none of my past, nothing of Rhannon at all. They. . ." He looked at Vespus, who nodded. "Her Majesty, Queen Melisia, and her council weren't as convinced as Lord Vespus."

"My sister suspected he was an imposter," Vespus added. "She worried he was plotting to make trouble between our countries. She had him arrested and imprisoned. They brought Beliss to the castle too and accused her of the same."

"So what changed my aunt's mind?" Rasmus asked. Vespus's expression darkened briefly, but he said nothing.

It was Mael who answered. "Besides the birthmark, Beliss had kept the outfit she'd found me in. After all those years, she still had it, tattered as it was. It was brought to the castle and examined and the tailor's label was found. Queen Melisia remembered what I'd been wearing. The embroidery on the collar, specifically. It was Rhyllian made, you see. By her own tailor, as a gift. Completely unique."

Silence fell over the table. Vespus gestured for the server to return, murmuring to him to replace the coffee.

"Where is it?" Charon asked. "The outfit? I don't suppose you still have it."

It was obvious he expected them to say it was lost, or destroyed during some kind of examination, and Sorrow

117

privately agreed, so she was surprised when Aphora reached into a concealed pocket in her flowing gown and pulled out a small parcel wrapped in gossamer-thin paper. She lay the package reverently on the table and delicately peeled the paper away, revealing a set of shorts, and matching tunic, in green and white, fit for a child. There was embroidery on the collar of the tunic, as Mael had said. Moonflowers.

Sorrow reached for the garments and Vespus moved, snatching them away.

"They're fragile," Vespus said coolly when Sorrow glared at him. "As you can imagine, the fall and the water took their toll. We've been protecting them carefully until we could hand them to the chancellor." From inside his robe Vespus drew a long glass stick, and used it to push a scrap of the white cloth back, revealing a label. "But you see here, the royal tailor Corius's label. You were there, Lord Day, were you not? You remember it."

Sorrow looked at Charon, whose face was stony as he gave a curt nod.

"Did the Rhannish ambassador know that you believed you'd found the lost child?" Sorrow asked.

"No," Vespus said firmly. "Ambassador Mira knew nothing. There was a very small inner circle who were aware of it until this morning, on Melisia's orders. She did not want Mira to be compromised. Mira was notified this morning, along with those who accompanied us to the bridge shortly before we began the journey."

"Why wasn't she there?" Sorrow asked. Mira had always attended the ceremony before, remaining on the Rhyllian side.

"She was asked not to attend."

Charon's tone was icy as he said, "You detained the

Rhannish ambassador so she could not attend the memorial?"

"Let's not get into that now." Sorrow's eyes pleaded with Charon's and he grudgingly nodded. "I still don't understand why you didn't tell us as soon as you were sure," she said to Vespus.

"Many reasons," Vespus said. "In the first, the practicality of it. What were we to say – we've found a boy who barely understands a word of Rhannish, who's never had a haircut or worn a pair of shoes in his life, but we believe he's the chancellor's lost son, can you prepare a suite of rooms? He couldn't read, had had no formal education, no experience of people; simply being in a room with Beliss, Aphora and I was enough to make him shake when we first found him. Then there was the situation with your father... Was it wise to expose Mael to your father, given his ... ah, difficulties?"

Sorrow didn't like the pause he'd left there. Didn't like the way it was exactly the right size to imply he knew precisely what those difficulties were.

"You didn't have to contact my father. You could have contacted my grandmother, while she lived. Or Lord Day. Or even me."

"I didn't want it." Mael spoke up suddenly, drawing their attention back to him. "When they told me who I was, I decided I didn't want to be Mael of Rhannon."

Sorrow took a breath. "Then who did you want to be? What was your name? To the woman, Beliss. She must have called you something."

"Ir bishi. She called me Ir bishi."

"It means 'he who was discovered'. Basically, 'foundling boy'," Rasmus said, his voice icy. "It's not a name."

"I didn't know that," Mael snapped, his eyes clouding. "It

119

was a name to me, until they told me otherwise."

Rasmus made no reply.

"I know how you feel –" Mael focused on Sorrow once more "– because it's how I felt two years ago. My whole world turned upside down; everything I believed I knew to be real was gone. I was angry and I didn't want it to be true either."

She stared back at him. "What's different now?" she asked softly. For a moment it felt as though the others in the room had vanished, not a breath or a murmur from any of them. Sorrow waited, her heart pounding fiercely without her knowing why, for his answer.

"I want to know where I come from. Who I am." Mael laid his hands on the table, palms up, the universal gesture of openness, and leant towards her. "I want to know my history and my family, if they'll allow it. If you'll allow it. I want to know the truth of who I am."

Without meaning to, Sorrow found herself leaning towards him too, nodding. With a start she realized she *recognized* him. Though she'd been born after her brother died, Sorrow was consumed by an unmistakable sense of knowing as Mael's eyes locked on to hers. He was familiar. She forgot where she was, forgot everyone else there, save for Mael.

"I want to come home," he said.

The Chessboard

Rasmus coughed loudly, and at the same time Charon rolled his chair away from the table and said, "I think we've heard enough for now."

It was enough to shake Sorrow from the reverie she'd fallen into at Mael's words. She blinked and sat back in her chair, her thoughts thick and syrupy.

"We're leaving?" she asked.

"We need to bring the rest of the council up to speed, and prepare for your father. I believe we know everything we need to." When Sorrow continued to stare at him, her confusion clear on her face, Charon spoke again. "Miss Ventaxis, we need to make our way to the Summer Palace. Now."

"It might not be safe to go," Mael said, and Sorrow looked back to him. "There might still be a crowd."

The sense of recognition was gone, and Sorrow found

herself frowning at Mael, an uneasy feeling tickling her spine as he stared back at her, his own expression puzzled, as though he felt it too.

"Allow me to send someone to the bridge to be sure it's clear for us." Vespus stood smoothly, planting both hands on the table.

"Us?" Charon said.

"Of course. We're coming with you. We agreed that."

As Charon sucked in a deep breath, Sorrow stood, suddenly filled with the need to be outside, away from these people, and the inevitable argument that was about to happen. Charon could handle it. She needed space to think.

"I'm going to get some air."

"I'll come with you," Rasmus and Mael chorused.

"I'd prefer to be alone," Sorrow said, not looking at either of them.

"Is that wise?" Vespus said. "Mael will go with you. You should have a chance to speak to one another privately. I imagine the next few days will present demands on both of your time."

"I'm not sure..." Charon began, but Sorrow shook her head, impatient to be gone.

"It's fine. We won't go far."

She didn't give him a chance to say anything more, instead marching from the table. Footsteps behind her told her Mael had followed, but she didn't slow for him, or acknowledge him at all.

The door to the inn opened, as though Melakis, still stationed outside, had expected her to leave. The sunlight was harsh after the dimness of the inn, and she had to stop to blink, and allow her eyes to adjust.

"We'll go and check the bridge."

Aphora's voice startled her. Sorrow hadn't heard her – or Lincel – who stood silently behind her, follow. Aphora nodded to Sorrow, then left them, Lincel following her.

Sorrow didn't say a word, walking the opposite direction to the one Aphora and Lincel had taken.

"We should stay where Melakis can see us," Mael said, but Sorrow ignored him, taking a narrow path towards the rushing sound of the river, hoping he wouldn't follow.

Her gown kept snagging on branches, and she tugged it free, hitching it up into her arms, walking until she emerged into a small clearing, high above the roaring water. She moved forward and peered down at it, the surface angry and alive. The ferocity of the river matched the churning inside her, and she watched it crashing against the rocky sides, leaving thick reams of foam behind.

"It's hard to believe I survived that," Mael said, beside her.

Sorrow didn't like how close he stood to her. It was too familiar, an easy invasion of her space, as though they hadn't met mere hours before. She took a step forward, standing on the edge of the cliff. Her annoyance spiked when he joined her.

"I wish I could remember something," he said. "Something definitive, that would prove it beyond doubt. Lord Vespus thought the birthmark, Beliss's testimony, and the outfit would be enough. And I hoped it would be, too. But Lord Day isn't convinced, I can see that. Neither are you, are you?"

Sorrow shrugged. She honestly didn't know what to think. Her mind swung like a pendulum between yes, she believed him, and no, how could she? Both possibilities left her feeling hollow. So she said nothing, staring down at the river.

"It's all right. I understand. I don't think I'd believe it either. Not at first, anyway."

She wished he'd go, leave her to unpick the knot of thoughts wound around her mind. If he was hoping to convince her now, he was mistaken.

"I'm sorry again, about the bridge. I didn't think about what it might mean for the people to see me." He paused. "Lord Vespus thought it would be a good thing. He told me what things have been like in Rhannon, because of what happened to me. He thought if the people saw me it might make them happy, especially given it was the anniversary of the fall."

Sorrow bit the inside of her cheek. Lord Vespus hadn't planned it because it would make the people happy; how naive was this boy? And yet something stopped her from snapping at him. It would be like kicking a puppy.

"I didn't know we were coming today, until late last night," Mael continued. "Perhaps we should have waited. I'm glad I finally got to meet you, though."

Mael raised his hand, as though he might touch her, and without thinking Sorrow jerked away from him.

And lost her balance.

Her left foot slid over the edge of the cliff, the mud giving way, and she locked eyes with Mael as her arms windmilled, a scream trapped in her throat. For a split second she was frozen, caught halfway between the ground and the river, and as her body arched backwards, pulled by gravity and momentum, she saw his intentions as clearly as if he'd announced them.

She'd been an idiot to go there with him, to fall for his sweet, innocent act. To allow him to herd her to the edge.

He was going to let her fall.

Then his hand gripped her wrist, and he yanked her back,

away from the edge. She crashed into him, sending them both tumbling to the ground, into a mess of leaves and dirt.

They landed awkwardly, Sorrow sprawled half on top of him, her knee hitting the ground with a painful thud, his hand still holding her with a force that would leave a ring of bruises like amethysts around her wrist later. The moment he let go she scrambled up, ignoring the throb from her knee, clutching her wrist in her right hand, staring at him. Mael watched warily from the ground, then slowly rose.

"I think one Ventaxis child ending up in the Archior is enough for five lifetimes," he said, a tremor in his voice.

Sorrow swallowed.

"I wouldn't have let you fall," he said softly.

She nodded, unsure if she believed him, her breath coming hard and fast as though she'd been running.

A noise behind her made her turn, in time to see Vespus and Melakis arrive in the small clearing. Sorrow's heart leapt into her throat once more, until Rasmus appeared after them.

All three Rhyllians looked at Sorrow and Mael's ashen faces, the leaves and twigs clinging to them, questions in their eyes. Vespus frowned.

As he opened his mouth, Mael stepped forward, standing between him and Sorrow. Blocking her from him, Sorrow realized. He was protecting her. He'd saved her, and now he was shielding her. Her stomach gave a little jolt at the knowledge.

"What news?" Mael demanded before Vespus could speak.

"The crowd is gone," the Rhyllian lord said, his gaze moving between Sorrow and Mael, full of questions.

Sorrow didn't wait for him to voice them, walking past them all, for the first time in her life anxious to be back in Rhannon.

Charon didn't say a word as they made their way back to the bridge. None of them did. Melakis carried Charon, and Aphora took the chair. Sorrow followed them, Rasmus silent at her side, with Mael and Vespus bringing up the rear.

Though Vespus had been right, and the Decorum Ward had dispersed the crowd, Sorrow still felt as if there were eyes on her as they descended the bridge into Rhannon. She kept to the very middle, moving slowly, mindful of the jade-green water far below her. But even that couldn't stop her thoughts turning to the Rhannish boy behind her, aware of his every step.

Say he *was* Mael Ventaxis, returned from the dead. He was right, the birthmark and the outfit were convincing proof. Not to mention how much he resembled the portraits. So, then, he'd come home, Harun would heal, and she wouldn't have to be the chancellor any more. Or ever.

Something inside her stomach tightened, and she stopped.

"What's wrong?" Rasmus asked, but she shook her head and began walking again.

She didn't want to be chancellor. So why did the idea of him taking over, taking her place, make her feel strange?

"Is there only one carriage?" Vespus's voice broke into her thoughts.

Charon waited until the twins had placed him inside that carriage before he replied.

"Why, yes, the others will have gone on to the Summer Palace. You understand, we had no warning of guests. But we'll send one back for you, the moment we arrive."

Vespus went statue-still and Sorrow had to fight to suppress a smile. In spite of everything else, it was good to finally have the upper hand over Vespus.

Vespus turned to her, his eyes flashing, and once again Mael placed himself in between them.

"You're good – I mean, thank you," Mael said, correcting himself. "We'll wait in the tower on the Rhyllian side for its arrival, won't we, Lord Vespus?"

"How long?" Vespus said, and though his voice was measured, the icy rage in his gaze betrayed him.

Sorrow let Charon answer. "Four hours? Two for us to get there, two for a carriage to reach you."

"And another two for us to join you. By which time the chancellor will have long since arrived."

Charon's nod was beatific.

"We could take a boat," Vespus said, turning to Aphora, who nodded.

"We'll wait." Mael spoke directly to Sorrow. "That's fine."

Vespus glared at him, but Mael merely smiled at Sorrow.

Sorrow knew she should offer something in return for the way he'd stepped in, but she couldn't bring herself to do it, still reeling from what had happened by the river, in the inn, on the bridge, all of it. She finally managed another awkward nod, and watched the coachman fold Charon's chair and place it on the back of the carriage, before she climbed in, moving over to make room for Rasmus.

Vespus reached forward and put a hand on his son's shoulder.

"Rasmus will travel with us," he said.

"But he's the ambassador to Rhannon," Sorrow said, as the coachman slammed the door shut and mounted the cab. Rasmus's eyes met hers through the window, a plea in them.

"Let attaché Corrigan have a chance to spend some time with his father," Charon said. "He'll join us at the Summer Palace. Drive on." He knocked the top of the carriage and Sorrow heard the crack of a whip.

"Charon, what—?"

"We need to talk about state matters and we can't do that with a Rhyllian present, even an apparently friendly one." Charon kept his voice low, barely speaking over the rumble of the wheels. "What happened when you were alone?" He nodded to where leaves still clung to her gown, and Sorrow picked them off as she replied.

"He said he wished the proof they'd offered was enough, but in our position he'd be sceptical too. And he. . ." She'd been about to say that he'd saved her, but the determined, sharp look on Charon's face made her change her mind. Charon didn't need to know about that. Nor that the whole morning had left her so confused that if someone told her black was white, in that moment, she might believe them.

"I don't know who that boy is, but he's not Mael Ventaxis. It's impossible. Mael is dead and has been for eighteen years. We have to maintain that truth. We mustn't lose sight of it."

Sorrow stared at him blankly.

"You can't think it's him?" He leant forward, his eyes locked on hers.

She couldn't meet his gaze. "He has the birthmark. Right there, on his neck. The outfit – Charon, they had the outfit. And he looks like the portraits. . ."

"For the Graces' sake," Charon snapped. "Anyone would think you wanted it to be him."

"Would it be so wrong if I did? To discover my brother, the reason the whole of Rhannon is broken, the reason my father is an addict, was alive?" Sorrow's reply was just as harsh.

"And the timing, Sorrow? That it was today, of all days."

"It's the anniversary of the fall."

"It's also the morning after I told you that you would have to depose your father. After a woman died in front of everyone of note in Rhannon. The same day we voted to make you chancellor presumpt."

Sorrow sat back in her seat. It was an unlikely coincidence. She knew she hadn't truly wished him back to life at the right moment to save her from it, but it was odd that of all the times he would reappear, it was today. A day or two later and he would have been coming back to a very different Rhannon.

"Many would kill for the kind of power you're trying to avoid," Charon continued. "People have. Your family have. And I'm sure Vespus would very much like Mael to be the chancellor."

Sorrow didn't understand. "Why would Vespus care who the chancellor of Rhannon was?"

Charon leant forward. "Do you know why Harun banished him?"

"No." Sorrow didn't. If she was honest, once she realized Rasmus could stay after his father left, she hadn't cared. She'd asked Rasmus, of course, but he hadn't known either. They'd decided it must have been because of Lamentia. They assumed he'd argued with Harun over it, as Arran Day and Coram Mellwood had, and, like those men, had been sent away for it.

"He'd been petitioning Harun for land, here in Rhannon."

"What?" Sorrow's eyes widened. She didn't understand. "Why would he want land here?"

129

"For his Alvus trees. Vespus has been attempting to build a thriving forest of them on his estate for decades, with weak results."

Sorrow nodded; she knew that. Rasmus had told her the wood, the sap, even the leaves were valuable. But they were rare, because they were hard to cultivate, Rasmus said. If it hadn't been for his father's ability with plants, he could never have made them grow at all.

"So he thinks the land here is better?" Sorrow said.

"It is. In the north of Rhylla there's not enough sunlight, few natural pollinators, nutrient-low soil... He asked Melisia time and again to grant him lands in the south, where it would be easier for him, but she refused to take it from people who already owned it."

"I take it Father refused him too?"

"On the contrary, he considered it," Charon said, surprising Sorrow again. "Until the Jedenvat reminded him of the rumour that Vespus had opposed the peace treaty because he believed Rhylla could win the war once Harun presided. He'd urged Melisia to fight on for decisive victory, hoping to claim the North Marches as his own – land which he could use to farm."

Sorrow's mouth formed an "O" of understanding. "So you think this is him trying for that land again? That he'd go as far as to put an imposter in power, all for what? A few miles of land?"

"With his puppet in office it wouldn't be a few miles of land, Sorrow. Why on Laethea would he be content with just that? It would be all of Rhannon. A chance to rule, like his half-sister. Don't forget, they have different fathers. Melisia's father was a king. Vespus's was only a minor lord. She goes on

130

to be queen and rule a country, and he... He gets his father's estate in the north. From what you know of Vespus, do you think that fulfils him?"

Sorrow shook her head.

"But this... Well, after what Harun has done, who's going to complain when the firstborn son returns from the grave and restores the land, even if he does have a Rhyllian as his right hand?"

"If this is true, then he's been planning this for... How long? Since he left Rhannon, if what they said about finding Mael two years ago is true."

"And does that not strike you as more than a coincidence too? He leaves, and almost immediately finds the lost heir? Now do you understand *my* scepticism?"

Sorrow nodded. She should have seen it before. Why would the half-brother of the Rhyllian queen be content to be the ambassador to a place like Rhannon? Someone raised in luxury that he couldn't inherit, and ambitious enough to encourage his half-sister to continue a war everyone knew she didn't want, so he could get some land. Would a man like that really give it up to live in Rhannon for eight years for nothing? So he'd changed tactics, intending to wheedle the land from Harun. And when that failed...

"We need to write to Queen Melisia. She should know what her half-brother is planning." Sorrow spoke decisively.

Charon's eyes were full of pity. "Sorrow, that boy has been living in her castle for the last two years. And at no point did *she* write to us. I'm not saying I believe she's working with Vespus on this," he added carefully, "but it's imperative we don't do anything that might alert him to our suspicions, until we know more. Which also means you can say nothing to attaché Corrigan when he returns, either. We can't be sure how much he really knows."

Sorrow opened her mouth to defend Rasmus. Then paused. Given Harun's parenting, she'd never questioned why Vespus would have been so happy to let his only child remain in a land far from home.

"Rasmus would have told me," she said aloud, speaking without meaning to. "If he'd known about Mael. He would have written. That's why Vespus let him stay. Because he'd already set this in motion. Found some boy he could use." Goosebumps broke out along her arms as she had a sudden sense of foreboding.

"Wait." Sorrow remembered the rest of what Mael had said. "He said he didn't know they were coming today, until late last night. They hadn't planned to come today but last night . . . something changed Vespus's mind."

Charon was right. Lincel must have written to Vespus straight away and told him what had happened with Alyssa. And Vespus had been at the Rhannish palace for eight years, long enough to predict how Charon would respond, the motions Charon would begin. He'd decided to reveal Mael today to thwart them.

And, she realized, he had. They wouldn't be going back to Istevar to depose Harun. Instead Harun was travelling to the Summer Palace, to determine if the boy Sorrow had just met was his long-lost son.

The Summer Palace

The Summer Palace had been called the Jewel of Rhannon; the former royal family and their entire court had moved there during the relentless summer months, bathing and enjoying the gardens, plucking dates and figs from the trees and splitting them open with their bare hands where they stood. It was a tradition the Ventaxis chancellors had maintained, inviting the ambassadors, the Jedenvat and their families to join them for a week or two.

The curlicue-patterned gates of the Summer Palace gleamed copper in the sunlight as they were pulled aside for them to enter, and both Sorrow and Charon fell silent as the carriage travelled the long path to the main palace building, preparing themselves for whoever would meet them.

Sorrow peered through the window at the palace, a three-storey building made of soft blue stone, though there were more windows than wall, at least on the facade. A sweeping staircase led up from the path to a set of azure-painted doors that always shocked Sorrow with their vibrancy. There was a large balcony above them, and higher still, a flagpole where the Ventaxis flag – now the Rhannish flag – sat permanently at half mast, the black heart surrounded by thorns, crowned with flames. Today it lay limp in the breezeless air.

They drew to a halt outside the stair, part of it covered with a smooth ramp for Charon's chair, and as they did a smaller door set inside the large ones opened. A short man with thinning dark hair and a kind face hurried down the steps. The warden – Sorrow recognized him from previous years, though it seemed he had trouble placing her, doing a double take before bowing to her.

"We've had a message, my lord, Miss Ventaxis." He handed a scroll of paper to Charon. "The bird arrived with it only a few moments ago."

Charon took it and moved aside, Sorrow following him, ignoring the Jedenvat and other nobles who had appeared in the doorway.

Charon cursed.

"What is it?" Sorrow asked, and he handed her the scroll.

Sorrow scanned the words. It was from Harun's steward, and it said that Harun was in much the same state he'd been in when Sorrow had left him earlier that day. There was no possible way he would make it to the Summer Palace tonight.

Sorrow repeated the word Charon had said, ignoring his raised eyebrows. "Vespus won't like it."

"Vespus has little choice in the matter."

Sorrow read on. Harun would remain at the Winter Palace

overnight, and his steward would make sure to keep him sober. In the morning he'd bring him north.

"Now what?" Sorrow said.

"We still need to address the Jedenvat before the Rhyllians arrive, let them know what happened in the inn. But first you need to tidy yourself."

Sorrow looked down to find there were still leaves clinging to her, and she could only imagine the state of her hair. No wonder the warden had seemed surprised when he'd seen her; she must look a fright.

"I'll send Irris when everyone is assembled," Charon said, and she left him, feeling a little embarrassed as she entered the main foyer.

The Summer Palace was beautiful, the floor made of pink marble, the slivers of wall between the numerous wide windows washed a soft eggshell blue. Even the roof was partially glass, to allow inhabitants and their guests to dine and dance under starlight when the long summer days of Rhannon finally darkened. Like the Winter Palace, it was preserved exactly as it was the last time Mael had been there. But unlike the Winter Palace, it was clean.

Shame filled her then. She should have done more to keep things under control. She shouldn't have let her father be an excuse. She caught herself resolving to do better when she returned and stopped, one hand mid-air as she reached for the banister, as she recalled she didn't know what she'd be returning from. Nor who might be returning with her.

Something emerald and venomous roused itself inside her stomach at that thought.

"We beg your pardon, Miss Ventaxis."

Sorrow turned, hand still outstretched, blinking, at two

young women who stood watching her. Sorrow guessed they were a year or two younger than her, dark-eyed, brown hair drawn back in long braids that reached their hips, long grey aprons over their black tunics. The elder of the two continued. "Can we do anything for you?"

"I need to freshen up; can you show me where I can do that?" Sorrow said, as the serpentine feeling in her belly fell quietly dormant.

"I'll show you to your rooms, Miss Ventaxis," the younger said. "Please, this way."

They passed through a set of ornate, thick doors into a wide corridor, a part of the palace she'd never been to before. The floor here was thickly carpeted, and Sorrow looked down to see her shoes were leaving orange dust stains in the cream pile. She paused, tugging the shoes off, ignoring the surprised look on the serving girl's face, and then took a step, moaning with the unexpected pleasure of the softness beneath her feet. The Winter Palace was carpeted, but it had also been constantly used over the last eighteen years, and not replaced. The carpet here was surely as pristine as it had been the day it was laid.

They continued on, passing doors that tempted Sorrow to open them. As in the grand hallway, the ceiling was glass, open to the sunset that was finally beginning above them, casting an orange glow on the walls.

Finally, the serving girl stopped outside a set of doors and, with a small curtsy, opened them. Sorrow stepped inside.

The room was dark but airy, and Sorrow suspected that the window and curtains had only recently been closed. She imagined the girls racing from room to room when they discovered that this year people wouldn't be coming to merely view the portrait but to stay overnight. Closing windows and curtains, trying to hide the evidence of their crimes.

The crime of wanting sunlight, and fresh air.

Sorrow liked the idea of a pocket of rebellion here in the Summer Palace, as she had her own in the Winter Palace. She liked the idea that the small staff here, forgotten most of the year, lived lives filled with secret pleasures behind the closed doors. Furniture upholstered in reds, blues, golds; windows and curtains thrown open. She hoped the girls had a Malice set, or other games and books they enjoyed secretly too. She made a note to send them some of her own personal games once she was back in Istevar.

Sorrow crossed to the drapes and pulled them aside to find a huge window behind them. She peered through the glass and found the room faced a garden she'd never seen before. Lush palms, thick grass, broad waxy leaves, all lit by the last of the sunlight.

A rush of vertigo hit her, and she drew back, taking a sharp breath. Looking down into the garden, even through the glass, reminded her uncomfortably of what had happened in Rhylla by the river.

"Are you all right, miss?" the girl asked, and Sorrow nodded, allowing the drapes to fall into place again.

She examined the rest of the room. There was a pair of cream couches, and Sorrow marvelled at them – the material looked so new, so clean. No holes or patches, no stains. The legs ended with the paws of lions, a table between them containing a platter of fruit, and a carafe studded with condensation. As Sorrow moved further in she saw two open doors, the one to the left revealing a bed furnished in white bedding – white! – so soft it looked to Sorrow like a cloud, and to the right a bathroom, the feet of the bath clawed to match the sofas.

The girl hovered nervously in the doorway. "Is everything to your satisfaction?" she said.

"It's lovely," Sorrow said. "Are we – where are we?"

"In the palace?" the girl asked, and Sorrow nodded. "We're in the chancellor's wing – also called the Goldcrest wing, but there was no bedroom assigned for you in the plans. This is one of the most important guest rooms, though."

"It's lovely," Sorrow said again. "I've only seen the staterooms before."

"Would you like a tour?" the girl asked shyly.

"Perhaps tomorrow," Sorrow said.

The girl nodded. "Can I do anything else?"

"No, except tell me your name?" Sorrow said.

"Shenai, if it pleases you, miss. My sister is Shevela."

"Have you always worked here?"

"Yes, miss. Our father is the steward. We were born here."

They had been lucky. To have grown up somewhere where they had the chance to live like this. "I'd like some fresh clothes," Sorrow said. "But that will be all. Thank you."

Shenai curtsied again, and then left Sorrow alone.

She wandered around the room, touching everything she came across: the brocade rope between the silk of the sofa and the wood of its frame, the cool eggshell-blue walls with their stucco detail. In the bathroom she lifted the unmarked jars that lined a small shelf and smelled them, one by one, unable to name most of the scents but a little bit in love with them all. The soft towels, the chill of the enamel on the bath. She ran the taps, cold, then hot, and marvelled at the smoothness of the plumbing, much less temperamental than in Istevar.

A knock at the door announced Shenai or Shevela's return, and Sorrow called for them to enter. She was surprised and pleased to find it was Irris instead, carrying a black gown.

The two girls embraced without speaking, holding each other tightly.

"Are you OK?" Irris asked, pulling back and holding her friend by the arms as her eyes roved her face.

The moment she released her, Sorrow slumped, suddenly drained, as though she'd been saving the last of her energy for this. "I don't know. I can't think. It's all happening too fast. And the moment I think I have something straight in my head, something else happens."

"You don't think he's really Mael?"

Irris's tone told Sorrow that, like Charon, she didn't believe it was possible. Sorrow wished she had their conviction. How were they so sure?

"He looks like the portraits, there's no denying it, and he does have the mark on his neck, though I suppose it could be a tattoo." Sorrow pulled her old gown over her head and took the new one from Irris, holding it tightly, her fingers twisting the fabric. "And there are some old clothes that Vespus says were what he was found in. But how could a little boy survive that fall? I looked down into the water. It's so high, and the Archior is so fast. He couldn't swim. And, as your father pointed out, the timing is one hell of a coincidence. My father being as he is. The Jedenvat's vote. Mael said he only found out they were coming last night. But, really, what is the likelihood of this all happening now by pure chance?" Her words were a stream of consciousness, tumbling from her mouth, and she wasn't sure if any of what she'd said made sense.

But Irris had understood. "Impossible," she agreed.

"He saved me," Sorrow blurted, apparently not finished.

"Who?"

"The boy. Mael. He saved my life. We went for a walk – I needed to get away – and he came with me. We were by the river, and I slipped. He could have let me fall. But he didn't."

Irris stared at her, and Sorrow shrugged. It was the only thing she couldn't fit into Vespus's alleged plan. The way Mael had stepped forward to protect her, not once but twice. The way he'd saved her. The sincerity in his voice when he'd told her he wouldn't let her fall. His overwhelming niceness. He didn't need to be nice to her. So why was he?

Irris shook her head. "That doesn't mean anything. He had to save you. If you'd fallen, everyone would have assumed he'd pushed you. To get rid of you."

"I suppose." But it didn't feel right. And it didn't explain why he'd moved to stand between her and Vespus. Unless – a new thought dawned on her – it was part of his plan to wheedle his way in. For all she knew, he and Vespus had planned those moments, so Mael could seem like a hero. After all, hadn't she thought their words in Rhylla had sounded rehearsed?

She wished she knew. She wished for a fact, something solid, instead of stories and speculation.

Though was more confused than ever, Sorrow stopped wringing the gown in her hands and smoothed it. "Thanks for this."

"Don't thank me yet. The Jedenvat are waiting for you."

Something in her tone made Sorrow stop in the act of pulling the new gown over her head. "What am I about to walk into?" she asked.

"Chaos," Irris said simply.

*

Irris kept a reassuring hand on Sorrow's back as she guided her to a seat in the hastily opened council room of the Summer Palace, but after that Sorrow was on her own.

The moment she sat down, the room erupted.

"Is it him?" Lord Samad was halfway standing, seemingly seconds from climbing over the table to grasp her. "Is it Mael?"

"Of course it's not," Bayrum Mizil scoffed at him. "Don't be ridiculous."

"If everyone could please remain calm. . ." Sorrow tried.

"How could a child survive that fall?" Tuva Marchant ignored her. "Ten men lost their lives diving in after him. Ten strong men who knew how to swim."

"*He* survived!" Samad roared, gesturing at Charon, as the vice chancellor's cheeks darkened with either embarrassment or rage.

"My lords and ladies, please. . ." Sorrow tried again to interrupt, but Samad and Tuva, who had never seen eye to eye, were too deep into their argument.

"If Sorrow had been born a son, would you be so keen to cling to this pipe dream of a dead child returning to life? No! This very morning, all of you —" Tuva paused to point a finger at everyone in the room "— voted to invest Sorrow. And now? Tell me, have you changed your minds?"

"How can we invest her now?" Kaspira said. "We have to know for sure whether the boy is or isn't Mael."

"He isn't Mael," Tuva shouted. "Mael is dead."

Sorrow finally sat back, watching the Jedenvat argue among themselves. The frequent angry glances Charon shot her way demanded she should do something, but she could see there was little point. They wouldn't listen. Not to her, not to each other. Not now. Better to let them get it out, before Harun came, before the Rhyllians arrived.

Besides, she didn't know what she believed, and she hadn't had a moment to herself to even think about it. So she stayed quiet, her thoughts turning again to how Mael had protected her. Smiled at her. She tried not to glance at the clock as Samad, Tuva, Kaspira and Bayrum continued to bicker; soon they might not be her problem at all. They might be his. All of Rhannon might be his.

And once again that sinuous flash of something acid green burned inside her, making her sit upright, the suddenness of the movement silencing the Jedenvat.

It was at that moment that the steward knocked on the door, appearing terrified, as he announced that Vespus's party, and the boy, had arrived.

"Bring him here," Lord Samad demanded.

"Yes, I'll take a look at him," Tuva said.

The steward shot a desperate glance at Charon. "Lord Vespus asked if they could go straight to their rooms, seeing as the chancellor isn't here."

"How did he know the chancellor wasn't here?" Sorrow asked.

The steward swallowed. "He asked... And I didn't know I wasn't supposed to say."

Charon took a deep breath. "Perhaps all of us would do better to get some rest and meet again in the morning. When we can control ourselves."

He shot a pointed look at Tuva and Samad, who both sat back in their chairs, still scowling at each other.

The steward left, and everyone turned to Charon, waiting.

"We need to present a united front tomorrow," Charon

said. "Put aside your personal beliefs and feelings, and think about what's best for Rhannon."

It seemed to Sorrow that this last was directed at her.

Sorrow went straight back to her rooms after the meeting, her body aching and her eyelids heavy. But for the second night in a row, the moment she climbed beneath the sheets, she was wide awake again. She tried, for a while, to trick herself into falling asleep, counting her breaths, in and out, telling herself stories. Sleep wouldn't come, and so she sat up, swinging her legs out of the bed, reaching for the robe that had been left for her.

She padded silently first to the table, pouring herself a glass of water, before crossing to the balcony. She'd left the doors open, and a cool breeze was blowing in, the scent of the river on it. She stepped out on to the cool marble structure and looked down, the garden shrouded in shadow, and silent. Above her thousands of stars glittered, and something close to peace, despite everything, settled over her. The night air cleansed her, stripping away her worries and fears, and the world was so still she might have been the only person in it. She found she liked that idea.

No more worry about her and Rasmus, no more rage at her father. No more frustrated empathy for her people. No Mael. Again that dangerous thought: *Would it be so bad if the boy really was Mael?*

She stepped back inside and put the glass down, belting the robe around her waist. She was restless suddenly, and full of energy, as though the moon had charged her. She looked at the double doors, and wondered if anyone was outside them, guarding her. Before she could really consider it, she'd opened them, finding the corridor beyond mercifully empty, save for two guards stationed at the end. She walked towards them, raising a finger to her lips. And then her feet were taking her out of her wing, her hand pulling the door gently to behind her, and she was ghosting through the halls of the Summer Palace.

14

Gone by Sunrise

She opened every door, stepped into every room. She didn't linger in her parents' old quarters, barely sparing a glance for the portraits that hung on the walls. She closed the door to Mael's old room the moment she realized what it was, deciding she'd had more than enough of him that day.

Every time she saw a guard, she did as she had done earlier, asking for their silence with a gesture, and it was granted, with a bow, or a nod, or sometimes no acknowledgement at all, as though they hadn't seen her. Sorrow met no one else on her travels. The Summer Palace kept a minimal staff; those who did work there would be fast asleep by now. The palace was hers.

Thanks to the glass ceilings, the pale walls, and the bright light of the moon, she needed no lamp, perfectly able to see as she pushed open the doors to the rooms beneath her own. She found the breakfast room. Beyond it was a patio, and she realized what she'd thought were windows were glass doors, every panel able to open out so breakfast could be enjoyed beside the gardens. Further still she found small salons, candy-striped chairs and games tables hidden beneath dust sheets, an old harp with warped strings that sounded like tiny screams when she plucked them. A gentleman's room, a pot-a-ball table at the centre, a small bar in the corner, which, when she opened it, still had bottles inside, sticky residue coating the bottoms.

Behind the grand hallway she found a ballroom with a huge floor for dancing, five chandeliers suspended above it, sconces at the wall to make it as bright or as dark as it needed to be. There were spiral staircases in each corner, leading to a balcony level with boxes where observers could sit and watch the dancing below, or secret themselves away for other pursuits. Sorrow's stomach twisted, and she left the ballroom swiftly, heading for the part of the palace she did know; beneath the swallow wing, where the walking gallery, main drawing room, and library were.

Her feet carried her to the main drawing room, and the handle felt cool beneath her palm as she opened the door. The room was day-bright from the full moon, and, as if it had been planned, a shaft of moonlight fell directly on to the covered easel that contained the latest portrait of Mael, as he would have been at twenty-one.

Sorrow crossed the room in three steps and ripped the covering away, unable to stop herself from gasping at the picture. He'd been painted standing, dressed in black, as always, a large vase of white lilies in the background. It was him. It was the boy Vespus had brought to the bridge. He could have been the model for it, the likeness was so exact.

Even the small details, she saw, things she'd never noticed before. One side of his lip curled up a little more than the other, giving him a faint but permanent smirk. His nose wasn't quite straight, listing a fraction to the left. The boy had been the same. Lacking in the symmetry that Rhyllians had – the thing that made them look so other, at first glance. Because they were perfect. Mael wasn't perfect. She'd thought he was, but no. Not quite.

There was a signature scrawled in the corner, dark paint against a dark background, and she tried to make it out. Cr... No, Gr...

The sound of footsteps jolted her from her staring, and feeling suddenly guilty, she tried to cover the picture, managing to get the sheet half over as the owner of the tread paused in the doorway.

Rasmus looked at her. "I went to your rooms," he said, a strange quality to his voice. "I've been looking for you."

Sorrow was about to walk towards him, to throw herself into his arms, suddenly needing him, when she stopped, disturbed by the blank expression on his face. Had Vespus said something after she'd left? Did he know something about Mael?

"What is it?" she asked, trying to brace herself.

"There's a balcony in my room," Rasmus continued, his tone flat and deliberate. "If it were the Winter Palace I'd never have opened the doors, but here it felt different. Like they wanted to be open. Bayrum Mizil is in the rooms next to mine, and he must have thought the same, because he opened the windows when he got back from meeting with you and the Jedenvat. He and Tuva Marchant had a lot to discuss." He stopped speaking and looked Sorrow straight in the eye. "When were you going to tell me you were deposing your father?"

Sorrow faltered, as though the floor beneath her had vanished. "I was going to tell you," she began. "I meant to tell you. . ."

"Don't," he barked, and Sorrow fell silent.

For once there was colour in his cheeks; a hint of rose lit his face. The set of his jaw was hard, jutting, teeth clenched behind pursed lips. His breathing was slow, too slow, she realized. It was controlled. He wasn't just angry, he was furious. And barely containing it. "When?" he ground out from between his teeth.

"As soon as I sign the papers," Sorrow whispered.

"No. When was this decided? Because I seem to recall seeing you last night. Spending much of it with you. So I assume it was after that? Because otherwise, you would have told me, right? You wouldn't have come to my room, to my bed, and not told me?"

Sorrow hung her head and spoke in a hushed monotone. "Last night, Charon told me it was going to happen. But it didn't become official until this morning, before the bridge. The Jedenvat met at dawn and voted."

"So when we . . . this was already in motion? By the time you came to me this was a done deal. And you said nothing." His violet eyes were cold as they met hers. "So last night was, what? Something to remember you by?"

Guilt and shame burned in her veins. "Ras," she began softly. "You're right. I messed up, and I should have told you. You have to believe me, I don't want this. You know I don't. But I don't have a choice."

"Don't you? Because if that boy is your brother, it looks a lot like you might have a choice."

"It's illegal between us."

"It hasn't stopped us before. It doesn't have to stop us now."

"Rasmus—"

"Stop saying my name. I've been begging you to talk to me for weeks. I knew – *I knew* – something was coming and I've spent every moment of every day trying to find a way to make it work. Trying to find a way of not losing you. I thought you felt the same. I thought. . ." He didn't finish, instead turning and moving away.

"Rasmus, wait," Sorrow called, fear making her voice high. It couldn't end like this. She couldn't lose him completely. She needed him.

He kept walking, and the shock of it rooted her to the spot. He was going to leave her there. But then he stopped, and turned back to her.

"What?"

"I don't want. . ." She didn't know how to finish. "You're my best friend," she pleaded.

"That's just it, Row. That's all I ever was. You never thought of me as more than that. And I was stupid enough to think that one day you might. To hope for it."

Sorrow couldn't breathe. As she looked into his desolate face, she realized she'd made a mistake – many mistakes. She'd told herself it was kinder to not talk about it, but all she'd done was lead him on. Every time she'd promised they'd talk, she'd made him believe there was something to talk about. When she knew there wasn't. That there could never be. And if she lost him now, there was no one to blame but herself.

"We knew this couldn't last for ever," was all she dared to say, the words a whisper.

He opened his mouth, then closed it, shaking his head. When he spoke, his voice was hollow. "I wasn't asking for forever. I wasn't asking you to be my bride, or my one true love. I was asking for *now*. What I wanted was a chance to see if there was something more to us than sneaking to each other's rooms, and being gone by sunrise. A chance. But I never had one, did I?"

He waited for her to respond. But Sorrow had nothing. His words beat against her skull until they made no sense, and all the while they stared at each other.

After a long time, when the silence between them had grown so much it might as well have been a wall, he turned and walked away, slowly, measured, his tread soft. She heard the faint click of the door as he closed, not slammed, it behind him.

Sorrow didn't know how long she stood there, her mind frantically searching for a solution, a way to bridge the horrible chasm that had opened between them. They'd argued before, of course they had – they'd been in each other's lives for the past ten years – but never, ever anything that felt this final.

When the door opened again, her heart leapt, only to plummet when Charon appeared, his wheels silent on the floor, fully dressed despite the hour. How long had he been out there?

"I was just..." Sorrow began, trailing off when he looked beyond her to the half-covered portrait of Mael.

Charon said nothing, moving into the room, his head canting to the side as he gazed at the picture.

"It's uncanny," he said, "in the true sense of the word, how much the boy they have looks like this."

Sorrow could only nod.

"What have you done?" Charon tore his gaze from the painting and looked at Sorrow. "I heard you. Both of you."

Sorrow's blood ran cold. "Charon. . ."

"You lied to me. To my face." The words were coated in ice, sharp like knives. "How could you be so stupid?"

"We never meant for anything to happen—"

"How long has this been going on?"

Sorrow paused. "Eighteen months," she said finally.

"And you've been to bed with him, Sorrow? For the Grace's sake, you're seventeen."

"So I'm old enough to be chancellor presumpt, but not to have sex?" Sorrow's rage flared then, and she whirled on the vice chancellor. "But, of course, the Jedenvat will have a hand in the chancellorship until I'm twenty-one. I guess I'm old enough to be your puppet, but not to take a lover."

Charon's bronze skin turned grey, and Sorrow immediately felt remorse. "I didn't mean it," she said instantly. "I take it back; I'm sorry."

Charon didn't reply for a moment, and Sorrow dropped to her knees, meeting him at eye level. "I'm sorry," she said again.

He reached out for her hand. "Sorrow. . ." He shook his head. "It's treason," he said softly. "It's not that you've . . . formed an attachment. What you've both done is treason, in the eyes of your respective countries. A death sentence, in Rhylla. Life imprisonment here, at the very least." He paused. "Do you understand the position you've put me in?"

Sorrow hung her head.

"I'm the vice chancellor of Rhannon. My job is to uphold all of our laws, to mediate the Jedenvat, and to counsel the chancellor. My job is to be impartial, and see that the good of Rhannon is served. Above all things. Above all people."

The bones in her legs turned liquid then, and she sat back on her knees, her hand slipping from Charon's grasp.

"But it's over now. We both swore that once I had to become chancellor, we'd end it." She could hear her voice becoming shriller and shriller. "Please don't punish him. I've already hurt him so much. There's no real harm done. No one knows. No one ever will. Charon, it's over. If you heard us you know that. He can't stand me now." The words felt like a knife in her chest, twisting, as fresh tears threatened to fall. Sorrow's eyes were wide, pleading, as she met the gaze of the vice chancellor.

"I have loved you as a daughter," Charon said. "To my detriment, it seems. I'm not going to have you arrested. Either of you. The country finding out the chancellor's daughter has been having an affair with the Rhyllian queen's nephew would be the final straw." He paused. "Rasmus is to go. Immediately. Back to Rhylla, and neither of you is to speak to, nor contact, the other again."

He reached out, leaning forward to cup her cheek. "I should have paid more attention," he said. "Does Irris know?"

"No." This time the lie was instant. "No. She would have been furious. She would have told you."

"That's something, at least. And I don't see that she needs to know. No one does. It will remain between us. I'll go to the boy and send him away, and that will be the end of it. After tonight, we won't speak of it again, and we will act as if it never happened. Get some rest." Charon withdrew his hand from her face and placed it on his wheel, turning it sharply. "Tomorrow is going to be a long and hard day and I need you to be ready for it."

Sorrow nodded, watching him as he glided across the floor.

"Cover the painting before you leave," he called from the doorway. "We're going to need it tomorrow. Oh, and Sorrow?" He kept his back to her. "Is there... Is there any possibility you're with child?"

"No," she replied, the skin on her face and chest burning. "We were careful."

He paused, and Sorrow had the sense he might say something. But then he nodded, and wheeled himself away.

She covered the painting and made her way slowly back to the Goldcrest wing, her legs leaden, her heart a rock inside her chest.

When she reached her room her gaze fell on the balcony doors, still open, the curtains billowing gently. She crossed the room and shut the doors, closing them against the stars, the cool night air, and the possibility of a life that she could never have.

She was woken by a cool hand on her forehead, and opened her eyes to find Irris Day leaning over her. The room was still dark; Sorrow didn't think she could have been asleep for more than an hour.

"Your father is here," Irris said softly.

Sorrow struggled to sit up, rubbing her eyes. "What time is it?"

"It's a little after four."

Sorrow was right – she'd finally tumbled into bed at three.

Her head muzzy; she stretched, shivering at the chill in the predawn air.

"And Rasmus has gone."

She was fully awake then, her head whipping around to meet Irris's concerned gaze.

"You didn't know?" Irris read her friend's expression.

Sorrow nodded slowly. "I knew he was going. Your father heard us. Arguing, late last night. About my becoming chancellor. He realized that we'd been..."

Irris sank on to the bed beside Sorrow, her mouth open.

"He's not going to punish us," Sorrow continued, surprised at how calm she sounded. "Or tell anyone. But Rasmus is banished and I'm never to see him again." Her voice cracked as she finished.

Irris said nothing, gently rubbing small circles on Sorrow's arm.

"I told him you didn't know," Sorrow said. "You're safe."

"I don't care about that," Irris replied hotly. "I care about you."

Sorrow leant against her friend. "I really hurt him, Irri. He said I never let him in. And he was right." Sorrow paused.

Irris lowered her forehead to Sorrow's shoulder. "Oh, Row. I'm so sorry."

Sorrow's throat tightened, and she willed herself not to cry. What right did she have to be upset, when this was all her doing? She should have been honest from the start, the moment he'd started hinting at a future. She shouldn't have slept with him last night; she should have told him what had been decided. She'd behaved like her father, burying her head in the sand and ignoring the issues at hand. This was her fault.

She pressed the heels of her palms into her eyes, screwing them shut, until the tears were driven back. Once she was sure they were gone, she cleared her throat. "Enough. We have Mael to deal with. Where is my father now?"

Irris straightened. "In his rooms, changing. And . . . Harun knows."

"He knows?" Sorrow stared at Irris. "About Mael? How? I wanted to be the one to tell him."

"He arrived with Balthasar. And Samad told Balthasar, who obviously told your father."

Sorrow swore. "So what do we do?"

"My father wants to meet with the chancellor before he has chance to see Mael, or whoever he is. Hence the very rude awakening. He wants the whole Jedenvat, and you, there."

"All right." Sorrow pushed the sheets back and swung her legs from the bed. "Let's get this over with."

It was still dark when she and Irris returned to the chamber the Jedenvat had met in the night before.

Charon was sitting opposite the door, so his was the first face Sorrow saw. She nodded to him warily, unsure of the reception she'd receive. But he was as good as his word, and he bowed his head to her as he always had, his expression carefully blank. Beside him sat Tuva, then Bayrum. They all greeted her with small nods of their own, which she returned, as she and Irris moved to take the seats beside them. It was then that Sorrow saw the other occupants of the table.

On Harun's right sat Balthasar, and he glared at her, hatred burning in his eyes as she took her seat. Samad and Kaspira sat further down along the same side, and it was opposite them that Sorrow and Irris sat.

Sorrow took the opportunity to look at her father.

It had been months since she'd seen him outside of his chambers in Istevar. Somehow, here in the Summer Palace, Harun looked even more ghoulish, his skin sallow and stretched like a corpse, the joints of his fingers pressing hard against the skin as he gripped the arms of his chair.

His nails were stained from Lamentia, lending them the appearance of rotting. His hair was thin, and combed over his skull, held in place with some kind of gel that made it look wet, arranged with a care that made Sorrow feel ill. He'd shaved, but whoever had done it had done a bad job; his beard was patchy and uneven.

Someone had dressed him in his ceremonial robes, and it was only when he stood that Sorrow saw how much her father had wasted away. Harun was a tall man, his shoulders broad; for all his hatred of war he had a warrior's form. But his robes, robes that had fitted him well enough a few years ago, now hung from him limply, like a shroud. He looked like a child wearing a costume.

"Daughter," Harun said in a thin, tired voice. "You're staring."

Sorrow blushed. "Father, forgive me. It's good to see you."

"Tell me about the boy," Harun said abruptly.

Sorrow had a name then, for the sickly, sharp feeling that kept twisting and writhing inside her stomach.

Jealousy.

Every time she thought of the boy returning to Rhannon, being Mael, her brother, son of Harun, heir to the Ventaxis dynasty, she was jealous. Harun might look like the walking dead, but he'd roused himself, dressed himself, for the first time in months at the mere thought that his precious Mael might still be alive.

He couldn't even look her in the eye.

"Tell me of him," Harun repeated.

She swallowed the bile in her throat and glanced at Charon, waiting for his subtle signal before she spoke. "You remember Lord Vespus, Father?" Harun scowled at the name with what Sorrow assumed was recognition, so she continued. "He came to meet with me on the Humpback Bridge, during the ceremony. He claimed he'd found a boy. Found Mael," she corrected herself.

Harun looked over her, his eyes feverishly bright.

"And had he?"

"I – I don't know."

"Show me the picture," he said to Balthasar, and the councilman rose from his seat, walking over to where a covered portrait leant against the wall. Sorrow hadn't noticed it before.

Balthasar lifted the picture, struggling against the weight and height of it as he carried it to a bureau at the end of the room. He grunted as he raised it, resting it against the wall. With a clumsy flourish he pulled away the sheet, revealing the painting.

"Did you see him?" Harun asked. "The boy?" He gestured at the painting. "Did he look like this boy?"

"I... There is a resemblance." She remembered what Charon had said in the coach, about Vespus's plans. And the boy's own words about the plan changing. "But that's hardly proof that—"

"And he is here, now? In the palace?" He spoke over her.

Sorrow lowered her head. "Yes."

"Your Excellency, there's no possible way this boy can be your son." Charon spoke firmly.

Harun turned on Charon. "And why not?"

"A child could not have survived that fall."

"You did." At Harun's words Samad shot Tuva a triumphant look.

"Barely. It shattered both of my legs. A child could not have survived it," Charon repeated. "Now, I'm sure there is no malicious intent on the boy's, or the Rhyllians' part, but you mustn't allow your love for Mael, and your grief, to cloud what you know to be the truth. I know you want it to be your son. But you have to face the very likely probability the boy is an imposter."

Harun nodded, as though considering the words. "Bring him to me. Now," he said. "I'll know if he's my son or not."

Charon let out an exasperated sigh, as Balthasar rose. "I'll fetch him, Your Excellency," he said, and Harun waved a hand to agree. Balthasar spared a final malicious glance for Sorrow before he left them, closing the door behind him.

A pall fell over the room, silent and threatening, like a storm. Sorrow saw then that the table was split clearly, almost comically, into two factions: those who she knew would be loyal to her if she asked it of them; Irris, Charon – though he shouldn't – Bayrum and Tuva, and those who would, for one reason or another, side with Harun. Despite their promises two night ago, she knew Kaspira and Samad were among that number. Two nights ago she'd been the best – the only – option. But now there was something new to consider.

Sorrow couldn't believe what she was seeing. They must

know what Vespus had done in the past. What he'd hoped to achieve. How could they trust his word now? Didn't they care what that might mean for Rhannon if Charon was right, and this was all part of a new scheme?

There was a firm knock at the door.

"Enter," Harun called, in a voice that shook Sorrow with its strength.

15

The Prodigal Son

Balthasar entered first, his complexion ashen, taking a spot beside the bureau where the portrait sat.

Then the boy followed, and it was as if the painting had been brought to life. He was dressed in black, in the Rhannish style of tunic and trousers, as if he'd just sat for the picture. The darkness of his clothes only served to highlight the brightness of his hair. He looked nervous today. The curiosity and confidence of the day before were gone: his shoulders were rounded, his eyes darting as he took in the room, moving from person to person. His gaze lingered longest on Sorrow; his expression brightened, his mouth beginning to curve, as though he was happy to see her. Before she had time to dwell on it, Harun stood, drawing the room's attention.

The almost-smile faded as Mael took in the sunken figure of the chancellor of Rhannon.

He turned to the doorway, where Vespus now stood, Aphora and Melakis with him, a faint sneer marring his lips. Vespus nodded at Mael, as though to urge him forward.

Harun did not need the same encouragement. His eyes were shining with tears, his mouth open in an "O" that showed his decayed teeth. He took a step forward, arms outstretched, flinching when the boy recoiled, too slow to mask his disgust.

"Mael?" Harun said.

After a beat, Mael replied, "Father."

His voice sounded flat, and Sorrow watched him swallow, saw him gird himself as he stepped forward to be embraced, looking more like a man approaching a gallows than his long-lost father. After all his pretty words yesterday about wanting to come home, she would have bet on him throwing himself into Harun's arms. She shot a quick glance at Charon, who returned it with his own grim look.

On the other side of the table, Samad and Kaspira were nodding, hands clasped before them. Neither of them seemed to notice Mael's reluctance. When Sorrow looked at Vespus, though, she saw he clearly had. His jaw was tight with emotion, his neck corded, and Sorrow had the strangest feeling he was trying to stop himself from pulling Mael back.

Mael was a little taller than Harun, and the chancellor reached up to take his face in his hands, pulling him down so their eyes were level. Sorrow saw the effort it took for Mael to allow this, to permit those thin, stained fingers to press against his skin, and she shuddered, grateful she wasn't in his place. Harun's expression was hungry; his gaze roamed all over the taut face of the boy before him. He stroked the birthmark on Mael's neck, and she pitied him then.

"Do you remember me, son?" Harun said. "Do you remember your mother and me?"

"I... I..." Mael tried to turn to Vespus, but Harun held him still, keeping them face-to-face. "No," he said finally. "I don't. I'm sorry."

Harun staggered back as though the boy had struck him.

"I'm sorry!" Mael said again. He looked away from Harun then, not to Vespus but to Sorrow, as though she could help him. She shook her head and his face fell, turning to Vespus, his expression pleading.

"You remember nothing?" Harun repeated, staring down at his hands as though they were dirty.

"He was an infant," Vespus said smoothly from the doorway. "Is there anyone here who can remember something from when they were so young?"

Harun turned with painful slowness towards the former Rhyllian ambassador, frowning.

"Why are you here?" he asked. "Did I not tell you if you ever set foot in my country again I'd see your head removed?"

"He's with me," Mael said swiftly. "Lord Vespus has taken care of me. I owe him a great deal. I owe all of Rhylla a great deal. I would be dead – truly dead – without them."

Harun stiffened, at his sides his hands curled into fists, and Sorrow saw the war raging in her father as he tried to decide whether his hatred for Vespus was greater than his need for this boy to be his lost son.

"You sound Rhyllian," Harun said.

"Yes." The boy didn't deny it. "But Lord Vespus made sure I was taught Rhannish, so I wouldn't shame you."

There was a long silence before Harun spoke again. "Leave

162

us," he said finally, his voice trembling. "I wish to speak alone with . . . this young man."

He hadn't used his name. Or called him his son. That was interesting. So Harun wasn't quite convinced yet. And when Sorrow's gaze once again shifted to meet Charon's, the quirk of his brow told her he'd noticed too.

Balthasar took a step forward. "Your Excellency, perhaps I—"

"I said leave." The hint of iron was back in Harun's voice, and Balthasar lowered his head at once. "All of you." He turned to look at them then, though his eyes glanced past his daughter. Sorrow ignored the sting beneath her ribs at the dismissal.

"I'm not sure—" Vespus began

"It's all right," Mael said. He nodded at the Rhyllian, until Vespus took a step back. Then he looked at Harun. "Why don't you and I break our fast together? We can eat, and talk, just the two of us. I'd . . . I'd like that."

Some of the tension left the room.

"An excellent suggestion." Harun's voice sounded thick. "We'll eat here. . . If you don't mind?" he added.

"Not at all," Mael said graciously. "I bow to your expertise."

"Excellent," Harun said. And then he smiled.

It was a terrible sight, his thin, chapped lips gaping wide, exposing the damage to his teeth from years of neglect. He looked like a madman, the smile a frightening leer, and yet something inside Sorrow yawned open, some black hole, some cave – a lonely, dark place that she would always occupy. Harun had smiled for Mael. She was outside of this. She had always been outside.

"Where is Rasmus?" Vespus called then, the name catching her attention. "I'll break my fast with him."

Sorrow kept her eyes down as Charon replied. "Rasmus has left Rhannon. He resigned his position last night."

"Why?" Vespus's voice was laced with suspicion.

"That's for him to say," Charon replied. "He offered to resign, and I accepted."

"Come," Irris whispered to Sorrow, urging her to move, as Vespus began to ask Charon exactly what his son had said, and where he'd gone. "We'll eat in my rooms. Father can join us there." She ushered Sorrow past the Jedenvat, and her father. Mael gave her a small smile as she passed, but she couldn't return the gesture. Instead she turned from him and strode away, as though it had been her decision to leave all along.

Harun and Mael were ensconced for hours. Breakfast, lunch, then finally supper came, and Mael remained locked away in the council room with Harun. To her surprise, Charon told Sorrow there was nothing they could do, so she might as well make the most of the palace. Hidden behind the high walls, Sorrow and Iris spent much of the afternoon wandering through the orchards and across vibrant green lawns, pointing out flowers to each other, avoiding any mention of Mael, Harun, Rasmus or what might be happening in the palace as they walked.

They sat on the edge of a fountain and kicked off their shoes, lowering their feet into the cool water, slapping gnats away when they tried to land on them. They pulled branches down towards them and plucked fruit from trees, wiping their sticky fingers on their skirts afterwards. When the sun reached its highest point, Shevela bought them sweet, tangy ices on sticks, and they sucked them as they lounged in the shade of the trees, staring up at an endlessly blue sky. The garden was home to a variety of bright-red-and-green bird with a wickedly curved beak, and they were awestruck when one landed a few feet away from them, regarding the girls curiously. When Sorrow whistled at it, it whistled the same tune back, to her and Irris's delight.

It was idyllic, but it was an illusion; every time Sorrow glimpsed the palace through the foliage it cast a cloud on the day; she remembered everything that had happened, and might still happen inside it. Too soon the spell was broken, and they drifted back inside, to learn Harun and Mael had not yet emerged, and would not let anyone in.

Without planning to, everyone at the palace ended up dining together for their evening meal, Charon, Bayrum and Tuva sitting with Sorrow and Irris on one long banqueting table, and Balthasar, Kaspira and Samad opposite them on another. Sorrow had a mean stab of satisfaction on seeing Vespus's irritation at being left out of whatever her father and the boy were doing. He sat with Aphora and Melakis at the far end of her table, and the three talked softly in Rhyllian. Sorrow didn't miss the fact that every time the doors opened Vespus sat up straight, only to slump when it was a servant carrying more bread or water.

The hour grew late; servants walked the room, turning on the gas lamps on the walls, lighting citronella candles to keep away any insects that had snuck in. Everyone had lingered, again, that unspoken synergy that meant if one left, they'd be the last to know if – or when – anything changed. Charon was at a table alone, going through papers with a frown and scratching notes to himself. Bayrum and Tuva had dug out an old set of cards from somewhere and were trying to play a game, though neither seemed to remember the rules, bickering softly as they muddled through.

Aphora and Vespus stood in silence at the far end of the room, both holding back a curtain, seemingly staring out into the night, while Melakis remained seated alone.

Balthasar and his cohorts were clearly preparing to settle in for the night, summoning one of the servers to bring them a carafe of wine, and glasses. He kept glancing at Sorrow, sitting near the windows, not bothering to disguise his wrath, before turning back to the others and muttering, causing them to look at her too.

"Are your ears burning?" Irris asked her, cooling herself gently with a fan she'd fashioned out of a napkin. "Because mine are, and I'm sure I'm not who they're speaking about."

"I didn't expect to see Balthasar here."

"Neither did we. I would have thought after Alyssa's death he'd have returned to their home to grieve."

"Who told him?" Sorrow asked.

"I couldn't say." Irris shrugged.

"It should have been me, or at least your father. I should offer my condolences," Sorrow said.

"I'm not sure that's a good idea," Irris warned. "He'll take this out on you if he can."

"It doesn't matter. I was there. And I'm ... I should have done it earlier."

She rose, and made her way over to the table, all of whom turned to her as one, with a predatory gleam in their eyes. Sorrow became aware that the room had stilled; Bayrum and Tuva fell silent, and there was no sound of pen scratching, or shuffled papers from where Charon sat. She took a deep breath.

"Senator Balthasar, I'd like to offer my condolences for the loss of your wife. Please let me know if there is anything I can do for you."

The senator stared at her.

There was a collective intake of breath, and during those few seconds Balthasar's olive skin darkened, and his eyes narrowed. His lips curled back, he bared his teeth, and Sorrow braced herself.

But the storm came from a different direction.

Before Balthasar could say a word, the doors to the dining room were thrown open. And there, in the centre, stood Harun and Mael, arms around each other's shoulders, faces lit with matching smiles.

Sorrow, Balthasar, all was forgotten at the sight of the two men standing together.

Harun looked reborn; he stood taller, prouder, his eyes were clear. Someone had neatened his whiskers, trimming them right back, and they'd removed the remains of his hair, his head oiled and shining. The shadows under his eyes seemed faded; his skin looked less dull.

Though it was his clothes that made Sorrow's heart falter and flutter in her chest.

Harun was dressed in a soft blue tunic over royal-blue trousers, gold chains around his neck. And beside him Mael wore teal, stitched with red. The brightness of the colours hurt Sorrow's eyes, hurt everyone's eyes, and they all blinked, looking at the pair from the side of their eyes.

"Bring us wine," Harun called in a clear, strong voice. "Open the curtains. Open the doors. For my son has returned."

16

Many Happy Returns

The clamour was not instant. Instead, a hush fell over the room as the impact of Harun's words sank in, the two men framed by the doorway like a tableau at the end of a play. Then, as though the council were an audience and had finally remembered they had a job to do, there was movement, applause, cries of delight and surprise.

Balthasar shoved past Sorrow, sending her stumbling, in his bid to be the first to reach Harun and Mael, as everyone descended upon the chancellor and the boy. Even the servants abandoned their posts and stepped forward, milling on the outskirts of the group.

Only Sorrow, Irris and Charon held back from the crowd. Charon wheeled himself away from the table, but paused halfway across the room; Irris moved to his side, placing a hand on his shoulder. Charon looked up at her, and Sorrow found herself turning to seek out Rasmus, needing comfort of her own.

He was gone, she remembered then. But Vespus was there, striding across the room, his own smile spreading as he moved, his arms held out in welcome, Aphora behind him.

Sorrow stood alone.

"Where is my sister?" a voice called, and the group parted, leaving Sorrow exposed before her father and, so he said, her brother.

"Yes, child, come forward." Harun did not take his eyes off Mael as he spoke.

Sorrow found herself moving, though she didn't want to, walking forward to be embraced by Mael. Someone patted her shoulder as the man who claimed to be her brother folded her into his arms – Harun, she realized, still keeping one arm locked around Mael, held fast to him. She heard the cheers of the people around them, half-hearted now she'd joined them.

Sorrow really was all she brought.

She tilted her chin upwards, and looked out, over their heads. She kept her expression clear, as though she was happy to be there. As though she celebrated with them, when inside she was cold.

Be careful what you wish for, a voice murmured in her mind. *You might actually get it.*

Mael finally released her, but put an arm around her and brought her to his side, so the three Ventaxises were standing together, facing the room. Charon and Irris had joined at the fringe, and offered identical looks of pity and concern.

"I have been blessed," Mael said, and though he didn't raise his voice, the chatter ended at once. "Eighteen years ago, I should perhaps have died. Many did, trying to save me, and others suffered." He offered a nod to Charon – clearly someone had told him how the vice chancellor came to be in a wheeled chair. "But by the will of the Graces, I survived and found a home and family in Rhylla. Two families –" he smiled at Vespus, who inclined his head "– and today I have found a third. My first family. In my first home. I don't think it was a coincidence that I fell on the day the peace treaty between our countries was signed. In fact, the more I think on it, the more I think it was by design. Because of it, I am a child of both nations. Eighteen years ago, my father sought to bring about a peace between Rhannon and Rhylla, and in me I believe that hope is fulfilled."

Hope fulfilled – not so humble now. The voice came unbidden again into Sorrow's mind, and she recognized it now. Rasmus. For a moment she was overwhelmed with longing for him. For his touch, and his presence. She wouldn't feel so bad, so alone, if he were there. No, she reminded herself. That's not fair.

Harun spoke. "I . . ." He faltered, and looked to his son. Mael nodded encouragingly, and he took a breath before continuing. "I have not been . . . myself, for some time."

Understatement, Imaginary Rasmus whispered to Sorrow.

"The loss of my wife and son shook me to the core," Harun was saying. "Left me in a place that was dark, with no way out, and no solace."

If only you'd had another child to care for and cherish . . . Rasmus's ghost muttered, and Sorrow's lips twitched.

"I have done things I'm ashamed of," Harun said. "Behaved in ways that didn't behove the chancellor of this great nation. I have let you and Rhannon down, and I owe my Jedenvat, and my late mother, eternal thanks for working so hard in my absence, and for keeping the land together."

Phew. For a second I thought he was going to mention you. That would have been awkward, the Rhyllian voice joked. But Sorrow wasn't tempted to smile any more.

"I vow, though, as of today, I am a new man. I will preside over a new Rhannon. For my son has returned."

The Jedenvat broke into applause at the end of the speech, and Harun nodded cheerfully, accepting their praise. They stepped forward then, eager to shake the hand of the chancellor and his son, and it was easy for Sorrow to allow herself to be moved aside, back to the outside of the group.

Someone called for wine, and the servants hurried away, returning with carafes and glasses, filling them to the brim and passing them around.

"What about music?" Mael asked. "Is there. . . Do you have music?"

"We shall have music," Harun roared, and the company cheered.

Melakis left the room, returning with a pair of cases, which he opened to reveal two Alvus wood violins. He claimed one, and Aphora lifted the other. They busied themselves stroking rosin down the bows, plucking the strings, and then, without saying a word, they raised the instruments to their chins and began to play, as though they'd only been waiting for the opportunity.

Sorrow had never heard live music before in her life, only ever the songs Rasmus had hummed to her, and she froze as the voice-like melodies of the twin violins filled the room. Someone handed Sorrow a glass of wine and she took it, though didn't drink, too transfixed by the sound. She could *feel* it, she realized, across her diaphragm and in her chest;

every leap and trill of it became part of her. The melody was happy, she could recognize that. Joyful and rousing, and there was dancing, real dancing.

She wondered if Rhannon had folk songs. She'd have to find out. Irris would know where to look. She could bring them back, they could hold—

She stopped herself as she remembered she wouldn't be the one bringing them back now. It would be *him*.

She scowled as Mael bowed to Irris, who looked horrified, but took his arm and allowed him to sweep her in small circles around the tables. Samad shrugged at Kaspira, and the two took up a stiff, formal posture, arms rigid, as they began to move. Harun looked at Sorrow, then held out a hand to Tuva, who tried to demur, but Harun wouldn't accept her refusal. He pulled her into an awkward stance and began to chase his son around the room.

No one asked Sorrow to dance.

It was the kind of party Rasmus had told her broke out in Rhylla all the time. Almost every time a group gathered, for whatever reason, at some point a violin would be brought out, and as though the music was a spell, the people would be compelled to dance and to revel. But not her. It was as if no one could see her.

She stood still in a room that moved and swayed and celebrated, but she might as well have been a ghost. The dancers whirled around her, the music played, and the others steadily drank, while she remained the eye of the storm.

No, someone had seen her.

"Living up to your namesake?" a voice hissed wetly in her ear, and she turned to find a bleary-eyed Balthasar lolling next to her.

She swallowed her reply, forcing herself to remain calm. Grandmama always said you couldn't argue with drunks or addicts, and the Graces knew she'd learned that lesson well enough over the last four months.

But it seemed Balthasar wasn't planning to leave without a fight.

"I won't forgive you for locking me away," he said. "I won't ever forget it. And I won't let you forget it either."

Sorrow bit her tongue, fighting the urge to tell him to get the hell away from her as she subtly scanned the room for help. Bayrum was sitting, seemingly chatting amiably with Kaspira while the others danced. There was no sign of Charon, and she frowned.

"I don't know what I'm happiest about." Balthasar's voice was softly slurred, and Sorrow's hold on her temper loosened with every word. "Mael returning, or your play for power being forever thwarted. No, wait. It's the second one. I don't care if he isn't the real thing. He'll do. Because he means I don't have to pretend to obey some uppity little bitch who should have died with her mother."

Sorrow's fury detonated, and she slapped him.

The whip-crack sound of her palm meeting his cheek was lost in the frenzy of the music, and no one noticed the warden of the South Marches stumble under the force of the blow. Sorrow's chest was heaving as she sucked in breath after breath, her palm stinging from the slap. She watched him rub his cheek in wonder, before vicious eyes met hers, and she recoiled as his arm began to rise, fist clenched, to return the blow. But then he mastered himself, and took a step back.

"I won't be the only one rejoicing that the Age of Sorrow ended before it could begin," he said, no longer sounding drunk at all.

He bowed to her, smirking, and turned, taking a new glass from a tray a servant was holding and staggering away. Sorrow realized she was shaking, her entire body trembling through shock and fright. She really thought he'd meant to harm her. And who would have stopped him?

The servant approached Sorrow, and she saw it was Shenai, eyes wide with concern. She'd seen everything.

"Are you all right, Miss Ventaxis?" she asked.

"Fine," Sorrow lied, though the tremor in her voice betrayed her. She took a glass from the tray and drained it, before saying, "Did you see where Lord Day went?"

"He left after the music started, miss."

"Thank you," Sorrow said.

"Can I... Do you need anything?" Shenai asked.

Sorrow shook her head, not trusting herself to speak again.

The music stopped then, and Shenai slipped away, ready to replenish glasses. Melakis and Aphora exchanged a glance, and then Aphora offered the violin out to Mael as Melakis offered his to Vespus. Mael smiled, and released Irris with a bow.

His fingers curled around the neck with ease as he tucked the body between his chest and jaw, and drew the bow across it. His song was softer, still happy, but a purer kind than the hedonistic glee Melakis and Aphora played with. Vespus matched him, carving out a melody to complement the song, and it was clear they'd played together before, often. The people gathered around them, no longer dancing or raucous, watching the two men play.

Irris came to join Sorrow, her cheeks flushed, a light sheen of sweat at her brow. "Where is my father?" she asked.

Sorrow gathered the final dregs of her composure together. "He left, apparently. When the music started."

There was still an edge to her voice, and Irris frowned. "Are you all right?"

Sorrow didn't want to tell her what had happened with Balthasar while she'd been dancing, nor how it had left her feeling dirty somehow. Tainted. Instead she tried for sarcasm, but the words sounded sour instead of wry. "How could I not be? My brother is returned from the dead, and my father is sober for the first time in almost two years. I'm overflowing with joy."

"Row. . ."

"Look at them all." She nodded to where everyone, even Bayrum and Tuva, stood watching the boy play violin. "This time yesterday they were at each other's throats. And now they're dancing, and I'm over here, watching them."

Whatever Irris was about to say was lost as the chancellor approached them and Sorrow froze. It had been years since she'd spoken to a sober Harun, and she had no idea how much of their other encounters he remembered. Whether he knew she'd drugged him. Shouted at him. Threatened him.

"Miss Day. Daughter."

Irris bowed, as Sorrow said, "Father," mimicking his tone. Not that he noticed.

"I'd like to speak to my daughter, if I may," he addressed Irris.

"Of course, Your Excellency." She dipped her head respectfully and left them, Sorrow watching her as she made her way out of the dining room, probably to find Charon.

Harun moved to stand beside Sorrow, a hand span

between them, watching Mael and Vespus play. He said nothing, keeping his attention on the boy, and as the silence stretched Sorrow's pulse began to race as she waited for him to say something, anything.

"Mael said I should speak to you," he said finally. "He seems to think I owe you an. . ." He paused. "Explanation," he said. "For how things have been."

How things have been? Rasmus's voice was back, and outraged, but Sorrow shushed him, and forced herself to focus on her father's words.

"He said you, along with Charon and the Jedenvat, had been doing your best to keep things together, especially since my mother died."

He turned to her then and she nodded, though she couldn't meet his eye.

"Well, you don't need to concern yourself with it any more," he said. "Mael is here now."

He walked away, leaving her standing there, braced against the wall for support as his words stabbed into her, over and over.

That was it? Was that her thanks? she wondered. After eighteen years of neglect, of living under the cloud he created, of growing up in a country that was a living graveyard. Less than forty-eight hours ago he'd been face down in a pile of drugs, out of his mind on them, and this was her thanks? For keeping the country going, and covering for him, hiding his addiction, this was all she deserved?

He hadn't even called her by her name, she realized. He'd called her "daughter".

She only knew her hands were curled into fists when the pain from her nails against the flesh of her palms broke through the haze of hurt and rage. She was shaking, her breathing shallow, sweat dripping down her back from the effort it was taking to not hurl herself after him. Sorrow focused on the pain, trying to centre herself. Bayrum, now talking to Melakis, shot her a concerned glance, but she shook her head, not trusting herself to stay in control if anything broke the fragile hold she had over her temper. She watched as Harun stepped forward to embrace his son again. It was as though he couldn't touch the boy enough. She hated him. She *hated* him.

"I wish you'd died," she whispered to herself as the song ended and Harun stepped forward to embrace his son. "I wish you were dead." In the moment she wasn't sure which of them she meant.

Somewhere beyond the room a clock began to chime, and she counted the bells, using them to bring her breathing back to normal. At the twelfth bell, she released a long sigh. A new day.

Sorrow realized with a start that it was her birthday. She'd been born two days after the accident. She was eighteen. She looked over to what was left of her family – her father and so-called brother, standing arm in arm, accepting congratulations and joy from everyone.

Yearning for Rasmus overwhelmed her, and she had to lean against the wall to stop from sinking to the ground. If he'd been there he would have danced with her; he would have fought to suppress a gleeful smile when she'd slapped Balthasar. He would be with her now, wishing her a happy birthday, telling her he'd come to her rooms, that he couldn't wait to hold her.

A lump formed in her throat then as she understood what she'd lost. And it was all for nothing, for now Mael had returned she wasn't needed. Her father had seemingly rallied, and if he faded again Mael was here to be chancellor. She closed her eyes, unable to stomach seeing them.

Movement at her side a moment later made them fly open.

Mael was standing beside her.

She looked at him, then around the room. Melakis had taken up the violin again, and he and Vespus were playing something muted, as the Jedenvat milled around and tried to pretend they weren't watching Sorrow and Mael. Balthasar closed in on Harun and began to talk, though Harun kept glancing back at his children, his envy of Sorrow evident in his sharp gaze.

"Why are you over here? Why don't you join in?" Mael asked. "You're not happy, are you?"

"I'm tired," Sorrow said. "The last couple of days have been eventful."

He nodded, accepting it. "Did he talk to you?" Mael turned, leaning against the wall with his shoulder so he could face her.

Sorrow remained where she was, facing out into the room. "He did. He said you were here now and I didn't need to concern myself with Rhannon any more."

Mael made a soft click with his tongue. "I didn't mean for him to say that."

Sorrow turned. She looked at him, this new-old brother, whose face she recognized from a lifetime of paintings. "What did you mean for him to say?"

"Just ... that you don't have to do this alone any more. You don't have to be responsible for all of it." He swallowed. "I know that to you Lincel is a traitor, but to me she was a lifeline. To me she was a link to my sister, and my father; every bird she sent was a gift. She was the one who told me about both of you, and Grandmother too." Sorrow flinched at the mention of her beloved grandmama. "She told me how much the Dowager First Lady did to lessen the harshness of our father's rule. And how you tried to fill her place after she died. I wish I could have known her."

Sorrow met his gaze levelly. His eyes were the same brown as hers. As their father's.

Everyone in Rhannon has dark eyes. So what? Sorrow shook her head and tried to concentrate.

Mael turned to where Harun was watching them. "He promised no more Lamentia. He sent a bird, while I was in the room, to Istevar, asking for his chambers to be stripped and cleaned, and for any trace of the drug to be destroyed. He wants to start again. He knows it will be hard, and that breaking the addiction won't be easy, but he says he wants to try. For us."

"For you."

"Sorrow." Mael's eyes were sad. "He's so ashamed of the way he's treated you."

"Ashamed?" She couldn't keep the disbelief from her voice. "You think he's ashamed?"

"That's why he can't look at you, or talk to you. He told me so. He's embarrassed by how badly he's let you down."

Sorrow blinked. "That's his excuse for his behaviour?"

Mael nodded earnestly. "He knows he's not been the father you deserve and it pains him to have let you down so badly, to have his young daughter look after him. He told me of the times you'd gone to him, cleaned him up after one of his . . . episodes and cared for him. And how he wept once you'd gone, wept for what he was doing to you. But he promised me he would make it up to you and we'd be a true family."

Sorrow swallowed.

"He must have woven quite the story if you believe that anything he told you was true," she said bitterly. "But I have seventeen – no, eighteen – years of experience that has taught me otherwise. Which you don't," she added, surprised at herself.

A look of hurt crossed Mael's face. "I don't expect you to forgive him straight away," he said stiffly. "And I don't expect you to believe or even like me, just like that, either; in fact, I'd be disappointed if you did. But things are going to be different now. You'll see." He took her hand before she could stop him and raised it to his mouth, kissing it. "Like I said, we're going to be a family. I look forward to getting to know you both."

He bowed then, and began to back away. "Oh, and, Sorrow? Many happy returns."

He turned on his heel and walked back to the others, who welcomed him with cheers.

As Harun reached to embrace him once more, she studied both of their faces. Harun's beard made it difficult, but there was no superficial resemblance between them; where Harun's nose was slightly hooked, Mael's was sloped. And where Mael's cheekbones were high and sharp, Harun's were flat, even in his thin face. Of course, it might be the gap in age that caused the difference.

Or it might not. . .

Sorrow had had enough – enough of watching, enough of thinking. She beckoned Shenai back to her and took a glass of wine from the tray, draining it in one. She wiped her mouth savagely with her sleeve, and replaced the glass with force. Nodding at the bewildered servant girl, she left, stalking past the group who'd now moved to sit around a table as though in their own personal inn, and left them behind.

Adrenaline coursed through her and she picked up her pace, running through the palace, startling the guards on the doors, who were almost too slow to open them for her. When she arrived back at her rooms she dismissed Shevela, who'd been waiting for her, and threw herself down on to the bed. Sorrow grabbed one of the pillows and screamed into it, holding it against her face as she shrieked, over and over, wordless cries, until her throat and lungs burned. She threw the pillow down and lifted it again, punching and pummelling it; it was Balthasar, and Samad, and Kaspira, and Lincel. It was Vespus, and Harun, and Mael. It was even Rasmus, who'd left her, even though he'd had to.

When the pillow exploded suddenly, filling the air with feathers, Sorrow stopped. She collapsed on to her back and watched the white down fall around her, on her. She remembered Rasmus telling her about the weather in the northern mountains of Rhylla, and how his people would attach wooden slats to their feet and slide down its icy slopes for fun. She closed her eyes, and let the feathers blanket her like snow.

She woke to screaming.

She sat up immediately, sending the feathers flying, and was already on her feet when the door to her bedroom was thrown open. She braced to attack, relaxing only slightly when she saw Irris there.

Her friend stood, momentarily silenced by the feathers

swirling around the room.

"What is it?" Sorrow gasped.

"Your father." Irris stared at her, her eyes wide and frightened. "It's your father, Sorrow. He's dead."

No Constant but Change

Harun had been found collapsed on his bedroom floor by his valet. On the dresser was a ragged pile of Lamentia, a used piece of card rolled into a tube beside it. It was obvious what had caused his death.

By the time Sorrow arrived, still dressed in the clothes she'd been wearing the day before, he'd been moved to his bed to give him a little dignity, his eyes closed, his hands resting on his sunken chest. The curtains had been drawn, and the lamps at the wall lit, and it was by this dim light, eerily reminiscent of his rooms at the Winter Palace, that Sorrow approached the bed to see her father.

He too was still wearing the outfit he'd worn to the impromptu party, and against his waxy skin the colours were hideous, the tunic marked with dark stains. Though someone had been thoughtful enough to clean his face, she could see dark flakes of blood by one nostril, and a smear of something white and crusted, making a trail from his eye. She turned away, remembering Alyssa.

She'd been in the room for a few seconds before others began to arrive in exactly the same manner she had, rushing to the room and halting on the threshold as though an invisible door stopped them, until their eyes found the corpse. Then they filed in, one by one, taking a spot around the bed. Samad, Kaspira, Bayrum, Balthasar: the entire Jedenvat came. They made space for Charon's chair when he arrived, but no one spoke, their heads bowed and hands clasped reflexively. The fact that no one was crying spoke volumes to Sorrow. The fact no one expected her to cry said the same thing.

She looked down at him, waiting to feel something – anything. Not grief, that would be asking too much. But some sadness, or at least pity? Even anger?

There was a trace, then, of regret. Not for him, but for who he could have been. Thanks to Charon, and her grandmother, she'd been parented. Loved, even. But Harun had given up eighteen years ago. He could have loved her. He could have chosen to live for her, and to build a better life for her. But he hadn't. So it was relief that crawled through her. Never again would she have to wonder when, or if, this day would come. Never again would she look up at a knock at the door, and brace herself for this news.

How callous you are, she thought. *Your only remaining parent dead, and you're barely sorry.*

He was a terrible parent, in fairness, Rasmus's voice whispered in response. *And if your roles here were reversed, he'd probably be doing a jig.*

Then Mael arrived. His hair was wild around his head,

as though he'd dragged his hands through it a hundred times. His eyes were wide, and when they found Harun he let out an anguished cry that pierced Sorrow. The Jedenvat fell back as he approached, and Sorrow saw Vespus appear in the doorway behind him, paler than usual.

"But he promised." Mael's voice cracked. "He promised he'd stop."

He looked at Sorrow, as if asking her to confirm it.

Here was the grief that was missing from the room. In a boy who never knew the dead man.

Before she could stop him, Mael gathered Sorrow into his arms, crying softly on to her shoulder. She could feel tears soaking into her tunic, his body racked with sobs. She patted him awkwardly, feeling almost embarrassed at his outburst, as though she was intruding on the grief of a stranger.

Which he was, she reminded herself. No matter what Harun had believed, this boy was still a stranger to her.

Over his shoulder she met Charon's eyes, surprised by the flat expression in them as they stared at Harun. They softened when they met hers, and he raised his brows as though asking if she needed help. She shook her head once, keeping a loose grip on the bereft boy in her arms.

Seemingly deciding the scene was too much, Bayrum bowed to Sorrow before leaving. The rest of the Jedenvat quickly followed, murmuring soft condolences as they went. Finally, when only Charon and Vespus remained, Mael released her, and Sorrow found herself taking a deep breath, drawing air into her lungs as though starved of it.

"I'm sorry," Mael said immediately, like a child.

"I, too, am sorry for your loss," Vespus said before Sorrow could reply. "For both of your losses."

185

"I don't understand." Mael's voice was raw. "He said he'd never do it again; he sent orders to Istevar saying every trace of it was to be removed from the palace. He signed papers that said taking it – even having it on you – would land you in prison. I saw it! I saw him sign and seal them."

Mael pushed his hands through his hair again, and Charon shot Sorrow an urgent look she couldn't read. To cover her confusion she pulled a stool out and sat next to the bed.

"That's the nature of addiction," Vespus said softly, sounding in that moment so much like his son that Sorrow shivered. "It makes you a liar. I'm sure in that moment Harun believed he could stop taking it. Then later, back here. . ."

They all fell silent, their eyes moving to the dead chancellor.

"I know this is a terrible shock," Charon said, his voice kind but firm as he turned to Sorrow. "But I'm afraid we have some decisions to make."

"Decisions?" Mael asked, his voice bewildered. "Oh, I suppose – the funeral."

Charon cleared his throat. "Well, yes. But, and I appreciate that it's not a pleasant topic, the fact remains that we now have no sitting chancellor. The priority has to be our security during the transitional period, while we arrange an election."

"Can't that wait—" Mael began, but Vespus spoke over him.

"An election? And whose name will be on the ballot paper?"

"I would have thought that was patently obvious. Sorrow's, of course."

"Sorrow's?" Vespus barked, looking her up and down. "Mael is the heir. Harun recognized him as his son. You were there. We all heard him say it."

"You said you weren't interested in the chancellorship."

186

Sorrow spoke directly to Mael, who was watching them all with startled eyes. "In Rhylla. You said you wanted to get to know your family."

"That was then," Vespus said coldly. "Things have changed since."

"So now you want to govern?" Sorrow ignored him, still focusing on Mael. Her chest felt tight, her pulse hammering as though she'd run a great distance. "Do you?"

Mael opened his mouth as though to speak, but Vespus held up a hand, silencing him, before he continued. "Obviously nothing has been decided yet. No one could have known Harun was going to die. But you can't suppose to deny what Harun said – the entire Jedenvat was there – so the fact remains he is the heir and if he wants to run for election, he may."

"There is no doubt what Harun believed," Charon said pointedly, as two red spots appeared high on Vespus's pale cheeks. "But regardless of who he is – or isn't – this boy doesn't know anything about the practicalities of governing. He knows nothing of the intricacy of government, has no relationship with the Jedenvat or the wardens, and the people know nothing about him."

"What do they need to know? He's the eldest child of the most recent chancellor."

"This isn't Rhylla, Lord Vespus. We're a democracy."

"A democracy? Where there's only ever one name on—"

The tightness in Sorrow's chest had become a band that was burning her now, and she lashed out, snapping, "Stop arguing over the still-warm corpse of my father. We can wait a day before we decide anything. We have other things to think of."

"She's right." Mael moved to stand behind her, placing a

hand on her shoulder. Sorrow fought the sudden urge to shrug it off. "Surely this can wait?"

"It can," Sorrow said without looking at him. "There is much to do. Notices need to be sent to all of the wardens, from their governing senator, to announce the death through their districts and counties. Today will be a national day of mourning." She paused, realizing it already was, as the anniversary of Cerena's death. "Full mourning. Schools and non-essential businesses should close and remain so until the day after tomorrow. Black armbands will need to be made; grant working dispensation to any tailors."

She reeled off the list of commands she'd had to give four months earlier, when her grandmother had died. Back then Charon had coached her on them, forcing her through her grief to stand up and do what needed to be done. He'd been proud of her, though he'd not said it aloud, and she could see the same look in his eyes now as he watched her take charge.

Vespus, on the other hand, did not look pleased.

Sorrow didn't care whether Vespus was pleased or not, and continued regardless. "The deacon of the North Marches will need to be summoned to bless my father's body and dedicate it to the Grace of Death and Rebirth before we can move him – ask Bayrum Mizil to send for her. The body will lie in state in the temple here. I think that's right – it's where my mother was taken?" She looked to Charon for confirmation and he nodded. "Then I think it's right he lies there too. Afterwards we'll have him taken back to Istevar and interred in the family crypt."

"And what do you plan to tell people was the cause of death?" Vespus asked, his voice quiet and dangerous.

Sorrow hesitated. "I... We'll say his heart gave out," she

said after a moment. "That the events of the past two days were too much for him."

"So you'll blame Mael for it?" Vespus said.

"No, of course not," Charon snapped before Sorrow could reply. "I'm surprised Lincel didn't tell you that the official line on Harun's absence from public life was that he had a weak heart – the result of his grief after the loss of his wife and son, made worse by the recent death of his mother. The Ventaxis family has a history of heart failure down the male line –" he glanced at Mael "– it's what killed Reuben, if you recall. Sorrow's suggestion is perfectly in line with the current message, and will save the face of the family without causing any more suspicion or fear in the people than is necessary."

Vespus's eyes darkened, but he said nothing.

Charon looked back at Sorrow. "I am sorry to ask this but if you're ready, Miss Ventaxis, there are papers that you'll need to sign to release funds for the funeral. You are the only living member of the Ventaxis family authorized to do so," he added, earning himself a vicious glare from Vespus, and a surprised one from Mael, who again looked as though he might speak.

Charon spoke before he could. "Miss Ventaxis? The papers?" he said. "We need to send them to Istevar."

Suddenly the message behind Charon's pointed looks clicked in Sorrow's mind.

Papers. Mael said Harun signed and sealed orders regarding Lamentia, but he hadn't said if they'd been sent. Had there been other papers signed without their knowledge – papers declaring Mael his son and heir? And if so, were they still here? Was that what Charon was trying to tell her?

"I'd like a moment alone with my father," she said.

Relief was evident on Charon's face. She'd guessed right.

"Yes. Of course. I'll wait outside for you. Gentlemen." He gestured for Vespus and Mael to leave before him.

As soon as she heard the latch fall into place, Sorrow rose from her stool, walked to the window and threw the curtains open, filling the room with light.

She went through his travelling cases first, ignoring how gruesome it was to be ransacking her father's room while his body lay on the bed behind her. When nothing turned up there, she began to rifle through drawers, some of the clothes inside so old they disintegrated under her touch. She pulled the bottom drawers of the two chests out, to see if anything had been hidden under them. She explored the wardrobe, climbing up to search the top, and feeling underneath for anything that might have been taped to the bottom.

She got on her belly and crawled under the bed, searching every corner, and then, in an act that made her stomach turn, she plunged her hands beneath the mattress and felt the entire bed, trying to ignore the dead weight of her father resting above.

Nothing. If he'd signed anything declaring Mael was his son, it had already gone to Istevar.

Sorrow stood, and looked down at her father. She knew the rules of grief, knew that she ought to be crying. He'd demand it of her, if he could. Force a pipe into her hand and insist she martyred herself for him. She thought back to last night, to the last thing he'd said to her: *Mael is here now.* She'd wished him dead, she remembered. She hadn't meant it. Not really. But now it had come to pass. The second time one of her wishes had come horribly true.

Sorrow gave the room a quick once-over before she allowed the drapes to fall back into place.

Charon, Vespus and Mael had remained in the passage outside, and they all turned to her as she left Harun's room.

"Are you all right?" Charon asked.

"Yes." She spared her father a final glance as she paused in the doorway. Already he seemed to be sinking in on himself; already there was a hint of decay in the room, something she hadn't noticed until opening the door had allowed fresher air into the room. "I think we'll need to move him, soon. It's going to get warm in here."

Charon's mouth pursed and he nodded. "There are ice chambers in the cellars; we'll have him taken there."

"Can I see him too?" Mael said then, a bright edge to his voice. "I'd like to say goodbye." When Sorrow nodded mutely, he strode past her, shutting himself in with Harun's body. Sorrow met Vespus's gaze.

And recoiled.

There was violence in his violet-coloured eyes, and in the faint curve of his mouth, horribly at odds with the situation.

"My condolences to you," he said, the right words, the tone so very wrong. "To lose two parents, eighteen years apart, on the same day. What a tragedy."

He bowed his head, then looked up suddenly, with the air of someone remembering something. It was so theatrical, so *hammy*, that Sorrow knew it was deliberate, and braced for whatever would follow. "And if memory serves me, today is your birthday too. Terrible. What are the chances? Still, at least you have your brother now."

Sorrow was determined he wouldn't get the last word.

"Yes, I do," she said as she stalked past him, her legs shaking despite the lightness of her tone. "So save your pity for Mael. For he only has me." She was barely aware of the hiss of Charon's wheels following her as her heart thundered inside her.

She knew Vespus's gaze followed her, and she was relieved when she turned the corner, out of his sight. She made her way back through the palace until she reached her own room.

The moment Charon closed the door behind him, Sorrow began to pace. "I couldn't find any papers, but I think we can assume that at the same time he signed the Lamentia decree, he will have signed a declaration that recognizes Mael as his son. Which makes Mael the obvious candidate for the chancellorship. And we know that will serve Vespus."

Charon nodded his agreement.

"Do you think. . .? Do you think it's possible they killed my father? I mean, once the papers were signed, they wouldn't need him any more. . ."

Charon looked thoughtful, and when he finally answered, his tone was measured. "I don't know. And because your father died as he did, we can't prove it. I don't like that Vespus kept the boy under wraps for two years, only to thrust him forward as we were about to depose Harun. And I don't like that Harun has died hours after declaring Mael his son. It – like all of this – is too sinister to be a coincidence. But your father is – was – an addict. We can never prove he didn't kill himself, albeit accidentally. Especially because we don't know where Lamentia came from in the first place."

Sorrow stopped pacing and pulled out a stool, sitting down so she could look into his eyes. "So . . . what do we do? When Mael says he wants to run for election – which he will – Samad and Kaspira will almost certainly support him over me, and so will Balthasar. If Bayrum, Tuva and Irris back me, it'll be a tie. You'll have to choose who gets to be on the ballot."

Charon paused. "No. You'll both run. You'll both be on it."

The skin on Sorrow's arms prickled. "There has never, ever been more than one name on the ballot."

"There have never been two eligible bloodline candidates willing to campaign. And unless we can prove he's not really a bloodline candidate, he's entitled to do so. I can't stop him. The rules are clear. And Vespus will fight to see that's acknowledged, mark my words. So you have to run against him."

Sorrow swallowed. Two candidates. One female, and newly eighteen. One unknown, and more Rhyllian than Rhannish. One reluctant competitor, and one likely imposter.

If only there was proof that he wasn't Mael Ventaxis.

There had been the moment in the inn where she'd felt a spark of . . . something. When she'd wanted to believe that the mark and the clothes and the portrait were cold, hard evidence. But that need was selfish, she knew that. The portraits could have been painted to look like the boy, and not how the real Mael might have looked. The clothes were Rhyllian crafted, and that made them unreliable – Vespus could have bribed or threatened the maker into creating a duplicate set. And the mark might be a tattoo – they weren't uncommon in other realms. None of it was true, unarguable proof.

For her own part, she was almost sure he wasn't Mael. But her almost-surety wasn't enough. Charon's absolute certainty that he couldn't be Mael wasn't enough. Harun had declared he was, and the only way to discredit that was to admit that Harun had spent the last two years under the influence of a substance, and that that had killed him.

The Jedenvat would be ruined. She would be ruined.

Charon fixed his dark eyes on her. "You said you didn't

want to be chancellor. That you weren't ready. This could be your only chance to escape that fate, if you want to. This boy could take your place."

It was so close to what Rasmus had said to her: "*if that boy is your brother, it looks a lot like you might have a choice.*" It would mean freedom. She could travel to the lands she'd dreamed of: Svarta, Skae. Rhylla. She could take time to decide who she was, and what she wanted to do. Maybe even try again with Rasmus, give him the chance he'd wanted. For one glorious moment she allowed herself that possibility. . .

And in doing so she would leave Vespus in control of Rhannon, with an imposter acting as his mouthpiece.

Vespus, who was so desperate for power, for Rhannish land, he made a play for it time and again. Vespus, who'd wanted the war to continue to secure it. He had no regard for the customs or people of Rhannon.

No regard for Rhannon at all. She'd seen the people, two days ago. Cowed and broken, dead-eyed and hopeless. Vespus wouldn't care about helping them. He'd watched with apathetic eyes as the Decorum Ward beat the crowd back. He wouldn't rein them in; he'd use them to keep control, to help him move the people from the land he wanted so badly.

She could have freedom, but the price was Rhannon. Charon, Irris, Bayrum, Tuva. They'd all suffer. And the people. . . She thought of her grandmother, and how hard she'd worked to temper her son's orders. And Irris, who'd set aside her own dreams to try to step up when she was needed.

And like Irris, she was the only person who could step forward now. The only person who might stop Mael, and therefore Vespus. It was her, or no one.

Sorrow walked to the window and drew back the drapes.

Charon had kept them closed, as the vice chancellor ought to. His room had a different view from hers, another side to the garden, and she recognized the pond she and Irris had sat beside the day before.

It was another beautiful day, one she hadn't known about, because the curtains were closed.

She remembered the plans she and Irris had made, lying on her bedroom floor, what felt like a lifetime ago. The growth, and the art, and the hope they'd scrawled across the paper. The connections she'd wanted to make with Meridea, and Skae, and Svarta. The return of colour, and music, and flowers. A land where windows were opened, and children laughed. Where people looked to the universities, and the guilds, and began to build hopes and dreams around them. The Rhannon she'd heard about in stories.

It was time to open the curtains. It was time to let the world back in.

She pushed the fabric aside and opened the window, filling the room with the sound of birdsong, as she walked back to Charon, who was watching her carefully.

"Rhannon can't take another chancellor like your father," he said. "I know it's terrible to speak ill of the dead, but it's the truth."

"I'm not like my father," Sorrow said. "I'm not weak. We need to find proof that Mael isn't who he's pretending to be. But I'm going to run against him regardless. Because I am a Ventaxis. And I will be the hundred and fifth chancellor of Rhannon."

The vice chancellor held out his hand, and Sorrow shook it.

PART TWO

"We must not look at goblin men,
We must not buy their fruits:
Who knows upon what soil they fed
Their hungry thirsty roots?"

—*Christina Rossetti*, "Goblin Market"

18

Luvian Fen

"Damn him." Sorrow raged at the morning circular in her hand, terrifying the girl who'd been serving her tea. "Sorry," she muttered, waiting until the servant had scurried out of the room before she continued. "He's done it again."

Across the breakfast table, a slim young man, wearing a sharp charcoal three-piece suit and silver-rimmed spectacles, paused in the act of smearing butter along a slice of bread, his knife held aloft like a baton. "I assume you mean Mael? What has he done again?"

"Released another statement that's the same as one of ours." Sorrow brandished the thin newspaper at him. "Fourth day in a row. Exactly the same." She used the paper to gesture at the wall, where Irris had pinned up the list of ideas that she and Sorrow had written back in Istevar, all those weeks ago.

"It's word for word what we wrote – appoint judges to make

decisions about criminals, and stop the Decorum Ward from doing it. I'm telling you, Luvian, we have a spy. Someone here is telling him our plans, and he's making sure he gets them out there first so people think they're his."

Luvian Fen shrugged. "OK," he said calmly, before continuing to butter his bread.

"Luvian!" Sorrow waited until he looked back at her. "You're supposed to be my advisor. Shouldn't you be a little concerned about this? He's putting our ideas out there before we have a chance to. You should let me release statements too."

Luvian put down the knife with an exaggerated air of tolerance. "Firstly, as I keep telling you, it will be a thousand times more powerful if you introduce your plans as a whole at the presentation next week, and then publish the entire thing in one go. The mourning period for your father ended three days ago; people are going to be preoccupied with what that means. As far as the people of Rhannon are concerned, the election campaigns will officially begin with your respective presentations. I suspect the only people reading your brother's statements are us, and the Jedenvat."

"Don't call him my brother; we still don't know if he is or not," Sorrow reminded him.

"My apologies," Luvian said blandly. "Secondly, of course we have a spy. Do you think I don't have spies in their camp?"

Sorrow blinked. "Wait – do you?"

"Obviously. Where do you think all my information comes from? And, yes, they will have spies here, who've probably read your manifesto." He nodded at the wall. "You have to admit, it was a little naive to pin it up where anyone could see it. But be assured there's nothing on there that they won't have thought of too – it's not that far-fetched that he had the same idea – he's taking advice from Vespus, after all, and that's how it's done in Rhylla. Lawkeepers make arrests, suspects are tried, a jury decides, and a judge determines the punishment, or not."

"But—"

"And if I thought your list could be used against us, I'd have taken it down. Luckily for you, it's predictably mediocre, and, if I'm honest, darling Sorrow, more than a touch idealistic. Though that's simply my opinion."

Fighting to stay calm, Sorrow replied, "Well, all your so-called information has turned up is the fact he prefers lemon curd to lime, writes with his left hand, and likes to sing while he bathes, despite having a terrible voice. Which is also predictably useless, in *my* opinion."

Believing she'd made her point, Sorrow took a large sip of coffee.

But Luvian was ready for her. "I've been meaning to ask, does that run in the family?"

Sorrow choked.

"I'm kidding!" Luvian tossed a napkin over to her as Sorrow scrabbled for a nasty enough insult to lob at him. "Lighten up, lovely." He paused again, and looked at her over the rims of his glasses. "Seriously, Sorrow, what did you expect? A servant conveniently overhearing Vespus and Mael laughing evilly together about how he absolutely isn't really the lost boy? Vespus isn't an idiot – he's been working on this for a long time – but the closer we get to the election, the more likely he is to make a mistake, because he won't be able to control it. You need to be patient. Gossip and rumours travel on swifter winds than truth does."

"The election is in seven weeks," Sorrow fumed. "I

don't have time to be patient. We've already lost four weeks mourning."

"I can tell the loss of your father has devastated you." Luvian raised an eyebrow, and Sorrow glared at him. He knew perfectly well how things had been between her and Harun. Undaunted, he continued. "As I keep reminding you, you don't need to prove Mael is an imposter to win the election. That's why you hired me. You said, and I paraphrase, 'I will automatically win if I can prove he's an imposter, but I want to win because I love Rhannon and he doesn't.' Then I said, 'You will win, because I am brilliant.' " Luvian smiled widely and went back to his breakfast. Sorrow had to stop herself from throwing the marmalade at him.

"Good morning, team." Irris swept cheerily into the room, carrying a small pile of papers and envelopes, and a large package, which she deposited in front of Luvian. "Your records arrived. And I have an exciting piece of news."

"Thank the Graces," Luvian muttered. "Someone needs it."

Irris turned immediately to Sorrow. "What's wrong?"

Sorrow shot Luvian a dark look as she replied, "The news circular is reporting today that Mael plans to introduce a judge and jury of peers system to Rhannon if he wins."

Irris's eyes narrowed. "But that's our. . ."

"Yes, yes," Luvian interrupted, seeing where the line of conversation was heading. "We've dealt with it. What's your news?"

Irris smiled, something that Sorrow, after four weeks of increasing smiles, was still not used to seeing so often. "You've been invited to a party." She handed an envelope to Sorrow.

As she opened it, Luvian came to stand behind her, reading over her shoulder.

"A Naming celebration for new princess Aralie, in Rhylla. How lovely."

"Well, I can't go," Sorrow said.

"Why not?"

"I. . ." Sorrow stopped, frowning.

Over the years, Queen Melisia had invited Harun, Sorrow and her grandmother to many festivals in Rhylla, and the dowager had always sent back polite refusals, knowing Harun would react badly to the idea of any celebrations, anywhere. But now. . .

"Can I go?" Sorrow twisted to look up at Luvian, hope swelling in her chest. "Shouldn't I be here, doing election stuff?"

Luvian raised an eyebrow. "'Election stuff'," he repeated.

Sorrow's cheeks heated. "I meant. . ." She trailed off.

"Please don't say 'election stuff' in front of anyone in Rhylla. Not to mention, my politically ignorant darling, that the queen will have invited leaders and representatives from every country on Laethea. Leaders you'll need to work with once you're chancellor. So, technically this is 'election stuff'."

"You can stop saying it now," Sorrow muttered.

"It also gives us a chance to be in Rhylla. In the castle. Where Mael spent the last two years. Where he will have been seen and heard. So it ties into both of your interests nicely: beating Mael, and uncovering his true identity. This couldn't be better if I'd planned it myself." He patted her shoulder and returned to his seat, a sleek smile on his lips.

"Wait, 'us'?" Sorrow glanced back at the invitation. "Plus guest," she read.

"Obviously me," Luvian said instantly.

Sorrow looked at Irris, who was staring at Luvian too.

"It has to be me," he said.

"Why does it?" Sorrow asked. "I want Irris to come."

"Ouch." Luvian raised a hand to his heart. "But in all seriousness, it has to be me. It's going to be a hotbed of tension, with all the world leaders, and Mael and Vespus, there. This is what you pay me for. To help steer you. To be the captain of your ship."

Irris sighed. "He might be right. Not about the captain part."

Sorrow couldn't say why she wanted Irris there – needed her there – to face the one person she didn't think she could face alone now.

"Anyway," Luvian said, as though the matter was settled, "enough party chatter. You have a presentation to prepare for."

Sorrow groaned.

"You'll thank me after." He winked.

The look Sorrow gave him would have soured cream, but she let Irris lead her from the room.

"Have fun," Luvian called after them, pushing his spectacles back up his nose and picking up the bundle Irris had given him.

Sorrow hadn't known what to make of Luvian Fen when they'd first met. He was barely out of his teens, though he had the sharp, shrewd eyes of a man who'd already seen and done a lifetime of deeds. He was dressed in grey – deliberately choosing the same shade she'd worn to her father's funeral, she realized later – his clothes all sharp lines: slim-cut trousers, a frock coat that flared over his narrow hips, a paler grey shirt beneath, only revealing itself at the starched cuffs and collar.

His dark hair was longer on top, shorter at the sides, the longer part constantly bearing the trails of fingers passing through it as he brushed it back off his face. He didn't look how she'd pictured a political advisor when Charon had suggested she employ one.

Luvian had completed his diploma at the Institute in the East Marches, one of Rhannon's two universities, passing not only with honours in politics but with the highest grade in the college's history. But when Sorrow, impressed by his credentials, had written to his tutors for a reference, all of them told her he had a reputation for being cocky and arrogant.

Irris struck him from the small list of interviewees because of it, but he'd sent a bird to Sorrow directly, pointing out his educational records were exceptional, and telling her that his "unconventional approach was what she needed, in this most unconventional of elections". Irris had criminal records searched for his name, but nothing came up, so Sorrow, having not taken to either of the other applicants, and with no other option, agreed to see him.

He'd arrived at the North Marches estate, where Sorrow was basing her headquarters, an aristocratic-looking man with golden skin, black eyes behind spectacles, and finely carved features. From his reputation Sorrow had expected someone bullish, tall and broad, in the vein of Meeren Vine, but Luvian was lithe and not much taller than her. He'd seemed nervous at first, asking lots of questions about the role, and she'd tried to reassure him. Until she quickly realized he was interviewing her, and not vice versa.

He'd quizzed her on her ideas for the future of Rhannon and her thoughts on the past, and she'd dutifully recited her hopes and recounted her grandmother's stories and how they'd fed her plans. He'd asked her in what order she planned to approach the embassies of other countries, and what trade lines she planned to open, or close. What she planned to overturn, and what she hoped to reinstate and introduce.

She wasn't prepared for it, and answered off the top of her head, with no way of knowing what he thought of her responses until he'd sat back in his chair, looked at her from over the top of his glasses, and said, "Very well. I'll be your advisor."

"There's one other thing you should know," she said, and he'd tilted his head, waiting. "I'm not convinced the man running against me is Mael Ventaxis. I think it's more than likely he's an imposter, and a puppet for Vespus Corrigan. I plan to find out who he really is, and expose him."

Luvian had given her a long look before taking off his glasses and cleaning them methodically on his sleeve. "Because if you can prove it, you'll automatically win?"

"Yes. No." Sorrow paused. "Yes, I'd automatically win. But . . . I don't think he's running for election because he cares about Rhannon. He's doing it because Lord Vespus told him he should, and because he thinks it's his place to. He said as much the first time I met him; he wants to belong, and Vespus has convinced him he belongs here." She took a deep breath. "But how can he belong here when he doesn't know it? He thought he was Rhyllian until two years ago, and everything he's learned about since Rhannon has come from books, or been taught by Rhyllians."

"But you've only known Rhannon as it is," Luvian said. "All you know of what went before is from books, and your grandmother's stories. So how does that make you more qualified than him?"

She looked down at her clothes, the grey tunic over darker trousers. Her voice was quiet when she spoke. "I tried on a dress two days ago. A green one. I'd worn colours before, my grandmama's old clothes. Locked away in my room, knowing no one would ever see me. A rebellion, if you like. One I expect a lot of young men and women have taken part in, hidden in attics and bedrooms."

She'd looked up to find him watching her.

"But this time I knew people would see me in it. That was the point, so I'd know what I looked like. And do you know what happened to me, as I imagined them looking at me in my green dress? I broke down. My heart went haywire; I was shaking and sweating. I got a rash, all over my chest. I thought I was going to be sick. Mr Fen, I've dreamed my whole life of wearing colour, and when it came to it I panicked because every fibre of my body told me it was wrong. Dangerous, even. He can't know how terrifying it is, that moment when someone knocks at a door and you realize the curtains are open. He can't understand the guilt that comes from smiling, because it's not how his life has been. The cultural changes he'll have to undergo to learn to be Rhannish aren't the same ones the Rhannish people will be going through. He won't be like them; their problems won't be his problems. Their fears won't be his fears. I don't think he'd be a worse chancellor than my father, but he's not the chancellor Rhannon needs right now. I really believe that."

"And you think you can do better?" Luvian asked.

"Yes," Sorrow said simply. "I can build the Rhannon the people deserve, because I'm one of them too."

He'd stared at her for a long moment, lips slightly parted, before they'd widened into a wolfish grin that both thrilled and frightened Sorrow in equal measure. "Well, Miss Ventaxis, it doesn't matter who Mael really is, or why he's doing this. With me on your team, you'll win anyway."

He was undoubtedly cocky, sly and incredibly arrogant, but he hadn't put a foot wrong yet.

And as for Irris... Sorrow didn't know what she would have done without Irris over the past five weeks. Irris had been steadfast throughout, helping her to convince the Jedenvat that a state funeral was inappropriate. She'd held her hand as a dry-eyed Sorrow watched her father's coffin be interred in the vault in Istevar, three days after he'd died. When Mael had stared at her across the room, Irris had moved to block her from his view, echoing the way he had stood between her and Vespus once. Protecting her.

Once the funeral was over, and an official mourning period of four weeks set, Irris had cheerfully handed her place on the council back to her brother, Arran, and moved with Sorrow to a new base in the North Marches. The Jedenvat ruled no one could campaign from the Winter Palace, and Sorrow had fought to be based in the north, close to the bridge. She wanted to know who came over it, and how often.

"You don't have to do this," Sorrow had told Irris while they were packing up their things at the Winter Palace, worried her friend was once again sacrificing herself for some greater good. The idea of Irris not being by her side pained her, especially with Rasmus gone, but she wouldn't force her. "If there's something else you wanted to do instead, you have to. I don't want you to stay out of duty. I know how much university meant to you."

Sorrow needn't have worried, though.

"I can go once you've won," Irris had beamed at her friend.

"Unless you plan to fire my father and make me your vice chancellor. In which case I accept."

"You rumbled me," Sorrow had replied. "Don't tell Charon yet, though."

"Your secret is safe with me."

"We'd better get started, then."

And so they had.

19

The Gift

Though she'd done her best not to show it, aware that most of Rhannon didn't know how bad things had been between her and Harun, Sorrow had spent the last four weeks itching for the mourning period to be over so she could officially begin campaigning.

She'd been disappointed to find that there wasn't very much to do – candidates simply gave a presentation to the Jedenvat at the beginning of the campaign, and then waited for the formality of election day to be over so they could get to work. She supposed it made sense when there was just one candidate – after all, the entire country would have to abstain in order for someone to lose, and the Jedenvat's approval was guaranteed in the face of one candidate – but things were different this time. She'd be competing for votes. And she found, to her surprise, that she wanted to test her mettle.

Rasmus had always said she was unnaturally competitive for an only child.

Luvian had told her how in Svarta the prospective fain – their version of a chancellor – would travel the land and visit the various tribes, asking what they needed and wanted and incorporating that into their campaign. And in Astria, the presidential candidates held rallies and galas to gather support. Sorrow thought both sounded like ideal opportunities to actually get out and meet the people, as well as to see Rhannon, and had asked Luvian to write to the Jedenvat, to find out how she would go about arranging it.

So when the Jedenvat had replied saying that, in honour of there being two candidates, she and Mael would give two presentations – one at the beginning for the public and one before the election for the Jedenvat – but otherwise *"recommended she adhere to the protocol"*, Sorrow was annoyed.

"What does that mean?" Sorrow had asked Luvian. "Is it a suggestion, or a command?"

"How on Laethea should I know?" Luvian replied.

"What's the worst that happens if I assume it's a suggestion?"

Luvian took a deep breath. "You lose the support of the Jedenvat for going against their clear wishes. Which, if you absolutely win the public vote, isn't an immediate concern, but will make you the head of a council who don't trust you. And if you don't win the public vote, and it comes down to the Jedenvat making the final call, you're, how should I phrase it . . . buggered. Utterly buggered."

The word Sorrow uttered in response made Luvian grin widely. "My, my, Miss Ventaxis. Where did you learn such language?"

"Fine," she fumed, ignoring him. "I'll give them their presentations. I'll give them the best ones in Rhannish history."

But now the time for the first presentation was almost upon her, all her swagger had vanished, leaving her feeling desperately unready and unprepared.

"So, the presentation to the people." Irris thumbed her way through her notes. They were in a small library, sitting at opposite ends of a plush dark-green sofa. "Stay away from anything controversial. Luvian says you should use this time to show the people you can be mature, calm and focused," she read from the paper in her hand. "You need to show them you're not like your father. Then the second one will be you in decisive, powerful mode for the Jedenvat. That'll be interesting." Irris looked up and grinned at Sorrow.

"Ha ha."

"The important thing is to stay cool. Don't get flustered."

"Irri, it sounds like you're expecting me to mess up," Sorrow said, half joking.

Irris didn't smile.

"Oh," Sorrow said.

"You're not used to speaking in front of crowds. And Mael is a consummate performer, currently playing the role of the prodigal son," Irris added. "Who knows how long he's been trained for this moment?"

"And if we'd found proof he was a performer, this would all be moot. We would be in Istevar, overseeing the renovations at the Winter Palace. Or finally enjoying the Summer Palace."

"You'd still have to do some work," Irris reminded her. "There would still be an election."

"But I'd be the only name on the ballot."

"We've found Corius, at least," Irris said.

Sorrow snorted, remembering Luvian's face when they'd learned the Rhyllian tailor, who'd made the suit Mael wore on the day he fell, was dead. "I'm only surprised Luvian didn't demand him dug up and interrogated. *He's hardly dead at all, a mere matter of weeks,*" Sorrow said, mimicking Luvian's drawl with uncanny accuracy.

"If it helps, my father would probably have approved it." Irris arched a brow. "He's worried about how little we've been able to find, too."

Sorrow began to smile, but it faded. "Someone, somewhere, preferably still alive, must know something. We need to know where Vespus is hiding this Beliss woman. And find the artist, Graxal..."

She and Irris had finally determined the signature on the portrait of Mael read *Graxal*, though that told them nothing. Sorrow had asked to bring it with her, but the request had been denied. Further questioning revealed the portraits were delivered to the Summer Palace on the eve of the bridge memorial every year, from an artist in Rhylla who wished that he, and the portrait's commissioner, remain anonymous.

Sorrow had announced she had no intention of respecting his wishes and demanded an address, determined to prove a link between the artist and Vespus, only to be told the address had been mysteriously lost, and her best bet was to wait and see if the artist delivered a portrait the following year. Luvian had applauded her "inventive" use of language after that pronouncement, too.

"I wish it would happen a bit faster. I wish we didn't have to be so secretive about it."

"Well, it might be easier to find things once you're in Rhylla," Irris said. "Luvian certainly seems confident."

"Luvian always seems confident," Sorrow muttered darkly. "I wish you were coming."

"Me too." Irris smiled before adding carefully, "Rasmus will be at the Naming, won't he?"

Sorrow had been trying not to think about it.

Rasmus had not attended Harun's funeral. Caspar, prince consort, came in Melisia's place, as Melisia had not long given birth to their much longed for second child. Sorrow had expected Rasmus to come too, given how many years he'd spent living in Rhannon, if for no other reason. But he hadn't – Caspar had arrived with Vespus, and some other delegates whose names Sorrow had already forgotten. Sorrow was too proud to ask Vespus why his son hadn't come, but afterwards, unable to stop thinking about him, she'd sent Rasmus a note, saying she was sad not to have seen him, and hoped he was well.

She'd waited every day since for a reply from him, and was finally beginning to accept it wasn't coming. That he was gone from her life. The thought left a sour taste in her mouth; she still regretted how things had ended, and she hated him not being around.

All through her father's funeral, the move to the North Marches, hiring Luvian – she'd missed him, used to him always being there, helping her, distracting her. Fixing her. His absence was a physical ache sometimes, driving every thought from her mind as she longed for him, miserable at the idea of never seeing him again. Now, six weeks after he'd left her standing in the library of the Summer Palace, the pain of missing him had faded, for the most part, but every now and then it flared again. Every now and then she would have moved worlds for one more selfish moment with him.

"Maybe he needs more time." Irris knew what – or rather, who – she was thinking about.

"Maybe." Sorrow didn't believe it, and the thought of seeing him on his own territory, dressed up for glamourous events, made her feel ill.

Then something else occurred to her. "What on Laethea do you wear to a Naming? Or feasts? Irri, I don't think I have any clothes for this kind of thing."

She'd had new clothes made for campaigning, tunics and trousers in bright colours, and even a couple of dresses. But they wouldn't do for something like this. Not if what Rasmus had told her of Rhyllian parties was true.

"Don't worry. We'll write to the Winter Palace today and see what they have," Irris reassured her.

The following morning, a trunk of gowns arrived from Istevar, along with some other packages for Sorrow, and a young, timid-looking seamstress who could barely look her in the eye. Sorrow and Irris pulled the dresses out and lay them along the sofas in the library, looking at them with increasing dismay.

"Try that one." Irris pointed to a silvery gown that was the least terrible of the lot.

"I look like Grandmama," Sorrow said, staring at herself in the mirror. "In fact, this probably was hers. I can't go to Rhylla wearing clothes that are eighteen years out of date. Or older. I need something modern."

She saw, then, the enormity of what lay ahead of her in trying to rebuild Rhannon. The country had been frozen in time for eighteen years. No new art, music, fashion. No new inventions or innovations. They were almost two decades behind the rest of Laethea. Luvian had said Meridea was on the verge of creating some kind of steam-powered engine that would eliminate the need for carriages and make journeys that once took weeks take mere days. The Rhyllian ballet and opera were world class, with people travelling from all over Laethea to see them. Even austere Nyrssea – the only place, Sorrow realized, these dresses might actually still be considered risqué – had made great leaps in medicine over the past five years. Only Rhannon, the very heart of the world, had stagnated. Slumbered. And now Sorrow had to wake it.

How, though? It was one thing to talk about making changes, but how on Laethea was she going to pull it off?

Overwhelmed, she flopped down in the gown, eliciting an outraged squeak from the seamstress. Sorrow turned to her.

"What do you think of this dress, really?" she asked her. "Be honest."

She looked between Sorrow and Irris, as though worried the question was a test, before she said, "You're right. It's outmoded."

Sorrow nodded. "Do you like clothes? Fashions, I mean? Do you know about them in other countries? I mean, you must, to know it's out of style."

The seamstress paused, her eyes wide.

"It's all right," Sorrow reassured her. "You won't get into trouble."

The girl spoke hesitantly at first, her confidence increasing as she relaxed into her subject. "As far as fashions go, Skae and Svarta don't really have them. They still wear the same old styles they've worn for ever. But that's because of the climate there. And Nyrssea likes women to be as drab as possible; Astria is the same. Rhylla, though, and Meridea... I've seen drawings..." She stopped abruptly, aware she might have said too much.

"Black-market drawings? Don't worry, I promise it's not

a trick," Sorrow said hastily. It truly wasn't. If anything, she was thrilled by the idea that, as she herself, and Shevela and Shenai at the Summer Palace had, this girl too had staged a small rebellion and pursued her passion, secretly, stealthily. Sorrow hoped that the same held true across Rhannon: that young women, and men, had sought out the knowledge and joy Harun had forbidden them. It would make her job much easier, if the younger generations had already begun laying the foundations to bring life back to Rhannon. "So, have you?"

The seamstress nodded.

"Good. Can you get in touch with the people who got them for you? Can you find out what's fashionable there now?"

"I already know," the seamstress said softly.

"Then do you think you can adapt them? Make new designs?"

The flash of guilt that blazed across her face told Sorrow she already had.

"What's your name?" Sorrow asked.

"Ines."

"Ines. Do you think in a week you could make me some new gowns according to your designs?"

"In a week?" The girl looked horrified. "Getting hold of fabric will take at least twice that, not to mention cutting patterns, and sewing. . ."

Sorrow's heart sank.

"What about repurposing these old gowns?" Irris said. "Could you remodel them based on your own designs? After all, the basic shapes must be similar enough; skirt, bodice, and there are trunks of old clothes – good-quality clothes – in the attics at the Summer and Winter Palaces. We could send for them, and perhaps if you have friends who could help? You'll be paid, of course. And there might even be future work for you?"

Ines looked over Sorrow, peering intently at the dress.

"Yes," Ines said finally. "I think I can."

"There," Irris said to Sorrow. "You shall go to the ball."

Glad the gown problem was solved, and reassured that, thanks to the illicit knowledge of the younger generations, catching up might not be so hard, Sorrow began to open the rest of the packages.

She was pleased to find letters from two former ambassadors – Stile of Svarta, and Magnir of Meridea – ostensibly writing to see how she was, but she could read between the lines enough to know they were offering to return as ambassadors if she became chancellor. She handed the letters silently to Irris, who skimmed them, and gave Sorrow a knowing look.

The final box was wooden, the joins sealed with wax, and she took it to the small desk and picked up a letter opener, chipping away at the wax covering the lid as Irris joined her.

"What is that?" she asked as Sorrow hacked at the seams.

"No idea. If there's a note, it's inside," Sorrow said.

She wedged the opener under the side of the lid and pushed up.

Immediately the girls recoiled, hands over their faces at the stench that rose from the box. Meaty, sweet and thick.

Dead.

Sorrow pulled her sleeve over her nose and mouth and peered inside.

There was some kind of animal in there; she could see fur, and a small foot with tiny claws.

"Don't touch it. I'll fetch Luvian." Irris sped from the room, leaving Sorrow alone with the box. She took another look, and retched. Who would do something like this?

20

Readily Unready

Luvian wrote to Charon, demanding he look into who had sent the dead kitten – for that was what he'd identified it as, his pallor grey, his mouth a thin line – to Sorrow, given that it must have arrived at the Winter Palace first. Irris was convinced it was Mael, or at least Vespus on Mael's behalf, and she'd written separately to Charon, suggesting it.

Sorrow had written to no one, still reeling from the fact someone could do something so unspeakably cruel to an animal, and also want her to receive it. Her own private guess was that it was Balthasar, or Meeren Vine, but she kept that thought to herself.

Charon replied, saying the box hadn't come from the Winter Palace; he himself had overseen the dispatch of the trunks and letters to her, and there had been nothing else. He concluded it must have been added when the horses were changed on the journey, and he told her he'd look into it.

Luvian asked Sorrow if she was sure it was addressed to her, and Sorrow told him it wasn't addressed to anyone, that it had simply been included with the rest of her mail. She brightened momentarily as she remembered that – perhaps it wasn't supposed to be for her at all – but it didn't appease Luvian. If anything, it seemed to make him more anxious. And it didn't change the fact an innocent animal had been killed.

"Unless it was a joke," she said, more to convince herself than Irris and Luvian. "Or intended as a pet?"

But the box had been sealed. Airtight. Even as she said it she knew she was clutching at straws.

"From now on, I open all your mail," Luvian had seethed. "This won't happen again."

Days later, Sorrow remained shaken by it. Someone had deliberately set out to frighten her, or warn her. Someone who would hurt a kitten to do it. And as hard as she tried, she found she couldn't stop thinking about it, especially at night. Couldn't stop seeing the box, and imagining the pain and confusion of the poor creature. She tortured herself wondering if it had been alive when it was put in the box, or killed before.

Night after night she lay in bed, listening to the golden-haired monkeys that gambolled over the roof, calling to each other, only to fall into a doze and imagine they were cats, looking for their dead friend. Then she'd wake, staring into the dark, until the sun rose and it was time to get up.

Finally, the night before the presentation, Irris suggested she use the sleeping draught she'd once used on her father, and Sorrow had agreed, annoyed she hadn't thought of it before. She couldn't afford to be groggy or slow when she spoke.

When she woke, it took her a moment to understand it was still dark, that she shouldn't be awake. Then she heard a sound, a scrabbling from above her, and she realized that was what had pulled her from her sleep. The monkeys.

There was a thud directly outside the balcony doors that led into her room, and Sorrow groaned softly. There were dozens of trees in the gardens, could they not play there instead of on her roof?

Then the door handle rattled lightly, and every hair on Sorrow's body stood on end. That wasn't the monkeys.

Someone was trying to get in.

For a single, impossible moment she thought it must be Rasmus, finally forgiving her, and that was enough to make her sit up, trying to blink away the fogginess from the sleeping potion. Her hand snaked out for the lamp by the bed, her fingers seeking the dial to light it.

She froze when she heard a chime of metal hitting tile, followed by an insistent rasping from the door.

The lock. They'd knocked the key out, and were trying to pick it.

Rasmus would have knocked.

Rasmus wouldn't come at all, she reminded herself.

Then she remembered the dead kitten.

She lunged for the lamp, desperate for light, knocking it to the ground. The crash as the light clattered to the floor was like cannon fire, blasting apart the silence of the night. By the time Sorrow managed to cross the room and pull back the drapes, the balcony was empty and there was no sign of whoever had been there. The gardens below were dark, and Sorrow bent down and picked up the key, staring at it as though it might hold an answer.

She'd fitted it back in the door, about to turn it, when she realized whoever had been there might not be gone. If they'd come over the roof, they could have returned there... Could be waiting...

She dropped the curtain into place and took two steps back. Her foot nudged the lantern and she looked down to find it hadn't shattered. She returned it to the bedside table, sitting on the bed and turning the dial enough to give a reassuring glow. *Go and wake Luvian,* she told herself. *And Irris. Tell them about the intruder. Tell the guards at the entrance to the wing.*

But she was so tired, the sleeping potion still thick in her veins, slowing her heart, tricking her into believing the danger had passed.

I'll rest for five minutes, she decided, leaning back against the pillows. *Just five minutes...*

The next thing Sorrow knew, golden light was streaming in through the windows, and she was lying on the bed, a sheet tangled around her. She sat up slowly, trying to understand why she felt strange. A kind of tugging in her stomach told her there was something she was supposed to have done, and she racked her brains for it. Snatches of dreams came to her, sounds and sensations, and she found herself staring at the window. There had been someone there, hadn't there? Or was it a dream?

She was saved from thinking too deeply about it by Irris knocking at her door. Irris kept up a stream of chatter as she poured them both cups of strong coffee, the mere smell making Sorrow feel alert. As the drink took effect, the memories of the night before became even hazier, like smoke drifting away from her, and when Irris began to reassure her briskly that she couldn't be any more prepared for the debate, the knots that formed in her stomach made her forget about the night completely.

Later that day, Sorrow sat backstage, in what Luvian told her had once been a music hall, hastily whitewashed and swept in the days leading up to the presentation. There was a brown patch of damp on the ceiling, and Sorrow found her attention drawn to it, her mind making shapes in it: a rose, a turtle. A face.

The venue was in Prekara, a district Sorrow had never visited. Prekara was an archipelago, jutting out into the sea, divided by service canals that neatly carved up the territory.

It was a county of ruffians, smugglers and thieves. More people lived on boats than in houses, easy to move around if need be. And there was often a need – almost a third of all those imprisoned in Rhannish jails hailed from Prekara. The watery, labyrinthine streets bred criminals, and it was the seat of felonious dynasties like the Finches, the Monks and the Rathbones. It was hardly an obvious or illustrious choice for Sorrow to present her plans for Rhannon.

The Jedenvat had chosen the district, and the venue, and Sorrow didn't know if it was a good thing or bad. Senator Kaspira held the district of Prekara, and she'd never warmed to Sorrow, or her grandmother either, and Irris had told her it was because Kaspira didn't think a woman should be chancellor, which Sorrow found somewhat ironic, given Kaspira was one of the most powerful women in Rhannon. So while this was a chance to win over a crowd that might mostly mistrust her, thanks to Kaspira's influence, she also felt vulnerable. For the third time since they'd arrived, Sorrow crossed the room to peer at her reflection in an old, half-silvered mirror still mounted on the wall, nodded, and returned to her seat beside Irris.

She was dressed in a deep-red tunic over dark blue trousers, and every time she looked down she was surprised by the colour, despite Luvian's insistence she wear something bright every day so she'd get used to it. She wished she'd never told him what had happened when she'd put on the green dress; the man remembered everything.

Irris had swept Sorrow's hair into a sleek knot at the base of her skull and lined her eyes with kohl, gifted to them by Ines, who'd got it through her contacts. Finally she'd added a coat of dusky red to Sorrow's lips. The idea, she'd told her, was to make sure she'd be seen all the way at the back of the hall.

Sorrow, who barely recognized herself in the mirror, didn't think anyone would miss her.

Luvian's eyebrows had risen the tiniest fraction when she'd met him in the hallway before the journey. His poker face was legendary; squeezing any kind of uncontrolled expression from him felt like a victory, and she was glad she'd caught it, had almost missed it as she'd been concentrating on navigating the stairs in her new heeled boots. He'd quickly mastered his face, casting a cooler eye over her when she reached the bottom, before nodding. Now he and Irris were sitting either side of her, Irris stroking her hand, while Luvian sat going through a pile of papers, pausing occasionally to add a marking to them.

"How are you feeling?" Irris asked.

Whether it was the hours of preparation she'd put in, the mask the make-up offered, or simply that it was too late to be afraid, Sorrow was surprised to find she was calm. "All right," she said truthfully.

On her other side, Luvian put down his papers and leant over, placing a hand on her arm. "Sorrow, you're going to be fine."

"I said I felt all right." Sorrow frowned at him. "I honestly feel fine. I'm ready for this."

"Now don't be cocky," he urged.

Sorrow couldn't believe her ears. It was unnerving to hear Luvian – wry, droll Luvian – be cautious, and she realized then she might not be nervous, but he was.

She pulled her other hand from Irris, and patted him. "Luvian, when am I ever cocky? I'm saying I feel OK. We worked really hard and because of it I'm ready. And it's very rich for you to warn me about being cocky."

He smiled. "I'm not cocky, I'm rightly confident," he said.

"So am I."

Sorrow stood, making her way to the door, barely stepping back in time as it opened and a middle-aged woman in a floor-length tunic, entered.

"Miss Ventaxis, a pleasure to meet you. I'm Ellyra Bird, and I'll be introducing you and your brother today."

"What?" Sorrow, Luvian and Irris all spoke at the same time.

Luvian rose smoothly to his feet. "What do you mean, Sorrow 'and her brother'?"

"Mr Ventaxis is here too. . ." She looked between them, frowning. "To deliver his plans. . ."

Sorrow stared at the woman. She was mistaken. She had to be. No one had said anything about her and Mael presenting on the same night. It was one thing to run against him the election, but to be pitted against him onstage. . . Her hands rose to her mouth and covered it.

"No," Luvian said. "We knew nothing about this. We weren't told he'd be presenting today too. This is unacceptable."

"I'm afraid it's out of my hands, Mr Fen." Ellyra Bird took a step back. "I'm sorry. I'll give you a moment to decide if you want to proceed." She left swiftly, closing the door behind her.

Luvian crouched in front of Sorrow. "What do you want to do?"

Sorrow's sense of calm vanished, leaving a high-pitched buzzing in her ears as fear swelled inside her, making it impossible to breathe.

Luvian placed his hands either side of her face and gently turned her to look at him.

"You can do this," he said. "It doesn't matter that he's here. It changes nothing. In fact, this is a chance to show them all that you're better than him. To show *him* you're better than him. These are your people, and you love them. Remember that. Hey –" he shook her slightly as her eyes slid away from his "– nothing has changed. You're still as prepared. OK?"

Sorrow nodded obediently.

It wasn't enough for Luvian, who leant in until his forehead was touching hers. "Say: 'I did not put on this excellent outfit and get my hair done nicely to hide backstage from that upstart.' Say: 'I lied earlier, I am cocky, because I'm going to blow them all away out there.' Say: 'My name is Sorrow Ventaxis and I am going to be the next chancellor, deal with it.' Come on, Sorrow. Say it."

She didn't know how he'd done it, but some of her fear had seeped away, enough for her to say, "I'm ready."

"Close enough," Luvian smiled, leaning back. "But, yes, you are."

"I'm going first," Sorrow said. "Tell them. I want to go first."

Luvian's smile widened. "Atta girl."

The Sons of Rhannon

Ten minutes later, they filed along a passageway, through a heavy door, and instantly the sound of a crowd assaulted Sorrow's ears.

"How many people are out there?" she whispered.

"Around a thousand," Irris replied.

"A thousand?" Sorrow choked on the words, her mouth dry as dust as her nerves returned.

"They took out the seats – it's standing room only. This is history in the making," Luvian replied, sounding far too chipper for Sorrow's liking.

She whipped around to face him, but he shook his head and pushed her towards a set of steps, up and into the wings, and her entire body was instantly bathed in a cold sweat, her stomach churning.

She peeped through a gap in the curtain, taking in the

crowd. Despite the relaxing of the laws, they still wore the same old, dark colours, though they looked a little more animated than the people who'd been at the bridge the day Mael returned. They turned to their neighbours and spoke softly to them, exchanging quicksilver smiles and embraces, as though still frightened to do so. It seemed Rhannon was finally returning to life, albeit fearfully.

Behind the crowd the Decorum Ward stood watch, Meeren Vine and fifty of his men and women lining the walls. Luvian had insisted on it after the package, and for once Sorrow hadn't felt like arguing. It didn't mean she disliked Vine, or what the Ward stood for, any less, but until they found out who had sent a dead animal to her, she would feel a little easier knowing there was some security nearby.

Even so, it turned her stomach to watch Vine caressing the leather baton at his waist as he spoke to one of his men.

"Ready?" Irris whispered in her ear.

Sorrow nodded, too afraid to open her mouth in case she threw up.

"You've got this," Luvian murmured on her other side. "Show them who Sorrow Ventaxis is."

Before Sorrow could reply, Ellyra called her name, then Mael's, and Luvian was shoving her out on to the stage to the sound of polite applause.

Mael walked out with a hand raised, waving to the crowd, and Sorrow remembered she was supposed to do the same. He was wearing dark blue trousers, and a long fitted blue coat – he looked like Luvian, she realized, the same precise tailoring and fitted, almost militaristic cut. As he neared the front of the stage, the row of gas lamps along the front lit his face, and she saw that he looked thinner, shadows under his eyes, his smile a little strained. He wasn't finding it easy, she thought. He was probably up half of the night learning the intricacies of governing a country he was a stranger to.

At that moment, Mael turned to her, and his smile widened. He looked genuinely happy to see her, despite the fact they were competing against each other. He mouthed, "How are you?" and she replied, "Fine," in kind, aware they were being watched. Most of the time, she thought his niceness was an act. But sometimes... She shook the thought away.

She focused on Luvian and Irris moving through the crowd, gently pushing past people, until they were in her sight line, both of them nodding at her, silently telling her she could do this.

Ellyra Bird stepped forward.

"Welcome, all of you. Tonight, history will be made in Rhannon. For the very first time, we have two eligible candidates for the chancellorship: Mael Ventaxis, son of the late chancellor, returned to us from the dead..." She paused to allow the audience to clap, before continuing.

"... and his younger sister –" Sorrow tried to keep her face neutral "– Sorrow Ventaxis. Tonight gives both candidates the chance to address the people, and present their vision for Rhannon. So without further ado, let us begin. Sorrow Ventaxis will speak first."

The room fell silent as all eyes turned to Sorrow.

She cleared her throat.

"Thank you for coming today. My name is Sorrow Ventaxis, and I believe I am the right choice to lead Rhannon forward as your next chancellor. The past eighteen years, and before, have been some of the most challenging in Rhannish history. I've been here with the people, living alongside them, under the same rules and laws. In fact, they're all I've known. But not all I believe. My beloved grandmother, the Dowager First Lady, told me how it was when Rhannon prospered. When we were at the forefront of science and medicine on Laethea. When we celebrated the Greening, and the Gathering festivals, when we came together for midsummer and midwinter. But you, the people, have taught me that the Rhannish are some of the strongest – if not *the* strongest – in the world. I have seen you weather the many, many storms that have battered you over the past eighteen years, and not break. We are a resilient and adaptable people; there is no trial we cannot overcome, there is no burden we cannot bear. I am one of you." Sorrow turned to the crowd. "I am bound to you, by history, and by blood. Now, I ask you to allow me to lead you into something better. Something more than the darkness of the past. A new Rhannon. For everyone."

"Lies," a male voice called from somewhere in the back.

Sorrow peered out into the crowd as they all turned, some murmuring, towards the speaker. At first Sorrow couldn't see who it was; then the crowd began to move, parting, until there, in the centre of the hall, three people stood isolated. They were hooded, crude leather masks covering their faces, leaving only their mouths free. One stood to the fore, a huge mountain of a man, the other two only slightly smaller, flanking him like sentinals. Not that it looked as though he needed them.

"Lies," the apparent leader of the trio said again.

The hair on the back of her neck rose, and Sorrow's gaze flicked to Luvian, who was craning to see what was happening. When he met her eyes he looked almost frightened, which worried Sorrow more than the men did. Luvian wasn't the type to scare easily.

The hooded men stepped forward, the crowd backing away from them as they did. They stopped six feet from the front of the stage.

"Can we help you?" Mael moved to Sorrow's side.

"Yeah. You can piss off back to Rhylla, and take your sister with you," the man said.

"Excuse me?" Sorrow's mouth fell open with shock.

"You heard." The man's attention returned to her. "We're done with the Ventaxis family. All of you." His voice rang through the hall.

Luvian waved at her, eyes blazing a warning, but Sorrow shook her head and focused on the ringleader.

"Who's 'we'? Who are you?"

"The Sons of Rhannon," the man replied, his chin rising with pride. "Your reckoning."

So these were the vigilantes who'd targeted the Decorum Ward? Sorrow looked at Vine, and watched him whisper to the man beside him. Then that man turned to his neighbour, mouth to ear as he passed on Vine's message. Though she hadn't thought it possible, in that moment Sorrow was grateful for him, grateful for the Ward. But she didn't understand why the Sons of Rhannon were shouting at her and Mael. They'd done nothing wrong.

Sorrow decided to try to reason with them. "I know you suffered under my father, but I'm not—"

"You know nothing," he shouted. "You hid in your palace while our children starved. For eighteen years you've stayed locked away, coming out once a year to throw a doll that costs more than some of us earn in a year into the river. No new jobs. No chances to better ourselves. Nothing to hope for or live for. Your dogs beating our kids when they smile. Look at you −" he thrust an accusing finger up at her "− in your red, standing up there, deigning to meet us. Telling us things will be better. Well, maybe they will. But not while a Ventaxis is in power."

"My father—"

"It's not about your father," the man bellowed over her again. "It's your grandfather, and his father, and his father before him. All of you Ventaxises. Sending us off to fight a war we didn't want. You make decisions and we suffer for them. And now you have the gall to stand here and tell us things will be different? How will they? Because the only change we see is there's two of you this time. What a choice."

There were more murmurs from the crowd, still standing watching the scene, but this time the shock was absent. Sorrow could see people nodding, and her stomach dropped.

They agreed with the Sons of Rhannon, she realized.

And she couldn't think of a single argument against them. So far, she'd done nothing to prove them wrong.

But Mael still had things to say. "The law of the land states that only a Ventaxis can govern. . ."

"Laws the Ventaxis family made," the man shouted. "Crooked, like all of your laws. You come in telling us you're better than kings, and then you behave just like them. We're tired of it. We're tired of you. We want a new Rhannon."

The atmosphere thickened as rumbles of support came from the crowd, who'd drifted back towards the hooded men, surrounding them, all of them watching her, just like at the bridge. Though this time, there was fire in their eyes. Burning low but steady as they waited to see what she'd do next.

Sensing this was her last chance to disarm the hooded men, unwind the coiled spring the room had become, she took a deep breath. "And you will have a new Rhannon," she said, pushing her voice out into the far corners of the room, continuing the speech she'd so carefully worked on. "One with colours, and light, and music. One with art, and growth. One with—"

"One without you," the man roared, and then, in a swift, synchronized movement, all three men reached beneath their cloaks and withdrew something, hauling their arms back, as the crowd recoiled from them.

Sorrow saw a flash of something clear and bright arching towards her, and then the stage before her burst into flame.

Both she and Mael staggered back, falling, as the hall erupted into screams of panic, the crowd suddenly realizing they might be hurt too.

Scrambling to her feet, she peered through the wall of fire to see that the three men had remained in the centre of the room, even as the rest of the people ran for the exits.

They watched her through the flickering flames, their eyes red beneath their hoods in the reflected firelight.

Then they moved. Towards the stage.

In shock, Sorrow searched for Meeren Vine. She spotted him by the wall, where he'd been all night. He was watching her. Sorrow was aghast. Surely he wasn't waiting for a signal? Why wasn't he—? She half raised her hand, and stopped.

She understood as he met her gaze with those merciless shark eyes that he wasn't going to help. This was his revenge for her behaviour in the Winter Palace, all those weeks ago.

The last of her courage seeped from her as panic took over. Her knees locked, her body froze, the Sons of Rhannon getting closer every moment, but she couldn't move. Couldn't do anything except stare at the man who'd betrayed her.

"We have to go." Mael tugged on her arm, as she stared at the captain of the Decorum Ward in horror. "Sorrow..."

The hooded men turned to the left, making their way to a small set of stairs at the base of the stage. There was something in their hands, something long and glinting.

Curved swords, she saw, as the leader pointed his at her and it flashed.

"Sorrow..." Mael pleaded.

A gout of flame licked the edge of her shoe, and she grabbed Mael's hand, instinct finally kicking in, and dragged him from the stage.

She led blindly, listening for footsteps chasing them. Her heart beat triple time, her body screaming at her to get away.

They found themselves in a dead-end passage, four closed doors along one side. Sorrow turned, pulling Mael back the way they'd come, freezing when she heard voices shouting.

Mael opened the nearest door and pushed Sorrow through it, following her and closing it behind them. Sorrow backed away until she reached the far wall, hand pressed to her chest, eyes fixed on the door. They were in some kind of empty closet or storage room, the walls bare save for scuffs and chipped paint, a small, dirty window high up allowing a little light into the room. There was no lock on the door, and so Mael braced himself against it, pushing the handle up and pressing a finger to his lips. After a moment, Sorrow moved to his side, leaning against it too.

"The door won't hold them if they find us." Mael spoke in a low voice.

"We have to find a way out. The fire..."

"You'll fit through the window. I'll help you."

Sorrow looked again at the window. She might get through it, but he wouldn't. "And what about you?"

He didn't reply.

She hesitated, debating furiously whether she should go.

Leaving him to face them alone...

No, she decided. Two against three were better odds. Even if they did have swords.

"Do you think they actually want to kill us?" Sorrow asked. "Or is this all to scare us?"

Deep down she knew it was a stupid question – people didn't throw fire and point swords unless they meant it – but she was desperate for some kind of reassurance.

Mael was silent for a moment. "I don't know."

They both fell quiet then, and Sorrow realized that they were pressed shoulder to shoulder, and for the first time she didn't want to recoil from his touch. He might not be her brother, but right then she was grateful not to be alone. Because she'd loathed her father, she had no difficulty understanding that the people would. Stars, if they'd risen up against him while he was alive she might have been tempted to join them.

But she'd never imagined it might have transferred to her. She'd spent so long crafting a speech she'd thought would please them, reassure them. She didn't know them at all. And now she might die here. Murdered by masked men, who despised her because of her name.

She leant harder against Mael, comforted when he pressed back.

Minutes passed, with no sound from outside, and Sorrow shifted her weight. Beside her, Mael did the same.

"Maybe we should go?" Sorrow said.

Mael shook his head. "We're safer in here for now. It's us they want."

She suppressed a shiver. Maybe it was the Sons of Rhannon who'd sent the dead kitten. It seemed likely.

"Have you heard of these people before?" she asked haltingly. "Or has anything happened to you?"

"No. Nothing."

Sorrow blew out a long breath. "It sounds quiet. I'm going to—" she began, but no sooner had she said it than they heard footsteps and shouts. Someone rattled the door and Mael pushed Sorrow back, covering her as he gripped the handle.

"The window. . ." Mael hissed. "Go. . ."

"Sorrow?" Luvian's voice was tight with panic. "Sorrow?"

"In here!" she cried, forcing Mael out of the way and throwing the door open.

Luvian was alone.

"Where's Irris?" Sorrow asked, looking around for her friend.

"Safe. Don't worry," Luvian said. "Are you all right?" He moved as though to embrace her, stilling when Mael stepped out of the room.

Before Sorrow could explain, an older man, tall and reed thin, with thick sideburns, rounded the corner and stopped when he saw them.

"You're all right?" he asked Mael, who nodded, then moved to the man's side, a slight tremor to his hands the only sign he was still shaken. Sorrow's own heart was still fluttering away inside her chest like a trapped bird, her knees locked to keep her from collapsing or running, her body torn between both.

"Captain Vine said he'd send someone to fetch us when it was safe to do so," the man announced to the group. "The fire is mostly contained, but we can't leave via the main hall. I'm Arta

Boniface, Mael's advisor. Glad to finally have the pleasure. I'm only sorry it's under such strained circumstances."

Sorrow took a halting step forward and gripped the hand Arta Boniface offered. "Sorrow Ventaxis," she said. "This is Luvian Fen, my advisor."

"I know Luvian," Arta Boniface said. "In fact, I taught him at the East Marches Institute."

Luvian's face was carefully blank as he shook his former tutor's hand. "Arta was the only professor to grade me less than ninety-five per cent on my final exams," Luvian said. "Have you left the faculty now?" he asked the older man.

"A sabbatical."

"Until after the election?"

Arta inclined his head. "Unless I'm needed afterwards." His tone implied he didn't expect to return to his old role.

They lapsed into silence. Sorrow wanted to ask Luvian what had happened after she'd run, wanted to tell him that Meeren Vine had stood by and watched it happen, but she didn't want to say anything in front of Mael or his advisor, didn't want them to think her weak. So instead they waited, until finally Meeren Vine himself and two other members of the Decorum Ward appeared. Sorrow's fury mounted as she saw his flushed cheeks and bright eyes. She might have mistaken them for signs of exertion, if she didn't know better.

He was excited.

"All clear," he said, inclining his head towards Sorrow in a way that made her blood boil. How dare he pretend to care?

"And the men?" Luvian asked, before she could say anything. "The Sons of Rhannon? Did you catch them?"

"Got away," Vine replied. He looked at Sorrow, and she

could have sworn she saw his lip twitch, as though he was trying to master the urge to smile, or smirk.

She decided not to give him the satisfaction of her anger. He knew, and he knew she knew what he'd done. Let him wonder when her vengeance would come. Because it would.

"What about the people?" Sorrow asked, keeping her tone as pleasant as she was able. "Was anyone hurt?"

She knew she'd scored a point when he blinked rapidly before replying. "There was a crush, to escape."

"Did anyone. . .? Is anyone. . .?" Mael asked.

"No one died," Vine said.

Sorrow was careful to keep her own expression neutral as she replied. "Thank you for your service. I don't know what we'd have done without you."

Again, that satisfying double blink of confusion, before he said, "Any time, Miss Ventaxis. I'll send some people back with you to the North Marches –" he nodded to the man and woman with him "– in case any of them are still around. They'll keep a close eye on you."

Sorrow heard the threat in the words, but understood too late what it meant.

Meeren Vine didn't like to lose.

"In fact," Vine continued, "you ought to keep a guard with you at all times, seeing as the Sons of Rhannon have it in for you. Commander Dain, you wouldn't mind sticking near Miss Ventaxis, would you?"

The female Decorum Ward shook her head wordlessly as Sorrow's heart sank.

Sorrow looked at the female guard. She was tall, two heads taller than Sorrow, and broad, her muscular frame obvious even beneath her black tunic. Her dark hair was shorn close to her head, like all of the Ward, and her expression was theirs too: chin raised and jutted, eyes unforgiving.

"I don't think that will be necessary," Sorrow said.

"Oh, after what happened tonight, I think it is. And Commander Dain is one of my finest lieutenants," Vine replied with a smile. "You'll be in very safe hands."

Clever bastard. The last thing she wanted after his display inside was to have one of his people with her, and he knew it. This was a warning not to say anything about what he'd done. And to remind her that he and his men were her only real protectors.

"What about Mael?" Sorrow said desperately. "He'll need someone too."

"It's in hand," Arta Boniface said, and Vine gave him a courteous nod.

Sorrow looked at Luvian, imploring him to do something, but he shrugged, an apology in his eyes. Traitor. "Let's go," she said tersely.

Vine inclined his head and turned, leading her, Luvian, Mael and Arta through the warren of corridors, Dain and the other Ward bringing up the rear. They finally arrived at a door leading out to a small side lane, where Irris was waiting with two more members of the Decorum Ward.

She moved to Sorrow's side and hugged her before taking her by the hand and saying, "The carriage is this way, come on."

Sorrow allowed herself to be led as the last of her adrenaline seeped away, leaving her shaking and cold.

"Sorrow," Mael called.

She turned to see him standing in the light of a gas lamp on the wall.

He looked small, sad, and very tired. She was lucky to be

going back to the North Marches with Irris and Luvian. Arta didn't seem like much of a friend, and Vespus was in Rhylla. She didn't know if he had anyone else. And she was surprised to find she hoped he did. Hoped he wasn't alone. Not tonight, at least. She waited for him to say something more, but then Arta Boniface took his arm and guided him away.

Meeren Vine stepped forward then, standing in the light Mael had just left. And unlike Mael, he didn't look sad or lost. He raised a hand to Sorrow, as though bidding her farewell. It was only once she was safely in her carriage, Luvian and Irris either side of her, that she realized his fist had been closed. Not a wave, but a gesture of victory.

22

To Ask, Not Answer

Dain sat with them in the carriage as they returned to the North Marches, preventing Sorrow from telling Luvian and Irris about Vine's actions – or lack thereof – during the attack. She didn't want the Decorum Ward commander reporting back to her boss; she wanted Vine to think she'd let him win, that she'd learned her lesson.

But inside she smouldered, her anger red coals that burned the whole way back. She kept replaying, it, over and over, fury and shame taking turns to assault her: how he'd turned away. How he'd smirked at her through the flames, while the Sons of Rhannon advanced. How, in that moment, he'd taken all of her power and made her beg for his help, and still done nothing. She'd been a fool to think he'd be so easily got rid of. And now he had someone watching her. Without meaning to, she shot Dain a filthy look, which the

Decorum Ward missed as she stared out of the window into the night.

Irris noticed, though, and glanced at her questioningly.

"This is Commander Dain, my new bodyguard," Sorrow told her. "Captain Vine assigned her to me."

"I see," Irris said, offering Sorrow a sympathetic smile.

Sorrow supposed she was lucky to have got this far without having a personal guard assigned to her, but then the hooded man had been right too – she'd barely left the palace before, and when she had, there had been a battalion of Decorum Ward between her and the people.

And the people had never tried to attack a Ventaxis before.

Nevertheless, the presence of the guard annoyed her, and, still shaken from the events at the hall, Sorrow pretended to doze on the journey home. There would be repercussions from this, she thought, as she leant against the carriage side with her eyes closed. More than being assigned a bodyguard. Twice she'd been targeted now. Would there be more? Or would Mael be next? She found she didn't like the idea of that, either.

Mael... Another thought was demanding room in her head, one she didn't want to give any credit to. But it wouldn't leave her: the way he kept defending her, even against Vespus. The way he was always so nice. The way he'd grieved when Harun had died...

The way he acted persistently like a big brother.

Even though he couldn't be.

By the time they arrived back at their headquarters, Sorrow's pretend sleepiness had become real, her body and mind utterly exhausted; she didn't think she could talk if she'd tried.

Luvian gestured for her to follow him into the library, but

she shook her head, barely able to put one foot in front of the other.

"Tomorrow," she said finally, her voice soft and slurred, and he'd paused, about to speak, and then nodded.

The last of her energy was spent shooting a dark look at Dain as she took up a station outside her room. She made sure to turn the lock loudly, and then, quietly, she placed a chair under the doorknob. The idea of Dain out there didn't make Sorrow feel secure.

Sorrow climbed into bed fully clothed, not even bothering to kick off her boots as she pulled the sheets up to her chin, for once wanting the weight and warmth of them. When she closed her eyes she saw the three men again, staring up at her. The fire blazing across the stage as they'd flung their missiles at her. She sat up, heart pounding, reaching into her drawer for the remainder of the sleeping draught she'd taken the night before. Three large sips saw her sinking into a mercifully dreamless sleep.

She woke earlier than she'd expected, the sun barely warming the room. The manse felt quiet and still as she sat up. Her feet hurt from being confined inside her boots all night, and she pulled them off, dropping them to the floor with a thud. She followed them out of the bed, crossing to where her trunks were packed and waiting to be loaded on to the carriage for the journey to Rhylla later that morning.

Would they still go? she wondered. After what had happened, was it too dangerous?

If only Mael hadn't appeared that day on the bridge, she would have returned to Rhannon after the memorial and signed the papers deposing Harun. She'd already be chancellor, or as near as. Last night would never have happened. Though the Sons of Rhannon had made it clear they were against all Ventaxises, so perhaps it might have done... Vine had said there was a crush. No one had died, but that didn't mean people hadn't been hurt. More pain at the hands of a Ventaxis.

Again she thought about how much she'd underestimated the work ahead of her. Luvian had been right to call her list naive. It was nowhere near enough to simply open curtains and bring back colour. She had to make them trust her – despite her name.

There was a kind of karmic resonance to the Sons of Rhannon, she realized, crossing the room to check the balcony door was locked. Her family had been a little like them, once. They'd been the ones trying to overthrow their supposed evil overlords, gathering allies and spreading the word across Rhannon. And they'd succeeded. The kings and queens who'd once ruled Rhannon had been destroyed, and replaced, by the Ventaxises.

So she had to learn from this. Or else be the bad guy on two fronts: former usurper, and present dictator. She needed to be better than her ancestors – more than them. But how?

She was the first to arrive at breakfast, and she dismissed the servants and told Dain to remain outside the room, closing the door on the large woman. On her way to the table she pulled the list from the wall, pouring herself coffee while she read through it, tearing a roll into small pieces, waiting for the others to join her.

Irris came first.

"I thought you'd still be in bed," she said as she sat opposite Sorrow. "I went to your rooms. Did you sleep at all?"

Sorrow shrugged. "I used the last of the sleeping draught and got a few hours. But I woke early anyway."

Irris looked at the pile of shredded bread on Sorrow's plate. "I take it that's representative of your thoughts on the Sons of Rhannon?"

Sorrow popped one of the pieces into her mouth theatrically, only to spit it straight back out into a napkin when it turned to mush, offering Irris an apologetic smile.

"How are you feeling?" Irris asked.

"Aside from the attempt on my life, and the knowledge my future people hate me?"

"The people don't hate you. The Sons of Rhannon do." Irris pulled the coffee pot towards her.

"The people agreed with them. They hate what I am. A Ventaxis," Sorrow replied. "And I'm not sure I blame them. Not after what my father and grandfather did."

"They'll see you're not like them."

"Only if I show them I'm not."

"And you will, when you win." Irris poured herself some coffee, and topped off Sorrow's cup. "I saw your bodyguard outside."

Sorrow grunted as she sipped her drink.

"I hate to say it, but I'm glad the Decorum Ward were there last night."

"I'm not – Meeren Vine ignored me during the attack." Sorrow cut across her.

Irris paused in the act of lifting her cup to her mouth. "What?"

"I didn't want to use the Ward, because I know the people hate them. I thought it would look better if I tried to handle it myself. But when the Sons of Rhannon threw those things, I raised my hand to call for him. He hesitated. He *smirked*, Irri. He did it on purpose. To prove a point."

"What point?"

"That we need them. I need them. Last night proved it, and Vine knows that. But as long as they're working for me, the people won't like me. So I'm stuck – vulnerable without them, hated because of them. Having one as my personal guard is only going to look like approval, and that's why Vine sent her." Sorrow nodded to the closed door that Commander Dain stood behind.

Irris sipped her coffee. "I'll write to my father and ask him if he can release one of the palace guards to take over once you return from Rhylla. You do need a guard, though, at least until the Sons of Rhannon are brought under control. You could have been hurt. Killed."

"I know," Sorrow said, a shiver breaking along her shoulders. "What was that they threw at me?" she asked.

"Quickfire," Luvian said from the doorway. "It's a powder that reacts with air after it's been agitated in water. Add it to a bottle, seal it, shake it, and throw it. The bottle smashes, flames ensue."

Sorrow and Irris turned to him, and Sorrow was stunned to see how unlike himself he appeared. His suit was crumpled, as though he'd slept in it, stubble shadowing his chin, the top of his hair an almost vertical shock of black.

"It's Rhyllian," he added, making his way to the table. "They use the dried version in their fireworks. You'll no doubt see it in action at the Naming."

"You're not still going?" Irris said. "Is that wise?"

"It's up to you," Luvian said to Sorrow. "I'll go along with whatever you say."

Though she wanted to go, she didn't relish the idea of being out in a carriage, easily attacked. She didn't want the Sons of Rhannon to try to finish what they'd started the previous night, when she was miles from safety, with only Dain, Luvian and the coach drivers to protect her. But if she didn't go, if she stayed in Rhannon...

"We're going," she said. "We'll just have to take extra care. The worst thing I could do is hide away. Too reminiscent of my father. And I don't want to lose the chance to see what we can find out about Mael."

She wondered then if he'd got back to his lodgings all right, and if he'd still go to Rhylla. Yes, she decided. He would. So she had to.

Luvian sat down and poured a generous cupful of coffee, ignoring it when it sloshed over the rim and stained the tablecloth in a pattern that reminded Sorrow of the mark on the music hall ceiling.

"Wait a second," Sorrow said, remembering something. "Did you just say quickfire is Rhyllian? So is this Vespus's doing somehow? The Sons of Rhannon are in league with him?"

Luvian looked at her with tired, red eyes. "No," he said firmly. Then, "It wouldn't make sense. Mael was on that stage too. Very risky to have your own puppet in the literal firing line. The Sons of Rhannon are a problem, but a separate one from Vespus and Mael. You do seem to attract trouble."

"I hardly do it on purpose," Sorrow said, and took a deep breath. She was ready to speak her thoughts from the night before. "But, while we're talking about Mael..."

"I thought we were talking about the Sons of Rhannon?" Luvian said.

Irris tutted at him, and turned to Sorrow.

"We know it's unlikely he's the real Mael," Sorrow began. "But is it possible he doesn't? That the way he behaves is because in his mind he is my brother?"

"No," Irris said instantly. "What? No. No, it's him and Vespus in this together, we know that."

"Do we?" Luvian said, dragging a hand through his hair, answering before Sorrow could. "I have to confess, it's crossed my mind before now, too. What if he believes he *is* the lost child? What if he believes what Vespus has told him, because he truly lived that life he told you about?"

"Think about it," Sorrow said to Irris, who was shaking her head. "All the times he's defended me, the times he's saved me. Last night he told me to run while he held them off. And he's always so obnoxiously nice. . ."

"It would make sense," Luvian said, leaning across the table. "More sense to raise a child into a story than to get an actor to learn a script later. If he'd only joined Vespus in the last two years, there would be Rhannish people who would know him. Parents, friends, neighbours even. It would be too risky."

"So what?" Irris's expression was thoughtful as she worked through their case. "He was stolen as a child, and given to this Beliss woman to raise, waiting for the right moment to bring him back? You said yourself, Vespus wanted the war to continue for his land, and then he tried to petition your father. Oh – what if he took advantage of Mael's fall and created a backup plan? A boy he could hide in Rhylla in case he needed him?"

Luvian nodded. "He'd be too young to remember where he really came from, and enough time has passed to make him unrecognizable to his real parents here. His appearance could have been altered to give him the birthmark – he could have been tattooed, or perhaps someone with a cosmetic ability added it?"

"Abilities can only manipulate things that already exist," Sorrow reminded him. "Ras could only get rid of pain that existed at that moment. Vespus can only work with plants if he has plant material to hand."

"Maybe Vespus found a kid with a mole on his neck?" Luvian suggested. "That would be something that existed. He could have had someone manipulate that."

Irris looked at Sorrow, who shrugged. It was the most likely explanation for it, barring the tiny possibility the birthmark was real. . .

"So what do we do?" Irris said. "Because whether he knows it or not, he's still almost definitely an imposter."

"I'm already working on it," Luvian said. "I sent for the reports of every child that went missing, or is thought to have died, but no body recovered, during the three years before, and three years after, your brother was lost. That's what was in the package that arrived last week. I've been going through them. We'll also need to take advantage of our time in Rhylla to see what we can find there. Ideally, we find Beliss, though I expect Vespus will have hidden her away. But there are other avenues to explore. I have a plan." Luvian reached for the coffee pot again. "So eat up. It's going to be a long day."

23

Unmasking

The plan, Luvian informed her as he rushed her to finish her breakfast, was to leave for Rhylla within the hour. They'd take a carriage to the bridge, and on the other side a Rhyllian carriage would collect them, to bring them to the capital city. But on the way they would stop overnight in an inn.

"Where is the inn?" Sorrow asked.

"Ah." For the first time since he'd entered the room, a spark lit Luvian's eyes. "We're staying overnight in a place called Ceridog. It's a small village, tiny school, a clay mine, the inn. Oh, but the clay mine is … unusual. It's what they call a Rainbow Clay Mine, very rare. In fact, it's the only one in Rhylla." He paused, reaching forward for a pear from the bowl on the table. "Ceridog is a very popular place for artists to live and work."

Sorrow understood then. "The artist who painted Mael's portraits is Rhyllian. You found him?"

"No." He looked momentarily chagrined. "But, seeing as we're passing that way – and it's such a hub for artists – who are we to turn down the chance to visit? If we happen to find the artist, and therefore discover who commissioned the portraits, and, if that person happens to be Lord Vespus, well ... that would be a bonus." He was sounding more and more like himself each moment, his expression brightening. "Obviously the primary reason for going is because I myself am an art lover; everyone knows it."

And despite herself, and everything that had happened the night before, Sorrow found herself smiling at him.

Luvian took a bite of his pear with a satisfied crunch.

The journey to the bridge was uneventful, though Sorrow's heart had hammered the whole way, expecting at any moment for more quickfire to be thrown, or the carriage to be ambushed. She was almost grateful for Dain's silent, hulking presence beside her. When she saw the bridge on the horizon, the white stone blinding in the morning sun, she relaxed. They'd be over the border soon.

It was too easy. As the carriage drew to a halt, she looked out of the window to see two of the Decorum Ward scrubbing at something on the ancient, mythical bridge.

Luvian's face tightened.

"What is that?" She turned to Luvian. But then she saw it.

Sons of Rhannon. In tall, red letters like blood. Like the tunic she'd worn the night before.

Luvian was out of the carriage at once, Sorrow following a split second later, with Dain hopping down from her seat beside the driver to join them.

"How did this happen?" Luvian demanded of the guards.

The men turned slowly, looking at Luvian, their eyes shifting to Sorrow and finally resting on Dain, offering her a respectful nod.

"We don't know," said one of the men; he was small, wiry, with pointed features.

"You don't know how someone managed to vandalize a bridge that is supposed to be under round-the-clock guard?" Luvian asked.

"It was dark. They were very quiet."

Luvian's face was thunderous. "I see."

Sorrow looked at the men. Their expressions were insolent, the same hint of a sneer Meeren Vine had worn gracing their lips. And she knew then that it was deliberate. That they'd wanted her to see this, before she crossed the bridge. Perhaps they'd even planned it. Last night hadn't been a one-off, but a beginning.

Sorrow's eyes darted to the woman beside her, her supposed protector, and her fear grew. Was Dain part of this? How much danger was she in?

Then, to everyone's surprise, Dain spoke. "What is this? Get this filth cleared," she said in a low growl.

The men looked at each other, clearly shocked, as Sorrow looked at the commander, an identical look of surprise on her face.

Commander Dain wasn't finished. "And you make sure it doesn't happen again. Because if it does, I will take it as an act of disobedience against me personally. And I won't like that one bit. Do I make myself clear?"

"Yes, Commander."

Dain looked to Sorrow and nodded, and Sorrow returned the gesture, still taken aback by the Decorum Ward commander's actions.

Luvian covered for her. "Come, Sorrow, we'll be late. Let's leave these good men to their jobs. It looks like they have a quite a lot to do, and the sun is only going to get hotter and higher."

With that he turned, taking Sorrow firmly by the elbow, guiding her to the Alvus gum waiting for them.

Sorrow said nothing else until they were both seated in a new carriage on the Rhyllian side of the bridge, Dain up beside the driver once more, and the carriage was on the move.

"They did it." Sorrow moved to Luvian's side and pitched her voice a fraction louder than the carriage wheels. "The guards, they painted it, and they wanted me to see. I think they're trying to align themselves with the Sons of Rhannon. I'm the common enemy to them both."

Luvian turned to her, staring for a long moment before he gave a single nod. "I think you're right."

"What do we do? If they control the bridge then they control who's crossing it. What if someone comes after us – me – when we're out there, miles from home?"

Luvian chewed his lip, falling silent as he contemplated. "We're safer there," he said finally. "We'll be safe at the castle; it's well-secured and there will be guards everywhere. And no one knows we're going to Ceridog apart from you, me and Irris."

"And the coach driver, presumably," Sorrow said.

"No," he said thoughtfully. "I didn't want to tip Vespus off, so I hadn't planned to tell him until we'd stopped. The inn is booked under a pseudonym, for the same reason. By chance, it'll keep the Sons of Rhannon off our tail. They won't know we're there, and they won't have time to get to you even if they do find out. Win-win."

Sorrow was impressed. "That's sneaky."

Luvian shrugged, his cheeks darkening. "Quite. In the meantime, you need to write to Lord Day. Tell him everything."

"I can't. He has to be impartial."

"This is impartial. This is the country's police turning on their potential leader. And that only ever leads to martial law. Sorrow, if Dain hadn't been there today, Graces knows what might have happened. You have to nip this in the bud. If they're being this blatant about it, they must already think they could win."

"Win what?"

"Rhannon." Luvian leant forward. "You're not only fighting Mael for the country any more. You're fighting the Sons of Rhannon too. As is he, but I don't care about that. I care about you, and they've made it pretty clear that they have a grudge against you. Without the power of the chancellorship behind you, you're vulnerable to them all. It's more important than ever that you win."

The rest of the journey to Ceridog was sombre, and silent, Luvian working through his list, circling cases he thought were of note, and Sorrow writing to Charon, then watching the Rhyllian countryside roll by.

She sent the letter when they paused to change horses, staying close to Dain while Luvian informed her and the driver of the change of plan. He didn't seem put out, only commenting that he'd have to stay in Ceridog overnight too, in order to take them the rest of the way to Adavaria the following day. Luvian, it seemed, had already thought of that, and had booked him a room at the inn.

"I didn't anticipate you," he said apologetically to Dain. "Though I'm sure they'll have something."

"I'll be fine on the floor outside Miss Ventaxis's room," Dain said.

"You can't—" Sorrow began, but stopped when Dain tilted her chin up, her jaw set, gaze steady. "Well, we'll at least get you a pillow," she said feebly, following Luvian back into the coach as Dain closed the door firmly behind her.

The inn was different from Melisia's – this building was four storeys tall, with black wooden struts studding the white walls, and tables outside. Luvian had reserved the two attic rooms for them, at the top of a crooked but private staircase, and a room on the floor below for the coachman.

Dain checked both Sorrow's room and Luvian's before she took up a position at the base of their stairs without being asked, and Sorrow shrugged and went to see what a Rhyllian bedroom looked like.

Before she could see her own, Luvian tapped her shoulder and beckoned her into his. It was small, and disappointingly unremarkable. A single bed slotted against the wall, a narrow wardrobe at the end of it. There was a bureau and chair opposite, and a door Sorrow assumed led to a bathroom. But it was clean, and bright, the window looking out on to the square below, swallows darting in and out under the eaves.

Sorrow watched as Luvian reached into one of his cases and pulled out a rolled canvas. She gasped when he unfurled it, using shoes, a hairbrush and a bottle of cologne Sorrow had no idea he wore to pin the corners to the golden wood floor.

This year's portrait of Mael. He'd taken it from the Summer Palace.

"You stole it," Sorrow accused. "How? When?"

"Hush. I'm about to say some very important things." Luvian knelt down beside it. "Pay attention. So, I'm going to assume you know very little about art, given the state of the nation for, quite literally, your whole life?"

Sorrow nodded.

"Then allow me to educate you, Sorrow, dear. The Rhannish style of painting is to use small strokes to create a whole picture. Up close it makes no sense, but at a distance the image can be seen. But the Rhyllian style is long, continuous strokes. That's one way we can be sure the artist really is Rhyllian. See?" He gestured at the painting and she saw what he meant.

"The paints themselves differ too. Rhannish paints are oil based. Whereas Rhyllian –" he brushed a finger along the painted hair of the portrait and held it up to her, so she could see the thin layer of brown dust there "– are clay based. And when clay dries, it leaves a thin layer of powder."

"And here we are in the clay paint capital of Rhylla." Sorrow remembered his words back in the North Marches, and Luvian beamed at her.

"Indeed. A place so prestigious, there is a Registry of Colours."

"OK, now you've lost me," Sorrow confessed.

In reply, Luvian drew a small knife from the pocket of his coat and began to scrape the dark paint from the birthmark on the portrait.

"What are you doing?" Sorrow watched in horrified fascination as he vandalized the painting.

He didn't reply, continuing until he'd made a small pile of purplish flakes, which he carefully lifted on to the tip of the knife, before tapping them into the centre of a plain silk handkerchief.

"As I was saying, Rhylla takes art so seriously it keeps a Registry of Colours. The Rainbow Clay Mines mostly yield primary colours, which anyone can buy and sell, and mean very little, but every now and then, the pigments in the rocks mix and create pure, naturally occurring secondary and tertiary colours. Of course, that happens very rarely, so the artists buy primaries and mix their own. But they're required to register the colours, and the paintings they used them on, with the Registry, so that art buyers can't be cheated. See, an unscrupulous artist could claim the purple they used in your portrait was genuine pure colour from the mines, something they paid a fortune to procure, and therefore have to pass the cost on..."

"I get it," Sorrow said. "So, we can take those scrapings to the registry and find out who registered them? And that will lead us to the artist, which will hopefully lead us closer to finding out who Mael is, or at least who commissioned the pictures."

"Got it in one, Sorrow darling."

A burst of pleasure shot through Sorrow at his approval. "How do you know so much about Rhyllian art?"

Luvian opened his mouth, then closed it. "It's what I would have liked to do, if I could have. If the option had been there for me," he said finally. "My grandfather was a great lover of art. He taught me."

Sorrow had never seen Luvian look sad before. Angry, cheerful, arrogant and annoyed. But never sad. She realized it was the first time he'd ever revealed anything about himself. His time at university was "educational", his family were "amicably estranged". He never spoke of friends, save to say he wasn't popular, nor of lovers or love interests, only focused on his work. All accounts from his time at university said the same. She'd assumed there was a tragic story there, some kind of falling out with his family, or maybe childhood shyness he'd only outgrown after university, because no one could accuse him of it now. To be honest, she'd stopped thinking about him as anything other than part of her, Irris and him, the team she hoped to win the election with. He'd slotted so seamlessly into Sorrow's life, barely causing a ripple, that she'd almost forgotten he was still mostly a stranger to her.

He seemed to realize he'd let his mask slip as he forced brightness into his voice and continued. "So I used the gift of foresight to become a political maven, with the intent of seating a chancellor who will make it possible for me to indulge my hobbies. And on that note, we have work to do."

There was no point in pretending they weren't who they were – the country was abuzz with the news from Rhannon and the fact that both candidates were attending the Naming, even though no one had anticipated them coming to Ceridog.

So they didn't try to be discreet, instead walking slowly through the town to the central square, Dain shadowing them closely. Though Sorrow felt horribly exposed, she tried to relax, reminding herself no one knew they were there.

She forced herself to pause and look in windows, as Luvian marvelled at the things for sale: books, jewellery, trinkets that could have no real use except to be looked at as they gathered dust, until eventually Sorrow's curiosity was real, and her enthusiasm too. All around them Rhyllians walked and chattered, sitting on tables outside cafés with small cups of steaming coffee, gossiping in their lilting language, looking happy and relaxed. On a street corner a tall olive-skinned Rhyllian pulled a shining silver flute from a case and began to play, as passers-by flicked silver coins into a hat he'd left on the ground. Two children darted forward to dance, and Sorrow found her mouth curving involuntarily.

There was so much room for pleasure in the world, Sorrow realized, as Luvian handed her a small cake, topped with cream and crystallized petals, that he'd ducked into a bakery to buy after she'd pointed it out in the window. This was what she wanted for Rhannon. For life to feel worth it, not just be toil and misery.

Luvian handed one of the confections to Dain, who stared at the cake as though unable to believe it was real. She ate it in three bites, but there was a reverence to them that Sorrow found oddly charming. She would never have expected one of the Decorum Ward to be so . . . human. Though she was loath to admit it, after what happened at the bridge, and now this, the woman was beginning to grow on her.

When Sorrow took the first bite of her own cake, she couldn't stop herself from moaning. She'd thought the feast at the inn was incredible, but it was nothing, *nothing*, compared to the rapture of sugar and cream that flooded her tongue now. She met Dain's eyes with a complicit, chocolate-coated grin, as she licked the cream from her fingers greedily, not wanting a single morsel to go to waste. Irris hadn't said it was like *this*. Sorrow was right to demand everyone give her cake, she thought giddily. There really ought to be cake every day.

When she glanced at Luvian, he was staring at her, rubbing the back of his neck, his lips parted, and she realized abruptly she wasn't behaving like a future chancellor. She swallowed the remainder quietly, making sure she appeared composed every time her advisor darted a nervous glance her way.

Though she'd find a way to go back to the bakery before they left.

After they'd spent enough time establishing themselves as curious tourists, and Sorrow had finally recovered from her cake, they headed for the Registry of Colours. It was two streets back from the square, an old-looking, golden-bricked building that dominated the leafy avenue.

Sorrow pulled Luvian away from Dain. "How do we play this?" she whispered.

"Straight. There's no point in lying, they'll see right through it. We say we're trying to trace the artist, and we know this is one of the colours they used."

"All right." She returned to Dain. "I'm sorry, but I need to ask you to wait here." She pointed to a wooden bench, positioned beneath a tree. "This is confidential. You can't come with us."

"I'm supposed to guard you. I have orders." When she'd spoken at the bridge her voice had been a commanding bark, iron-lined and brutal. But now her voice was soft, sweet even, at odds with her muscular frame.

Sorrow looked at her more closely then, at her clear, bright skin, her delicate nose and large, thickly lashed eyes. She couldn't be much older than Luvian, perhaps mid-twenties. Her cheeks still had a childlike roundness to them, and again Sorrow thawed towards her. She wasn't the battle-hardened monster Sorrow imagined all the Decorum Ward were.

"I'm sorry, Dain. I can't tell you why you can't come, but that's *my* order. Please," Sorrow tried.

Dain gave her a long look, and then nodded. "Very well. I'll wait." She sat on the bench, knees apart, hands resting atop them.

"Call me deluded, but I think Vine might have accidentally assigned me the only decent member of the Decorum Ward," Sorrow murmured to Luvian as they approached the door to the registry.

"Miracles do occasionally occur."

He pulled the cord that hung beside the door, releasing it when a deep bell chimed behind the thick wood. A moment later, the door swung silently open and a young Rhyllian woman stood there. Like Rasmus, she was adorned in jewellery, her ears lined with hoops, another in her left nostril, and one piercing her left eyebrow. Her paint-splattered fingers were full of rings too, and through a tear in her equally stained tunic, Sorrow spied another ring through her belly button. The girl looked from Sorrow, to Luvian, then back to Sorrow, before frowning.

"We have some paint fragments we'd like to match," Luvian began, in Rhyllian.

"I know who you are," the girl replied in heavily accented Rhannish. "You're here about the portraits. Of the lost boy returned. You want to know who painted them."

"Yes." Luvian blinked. "But how—"

"It's me," the girl said, leaving Luvian gaping like a fish, and Sorrow stunned into silence. "I paint them. Well, I painted the last one, at least. You'd better come in."

She stood back to allow Sorrow and Luvian to enter, and they did, stumbling through the doorway.

They stood in a light, airy hallway dominated by a white wooden staircase that curved like the spirals of a shell, narrowing as it joined the floor above. The floor was tiled, also white, and the girl's bare feet made no sound as she walked past them, heading to a small door set back in the wall.

"Were you expecting us?" Sorrow asked, bewildered by the fact she'd been there, as though waiting for them.

The girl gave her a scathing look over her shoulder. "I was passing the door when you rang the bell. This way," she said.

Sorrow and Luvian exchanged a confused glance before following.

The Rhyllian didn't bother waiting for them as she moved silently down a corridor, turning left and vanishing around a corner. By the time they reached that bend, she was about to disappear around another, and so it continued as they chased her through a warren of identical passages, until at last they came to a corridor halted by a wall at the end, the girl nowhere to be seen. Nervous, they edged down the passage, pausing as they drew level with an open door. When they peered into the room beyond, they found the girl in there, throwing sheets over canvases.

They hovered in the doorway, something about the space forbidding them from entering without permission. It was a studio, that much was clear. But it was also a home; there was a low, narrow bed in the corner that hadn't been made, a small table covered in dirty dishes, clothes in rainbow colours thrown over a mannequin and heaped on a chair.

"Come in," the girl said, apparently more concerned with hiding her work than the evidence of her life. The girl lowered herself to the floor, crossing her legs under her in a smooth motion. "I don't have any refreshments to offer," she said bluntly.

"That's all right," Sorrow said. She walked over to the girl and sat opposite her, Luvian kneeling beside her, trying to remain calm. Finally they'd found the artist. Finally she'd get some answers about Mael. "So, you're Graxal?"

"No."

Sorrow paused. "But you said you were the artist."

"I am. Now. But Graxal isn't my name. It isn't a name at all. It's two names, made one. My name, Xalys. And my mother's, Gralys. She was the artist, and when she died, I moved here and took over her work."

Sorrow hadn't been able to look at the signatures on the older portraits, back in the Winter Palace, before she'd left. She'd taken it for granted it was the same signature, same artist. Graxal. Gralys.

"I'm sorry for your loss," Sorrow said finally.

The girl – Xalys – shrugged. "It was too soon."

Sorrow left a respectful pause before she asked her next question. "So your mother was the person who originally painted the portraits of Mael?"

"Yes." Xalys looked at them with silver eyes. "Until this year – she died before she could finish. So I finished for her, and signed it from us both." She paused. "I suppose your next question is who commissioned the paintings?"

"Exactly," Sorrow said.

"Lord Vespus Corrigan," Xalys said. "Though I suppose I can technically call him 'Father'."

24

Something Long-Term

"Your *father*?" Sorrow stared at the girl. She'd expected Vespus to be the answer to the question. But she hadn't expected this. "Vespus is your father? Rasmus is your brother?"

Xalys raised her eyebrows. "Half-brother. Lord Corrigan married Rasmus's mother when I was six. He was never married to my mother."

Sorrow was stunned, momentarily forgetting why they were there as she stared at the Rhyllian woman before her, trying to find Rasmus, or Vespus, in her features. Rasmus had no idea this woman existed; he'd often wished for a brother or sister, despite Sorrow's dark warnings that they could be more trouble than they were worth.

"So *Lord Vespus* commissioned the paintings?" Luvian's tone was a nudge, warning Sorrow to pay attention, and she shook off her shock and focused on what Xalys was saying.

"Yes. As a gift for your father, from the people of Rhylla."
Xalys looked at Sorrow. "To express our condolences for what
happened at the bridge. You didn't know that?"

"The records of who painted it were lost," Sorrow said.
"We were curious about who did the work, year after year. And
how the tradition began. It was pure luck to find you here. We
thought we'd have more of a search on our hands."

"They're really something," Luvian added. "The pictures.
It must have been challenging to imagine him."

"For the first one we worked from a Rhannish painting.
When they're that little, they don't change very much."

"What about as he got older?" Sorrow asked, following
Luvian's lead.

"A combination of guesswork and pictures of the chancellor
and his wife. And a model Lord Vespus brought."

Sorrow froze. "A model? A Rhannish one?" To her ears she
sounded too curious; she could hear the desperation in her
voice, and she held her breath, waiting to see if Xalys noticed.

But it seemed not, as the Rhyllian replied, "I don't know.
I was never allowed to see him; Mama always sent me away
when they came. He came for a few years. Then he stopped,
and Vespus told my mother what he wanted changed."

Luvian spoke before Sorrow could. "Such as?"

"Nothing especially. Comments on the length of his hair,
the size of his lips, the tilt of his nose. It's hard, sometimes, to
predict how a child will look, especially through their teens.
Vespus said the very same about Rasmus – that he'd changed
into a boy he didn't think he'd recognize. He said he didn't
want that for your father."

Sorrow turned to Luvian, who met her gaze with his own
bright eyes.

"Did he?" Luvian murmured. "How interesting. I wonder where the model is now?"

"I couldn't tell you. Lord Vespus probably could."

"We'll be sure to ask when we see him at the Naming," Luvian said.

Sorrow nodded, her whole body buzzing with this new knowledge. There had been a model. Someone had sat for the paintings. Someone real. And they'd stopped going after three years... So the model would have been around seven. Young enough, perhaps, to not remember doing it. Sorrow couldn't remember anything specific from her seventh year; it was only after Rasmus had arrived that she had real memories of her childhood... So the Mael she knew might have been the model... And if he'd stopped going, was it because Vespus didn't want him to remember doing it?

Even if the model wasn't Mael, but some other child, Xalys had practically proven Vespus had been planning this for years. Why else would he do it? Sorrow fought back a grin at this realization. Finally, they had something.

"Does he look like her work?" Xalys asked Sorrow, interrupting her thoughts. "Mael, the real one. Were we close?"

"He's identical," Sorrow said, unable to keep her glee from her voice. "It's incredible."

Luvian rose to his feet then. "Well, that's cleared that puzzle up. Now we know who our mysterious benefactor is, and the gifted artist. Thank you for your time." He offered Sorrow a hand, hauling her up with surprising strength as Xalys gracefully unfolded her limbs and stood too.

"Can you find the way out?" Xalys asked.

"Not a chance," Luvian replied cheerfully, and the Rhyllian girl smiled.

For the first time, Sorrow recognized Rasmus in her face, and her stomach gave a gentle flip in response.

Xalys led them back along the winding passageways, until once again they were standing in the entrance hall. Two other Rhyllians were descending the spiral stairs, and they looked coolly at Sorrow and Luvian but said nothing as they passed them, disappearing into the warren of rooms and studios beyond.

"Thank you." Sorrow echoed Luvian's words as Xalys pulled open the main door to the street.

"Enjoy the Naming," Xalys said.

"We will."

"Oh, and if you're looking for somewhere to eat tonight, there is a place on the other side of the square, on Crown Street, called Anwyn's. It sells kishkies; they're a pastry peculiar to Ceridog. You should try them while you're here."

"Thanks again," Sorrow said. "I mean, you're good to us!"

Xalys closed the door then, seemingly deciding the goodbye was over.

"To the inn?" Luvian asked, and Sorrow nodded, trying to contain her happiness.

They remained silent as they retraced their steps back through the bustling square to the inn, collecting a bored-looking Dain on the way. They told the bodyguard they were going to rest before dinner, and left her outside the floor once more. Sorrow opened her door, counted to three, then closed it loudly, before sliding into Luvian's room and silently latching it shut.

He was already sitting at his desk, coat sleeves rolled up, a pen in his hand and a frown at his brow. She sat on his bed and watched as he began to go through his ever-present list of children, crossing things out before writing something else, underlining that and drawing arrows between words. There was a breeze dancing through the open window, and he tutted at it, as though that might make it stop, trying to pin the sheets down and write at the same time. She wanted to ask why he was working on the list now, why then of all times, but something in his posture made her wait until he'd put his pen down and sat back.

"Is now really the time?"

Luvian jumped, as though he'd forgotten, or not realized, that she was there. "What?" He ran a hand through his hair, causing it to stick up like the crest of a bird.

Sorrow nodded towards the papers. "To do that?"

He gave her a long, unreadable look before replying. "There were over fifteen thousand children reported missing or presumed dead during the seven years I'm looking at."

"Fifteen thousand?" Sorrow was shaken.

"Relatively it's a small amount, especially for a country with a population of almost twenty million people. But still, a lot," he added hastily, when Sorrow gaped at him. "So whenever I have time to do this, it's time to do it. Besides –" he paused, taking off his glasses and cleaning them on his tunic "– it helps me focus. It's something solid."

"So is what we learned from Xalys," Sorrow said.

Luvian paused, and put his glasses back on. "Oh, that's something," he said, confirming what Sorrow had realized earlier.

"So. . ." Sorrow didn't understand why he wasn't as pleased as she with what Xalys had told them.

"We still have no proof that Mael is an imposter. All we know for certain is that Vespus commissioned the portraits, and, in the early days, had someone model for them. We don't know who the model was, Xalys never saw him. He might not even have been Rhannish – it could have been Rasmus, did you think of that? Perhaps the reason Xalys had to stay away was so she didn't meet her brother."

"But—"

"But nothing, Sorrow. It's confirmed our suspicions, and raised a lot more questions. That's all."

A lump formed in Sorrow's throat and she swallowed, forcing it down to say, "So finding the artist was pointless, despite everything she said."

Luvian wrinkled his nose. "It depends on what the point is. If it was finally proving Mael is an imposter, yes, it was pointless. But what it proves is that Vespus has been behind the portraits from the beginning. He ordered them five years before he became the ambassador. And he clearly wanted it to remain a secret. Why?"

"I don't know. Because he's an evil puppet master who likes to toy with people?"

"Exactly," Luvian said, to her surprise. She was being facetious. "A puppet master, pulling the strings. So we need to know what strings he holds. Understanding that will lead us back to Mael, or whoever he is. We know Vespus is the queen's half-brother, and that he owns an Alvus tree farm in the north of Rhylla. That he was the ambassador in Rhannon for seven years—"

"Until he was banished for trying to manipulate my father into granting him land in Rhannon," Sorrow added. "He first went after it during the war, trying to convince his half-sister to not sign the treaty unless the North Marches was granted to him. Charon said it was something to do with the conditions in the north of Rhannon, and the south of Rhylla being the best place for Alvus to grow. He needs the land there for it."

"But Melisia wouldn't give it to him. Either in Rhylla, or Rhannon. That sounds like Melisia doesn't care if her brother's business fails."

"I suppose."

"Which means she doesn't support it, for whatever reason." Luvian twisted round and made another note on his papers. "So he tried to prolong the war, and was denied. Next, he asked his sister for the ambassador's job, and started working on Harun, who eventually sent him away because of it."

"And in the meantime, he'd already started grooming a boy to be Mael, and Rhannon to accept him through the portraits, as another backup," Sorrow said.

Luvian nodded, then frowned. "This is a huge amount of effort to go to just to get some land to grow trees on. He's a lord – half-brother to a queen."

"Maybe that's it. It's pride. Something only he can do, with his ability. Maybe he wants to be seen as special, or worthy in his own right. The only person in the world who can grow Alvus trees?"

Luvian shook his head. "It seems a remarkably unambitious goal for someone like Vespus. Get some land, be a great farmer... And like I said, so much work. Eighteen years of scheming and planning."

"Charon said it wouldn't just be land. It would be all of Rhannon. If he put a puppet ruler in charge, he could rule Rhannon through them, as his sister rules Rhylla," Sorrow finished for him. "Maybe that's his plan. He wants to play at being king, make himself Melisia's equal."

"Maybe," Luvian said, but he didn't sound convinced.

Sorrow was suddenly exhausted, too many thoughts in her mind. She lay back on Luvian's bed, and sighed. She hadn't expected it to be easy to unravel the mystery of Mael, but all their leads so far – Corius the tailor, long dead; the mysterious painter – had led to nothing but more doubts. There was no sign of the woman who'd supposedly raised Mael. The only solid thing they had was Vespus being in the background, pulling the strings, weaving his web. That was a problem, and one she planned on dealing with.

But still, she wanted, *needed*, to know whether or not the boy was a fake. She had to know one way or the other. She'd been on the bridge, seen the Archior, and she knew logically he couldn't be, but as long as there was the tiniest doubt in her mind, she'd never rest.

All those times he'd smiled at her, defended her. He'd tried to make Harun apologize to her. He'd offered to sacrifice himself to the Sons of Rhannon so she could get away.

He believed he was her brother. He wanted to be.

And in the darkest, most secret part of her heart, buried so deeply she could barely acknowledge it, she realized she no longer hated the idea of it.

Even though she knew it was impossible, even though he was trying to take her job, and her home, and Rhannon from her. . .

Because if he was her brother, then she wasn't alone.

But she couldn't let him in until she knew for sure.

She couldn't do anything until she knew for sure. So she had to find out who he really was.

"What's the plan, then?" she asked.

"Focus on 'election stuff'."

Sorrow heard the smile in his voice and reached for one of his pillows, throwing it at him.

"Concentrate on wooing everyone at the Naming, and then channel that into efforts in Rhannon." The pillow landed back beside her head, and Sorrow tucked it beneath her.

"And what will you be doing?"

"I will be using my enormous brain and intellect to cope with being your advisor *and* continuing to investigate Vespus, and Mael." He paused, and then the bed dipped as he sat beside her. She turned to look at him.

"But I don't want you to get bogged down in that obsession and sabotage your own campaign. Especially now you have the Sons of Rhannon to take on that duty." He smiled at her. "If we can somehow prove he's an imposter, then the election is undoubtedly sewn up. But, even if we can't prove it, I think you can win anyway. I *know* you can. So your job is to focus on that."

Sorrow reached for his hand and squeezed. "You're a good advisor. A good friend. I'm so glad to know you," she said as she released him.

Luvian stiffened, closing his eyes, and Sorrow wondered if she'd upset him. "Of course you are, who wouldn't be?" he said finally, opening his eyes and sitting up. "Let's go and find these kishkies."

They took Dain with them to the restaurant Xalys had recommended, asking for a table for three. She seemed confused to be included, and Sorrow couldn't blame her, given the way she'd treated her so far. Sorrow was ashamed of her behaviour, and so she made an effort to talk to her while they waited for their food.

"Where are you from?" Sorrow asked.

"The East Marches," Dain replied.

Sorrow waited to see if she'd add anything else, but when it became apparent she had no plans to, she asked, "What made you choose to join the Decorum Ward?"

"It's a job," she said in her soft-as-velvet voice. "Papa is dead, Mam's not up to much and I'm the eldest of five. We needed money, and it pays. Besides, there aren't a lot of jobs out there and I'm... Well, I'm big. It made advancing through the ranks a lot easier. And the higher you go, the more money there is, so..." She trailed off, head lowering a fraction, and Sorrow's heart twisted in sympathy for her.

She knew what it was to have few – or no – choices about the path your life took. Dain was doing what she had to, for herself and her family, and that was something Sorrow had come to understand. And if Dain felt that way, perhaps others in the Decorum Ward did too. Perhaps they needed a chance somewhere else.

"Do you like it?" Sorrow's voice was soft.

Dain stared at her, and Luvian turned to her too.

"I don't like throwing my weight around," Dain said, her voice barely a whisper. "I don't like bullies. Or cowards. The two tend to go hand in hand. I don't want to become one."

Sorrow understood then why Dain had stood up for her at the bridge.

She smiled at her guard. "A lot of things are going to change when I win the election," she said as their food arrived. "For everyone. For you, if you want. I'll probably need a constant bodyguard, someone I employ."

Dain nodded, her eyes lowered, and Sorrow reached for one of the kishkies.

The pastries were nice, lightly spiced meat inside a flaky shell, dusted with icing sugar. The combination of flavours and textures was strange but incredibly tasty, and the owners were delighted to have Rhannish guests. They'd brought out more varieties than the table ordered, and plied them with honey wine. Like all Rhyllians they spoke Rhannish, and Sorrow leant over to Luvian and told him that when she was chancellor she wanted to make learning Rhyllian available to everyone.

"All the languages," she'd said, her voice slurring gently. "All of them. If I had an ability like the Rhyllians, it's what I'd want. Imagine it." She tried to say something in Rhyllian, mangling the phrase and causing the Rhyllians at the table next to theirs to look disgusted.

"That's enough wine for you." Luvian looked a little worse for wear himself. For once he'd taken off his frock coat and was sitting in his shirtsleeves, the cuffs rolled up to his elbows, revealing surprisingly toned forearms. He tried to take her glass from her, but she slapped his hand away, and drained the contents.

"That's enough wine for me," she said as she put the glass down a little harder than she'd meant to. "Come on, we have an early start."

It was the wine that made Sorrow do it.

They were walking back, chattering loudly, when Sorrow saw the shop. The sign on the door said open, and so she paused, bending down, pretending to adjust the buckle on her shoe.

"Are you going to be ill?" Luvian turned and asked.

"No, my feet hurt. New shoes."

"Do you need me to carry you?" He looked serious.

"No, I'd snap you like a sapling. I'll sit down for a minute. You go on, Dain can walk with me."

Luvian shrugged and began to head to the inn, pausing once to look back at her. She made a pantomime of grimacing and rubbing her heel, watching through her hair until he'd turned a corner and was out of sight. Then, looking at Dain, she pressed a finger to her lips and beckoned her towards the shop.

When they arrived at the inn, Luvian was standing at the bar, having an animated conversation with the barkeep, and he turned to wave Sorrow over.

She pointed at her shoes, faking a limp, and then disappeared up the stairs to the corridor the Rhannish party had hired for themselves, Dain guarding the corridor this time not from danger but from her advisor, while she slipped into Luvian's room and left a parcel on the bed, smiling to herself.

She'd bought him a set of clay paints, three brushes, and a small sketch pad. She didn't know why, only that she'd wanted him to have them, because once he'd wanted to be an artist and maybe it wasn't too late. She wanted to give him something to thank him. Something to give him the hope he'd given her. The same kind of friendship. For the first time since she'd lost Rasmus, life felt as though it had something worth fighting for in it again that was more than revenge. Something long-term.

25

Adavaria

Adavaria was a maze of dense stone streets and cobbled pavements, so different to Rhannon, and Sorrow drank it all in. Where Rhannish houses and shops were usually squat, white buildings, spaced apart to help the heat escape, Rhyllian buildings were tall, at least two storeys, pressed together in rows with only the occasional alley to separate them. Chimneys emerged from the slate roofs, perches for the maglings – dark, small birds that were considered pests by the Rhyllians, but that Sorrow, who'd never seen them before, found oddly sweet.

It was a pretty town, Sorrow realized, as they moved slowly along, progress hampered by pedestrians and other carriages. Doorsteps were scrubbed clean, lined with mats decorated with Rhyllian script. Outside one door a fat orange cat lazed, watching the carriage with an unimpressed look on its squashed face. The doors themselves were painted brightly; cheerful curtains framed windows that housed window boxes full of flowers Sorrow didn't know the names of. There were wreaths of flowers on every door too, and Luvian told her they'd been made especially for the Naming, and would be tossed down to carpet the streets when the queen and her husband took baby Aralie on her first tour of the country.

Sorrow admired it all. It would be easy to make Rhannish towns look as lovely as these, and she asked Luvian to add it to her plans.

People turned curiously as the carriage made its way along the wide streets, pointing it out to each other, some even waving. At Luvian's quiet command Sorrow waved back, surprised when the people responded, more of them turning, coming out of their homes and from shops to see what the fuss was about.

"I wonder if we could do the same thing on the way home," Luvian said, pulling out his ever-present notebook.

"Here? Or in Rhannon?" Sorrow remembered the Sons of Rhannon, and thought of all the things that could be thrown at her, or fired at her, as she leant out of a carriage.

He looked thoughtful. "Yes, in Rhannon too. Dain will be there, and it'll make you look confident and unafraid. Good leadership qualities."

"Great," Sorrow said through her teeth as she smiled out at the rows of Rhyllians.

By the time they arrived at the castle, both of Sorrow's arms ached from waving. They drew up to the gates, and Luvian gave their names to the forbidding-looking guard who approached the carriage with a slim folder in his hands, crossing them off as he found their names on the list within.

"Who's that?" He nodded to Dain.

"My bodyguard, Dain. . ." Sorrow realized she had no idea if Dain was a first name, a surname, or even a nickname.

"Dain Waters, sir," Dain offered. "Commander Dain Waters."

The man looked at his list. "We weren't expecting a third member of the second Rhannish party."

"Surely we're not the first to bring staff?" Luvian said.

"You're the first not to tell us," the Rhyllian said, deadpan.

"She's a new addition," Sorrow said. "I don't know if news reached you of the incident in Prekara two nights ago, but I was attacked. Commander Dain was assigned to me for my protection that night."

The guard gave her a long look, and then silently passed the list, and a pen, through the window.

Sorrow wrote Dain's name, and role, and where she was from, beneath her own details, and handed the folder back to the man, who read it, and then raised his hand to open the gates.

"Enjoy your stay, Miss Ventaxis." The man's voice was a fraction warmer as the carriage lurched to life and they entered the castle complex. "Welcome to Castle Adavaria."

Castle Adavaria was situated on an island, at the end of a long, narrow drive over the water. Luvian leant out of the window, peering into the huge lake that surrounded the castle.

"What are you doing?" Sorrow asked.

"Legend has it there are merrow in there. Merpeople. They help guard the castle by sinking any boats that try to reach it and eating the sailors."

"That's not true."

"Only one way to find out," he grinned.

She didn't believe him – surely Rasmus would have told her

about it – but that didn't stop Sorrow gazing out of the window too. She did feel safer here, though, she realized. No one could get to the castle over land without dealing with guards, and even if someone did manage to row across the lake, the fifteen-foot walls that bordered the island would deter anyone from trying to get into the castle, where they would only face more guards anyway.

Though the entire complex was referred to as "the castle", it was actually multiple buildings acting as satellites around the main keep, which was home to the royal family. The keep was the oldest liveable part of Castle Adavaria, built as a replica of King Adavere's castle, which had long since fallen victim to the weather. The rest of the complex was a hotchpotch of buildings: working spaces and chambers, guest quarters, the palaces of nobles who lived at court, servants' housing, a theatre, and even a small market square, all showcasing centuries of Rhyllian architectural trends: pastel walls, soaring columns, exposed beams.

"All of the buildings are connected by those paths," Luvian told her with a tour guide's certainty as she stared at the covered walkways that stretched between the buildings. "Adavaria has the second highest annual rainfall in Rhylla, so it makes sense. There's even a kind of awning that rolls down to cover it completely, in case the rain falls at an angle. It has windows cut in and everything."

"Fascinating," Sorrow said, more sharply than she meant to as she spotted a tall Rhyllian emerging from the main keep. A heartbeat later she saw it wasn't Rasmus and relaxed slightly. "Sorry," she said to Luvian when she saw his wounded expression. "I'm anxious to finally get out of this carriage."

As she said it, the carriage rumbled to a stop alongside a

flight of stone steps leading to a small, pastel-blue palace. The doors at the top of the stairs opened at once, and a Rhyllian woman with pale gold hair appeared, resplendent in a purple long coat and carrying a slim folder, tripping down the stairs and opening Sorrow's door.

"*Arventis li Rhylla*, Miss Ventaxis. Welcome to Rhylla," she said in Rhyllian, then Rhannish. "We're delighted to have you here. My name is Deryn. And you must be Luvian Fen," Deryn said as Luvian climbed out. "*Arventis li Adavaria*. Be welcome in our land and home."

She paused as Dain climbed out. "We weren't expecting a third person. . ."

"No, this is Commander Dain, my bodyguard. After an incident in Rhannon we thought it prudent," Sorrow said.

"I'm not sure we have room. . ."

"I can sleep on the floor of Miss Ventaxis's quarters," Dain said.

"You cannot." Deryn looked outraged at the mere idea of it. "We won't have guests on the floors like animals. I'll see what I can do."

"You are kind," Luvian said in Rhyllian.

Deryn appeared slightly mollified by his use of her language. "Yes, well. Shall we?" She led them up the stairs, Dain following silently, into the hallway of the castle. To the right Sorrow could see a cosy parlour, the walls covered in rose-patterned paper, tall vases of the same bloom on the tables dotted between damask-covered chairs and love seats. In the corner stood a small bar, complete with attentive-looking Rhyllian butler, who nodded at them as they passed.

"We call this building the small palace," Deryn said as she opened a door on the left to reveal a small but well-stocked library, before leading them to a short passageway lined with abstract prints, and up a well-worn staircase to the second floor. "Long ago it was used as the home of the royal children, but Her Majesty's great-grandmother changed the practice and kept her children with her at the royal palace. It's been used as guest quarters since, though this is the first time it's been full." She gave Dain a concerned look.

The jab was not lost on Sorrow, but she ignored it.

"Who else is here?" Luvian asked.

"Miss Ventaxis's brother, of course. We have, due to the political situation in Rhannon, allocated Mr Ventaxis and his party rooms in a different part of the castle complex. We thought it best."

Sorrow wondered whether those quarters were in Vespus's private palace.

Deryn continued. "The Duke of Meridea and his consort will join us for the Naming and the ball. The Astrian and Nyrssean ambassadors are representing their leaders – sadly the leaders themselves could not attend – and so are staying in their usual accommodations and are, of course, already here."

"What of Svarta?" Sorrow asked.

"Fain Darcia herself is due to arrive later today, as is the Lady of Skae." Deryn paused outside a door, then opened it, ushering them in. "As you can see, you have your own sitting room, and your bedrooms are marked for you." She nodded to the doors on each side of the room. "We hope it's not an imposition, but – as I said – space is limited so we had hoped to house Fain Darcia in the small palace too. She's travelling alone, and will have separate quarters."

Sorrow nodded her acceptance eagerly. She'd never met the Svartan leader, but she'd liked their ambassador very much, and she'd spoken highly of the Svartan fain. Svarta had always intrigued her.

Deryn appeared relieved, and continued. "And Lord Day will be the guest of Ambassador Mira, of course."

"Charon is coming?" Sorrow's heart lifted at the idea of seeing him.

"Indeed, though sadly only for the Naming and the ball. Again, the climate in Rhannon made Her Majesty believe it prudent to have a neutral Rhannish presence. Actually –" she turned to Dain "– that gives me an idea. We've had to make special arrangements for Lord Day, on account of his chair. Perhaps we can create a similar setup for you."

Dain shrugged, and Deryn frowned.

"Of course, we heard of the incident two nights ago. Her Majesty wants you to know that the palace compound is very secure," Deryn said, glancing at Dain from the corner of her eye. "You'll notice that neither Her Majesty nor the prince consort or princess have bodyguards. That's how much faith we have in the palace guards, and our other security systems. Castle Adavaria has never been breached, by land nor water."

Luvian gave Sorrow a knowing look, and she had to refrain from rolling her eyes. There weren't merrow in the lake.

"I'm sure I'll be fine," Sorrow said. "And I have Dain." Sorrow smiled at the Ward, and her cheeks turned dusky.

"I rather hope you won't need her," Deryn replied, and it was Sorrow's turn to flush as she wondered if she'd insulted her hostess.

"No, of course not. While we're here Dain can relax."

"Very good," Deryn replied. "Though it wouldn't be appropriate for you to attend the festivities, you must feel welcome to use the parlours downstairs." She addressed Dain directly before speaking to them all. "Her Majesty says you're free to use the grounds, but she asks that you respect the privacy of the castle residents and remain on the paths. The guards won't take kindly to people being where they're not expected. Dinner is at seven; if you could please meet downstairs in the hall, someone will come to escort you to the main keep. I think that's all... Unless you have any questions?"

"None. Luvian?"

"I'm good."

"If you'd like to follow me, I'll see what I can do about rooms for you." Deryn spoke to Dain, who turned to Sorrow with a questioning look.

Sorrow nodded, and the Rhannish and Rhyllian women left.

"I don't think Deryn has a good grasp of what bodyguard means," Sorrow said.

"I think she was insulted you thought you'd need one here," Luvian replied.

"What should I do? I mean, the point of her being here is to guard me."

"Hard to argue that when you left her on a bench in Ceridog because it suited you," Luvian said. "And Deryn is right. The castle complex – Rhylla in general – is the safest place in the whole of Laethea. Historically there has never been a breach of the walls, never an attack here."

Sorrow narrowed her eyes at him. "Did you actually read some kind of guidebook before we came?"

"Yes. Because I like to know about the places I'm going. Ignorance is nothing to be proud of, Sorrow dearest. Now, I think I'll go and investigate my room." He smiled winningly and left her.

Sorrow rolled her eyes, and turned to the door labelled for her in beautiful script. It was small but elegant, a carved bed with a headboard that looked like a scroll in the centre, a wardrobe and dressing screen made with the same golden wood. Alvus, she expected. She crossed to the window to see what view she had.

She regretted it instantly. Rasmus – there was no mistaking him this time – was walking away from the guest quarters, heading towards the main keep. Beside him was a young Rhyllian woman, fair-haired as he was. Longing tugged at Sorrow. Though she'd tried to prepare herself to see him, she hadn't realized just how strange it would be. Nor how sad it would make her.

As though he sensed her gaze, Rasmus turned, looking directly at her, and Sorrow ducked back, pressing herself against the wall, her heart slamming against her ribs as though she'd been running. Luvian chose that moment to appear in the doorway, a steaming earthenware cup in his hand.

"Coffee?" he began, then frowned. "What are you doing?"

"Nothing." Her voice was high and tight, like a violin string.

Luvian wasn't convinced. "Right. . . Just casually standing pressed against the wall?"

"Yes. No. No, thanks, to coffee." Sorrow stepped away from the wall and tried to calm herself. "I think I might lie down for a bit."

Luvian shrugged, but his eyes were narrowed thoughtfully. "Do you want me to come and get you when it's time to go?" he said finally.

"Thanks, yes."

He stayed there for a moment, and Sorrow waited for him

to say something else, but he didn't, merely turning and closing the door as he left.

Sorrow turned immediately back to the window and peered out, but Rasmus was gone.

Instead of resting, she'd locked herself in the bathroom and tried to groom herself into calmness.

With painstaking care, she lined her upper eyelid, keeping the wings small and sharp, only having to start again three times, which felt like an achievement. She'd already decided there was no point in lipstick if they were eating, but once her eyes were done, she thought her face looked out of balance, the drama of her eyes versus the normality of her mouth. So she smeared on a rich red, only to wipe it off a moment later. Too much. Unless she added more eyeliner...

No. She forced herself away from the mirror. Her make-up was fine.

Rasmus had never seen her with make-up on – not that he was the reason she was doing it, she told herself. Putting on make-up was like putting on armour – a mask to hide her worries about seeing him, and also Mael, the election, and the Sons of Rhannon. How could anyone with kohl-lined eyes, or bright red lips, be thought of as afraid?

And it wouldn't hurt for him to see her looking good, so he'd know she was all right.

She released her hair from the braid she'd worn to travel in, running her fingers through the soft waves, allowing them fall naturally down her back, though she slipped a hair tie over her wrist.

Ines had fashioned a soft teal gown for this first supper, as it was known to be one of Melisia's favourite colours. The gown was simple, a sleeveless column with a modest V-shaped neckline in front and back, falling into soft folds to her ankles, a braided gold rope around the waist. Mercifully, Irris had paired it with flat gold slippers, and Sorrow was grateful to slip her feet into them. She found the shawl her friend had included, and was mulling over whether to put it on, or wait, when Luvian knocked on her door.

"Coming," she said, turning as he opened it.

"Are you— Wow."

"Am I wow?"

"You look. . ." He waved his hands at her as though that said it all. "Your eyes. . ." He gestured again.

"Does it look bad?" Sorrow asked, suddenly worried by his reaction. "I tried to do it how Irris did it for the presentation, but I embellished a bit. Because it's a party. . ."

"No," he said slowly. "It looks good."

Mollified, she took his arm when he offered it and they made their way down to the rose parlour. They were the first there, save for a manservant serving drinks and Dain, a glass of amber liquid in one hand and a book in the other, looking for all the world as though she belonged there. She stood guiltily when they entered, but Sorrow waved her down, moving to stand beside her as Luvian went to the bar.

"What are you reading?" she asked.

She held it up so Sorrow could see the cover. "*Adavere and Namyra*. I love that story."

"It's all they had in Rhannish," Dain said. "Miss Ventaxis, if you need me to come—"

"It's fine. I'd prefer not to insult the queen by implying I don't think her castle is safe."

"I don't want to be accused of neglecting my duties," Dain said, a faint edge to the words.

Sorrow understood. "I have no plans to mention this to Meeren Vine," she told her. From the way the tension in her jaw loosened, she knew she was right. "Enjoy it," she added with a smile.

"I will, Miss Ventaxis."

"Where are you sleeping?"

"The library." The woman's eyes lit up at the word, and Sorrow gave in fully to liking her. As soon as they got back to Rhannon, she'd ask her to leave the Ward, and become her personal guard permanently.

Luvian joined them, with a small glass of wine for her, and she was grateful. She'd thought she'd mastered her fears, locked them behind layers of eyeliner and chiffon, but now, with only a short walk between her and seeing Rasmus, she found she wasn't steady at all.

When Luvian handed her the glass, he noticed her shaking hands.

"Nervous?" he asked.

There was little point in denying it, so she nodded.

"Just remember..." he began, but then fell silent as Fain Darcia – for the tall, slender woman with bone-white skin and silver fur at her throat could be no one else – glided into the room, coal-black eyes settling immediately on Sorrow. She smiled and crossed at once to her, and Sorrow and Luvian bent deeply at the waist in greeting.

"Miss Ventaxis," the northern woman said in Rhannish, once again shaming Sorrow for her own lack of language skills. "I am happy to meet with you."

"And I you." Sorrow took the hand she offered in hers. "I heard so many good things about you and your country from Ambassador Stile."

"She spoke of you too. With much fondness. She was sad to leave you, but . . . you know, these things." She turned then to Luvian. "And this must be. . ." She paused. "No, I don't know. Who are you?"

"Luvian Fen, my lady." He bowed again, rising when she offered her hand.

"You may call me Darcia," the Svartan said. "Both of you may; we are friends." Darcia gave her drink order to the manservant and waited while he prepared it. When he handed it over, it was a thick, black liquid that smelled like aniseed. Darcia took a hearty swig and wrinkled her nose.

"Bah, not like at home," she said, offering the glass to Sorrow.

Sorrow took a tentative sip and coughed, her cheeks turning scarlet, eyes watering, as the liquid blazed a fiery trail of lava down her into her stomach.

"Too mild," Darcia said. "Weak, southern stuff. When you come to my home as the chancellor I'll give you the real thing. It'll keep you warm through our cold nights."

Sorrow, her voice burned clean away, could only nod. She was saved from replying at all when a liveried woman appeared in the doorway.

"If you'd like to follow me, your carriage is here."

26

A Taste of Mania

The assembly hall in the central keep was intimidatingly grand, built to impress or inspire, exactly how Sorrow imagined a temple or sacred space would be. The ceiling was high and vaulted, ornate buttresses arching out from between the stained-glass windows. Rasmus had said the windows told the story of Adavere and the Humpback Bridge, and Sorrow saw it there, fourteen tall, colourful panels recounting the tale of how he tricked the stars detailed in the candlelit glass. Ten large columns supported the ceilings, each one wrapped with white silk that glowed like moonlight, creating a central space, filled with round tables, where the welcome feast was to take place.

Sorrow couldn't see a high table, nor any of the Rhyllian royals – including Rasmus – amid the chattering people, and it puzzled her, until she noticed an empty table at the centre of the room and wondered if the Rhyllian royals sat amongst their guests, as though they were all equals.

A servant showed them to their table, and Luvian pulled out her chair, but before Sorrow could sit, a hand gently touched her shoulder, and she turned to find Mael standing there, smiling at her. She allowed herself to give him a small smile back – it wouldn't hurt to be nice – and was rewarded by his own widening grin.

"You came," he said. "I didn't know if you would, after what happened. How are you? You got back to the North Marches all right? There was no more trouble?"

By the time he'd crossed the bridge, the graffiti was gone, Sorrow realized. Should she tell him that the attack hadn't been a one-off?

He continued before she had chance. "I asked Arta if we should offer to travel with you, safety in numbers and all, but he said it wouldn't be right. I think he sometimes forgets we're brother and sister, and not simply rivals."

The annoyance that usually burned through her veins whenever he called himself her brother was absent, but before she could dwell on it, a fanfare echoed through the room, and everyone rose to greet Queen Melisia and her family.

She entered first, in a flowing gown of silver that clung to the remains of her pregnancy curves, a coronet glittering on her brow. Her consort, Prince Caspar, came next, also in silver, holding an infant swaddled in green in his arms. Then a pretty blonde girl – Sorrow's heart stuttered – on the arm of Rasmus, and it dawned on Sorrow she must be his cousin, Princess Eirlys, and that's who had been walking with him earlier.

Vespus brought up the rear, and beside him was Aphora, the woman who'd been at the bridge and the inn, the day they revealed Mael. Sorrow wondered if Vespus was in a relationship with Aphora. From the way the dark-skinned Rhyllian woman gazed at him – part pride, part possession – and how his hand skirted low on her back, caressing the exposed skin, she surmised yes.

Melisia paused to greet her guests as the royal party made its way through the room, her face lit with pleasure as she shook hands and, more often than not, embraced her visitors. Sorrow watched her carefully, noting how she made sure to speak to every single person, and how they glowed a little after she had.

"Mael and Sorrow Ventaxis," she said in a smooth, melodious voice when she reached them. "Thank you both for coming."

She held out her hand to Sorrow, who shook it with as much warmth as she could muster, only to feel slighted when Mael stepped forward and hugged her

"You look radiant, Your Majesty," he said as he released her, before nodding a greeting at the prince consort.

Melisia laughed, and turned to Sorrow. "Last time your brother saw me I was the size of a house, and itching to have my body back."

"Not at all. You looked as fierce and lovely as ever," Mael replied. If anyone else had said it, Sorrow would have sneered at their insincerity, but she suspected Mael's words were genuine, and from the way Melisia rested a hand on his cheek, before passing along, it seemed she thought so too.

As the queen and prince consort passed, Sorrow braced herself to speak to Rasmus. But at the last moment he turned away, saying something over his shoulder in Rhyllian to Aphora. Sorrow's skin burned with embarrassment.

He'd ignored her.

"Miss Ventaxis." Vespus's voice was silky as he drew level with her. "How good to see you. Colour suits you. And, Mael, how wonderful to have you back within these walls."

He embraced the boy and lingered with him, speaking in rapid Rhyllian, with Mael replying just as fluently. Back and forth, with Sorrow watching them, the gestures of their hands as they spoke as synchronized as a dance.

"Sickening, isn't it?" Luvian leant over and whispered in her ear. "Poor Xalys is better off out of it. They look more like father and son than him and his actual son."

They both looked at where Rasmus stood alone, his fingers flexing and straightening, the silver rings flashing with each motion, as he watched his father and Mael.

"How far exactly could a Rhyllian alter someone's appearance, if they had the ability?" Luvian asked. "After all, it would technically be manipulating organic matter..."

"What are you getting at?" Sorrow said.

"Well, we just discovered Vespus has a secret daughter. What if I'm wrong, and he didn't take a child from Rhannon? What if Mael is another of Vespus's children, made to look Rhannish?"

Sorrow shook her head. "It's not possible. I told you: it only works within the confines of what already exists. A mole could be increased to look like a birthmark, yes. And maybe, if a Rhyllian had the right complexion, the skin could be darkened so it looked Rhannish. But they couldn't change the ears. Their shape is too fundamental to alter."

"How can you be sure?"

Sorrow fell silent. She was sure because she'd asked Rasmus about it once, not long after they'd first slept together.

Back then, with her grandmother still alive and strong, she'd been paralysed at the idea of having to give him up, and unconcerned about Rhannon, so she'd tried to hatch a plan where they could be together. No one would accept them as they were, but what if they looked different, she'd told him eagerly. What if they could find someone to make him look Rhannish, or her Rhyllian?

He'd held her very close as he'd explained it didn't work like that. That someone with an ability in glamour might be able to make hair shinier, plump lips, deepen eye colour, or lighten it. But only in so far as it already existed. They couldn't make blue eyes brown; they couldn't make a tall person short. The abilities didn't allow for changes to something or someone's fundamental being. That's why Vespus had such trouble growing Alvus – he couldn't alter its innate needs to make it adapt to the soil in the north of Rhylla. So, he told her, no one could make his ears rounded, or hers like arrow tips.

"Because I was told once," she said finally. "And besides, there's a registry for all the abilities. Even if it was possible, it would have been recorded there, and I'm sure it's the first thing the queen would have checked when he came here."

Luvian shrugged. "I'll stick with going through the list of Rhannish missing children and—" He stopped suddenly, eyes narrowed behind the lenses of his glasses. "They do love their registries here, don't they. . .?"

"Where did that come from?" Sorrow asked. "And what's with that look? You look very scheme-ish."

"'Scheme-ish' isn't a word. Though I suppose once you're chancellor you can make up all the words you like."

"Don't try to change the subject," Sorrow warned. "I know you too well."

He peered at her over the top of his spectacles. "Do you, now?"

"Yes. You and your – what was it? – your fearsome mind?"

"My fearsome mind?"

"Or whatever you were bragging about yesterday. There's so much you have to say about yourself that sometimes I forget..."

His expression became amused, a single brow arching. "Ah, you mean my massive brain and intellect?"

"In fairness, 'fearsome mind' sounds like the sort of thing you'd say in reference to yourself."

"Envy is such an ugly emotion, Sorrow darling," he replied, and she laughed.

It was only then she realized that Vespus and Mael had fallen silent and were watching them.

Rasmus, too, was watching, his jaw clenched tightly as he looked between the two of them. Then he turned away, sitting down and waving for a servant to come fill his glass.

Sorrow sat then, busying herself with her own wine, as Luvian lowered himself next to her.

"What was all that about?" he leant over and murmured.

"No idea," Sorrow lied.

She could feel Luvian watching her, waiting for more, and in response heat broke out across her body. She was saved when Melisia stood, and the rest of the room fell silent, Vespus hurrying to his seat as Mael took his.

She spoke first in Rhyllian, then Meridian, Svartan, Skae, Astrian, Nyrssean and finally Rhannish, and Sorrow could only assume she said the same thing each time: "Greetings, friends, and know you have our sincere gratitude for travelling here for the Naming Day of our new daughter. Please be welcome at our table and hearth, feast and rejoice with us. There is nothing so precious as a new life, and we are honoured to share this with you."

The room erupted into applause, and Melisia bowed then sat down. The moment she did, wide doors at the end of the room opened, and the feast began in earnest.

Sorrow found her eyes drawn to Rasmus, whose gaze flickered briefly to her, then away. Instead he turned to his cousin and fixed her with a smile so bright it could have lit the room, and jealousy stabbed somewhere near Sorrow's heart. She speared her fork viciously into her chicken. She had no right to feel bitter, she told herself angrily. None at all.

It wasn't enough to make the feeling go away, though.

Dinner was followed by a drinks reception, the party moving to another room without formal seating, allowing everyone to mix. Melisia and Caspar retired for the night, leaving the others to enjoy the celebration. When Vespus made a beeline for Mael, Aphora on his arm, Sorrow headed to the other side of the hall, to Darcia, and Lady Skae.

Luvian had vanished, complaining of toothache, so Sorrow busied herself asking Darcia to teach her a little Svartan. *Take that*, she thought; while Mael stuck like glue to his Rhyllian friends, she was forging links with leaders from other countries. Luvian would be proud.

Across the room, Rasmus laughed, and the sound was like a knife in Sorrow's back. That laugh that she'd only ever heard muted, hushed, in the Court of Tears was unleashed here, loud and alive. She'd never heard him laugh like that before. Though she told herself not to, she turned to see him standing with Eirlys, whose own face was creased with mirth, her shoulder shaking silently. Beside them a third Rhyllian with red hair was laughing so hard his cheeks were shining with tears. She barely recognized Rasmus, his eyes screwed shut, his mouth leering as he gasped with laughter.

She looked away, a cocktail of sadness, envy and annoyance confusing her. Was he behaving like this to get to her, or was it arrogance to imagine he even still cared?

"They've been drinking Starwater." Darcia shook her head. "Silly children."

"Starwater?" Sorrow asked. She'd never heard of it.

"A trend with young Rhyllians. Rich young Rhyllians, at least. It's made from the fermented sap of the Alvus tree. Very strong. A little makes laughter come easy. Too much will make you very ill. Well –" she paused "– not them. But my ambassador sent me some, and it did not agree with me. And I am not –" she fumbled for the Rhannish word "– weak, when it comes to drinking."

Sorrow made a mental note to avoid Starwater if ever she was offered it. If Darcia, who drank that dark aniseed alcohol like it was milk, couldn't handle it, there was no chance Sorrow could. "What does it taste like?"

"Mania," Darcia said, and Sorrow wondered if she'd got the word confused. Mania wasn't a flavour. "If the queen sees them with it, she'll be furious," she continued.

"Doesn't she like it?"

"Not one bit. They wouldn't dare drink it if she was still here."

Sorrow looked back at Rasmus, one hand over his mouth, the other clutching Eirlys's shoulder as he laughed. He looked out of control, wild; for the first time his pointed ears and fey eyes made her uneasy. Perhaps Darcia was right, and it was the taste of mania. As she watched he gulped down more of the liquid, his eyes glittering with something deep and uncontrollable. It was a side to him she'd never seen before and she didn't like it.

"Bathroom," she said, excusing herself.

A guard pointed out the direction to her, and Sorrow was relieved to be away from the noise and atmosphere of the Great Hall. She lingered in the cooler room, running her wrists under the tap, allowing the cold water to slow her heart.

The door burst open, and Princess Eirlys stumbled in. Her cheeks were bright red, her eyes sparkling. She grinned at Sorrow.

"I apologize. The door wasn't locked."

"I'm finished," Sorrow said, edging past the Rhyllian girl and back out into the corridor.

Rasmus was there, obviously waiting for Eirlys. The moment he saw Sorrow he began to walk back down the corridor.

"Rasmus?" she said, before she could stop herself.

He took two more steps before stopping, his shoulders high, spine ramrod straight as he turned slowly and looked at her. He'd pulled the tie at his throat loose and opened his jacket, exposing the white shirt beneath, the laces undone. In his left hand he clutched a small bottle, half full of clear liquid.

"Hello," she said.

His face, which was carefully arranged into a bland expression, faltered for a moment. "Hello. How are you enjoying the party?"

"It's lovely."

"And Rhylla? How are you finding my country?" His

accent had changed, she realized, since she'd last spoken to him. He sounded more Rhyllian now, more rolling "r"s and lilting tempo.

"It's beautiful." Sorrow could have kicked herself at the stupidity of her replies.

He took a step closer to her, looking her up and down, and her heart exploded into a tattoo of rapid beats. "You look well," he said finally.

"Thank y—" She stopped herself. "That is kind of you to say," she finished.

He nodded, as if it didn't matter, as if he didn't expect her to reply the Rhyllian way, before raising the flask in his hands to his lips.

Immediately his eyes changed. They looked metallic, somehow, the violet becoming steely. Her stomach tightened in warning.

"It's Starwater." He followed her gaze to where it rested on the bottle.

"I figured. Fain Darcia told me about it."

It wasn't a hint that she wanted some – after what Darcia said she had no desire to poison herself – but he held the flask out to her as if it had been. She hesitated for a moment, then took it, holding it loosely.

"I was sorry to hear about your father," Rasmus said, unblinking eyes fixed on hers. "I would have written, only Lord Day made it very clear that word from me wasn't welcomed by you. That it wasn't *appropriate*."

It was the first time any hint of emotion had coloured his voice, but it was bitter, his accent clipping the words so they felt like hailstones. "No one would have thought it inappropriate for you to offer your condolences to the daughter of a man whose home you'd lived in for the past ten years."

"We sent a wreath."

Sorrow choked on thin air, forgetting to be careful. "Oh, well, that's all right then." When he stared at her with a patient, blank expression, her ire rose. "This was a mistake," she said. "I should have known better."

"I'll bid you goodnight, then." He tried to leave, but Sorrow couldn't stop herself.

"Rasmus. Can't we... Can't we be friends? I still care about you." The words fell from her lips before she could stop them, and she knew even as they did it was the worst thing she could have said.

"Care about me?" His face drained so abruptly of colour it scared her. "*Care?* Stars, Row, why don't you stab me in the heart and be done with it?" He turned and strode away.

"Rasmus, please," she called desperately, knowing that if she let him walk away now she would lose him for ever. "That's not what I meant. Ras, I'm trying – please listen to me."

But he kept moving, and Sorrow looked down at the bottle, still clutched in her hand, and made one final attempt to stop him.

"You forgot your Starwater," she called after him.

He paused, and half turned, his profile caught in the lamplight, and Sorrow breathed a sigh of relief. Now she could explain—

"Keep it. I know better than anyone how you like to experiment with Rhyllian things."

His words struck her like a punch, and Sorrow folded in on herself, gasping. Rasmus walked away without a backwards glance.

At the sound of Eirlys fumbling with the handle of the

bathroom door, Sorrow picked up her skirts and ran back to the Great Hall, to find Darcia and Lady Skae waiting for her.

The two northern leaders chatted happily on the journey back to the small palace, and Sorrow let their words fly around her, nodding and smiling in the right places. She even stayed in the parlour for a drink with the two of them, somehow managing to participate, until Lady Skae made her excuses and left.

When they finally went to their beds, Sorrow left her dress and bag in a heap on the floor. She lay on the bed and stared at the ceiling, her heart breaking as she finally admitted the truth to herself. The real reason she'd never considered a future with him: not because he was Rhyllian and she was Rhannish. Not because of duty. She knew exactly what he'd wanted her to say. She'd known he'd waited years for her to say it. But she couldn't. She didn't love him. Not the way he'd needed her to. She'd wanted him – craved him, even – loved him as a friend, trusted him more than almost anyone. But she hadn't been in love with him. And if she was honest – really honest – she wasn't sure she could love anyone that way.

Sorrow, for that is all she brings us, a voice whispered in the dark.

For once it wasn't Rasmus's voice in her head. This time it sounded like her own.

When she woke the next morning Luvian was gone, the door to his room open and his bed neatly made. Once she was dressed, and had eaten, Sorrow went to find him, but he wasn't in the parlour or the library. She wondered whether to search the grounds, but a light drizzle, and the worry she might bump into Rasmus, put paid to that idea. If she never saw him again it would be too soon. She was already planning to fake an illness to get out of the second dinner that night.

At a loss for what to do with herself, she retreated back to her rooms. She found the pile of Rhannish records Luvian had been going through on the table in their private parlour, and, remembering what he'd said about the vastness of the task, she decided to see if she could help.

They made for gruesome reading, and once again Sorrow realized how little she knew of everyday Rhannish life. It seemed children fell into wells, rivers, or vanished into woodlands with something close to regularity. They were presumed eaten by desert cats, jungle cats, snakes and even, in one case, tiny carnivorous lizards that dwelt on the coast of the West Marches. Children who'd left their homes in the morning and simply not returned. Babies seemingly snatched from their cots, or from beside their sleeping mothers. Children who'd been last seen talking to strange adults, taking their hands and vanishing for evermore...

Sorrow almost put the records down, not wanting to know any more. But then she forced herself to pick them back up. These were her people. She needed to know about these things, might be able to help, somehow, provide money to cover wells, and for fences for villages where animal attacks were likely. Besides, if she found him in here, she'd know for sure that he wasn't Mael. She could get on with the election, and her life, with an easy heart. She began to go through the reports.

Luvian, it seemed, had narrowed his search down to

missing children from the North Marches, which Sorrow supposed made sense. Easier to take a child from close to the border than from deeper in Rhannon. She started to mark them off, following Luvian's lead, crossing out any from outside the border state, and any who were female.

Sorrow was so engrossed in the work that she didn't hear Luvian return until he spoke.

"There you are," he said.

Sorrow narrowed her eyes. "What do you mean, 'there I am'? I've been here all day. It's you who's been off, Graces know where."

"Ah, yes, you're quite right. I have been mysteriously absent," he beamed.

He sat opposite her, kicking his long legs up on to the table and removing his glasses, polishing them theatrically.

Sorrow knew what he was waiting for, and she ignored him.

Luvian squinted at her and pushed his glasses back on to his face, and despite how upset she still felt about Rasmus, and how heartsick over the missing children reports, she almost smiled.

Five, four, three, two... she counted.

One.

Right on cue, Luvian said, "Don't you want to know where I've been?"

Sorrow shrugged. "I'm sure you'll tell me in your own sweet time." She smiled.

He scowled. "I ought to make you wait. But I'm going to take the higher ground, because I'm a better person. Do you remember yesterday, during dinner, when you were talking about the abilities? You said there was a registry for them. And I said they had registries for everything?"

"Yes. . ." Sorrow said slowly, leaning back against the carved arm of the sofa.

"They keep lists of everyone who visits. That's why they were so put out about Dain. She wasn't on their list. So they added her." He paused. "And you know who else would have been on a visitor list? Beliss. You told me the queen had her brought here. Ergo, she must have been put on a register."

"You found her?" Sorrow stared at him. "You really found her?"

He nodded. "I skipped the drinks last night and went to find one of the guards. I told him I thought there had been a mistake on the register about my address, and he told me I'd have to go to the registry, right here in the complex, to correct it. He also told me it was closed for the next few days for the Naming. So, this morning, at the crack of dawn, I went there."

For a moment she was puzzled. "But if it's closed. . . You broke in? Luvian! If you'd been caught. . ."

He smiled winningly, in a way that suggested the idea of him being caught was preposterous. "Then you would have had to fire me for misconduct and have me arrested, and release a statement saying you didn't know about it, and it wasn't done on your orders."

"It wasn't!"

"Good. You wouldn't need to lie. Anyway, Madame Beliss lives in a charming, if unoriginally named, little place called Cottage Near the River, in the county of Starsia. So, I propose we send a bird to Irris and prolong our trip here. Take another detour on the way back to Rhannon."

"You're a genius." Sorrow shook her head in awe. "Insane. But a genius."

"Why, thank you. Now, you can go and get ready for tonight's dinner. But be sure to continue ruminating on my genius as you do."

Sorrow's joy immediately soured.

27

Greetings from Rhannon

The dinner went smoothly enough, with Sorrow tactically delaying herself and Luvian so that everyone was already seated when they arrived, and leaving as soon as it was over, claiming she felt ill. It wasn't even untrue; being in the same room as Rasmus, even though he didn't so much as look in her direction, left her shaken and vulnerable.

So when Charon Day entered the ground floor parlour the following morning, Sorrow almost threw herself into his arms. She'd declined the offer to go on a celebratory hunt with the other guests, and had remained in her rooms, intent on brooding some more on the night before. But several birds had arrived for Luvian throughout the morning, turning their private parlour into part aviary, part office, and making it impossible for her to concentrate.

Luvian arranged the papers they'd brought into some order

only recognizable to himself, and when Sorrow, deciding she might as well make herself useful, had tried to reach for one, he'd snatched it from her and told her to go away and let him do his job, only to call her back a moment later and shove his infernal missing child reports into her hands.

"You can carry on going through these," he said, effectively dismissing her as he returned to his new tasks.

Miffed, she'd retreated to her room, only to be shooed out by Rhyllian maids armed with clean linen and dusters, muttering darkly as they began to tidy the room. And the main library was now Dain's bedroom; she couldn't exactly go and commandeer it to work in.

She'd eventually hidden herself away in the rose parlour with a pot of moonstar tea and the reports. She was going through them, her heart aching more and more with each child, when she heard the familiar whisper of wheels on the ground, and she looked up to see the vice chancellor of Rhannon.

"Charon," she cried, putting the papers down with indecent haste, crossing the room in three steps and kneeling in front of his chair. Charon applied the brakes and took Sorrow's face in his hands.

He didn't speak at first, scanning her with practised eyes, nodding to himself as he took her in. Though it had only been little over a month since she'd last seen him at her father's funeral, she did the same, checking him over for signs of strain or tiredness. She was pleased to see he looked well: bright-eyed, relaxed . . . and unmistakably happy to see her as his face broke into a grin. She drank the sight in, already feeling more settled, more capable, now he was here. Then a thought came to her, and she frowned.

"Are you allowed to be here?" she asked. "I mean, you can't be seen to be supporting me. This might look bad."

Charon raised a brow. "I hardly snuck in." He glanced down pointedly at his chair. "Besides, I've already been to see Mael, so there can be no accusations of favouritism."

"You went to him first?" Sorrow tried, and failed, to hide her hurt as petty envy needled her.

Charon's expression was one Sorrow knew well from her childhood – one part infinite patience, one part exasperation – and his tone was long-suffering as he said, "If I'd come here first I'd have to leave you, to go to him. . ."

"Oh. Of course." Reassured, Sorrow returned to her spot on the sofa, smiling as the butler discreetly slipped out of the room, giving them privacy. "So, I suppose we can't talk about the election?" she said, and Charon nodded. "That narrows the field considerably," Sorrow said as she tucked her legs beneath her.

"I'd very much like to hear exactly what happened in Prekara. Your note wasn't terribly heavy on detail."

"Stars, Charon, it was awful." She relayed to him her version of events, starting with the appearance of the hooded men, the shouting, the fire, Meeren Vine's pause before he came to her aid, ending with Commander Dain's assignment at Vine's insistence.

"Where is she now?" Charon asked. "Isn't a bodyguard meant to do exactly that?"

"The library. Deryn – the Rhyllian who greeted us – was offended at the idea I'd brought a guard, but she was quick to accommodate her. She had the library set up as a makeshift bedroom. And Dain seems to love it. She's quite the bookworm. And, as everyone keeps telling me, I'm perfectly safe here."

Charon opened his mouth, as if to speak, and then closed it.

"What?" Sorrow asked.

"Nothing."

"Tell me." She knew him well enough to know he was lying.

He pressed his lips together, seemingly thinking, and then said, "There was a break-in, at the house you've been using in the North Marches. The night you left for Rhylla."

Sorrow's heart stopped. "What do you mean? Wait, Irris was still there; is she OK?"

"She's fine, don't worry. In fact, she's here too; she came with me. She wanted to come straight to you, but I asked her to let me speak to you first. I've left her unpacking, so by my estimate she'll be here in ten minutes and our belongings will remain in their trunks." He smiled.

Sorrow's mood lifted temporarily at the thought of her friend being here, but fell again almost immediately. "Who broke in? Do you know? And how?"

Charon paused. "They came through your room. Through the balcony door. And I suspect, after what happened in Prekara, that it was the Sons of Rhannon."

His words picked at something in her memory then. Monkeys on the roof, metal hitting the tiles...

Charon continued, bringing her back to the present. "Irris was still awake, when it happened. She heard sounds coming from your room, and knowing you'd gone, took some of the servants and a large knife with her to investigate. By the time she arrived, there was no one there but the balcony door was open. The lock had been picked. I've ordered it repaired, and additional bolts added, but I think it best to move when you return to Rhannon. To somewhere more secure. Bayrum Mizil would offer his manse. Or there's the Day seat in the East Marches."

"Stars. . ." Sorrow said, as understanding chilled her to the bone. They'd come for her in the night, when they knew she'd be alone. And vulnerable. So they did mean her real harm; it wasn't just public threats and graffiti. She shivered and crossed her arms.

"And I have a man ready to take over as your bodyguard once you return," Charon continued.

"Actually. . . Assuming she's not a spy for Vine, I think I'd like to keep Dain," Sorrow said, as Charon's thick eyebrows rose. "She stood up for me at the bridge, and she'd welcome it, I'm sure. Plus, it might go a long way to appeasing the Decorum Ward when the time comes if they see me employing their former colleagues—" Sorrow stopped as Charon held up a hand. "Too close to election talk?" she said, and he nodded. "Sorry. Should we tell Mael about the break-in?" Sorrow asked suddenly, ignoring the look of surprise on Charon's face. "They're probably after him too. I know he's more or less an enemy of sorts right now, but I don't want him murdered in his bed," she added when he continued to stare at her.

Charon nodded. "I suppose we should. I'll speak to Arta Boniface later. But for now, tell me about Rhylla. How are you enjoying it?"

"It's beautiful," Sorrow said. "I still can't get over the food. I feel like I'm actually eating colours sometimes, everything is so tasty and vibrant. And I met Fain Darcia and the Lady of Skae. I think I made a good impression on them."

Charon shot her a warning glance and Sorrow swallowed an impatient sigh. This was harder than she'd thought.

"Have you seen Rasmus?" Charon asked, watching her closely.

Sorrow nodded. "You needn't worry. He hates me. He can't even look at me." She remembered his words from last night and felt her chest contract as sadness rose like a tide inside her.

"I never wanted that," Charon said. "And for what it's worth, I am sorry. Really," he said, when her eyebrows quirked, betraying her scepticism. "So, any other news?"

"Oh," she remembered. "We stopped on the way here in Ceridog, for . . . a reason. And we're going to see some of the south before we return, for the same reason." She didn't know how much she could, or should, say about Mael here, so she gave Charon a deliberate look.

"That's the last avenue you have?"

"Yes. No." Sorrow's gaze fell on Luvian's reports. "Luvian pulled all the reports of children who went missing around the time—"

Charon jerked so violently Sorrow was afraid he'd tip out of his chair. Her words died in her mouth as she reached for him, but he shook his head, bracing his hands on the armrests, and took a deep breath.

"Are you all right?" Sorrow asked him.

He nodded, but Sorrow didn't believe him. Though his expression hadn't altered, he was noticeably paler, his temples and upper lip glistening as sweat bloomed there. His knuckles were white as he gripped the armrests.

"I'll fetch someone." Sorrow half rose, but the vice chancellor waved her down.

"No," he said, then again in a stronger voice. "No. I'm all right. Just an odd moment. No doubt from travelling so far without a real rest. I'm fine. What were you saying?" he asked.

"Something about missing children?"

"Let me get you some water, or maybe something to eat?"

"I'm fine, Sorrow. Please, carry on."

She sat back slowly, pausing before she answered. "We think it's probable that Mael doesn't know he's an imposter. In which case he would have been taken from Rhannon as a very little boy. Luvian thinks we might be able to find him. So we're looking for a child who went missing from the North Marches, in the two years after the accident."

Charon sat back in his chair, resting his hands in his lap. "How will it prove anything?"

"We'll know where he came from," Sorrow said. "We'll know who his parents are and who he really is."

I'll know who he really is, Sorrow thought. *I'll know.*

His eyes moved again to her reports. "And then what? What if you find a child in there, right place, right time? What will you do? Go to the parents and tell them you believe their son is alive but thinks he's the son of the chancellor?"

Sorrow couldn't understand why he seemed so angry. "Yes, of course. It might help us prove he's an imposter. If he looks like one of them, or they recognize him. . ."

"Your father recognized him," Charon said sharply. "Your father was convinced he was his child. What parent wouldn't want to believe it? They'll see what they want to, as Harun did. And you'll be accused of trying to sabotage his attempts to win the election."

"I'm doing this for the election. If I can find him—"

"You should be focusing on winning it," Charon snapped.

They were Luvian's words too, the same old message, but right now they sounded like an attack. An accusation. Sorrow couldn't think of a response.

"Perhaps I should go," Charon said.

Sorrow's jaw dropped. "You're leaving?"

"I'm tired, from the journey, and in some pain." He nodded to his legs. "It's making me ill-tempered." He tried for a smile, but Sorrow couldn't return it.

He snapped the brakes off and turned the chair. "I'll rest for an hour or two and see you at the Naming this afternoon."

Sorrow scrambled to stand, to walk him out, but he shook his head.

"No, you stay there. But I'd advise you to give up that foolishness." He nodded to the abandoned reports. "And I'll be having a word with Luvian Fen about it too. Focus on your campaign."

With that he gripped the wheels of his chair and propelled himself out, leaving Sorrow staring after him.

She'd never seen him that flustered before, never seen him falter; not when her grandmother died, not when Alyssa overdosed. Not when Mael appeared, or even when Harun had passed. For the first time in her life, she doubted her mentor, the man who'd truly been a father to her, who'd raised her and taught her and protected her.

Because she didn't believe him. He wasn't in pain, or tired. Or if he was, that wasn't what was behind his behaviour.

Sorrow wasn't proud that she was an accomplished liar, but it had left her with the ability to know when others were being dishonest too.

In that moment, Sorrow was certain Charon was hiding something from her. And that he was afraid.

28

Blessings and Curses

But Sorrow had no time to try to understand why. Within moments of Charon leaving, Fain Darcia and Lady Skae returned, ruddy-cheeked and beaming from the morning's ride.

Darcia sat beside Sorrow, who barely managed to get the papers out of the way as she did.

"Ah, Sorrow. . . It was magnificent." Darcia took her drink from the butler's hands and sat back. "Almost as good as the hunts back home."

"Not quite, though," Lady Skae agreed.

"No. Horses are not as good as alces for riding," Darcia said.

"Alces?" Sorrow asked.

"Like a deer, but bigger. Much bigger. Faster," Darcia said. "We use them to hunt wild rangifer, pinnipeds, alba bears, you name it."

Sorrow allowed herself to be drawn into a conversation about how the northern women hunted, happy to let the two tell her about their traditions, the beasts they killed for food and skins and bones, trying to distract herself from what had happened with Charon. She didn't want to doubt him, didn't want to think of him as someone calculating, or with secrets. There were too many secrets going around these days, and too few people she could trust.

The distraction worked, though Sorrow only realized how well when Irris rushed into the room, apologizing for taking her time.

Sorrow squealed when she saw her – she'd missed her, despite last seeing her three days ago. Irris held her tightly, and the two hugged each other.

"I'm so glad you're here," Sorrow said fiercely in her friend's ear. "Are you all right? Charon said there was a break-in at the house, and you were there."

"I'm fine. Totally fine. What about you? What news do you have?"

Sorrow knew Irris was not just asking about the Sons of Rhannon, and what had happened at the bridge, but about Rasmus too, and what she and Luvian had found in Ceridog.

"I'll tell you everything. And you can tell me more about —"

Darcia cleared her throat in amusement.

"Sorry," Sorrow said, releasing Irris, muttering, "Later," again in her ear as she did.

Sorrow introduced her friend to the foreign women, and all three began to tell Irris what she'd missed, only stopping when Luvian appeared in the doorway, already dressed in a peacock-blue frock coat, frantically reminding them all they had to be ready to leave in half an hour for the Naming ceremony.

The Naming was being held on the outskirts of the complex, in a building that to Sorrow's eye could have used a little cleaning, hypocritical as that made her. It looked like the wild and disobedient sister of every other building she'd seen in Rhylla, the grey stone worn and crumbling, ivy running rampant over it, instead of falling in manicured curtains. Parts of it were clearly falling down, roped off to keep people from climbing on them. It was only when they got closer that she realized what it was, and why it was significant.

"Adavere's castle," she murmured, more to herself than to Irris or Luvian as they'd stepped out of their carriage.

It was the ruins of the first king's home, the place he'd shared with his Rhannish wife, until she ran away. All that remained now of the massive former castle was the keep, and even that was missing part of the roof.

"Why don't they try to repair it?" Sorrow asked Luvian.

"All things must crumble," a voice remarked, and Sorrow turned to see the red-haired Rhyllian man who'd been drinking Starwater with Rasmus and Eirlys at the welcome feast. "It's natural. And good to remember it, sometimes. Harcel Argus." He held out a hand. "Or Baron Argus, if you want to be formal. Which I don't. I haven't had the chance to introduce myself to you yet. You're Sorrow Ventaxis, are you not?"

"I am," Sorrow replied, taking his hand. "It's a pleasure to meet you."

"Likewise." He turned to Irris. "I don't believe I saw you at either dinner – am I wrong? Or just a drunk?"

"No, I arrived this morning." She smiled. "I'm Irris Day. I used to sit on the Jedenvat for the East Marches."

"Of course. You must call me Harcel, Miss Day."

"Then you must call me Irris," she smiled, and Harcel raised her hand, as though to his lips.

Irris was having none of it, though, and gently but firmly twisted her wrist, forcing him to shake her hand instead.

The baron, to his credit, easily went along with it. He greeted Luvian then, and Sorrow decided to leave them to it, linking her arm through Irris's.

"Come on," she said. "Let's find somewhere good."

"Actually, I'd better wait for my father," Irris said apologetically. "He was a bit strange when he got back from visiting you and Mael. Was he all right when you saw him?"

She didn't know what made her do it, but Sorrow nodded, and Irris shrugged.

"Maybe it was the travel. It was a horribly long way; he's stuck at the mercy of helpers to get in and out of the carriages. I'll come find you afterwards. Oh, and we should get ready for tonight together," Irris promised, and Sorrow left her, hurrying to catch up with Luvian and Harcel, who were still talking.

Sorrow expected Harcel to go and sit with his own people. But he seemed quite happy to remain with her and Luvian. She saw Mael and Arta sitting on the right-hand side, and Fain Darcia and Lady Skae two rows behind them, so she turned the same way, sitting behind a man with skin a few shades darker than her own: the Duke of Meridea.

He turned the moment she was seated and offered a hand. "Miss Ventaxis, how nice to finally meet you."

His Rhannish was flawless, and again she was ashamed of her own lacking language skills, even more so when Luvian smiled easily and said, "*Dirnisha sula rallia meter.* So good to meet you."

He turned to Sorrow, smiling pointedly, and she repeated

the phrase he'd said, much to the delight of the Duke of Meridea.

"Ah, you speak Merish," he beamed.

"Sadly not," Sorrow said. "I'm afraid I copied what my friend said. But I'm hoping to learn much more soon."

From the corner of her eye she saw Luvian give a small, satisfied nod.

The woman beside the duke, her close-cropped hair not unlike Dain's, and elaborate jadis earrings cuffing her ears, turned then, and Sorrow greeted her the same way, earning herself a large grin from the Merish woman.

"My consort, the Lady Iola," the duke introduced his companion. "This is Miss Ventaxis."

"Please, call me Sorrow."

"Of course, Sorrow. I'm hopeful I'll have the chance to talk more to you at the feast tonight," she said, before turning back to her husband and lapsing into rapid Merish.

Relations between Rhannon and Meridea had been tense since Meridea's refusal to side with their nearest neighbours during the Eternal War. Sorrow knew from her grandmother that Reuben had blasted them for it, and of course Harun had made no attempt to heal any wounds. But it seemed the duke and his consort had no interest in maintaining grudges, and Sorrow made a note to definitely seek them out that night.

Luvian excused himself, and Harcel followed him, leaving her alone, and Sorrow took the opportunity to examine the room. The walls were bare, patched with moss, and the flagstone floor was peppered with shoots and leaves, as though nature was trying to claim the building for its own. It was as sparse inside as out, set up with rows of wooden benches, creating a wide aisle between them. She found she recognized a lot of the faces already seated, nodding and smiling at those she made eye contact with. At the front was a small altar, bare of anything except a silver or pewter jug, and a large stone bowl. Mael turned around, pulling her gaze to his. They exchanged smiles, and Sorrow remembered the break-in. She'd have to make sure he was told, it was only fair. She was certain if their positions were reversed, he'd tell her.

She searched then for the Rhannish vice chancellor, spying him near the back in a space that had been cleared for his chair; Irris was beside him, talking to a tall man in the stark costume of the Astrians. Charon stared rigidly ahead, and Sorrow got the impression he was deliberately avoiding her gaze. She frowned, trying to catch his eye. He was scaring her a little.

Movement to her side made her turn, but instead of Luvian she found that Harcel, the red-headed Rhyllian, had hastily taken his spot.

"It's about to begin," he said, by way of explanation, and no sooner had he said it than Vespus, again with Aphora by his side, followed by Rasmus and Eirlys, swept down the aisle and took their seats at the front. Sorrow looked away as Rasmus passed, annoyed at how her skin flamed with embarrassment.

Then, at some signal Sorrow missed, everyone turned to the doors as Melisia and Caspar entered the room. Both wore white, and the babe in Melisia's arms wore gold. They made their way slowly up the makeshift aisle to where a priestess of some kind had appeared, clad in a blue shift, beside the altar. Melisia handed the baby to the priestess, who began to speak in rapid Rhyllian. Sorrow didn't even try to follow the words, instead focusing on the feeling and the beauty of the ceremony.

She was surprised when envy gripped her as she saw how carefully they all handled the child; as though she was the most precious thing in the world. She wondered if her mother would have held her so tenderly if she'd survived. Perhaps she might have grown to love her daughter once the pain of childbirth faded, regretted naming her Sorrow.

The priestess anointed the child with clear water from the bowl, and then spoke one final time, before saying, "Aralie."

Almost everyone in the room replied, "*Arventis*, Aralie."

"Welcome, Aralie," Harcel leant over and translated.

Sorrow didn't tell him it was one of the few Rhyllian words she knew. "Beautiful name," she murmured instead.

"It is. In Rhannish it would mean something like 'she who flies the highest and sings the sweetest'."

"Like a kind of bird?"

"Perhaps." The red-haired baron shrugged.

They all rose as Melisia and Caspar returned down the aisle with their newly named daughter, followed by Eirlys, Vespus, Aphora and Rasmus. Sorrow kept her eyes fixed on the tiny hand waving from the blankets in Melisia's arms, turning back to Harcel when Rasmus drew level with them.

"What happens now?" Sorrow asked the baron.

"Now baby Aralie will receive her blessings from those Her Majesty and the prince consort have chosen to bless her."

"Blessings?" Sorrow had spoken to him to give her something to do while Rasmus passed, but her curiosity was piqued. She didn't know what blessings were.

The room began to empty, those not invited to the private part of the ceremony eager to find the wine and toast Aralie's health, and Harcel gestured for her to follow the crowd outside.

"Yes. You know that some Rhyllians have abilities?" he asked, steering her to where a table had been set up beneath a large tree and glasses were being filled. Sorrow picked up a glass and handed it to him, taking one for Luvian until she saw he'd been waylaid by Fain Darcia, so she kept it for herself and allowed Harcel to find a space for them, away from the main throng hovering near the door.

"I do, of course."

"Well, it's tradition in Rhylla to ask those whose abilities you find particularly admirable, or worthy, to bless your child, in the hope it will foster a good ability in them." He took a sip of his wine, and Sorrow did the same. "Of course, that's not how it works. These days only one in seven Rhyllians has an ability, and it doesn't follow a logic. Fathers without an ability can have children with one, a pair of twins might find one has an ability, one does not." He turned and looked around the room. "There, see."

Sorrow followed the gesture of his glass to where Aphora now stood with Vespus, and the man who'd been with them at the bridge all those months ago. Her brother, Melakis.

"Twins," Harcel continued. "The girl has a gift, but her brother doesn't. And yet they were both blessed by the same people, born to the same parents. We're not a naturally discriminatory race, and yet the abilities do mark differences that sometimes have an impact. Melisia would tell you otherwise, but then who discriminates against a queen? No, she's fine. But some of us are less valued, in some circles, for our lack of ability."

He looked across the room to where Eirlys was standing

with Rasmus, the pair doing their best to be subtle as they poured something from a flask subtly into their drinks. Starwater, she assumed. They toasted each other and drank, Eirlys sucking an ice cube into her mouth, grinning at her cousin, whose lips curved in response.

As Sorrow watched, Eirlys trailed a hand over the back of a chair, leaving a patina of ice crystals in its wake. So she could wield coldness, Sorrow deduced. Not really useful in a land that bordered the Svartan sea at the north, but probably in demand over high summer.

When Sorrow looked back at Harcel, there was a wistfulness on his face, and Sorrow wondered whether it was for the girl, or her ability – she noticed he had mentioned no ability of his own.

"I'm surprised Her Majesty didn't choose Lord Corrigan and his son to bless Aralie, given that they're family," Sorrow said carefully.

Harcel frowned. "Well, healing isn't one of the most sought-after gifts. There are pills and potions that can alleviate pain as well as what Rasmus can do."

He was jealous, Sorrow realized. So it was the princess Eirlys he liked.

"No," Harcel continued. "Her Majesty and the prince consort will have chosen carefully who gives the blessings, and it would never have been Rasmus or his father."

Sorrow kept her voice light and level as she replied. "Really? I suppose because Lord Vespus is only Melisia's half-brother? And so Rasmus is only a half-cousin?"

"It's nothing to do with that," Harcel was dismissive. "None of the blessers are related to Aralie. It's political, Miss Ventaxis – something you must understand given your new situation. It's all about appearance and meaning. Who they've chosen sends a message about who's in favour, and also what qualities they have decided are to be celebrated. Rasmus resigned his role in your country and left without warning. The queen isn't happy with him."

Sorrow's chest tightened guiltily. It was her fault Rasmus wasn't in favour right now. But, she realized, Harcel had said Vespus wasn't in favour either. Was this because of the Alvus farm, or something more? Did Melisia suspect what her brother was trying to accomplish with Mael in Rhannon?

"True," she replied. "But what has Lord Vespus done?"

Harcel gave her a sharp look, though whatever response he'd been about to make was lost to the fanfare as Melisia, Caspar, the baby and three other Rhyllians left the ruins and joined them in the courtyard. The guests broke into applause, and Sorrow looked at the three Blessers: a Rhyllian woman with the white hair of old age, a younger woman who stood proudly, meeting the eye of anyone who looked at her, and a young man who looked both thrilled and terrified simultaneously, his pale skin alternately flushing pink and then blanching white as he gazed at the queen and then the clapping crowd.

When the cheering had died away, Melisia spoke, first in Rhyllian, then again in the languages of those gathered.

"We will now adjourn back to our rooms to rest, relax and celebrate in private before the ball tonight. We look forward to seeing you there," Melisia finally said, working her way through the spectrum of languages her guests spoke.

When the royal party, including Eirlys, left, Harcel visibly slumped.

"I'll see you at the ball," he said, sloping off after them, joining a group of laughing Rhyllians.

Sorrow looked around for Irris, but couldn't see her. Then Luvian appeared by her side, an odd look on his face.

"Have you seen Irris?" Sorrow asked.

"She was talking to Rasmus earlier. Maybe she went to start getting ready for tonight."

Sorrow blinked. Surely Irris wouldn't have left without her? What was wrong with the Days today? "Oh. Well where have you been?" she asked. "More breaking and entering?"

"How dare you besmirch my good name?" Luvian replied. "And, no, actually I was getting told off by Charon Day. I had to go to the bathroom, and when I came back it had started, so I sat next to him and he collared me afterwards. He's not happy with me. I'd go as far as to say he's outright furious with me. Apparently I'm not being paid to waste your time on a wild-goose chase."

Sorrow swore. She'd meant to warn him Charon planned to speak to him but had forgotten.

"Sorry," she said.

Luvian looked at her. "He's wrong, you know. I mean, not totally. Obviously finding out who Mael really is isn't enough on its own, and we know that. But that, combined with finding Beliss and getting her to admit she raised a stolen child given to her by Vespus, will be enough. And it will give him somewhere to return to afterwards. If we can match him to a missing child, and have Beliss's confession, that's enough."

"So you think we should continue looking through the reports?"

Luvian nodded. "But Lord Day doesn't need to know," he added. "He made it very clear we were to stop."

Suspicion made her narrow her eyes.

Why? she asked herself. His reason, his insistence, didn't make sense. So what if she whiled away a morning reading an old list? There was nothing else she could have been doing. Why did he want them to stop looking into it?

"I think Darcia and Skae plan to start the party early," Luvian said as they made their way back to the carriage. "Shall we join them? Do a little more for diplomatic relations?"

"You go," Sorrow said, a plan forming. "I have a headache."

Luvian shrugged. "Are you sure?"

Sorrow nodded.

They parted, Luvian joining Lady Skae and Darcia in their carriage, and Sorrow taking her own, alone, back to her quarters. Dain, who had been dozing in the Rhannish party's private parlour, looked up when she entered, but Sorrow repeated her lie about having a headache and retreated to her rooms, where she picked up the reports she'd left there earlier.

She never had been very good at following rules.

29

Succedaneum

She found it so fast it was as though it had been waiting for her. There, on the page after the one she'd been looking at that morning, two days after Mael had fallen from the Humpback Bridge, she found the missing child.

But not a son. And not a toddler.

A baby. A girl, taken from a hospital in the North Marches hours after her birth, while her mother was sleeping and the nurses were occupied with another, difficult birth in the very same building.

The hospital Sorrow had been born in. The night Sorrow had been born.

Her grandmother told her she'd been a miracle child, snatched from the jaws of death. She'd told her how she'd offered anything to the Graces if they'd bring her back. The story had warmed Sorrow as a child, this proof that someone had loved her enough to want her to stay. Her father couldn't have made it clearer he didn't love her, didn't even like her. He never used her name, always "daughter". An accusation. Or perhaps a question. . .

Sorrow stared down at the page, her vision swimming. It was a coincidence. It had to be.

But there was a chill in her bones, a deep, heavy pooling of dread in her stomach.

She had to find Charon.

She hurried from her room, ignoring Dain when she asked if Sorrow was all right as she passed. She left the small palace and began to run, the piece of paper gripped in her hand as she followed the covered walkways. She should have asked him where he was staying – wait, what had the woman, Deryn, told her? With Ambassador Mira. Charon was staying with her.

Sorrow saw two Rhyllian guards walking ahead of her and sped up, slowing when they turned at the sound of her feet pounding the gravel.

"Ambassador Mira's quarters?" she panted. "I need to find them."

The men looked between themselves, silently conferring, before one pointed towards a small palace, painted a soft green. "There."

"Thank you," Sorrow gasped, forgetting Rhyllians disliked the simple phrase and breaking into a run once more.

There was another guard outside, and he moved to block her path as she approached.

"I'm Sorrow Ventaxis," she said as she drew up before him. "I understand the Rhannish vice chancellor is staying here. I need to see him, urgently."

She wondered how she looked to him, still dressed in the

pale blue gown she'd worn to the Naming ceremony. She could feel her hair had fallen loose from its knot atop her head as she'd run, knew her face would be flushed, her eyes wide and panicked.

The man gave her a once-over and, apparently deciding she wasn't a threat, stood aside, and Sorrow entered the ambassador's palace.

The layout of the ambassador's palace seemed the same as the one she occupied, so she turned to the left and followed a short passageway down to where the rose parlour was in her own quarters. As she'd hoped, it was the same here, though instead of roses the walls were patterned with birds, vases of feathers instead of flowers, but the room was empty of the vice chancellor.

At the sound of her footsteps a butler appeared from a small door behind the bar area.

"Can I help?" he asked in Rhannish.

"Is Lord Day here?"

"Yes, miss. I believe he's in his rooms. From the hallway, follow the corridor down; it's the second door on the right."

Sorrow nodded her thanks, turning back and heading to the room she'd been directed to, heart beating in time with her hurried footsteps.

She took a deep breath, and knocked on the door.

"Yes?" Charon called.

Sorrow went in.

As in the small palace, the room was a library, now adapted into a bedroom for Charon, so he could come and go as he pleased without needing to be carried up and down stairs. There was a low bed, and a small sitting area, and a screened part that Sorrow assumed was for bathing or dressing. But at that moment she didn't care about the setup of the room. She didn't care about anything but getting an answer to the question that was bubbling through her like poison.

Charon was sitting up on the bed, the chair parked beside it, his legs under a light blanket, a book in his hands. The window was open, birdsong and the low buzzing of bees drifting in through it, and the room smelled of the roses that grew outside. Charon frowned when he saw Sorrow, opening his mouth to speak.

Then he saw the piece of paper in her hand, crumpled and ragged.

Without saying a word, he swung himself off the bed and into his chair, rolling to meet her in the middle of the room. He met her gaze steadily, though she could see the fluttering of his pulse at his throat.

"Tell me..." Sorrow began, but didn't know how to finish. "On the day I was born, a baby girl vanished from the hospital—"

"Sorrow..."

"No." Her voice was high, still breathless from running. "Let me finish. A baby girl vanished the night I was born. And I was born with the cord around my neck, wasn't I?" she asked as Charon lowered his head. "That's the story. Grandmama revived me when the midwife froze. Whisked me out of the room to save me. And she did. I lived."

Charon said nothing.

"Or did I die?" Sorrow said. "Rather, did the real Sorrow die? And my grandmother took me instead, to take her place. Is that why you didn't want me to look at the reports? Not because it was a waste of time, but because of this?"

Still he didn't speak, his eyes locked on hers, his mouth

pressed together. On the wheels of his chair, Charon's knuckles were white.

"I'm an imposter," Sorrow said.

"No." Charon spoke then. "You're not an imposter."

"So I'm wrong? This is a coincidence?"

"Sit down."

"No."

"Sorrow, please. Sit. If you fall I can't catch you."

If it hadn't been for the fact her bones felt as though they were made of spun sugar, she would have remained standing to defy him. But she didn't trust them to hold her for much longer, so she sat, collapsing into a chair covered in gold silk, as Charon moved opposite her.

"I want to hear it all. The whole truth."

Charon gave a single, deep nod.

"I didn't know until afterwards – that's not an excuse," he said. "But I want you to know it wasn't a scheme. None of it was planned, by anyone. And by the time I found out it was too late to do anything without destroying the country. I was in hospital myself when it happened." He gestured down at his legs. He would have been bed-bound, the bones in his legs shattered beyond repair when he dived after Mael.

Sorrow said nothing, waiting with a face like stone for him to continue.

"To the best of my knowledge, the infant I met when I returned to the Winter Palace almost a year later was Cerena and Harun's child. I had no inkling until four years after that, when your grandmother told me." He lapsed back into the old terms. "Harun had shown no interest in you at all, and your grandmother came to me. It must have weighed on her so heavily. She'd got into her head that Harun could sense you weren't his, because he wouldn't see you, wouldn't hold you. I tried to reassure her that his disinterest was because of his grief . . . and then she confessed what she'd done."

"She stole me." Saying the words aloud did nothing to make them easier to bear.

"She took the baby – Harun and Cerena's real daughter – from the room, but she was clearly beyond help. She said she didn't know what to do; she kept walking and then she passed a room with a sleeping child in and it was done. She took her – you."

He made it sound such a simple thing. Explained in just a few words the actions of a few moments. Sorrow shook her head, trying to clear the low buzzing there.

"What happened to the other baby?"

Something like shame, or regret, flickered over Charon's face. "She hid her, in a cupboard."

Sorrow choked, her hands rising to cover her mouth.

"She went back for her," Charon said hastily. "Graces, Sorrow, she didn't leave her there. She secreted her out, and into Cerena's coffin. They're buried together."

He paused, and Sorrow closed her eyes. That poor baby. Her poor parents. Surely they'd raised the alarm? Surely they'd demanded to know where their daughter had gone?

"How did she keep it quiet?" she asked.

Charon understood what she meant. "Mael and Cerena had just died, the country was in shock. No one cared about a missing child, even one taken from the same hospital you were born in. The people were just grateful it wasn't you."

"But it *was* me," Sorrow said, her eyes flying open to meet his.

He held her gaze for a moment, then looked away.

"Who are my real parents? Did she tell you that?"

330

Charon hesitated, clearly debating whether to answer or not. "A young couple, from the North Marches," he said finally.

"Do they have other children? Do they still live there?"

"I don't know. I never asked for more information than that. I didn't want to know."

"You didn't want to know?" Sorrow couldn't stay seated any more, launching to her feet and beginning to pace.

"Sorrow, listen to me. You were five years old when I found out. Five. You'd fallen asleep in my arms more times than I could count; my name was the third word you ever said. My own children doted on you, Irris couldn't be kept from your side. Arran stood watch over you when you were ill. As far as I was concerned, you were Sorrow Ventaxis."

"But I wasn't!" Sorrow's voice rose as hysteria gripped her. "I'm not."

"What was I supposed to do?" Charon replied. "Cast you out? Tell Harun? Your grandmother would have been executed."

"She wasn't my grandmother!"

"She was in every way that counted."

"She stole me! From innocent people. Stars, Charon, of anyone, how can you defend this?"

"I'm not defending it. I'm explaining it."

Before he could say anything else there was a knock at the door.

Sorrow and Charon exchanged a brief glance, and Charon wheeled himself to the door.

Irris stood on the threshold.

"Is everything all right?" she asked Charon. "Sorrow?" She looked into the room. "What's going on?"

"It's fine. We're fine," Charon said. "Go and get ready for the ball."

Irris looked at Sorrow, and it took every ounce of self-control she had to nod that she was all right.

"It's just a disagreement," she said, her voice shaking. "I'll tell you later."

Irris looked between the two of them, her disbelief evident in her frown and the set of her mouth. Then she shrugged, saying nothing else as she turned and left. Charon closed the door and then rolled to the window, closing that over too.

"Sorrow. . ." he said as he moved back to her.

"That's not my name. That's the name of the dead girl. I don't know what my name is."

"Your name is Sorrow," Charon said.

"For it's all I bring." She turned to him. "That's what she said, Cerena, isn't it? Sorrow is all I bring. Stars, what if she knew? What if the last thing she knew was that I was a lie, that the daughter in her arms was a substitute? After all, my name is practically a prophecy."

"Please, calm—"

"If you tell me to calm down I will scream."

He held up his hands. "Sorrow, believe me, had I known at the time what your grandmother had done, I would have done something. Had you smuggled back to the hospital and returned to your . . . to those people. But as I said, you were five when she confided in me. Too late to undo what had been done without breaking Rhannon completely. The nation knew you as Sorrow Ventaxis, the last scion of the Ventaxis family. It was far too late to do anything other than make the best of it."

"And my real parents. Do you suppose they made the best of it?"

Charon shook his head mutely.

Sorrow made her way back to her seat. "Who else knows?"

"No one. Your grandmother only told me. And I know you might not want to hear this now, but she loved you. As far as she was concerned you were her true granddaughter. She knew what she did was wrong, but I don't believe she ever regretted it. And. . ." He paused. "You're the true Ventaxis heir. You might not be a Ventaxis born, but you're Ventaxis bred. You've been raised that way."

"How can you condone this?" Sorrow said on a breath. "It's your job to make sure that the laws of Rhannon are upheld. I'm not a Ventaxis. I can't run for election any more."

"It's my job to make sure the needs of Rhannon are served before anything and anyone else. No individual is bigger than Rhannon; only Rhannon matters. I've told you that a thousand times," Charon said. "You have to run. And you have to win. Or Rhannon will fall under Vespus's control."

"How is this any different to what Vespus is doing? I'm the same as Mael. Raised to be something I have no right to be."

"It's not the same. You have lived your whole life Rhannish, as Sorrow Ventaxis."

"It wasn't my life to live!" Sorrow said.

"It's too late to think those thoughts, Sorrow. This can never come out." Charon's eyes were wide. "You can't reveal this. Not now. Not ever."

She knew they couldn't. Especially not now, not with the Sons of Rhannon and their stirring up of hatred against the Ventaxises. It wouldn't take much to ignite the fire they were kindling under the people of Rhannon, she'd seen that at her presentation. There was an undercurrent of hatred running through the heart of Rhannon. The people were already on edge. The slightest spark could cause an explosion that would devastate the land. Bad enough that after too many years of suffering and deprivation they were now playing witness to a fight for the chancellorship. Two Ventaxises battling for the role.

No. Not two.

Because she wasn't a Ventaxis.

She didn't know, still, whether he was – not for sure.

But she knew, without doubt, that she wasn't.

The knowledge sank into her, and she doubled over, gasping for air.

She heard Charon move, felt his hand on her shoulder, and she wanted to shrug it off. He'd lied to her, almost her whole life. And yet he was all she had and she couldn't push him away. Not then, at least.

The sobs were deep, coming from somewhere inside she hadn't known existed. She'd never been someone who cried easily, or at all. As a child she'd raged and seethed when things didn't go her way, but never cried. When she'd fallen over or hurt herself, she'd remained stiff and silent, biting her tongue to keep from crying. Even when her grandmother had died – *not her grandmother* – she'd felt broken, bereft and empty, but she hadn't cried. In a country once caged by grief, not crying had seemed an act of rebellion. Yet now all she could do was cry, convulsing as weeping engulfed her body, her mouth open in a silent moan as tears fell. Her hands were fists, beating softly at her knees as she wept a lifetime of tears, until the well was dry and she was hollowed out, empty of everything.

All the while Charon kept his hand on her shoulder. He didn't rub it, or offer any words. He was Charon, her all-but-father, as stoic and steady as he'd always been. There, always there.

She wanted so much to be angry with him. But her rage had leaked out too, washed away by her tears.

She looked up, her throat aching from crying, her face puffy and tender from the salt water that had flooded it.

"My girl," Charon said.

Then she moved, allowing herself to be held by him. Needing it.

When she finally pulled away, embarrassed, she scrubbed at her eyes furiously.

Her voice, when she spoke, was a crow's song, croaking and harsh. "What do I do?"

"What you've been doing."

"And if I win?"

"Then I'll be a happy man because Rhannon will finally have the chancellor she deserves." Charon said. "You're Sorrow Ventaxis. It's who you were raised to be. Nothing has changed."

He was wrong. Everything had changed.

She had more questions. More she wanted to know. But her tongue was lead in her mouth, thick and heavy. She rose to her feet, forcing him to roll his chair back to look up at her.

"I'd better get ready for the ball," she said.

"Sorrow. . ."

"I'm . . . I need time," she said. "Please."

Charon nodded.

He wheeled ahead of her to the door, turning his chair to block her path.

"Don't tell anyone," he said. "I know it's a lot to ask, but you can't. Not Luvian, not Irris. No one. Please, trust me."

Trust him. . . How could she, when he'd lied to her for most of her life?

"I'm here for you," he said. "Whenever you need."

She believed him in that, at least. He held up a hand and she took it, reaching for the door handle with the other. Then she left him, left the ambassador's palace, walking back to the small palace in a daze. When she got there she couldn't recall if she'd met anyone on her journey back, or spoken. She heard voices from the parlour but ignored them, climbing the stairs to her room. Mercifully Dain had gone, and Luvian was still out. Sorrow closed the door to her bedroom and lay on the bed, eyes open but unseeing.

Somewhere out there her real parents might be living their lives. She might have siblings, cousins, grandparents. They might even have been at the presentation, she realized. Or at the bridge. . . The young woman with the baby; that could be a sister, a niece or nephew. Suddenly every Rhannish face she'd seen looked a little like hers, a parade of them behind her eyes, face after face with her lips, her eyes, her chin. She'd always thought she looked like Harun, but she was no more his than Mael probably was.

And what a dark thing that was. To have to fight him, knowing she deserved it no more than he did. Less, because he at least still thought he was a Ventaxis. Stars, with the way things were going maybe he *was* really Mael Ventaxis.

She lay there, unmoving, long into the afternoon, until the sun dipped, bathing the room in a soft gold light.

She heard Luvian's return, heard the shuffle to his steps that told her he was maybe a little drunk. She heard him go into his room, heard drawers opening, heard the splashing of water as he washed. He whistled softly, his pitch perfect.

Still she didn't move, lying on the bed as though she was a corpse, as dead as the girl whose place she'd taken.

"Sorrow?" Luvian knocked on the door and opened it without waiting. "Sorrow, is your head—"

He cursed when he saw her, rushing to her side, pressing his hand to her forehead.

"Sorrow? Graces, you're hot. Shall I send for Irris?"

"No." Her voice was still hoarse. "I'm fine."

She made to sit up, and Luvian sat on her bed, watching her with naked concern.

"Sorrow, I don't think—"

"I said I'm fine. What time is it?"

"Seven chimes."

"I'd better get ready."

"For the ball?" Luvian asked. "Do you think that's a good idea? Look, you stay here; I'll send someone to fetch Irris, and she can sit with you until you feel better."

"It's a headache." She could hear the flat tone to her voice, saw the worry in his eyes. "Give me half an hour."

"I'll stay with you, I don't mind."

"Half an hour," she said again.

Luvian paused, as though he might argue, and then nodded, rising silently and leaving her. He closed her door, and she heard him moving about, but he wasn't whistling any more.

Sorrow swung her legs off the bed and crossed to the wardrobe, every step as heavy as though she was moving through honey. She took out the dress Irris had assigned and changed into it, letting her old outfit fall to the floor like a skin she'd shed.

The dress was sleeveless, gossamer-thin gold silk, the fabric pretending at sheerness. The neckline was a slash that ran from shoulder to shoulder, the slim, fluted skirt grazing the floor. She was more covered than she had been on either of the previous nights, yet the colour of the dress, so close to her skin tone, and the way it clung to her form before flaring over her hips, made her seem, at first glance, so much more exposed. It was beautiful – a weapon of a dress; Ines's work was exceptional – and Sorrow had been looking forward to wearing it, knowing it would draw the eye. A gown fit for a future chancellor.

Not a pretender.

If she'd had anything else to wear, she would have buried the dress at the bottom of her trunk and wished never to see it again.

She walked to the mirror, ignoring her body from the neck down, and pulled her hair back into a severe chignon. She lined her eyes, drawing the wings into savage points, coated her lashes in black paint and daubed her mouth with scarlet lipstick, once again creating a mask to hide behind. When it was in place, she opened her bedroom door.

"Ready," she said.

Luvian's eyes were wide, almost frightened, as he took in the woman who stood before him. For a moment it was as though he hadn't recognized her.

Sorrow knew how he felt.

30

Outside, Inside

The ballroom had been transformed into a lush, green, impossible affair. The stone walls and the stained-glass windows Sorrow admired had all vanished behind a curtain of fragrant ferns and leaves. Above their heads a tangled network of vines masked the ceiling and wound around and through the buttresses, playing home to brightly coloured birds that darted like tiny comets between the foliage. The flagstone floor had been covered by soft, springy moss, and many of the guests were taking advantage of it, moving barefoot through the room, shoes dangling from fingers, or left somewhere for later.

Over a hundred oil lamps hung suspended from the roof, lighting the room, though much of the outskirts were in shadow, and Sorrow could see people moving there, silhouetted against the living walls. And as she and Luvian moved into the space, she saw tiny green lights glowing in between the leaves. Starflies, she realized. Rasmus had once told her he kept some in a ventilated jar by his bed at night as a child, catching them at sunset and releasing them the following morning, falling asleep to their dancing.

The entire hall was a natural grotto; even the tables and chairs had been replaced by large tree trunks and stumps, some with screens of grass partially around them, allowing for privacy. Beneath the delicate sound of a Rhannish pipe and violin playing softly, Sorrow imagined she could hear the burbling of water, a pool or a waterfall right there inside the room.

It was stunning; even in her numb, lost state Sorrow could see that. But though she knew it, objectively, to be wondrous, she felt nothing. No joy or marvelling at this unexpected, magical transformation. Not even the sight of the starflies that she'd long coveted was enough to pierce the shell that had formed around her after Charon's confession.

Unlike Luvian, who'd pulled her to the walls to run long fingers through the fronds, shaking his head, his smile childlike and wide, as the Starflies danced around his hands.

"This must have been Vespus," he murmured to Sorrow, snagging them both a drink from a passing waiter. "He must have used his ability to do this. I know we said it was pretty useless, but we might have been wrong. This is amazing."

Sorrow took the glass he offered and drained it in one.

"Steady," Luvian said, though he took the empty one from her and gave her his. "What do you want to do? Circle around, say hello? Find Irris and Charon? Sit and eat, and then go chatting? Or we could dance?" He gestured to where the Duke of Meridea and his consort were already moving gently to the music.

"Sit," Sorrow said. Definitely no Charon. And she didn't know what she was going to say to Irris – Irris knew her too well to believe a headache could be behind Sorrow's expression. Despite the make-up, she looked as though she hadn't slept for days. Sorrow wondered how Charon had explained their fight, and also whether he'd told Irris to leave her alone, and that was why she hadn't come to get ready with her.

Luvian took Sorrow's elbow, guiding her to one of the tables partly shielded by a wall of tall grass. He sat beside her on the log, watching as she drained the second glass.

"Sorrow, unlike our fine Rhyllian friends I'm not gifted with either an ability, or the skill of mind reading, so you're going to have to spit it out," he said. "Something's wrong. Don't lie. Tell me."

"I'm fine. I told you already, it's a headache."

"Still? Can't you take something? What if I find Rasmus; he can heal, right?"

"No," Sorrow barked. "Just . . . forget it, Luvian. I'll be fine. As soon as you stop coddling me."

His mouth pursed, his brows drew into a frown as he looked at her, before giving a carefully uncaring shrug.

"I'll leave you in peace," he said stiffly, and rose, striding out towards where Fain Darcia was standing with a circle of Rhyllians. Sorrow watched as they made room for Luvian, as he slotted easily into the group, and the conversation. Fain Darcia leant towards him and spoke, and Luvian gestured to her. Sorrow looked away.

A waiter passed and she took another drink, cupping it in both hands. She scanned the room for Charon, wondering if he'd managed to navigate it in his chair. Thoughtless of Vespus, really, she realized, to create an environment the Rhannish vice chancellor couldn't manoeuvre with ease. Knowing Vespus, it was deliberate.

Lord Vespus was standing beside his half-sister and Prince Caspar, hands behind his back, seemingly enjoying a conversation with them. Prince Caspar held Aralie in a sling across his chest, leaving his hands free to gesture as he told his wife and Vespus some story. There was no sign of any tension between them, and Sorrow wondered what the red-haired baron, Harcel, might have said about his seeming lack of favour, if they hadn't been interrupted.

"Hello." She turned to see Mael peering around the side of the screen. "May I join you?"

Sorrow shrugged, and Mael sat where Luvian had before.

"I saw your advisor go over there, and Arta is at the buffet, so I thought I'd come and see how you were before someone insists we don't talk."

"I'm fine," Sorrow said without looking at him.

"Isn't this brilliant?" Mael continued. "Lord Vespus did it, as a Naming gift for Aralie."

"It's not so brilliant for Lord Day. He's in a wheeled chair. I can't imagine the ground is easy for him to travel."

"Oh, no, the plants withdraw when he moves, look." Mael pointed to where Charon had steered into view, Irris beside him. As Sorrow watched, the moss seemed to part in the path of his chair, allowing him to pass.

He turned to see Sorrow and Mael sitting together, and frowned, but Sorrow returned his gaze levelly, giving nothing away, until he gripped his wheels and moved deeper into the room. Irris looked between them both, and raised questioning brows. So Charon hadn't explained their fight, then.

For a moment Sorrow wanted nothing more than to cross the room and pull Irris aside. Irris loved Sorrow enough to tell her the truth; Irris always cut to the heart of an issue like a knife through butter. Irris pulled no punches, never balked, never quavered. Irris would soothe her, rally her, as she always did.

But what could Sorrow say to her? Irris couldn't know the truth; Charon had been explicit in that. And Sorrow didn't think she could lie to Irris's face. So she shrugged, and saw hurt flicker over Irris's face. Her mood darkening further as her friend hurried after Charon, she tuned back in to what Mael was saying.

". . . so Lord Vespus instructed them to do it," Mael said, and as Sorrow watched the moss moved seamlessly back into place in Charon's wake.

"How very good of him."

"You really don't like him, do you?"

Sorrow's tone was bored as she replied, "What on Laethea gave you that impression?"

"And you hate me too," Mael said suddenly.

Sorrow turned to him. "No," she said honestly. "I don't hate you."

She had, for a while. Well, she'd hated the brother who'd died, and was therefore always perfect in her father's eyes. And she'd hated the boy at the bridge, and the boy who'd stood beside Harun the night he'd died. She didn't hate this boy. Whoever – whatever – he was.

But he couldn't know that.

"It's all right," Mael continued, when Sorrow remained silent. "I understand. What you went through, growing up, because of me. What you're going through now, again, on my account. I'd probably hate me too. It wasn't my idea, you know, to run against you."

"Then why are you?" She was truly curious. If what he was saying was true, then he did it knowing it would make her feel bad towards him, and yet he persisted in trying to befriend her. It made no sense.

"Because it's my responsibility to," he said simply. "I wasn't lying when we first met and I said I wasn't interested in being the chancellor. I truly wasn't. I thought I'd come home, and Father would get better, and start to fix Rhannon. Lincel had told us what life in Rhannon was like, and I believed if I came back, things would change. Because it was my fault, in a way. Me being gone was what started it all."

He paused, as if waiting for her to deny it, but Sorrow didn't reply, her eyes fixed on the far end of the hall.

Mael sighed, then continued. "But he died. He didn't have a chance to fix anything. So the task of healing Rhannon is my responsibility. It's on me. I caused it, I have to mend it. I have to run against you, to prove to the people that I know that. If they don't choose me, so be it. But how could I ever face them if I didn't stand up and say to them I'd at least try to make things better, after they suffered so much for me?"

She believed him. Quite simply, and quite suddenly, she believed him. She'd never had a chance to hear his presentation in Prekara. She'd assumed he was saying the things she'd written in her manifesto, about wanting to heal the country, and its people, because he thought it's what might help him win. But he meant it; every single word was drenched in sincerity. He had the same light behind his eyes that Luvian got when he was urging her to do something. That look of total and utter dedication, come what may. He really wanted to fix things. He really thought he could.

"How could I face you, too?" he continued. "You suffered, perhaps most of all. I hate that. You're my little sister."

She couldn't help the harsh bark of laughter that escaped her.

The light in his gaze dimmed, and he swallowed. "I hope, when this is over, no matter how it ends, we can move past it. I won't hate you if you win. I'm doing this because I think it's right." He rose and looked down at her. "And I won't give up trying to make you like me. Or caring about you. We're all the family each other has, and that means something to me."

He walked away, only the barest slump to his shoulders.

She envied him. He truly believed he was Mael Ventaxis, not a shred of doubt in his mind. She realized then that she'd inadvertently done to herself what she'd hoped to do to him. In trying to prove he didn't deserve a place in her life, she'd destroyed herself. It didn't matter now, whether he was or wasn't Mael Ventaxis. Because she wasn't Sorrow Ventaxis.

As she watched him go, she caught Luvian's eye, head tilted in inquiry. She nodded to say she was all right, though it was far from the truth.

She could see Luvian making his excuses to the group, planning to return to her, and she didn't want it. Didn't feel she could take him being light, and droll, and making clever comments. She didn't have enough in her to laugh at them. No, Luvian wasn't what she needed.

Sorrow rose swiftly and moved behind the tall grass, pausing to put her glass down before moving deeper into the room, taking advantage of the low lighting.

Across the room Mael had joined the Duke of Meridea and

another man, who Sorrow assumed from his floor-length coat and the gold tattoo across his forehead was the ambassador of Nyrssea. She stood behind a palm and watched as they talked, Mael as at ease with them as Luvian had been with his crowd.

And she knew that this time last night, she could have been the same. Could have joined a group with confidence, because she belonged there. Belonged in this room of dukes and queens and ambassadors and politicians. Was their equal. But now she knew the truth. She was a cuckoo in the nest.

That was why she'd thought she'd recognized Mael, she realized, all those weeks ago. It was like calling to like. Imposter to imposter. Fool to fool. Two silly children who thought they knew what they were because they'd been told it. And now here they both were, fighting for a seat neither had the right to hold, both the puppets of people who'd decided their fates for them, whether for good or ill.

Mael and the Nyrssean clasped forearms, beaming at each other, before Mael left them, crossing the indoor woodland to where Lord Vespus still stood beside his sister, bowing before the queen, who welcomed him with a large smile. As Sorrow watched, she turned from Vespus, drawing Mael with her, Caspar following them, and a dark look crossed Vespus's handsome face, his hand rising to smooth his hair back behind a pointed ear before he strode away, to where Aphora stood feeding one of the ruby-and-emerald birds with crumbs from her palm.

Despite everything else that was happening, her curiosity was piqued. Why was Vespus out of favour with Melisia? Was it a new development, or an older resentment?

Sorrow looked for the baron, only to see him standing with Eirlys and Rasmus in the far corner of the room. Both Rasmus and the princess were dressed in metallic finery; Princess Eirlys in a gown of gold and Rasmus in a frock coat of silver, over midnight-blue trousers.

As though he felt her gaze, he turned, his violet eyes meeting her dark ones across the room. Sorrow looked away first.

Heart sore and alone, she left her post in the shadows and moved towards where a buffet was being served by Rhyllian chefs and began to fill a plate, noting with little interest that florals and botanicals were the theme of the meal. Cream soups in tiny glass tureens topped with purple and yellow blossoms. Salads made from a mixture of leaves and blooms, breads with herbs and seeds baked through. Slices of rare beef with rosehip sauce, minced lamb and rosemary wrapped in vine leaves. And the desserts ... lavender and lemon cakes, rose and pistachio pudding, geranium ices melting in pools of liquid hot chocolate...

She took her plate and retreated again, trying a little of this and that, finishing the lot without meaning to. She hadn't known she was hungry. Rhyllian food seemed to do that to her.

It was as she licked the last of the lavender syrup from her fingers that she became aware of eyes on her, and knew before she looked up that it was Rasmus.

He was alone, leaning against the wall, the leaves behind him curling around his body, as though they knew him. Her heart gave a thump, and she stilled with the instinct of something knowing it was being hunted. Slowly, she rose, leaving her plate, skirting around the table and moving towards the back of the room, her pulse speeding as she did.

Rasmus followed.

31

A Personal Eden

He kept to the other side of the hall, stalking her along its length, his eyes never moving from her. When she paused to exchange greetings with someone, he waited. As soon as she moved again he did too, matching his pace to hers.

Sorrow's heart thrummed in her chest. What was he doing? Why was he doing it? Starwater, she assumed, it had to be. He'd drunk the liqueur again and it had made him reckless. But how reckless? Did he plan to confront her, in front of his family, and their guests? Or perhaps he was trying to intimidate her, remind her this was his place.

She weaved through the dancers, but her dress made her feel like a target, and she knew he was still there, waiting for her to emerge. As she freed herself from a twirl Fain Darcia had drawn her into, there he was, lips slightly parted, eyes unblinking.

Enough, she decided. She didn't need this, not today.

She glanced around and spied the bubbling pool she'd heard earlier, hidden away behind a trailing curtain of ivy. She looked at Rasmus and jerked her head towards it, before making her way over, disappearing behind the greenery.

A moment later he joined her.

"What are you doing?" She went on the attack immediately. "You made your thoughts about me perfectly clear. I've been trying to stay out of your way."

He fixed her with glittering eyes. "People think it's strange we don't talk. They're speculating we fought, and that's the real reason I left Rhannon."

"If you wanted to avoid rumours, you should have spoken to me openly, not hunted me across the hall."

"That's not what I want." His voice was low, his expression searching as he looked her up and down, scanning the dress that now felt too flimsy.

"Then what?" She forced the words out through a mouth suddenly as dry as Astria.

"I was..." He turned away, walking to the other side of the pool. "I spoke to Irris earlier, after the Naming. She asked if I'd spoken to you and I confessed I had. And not very well. My behaviour two nights ago was hideous. I was hideous. The Starwater..." He trailed off. "Clichéd to say 'I was drunk', but it's not totally a lie."

"Are you apologizing because Irris told you to?"

"She told me to leave you alone, actually. But I can't. Not until I've apologized. So, on that note, I shouldn't have spoken to you as I did. I was drunk, and childish. I beg your forgiveness."

Sorrow left it a beat before she replied. "I understand why you acted like you did."

"That doesn't make it right, and I'm sorry," he said,

emphasizing the Rhannish word. "Especially for my parting shot. That was low, and untrue."

"It was," Sorrow agreed.

Rasmus lowered his head, and Sorrow walked around the pool to face him.

"For what it's worth, I'm sorry too. For not telling you straight away when I knew what was going to happen. I should have. I owed you that. And I'm sorry I didn't listen to you, when you asked me to. I think I knew how it was going to go, and I knew if we spoke I'd have to say something then. It was cowardly, and you deserved better."

He was silent for a long moment. "Forgiven, then?"

Sorrow held out a hand and he took it.

The second his fingers wrapped around hers she knew what she wanted. Needed. He could fill the chasm that was threatening to split her in two; hadn't he always been able to distract her, to soothe her? Heal her?

Her eyes locked with his, and then they were moving, as if they'd planned it that way all along: Sorrow reaching up as Rasmus bent down, their lips finding each other's as though they'd never known anywhere else.

He moved her back, back against the wall, and the leaves welcomed her, welcomed them both as he kissed her.

Their hands returned to those places they knew so well, falling back into a rhythm that was part dance, part homecoming: hers in his hair, cupping his face, his at her waist, pulling her flush against him, her skin humming under his touch. He moaned when she pressed into him, breaking the kiss to lick her throat, grazing his teeth over her collarbone as she let her head fall back and her eyes flutter closed.

A loud laugh nearby forced them apart, the jewel-coloured

birds above them twittering loudly as they flew away. Rasmus's eyes were glazed, his face flushed. They looked at each other for a long moment.

"That was foolish," Sorrow said. "If we'd—"

"Leave. Leave the ball." His voice was whisky-rough and rich. "Follow me."

Sorrow nodded.

He tore a handful of leaves from the ivy and left her. She crouched down, splashing her face with the cool crystal water. She couldn't go. She shouldn't go.

She went.

She was blind to the rest of the party as she made her way after him, and this time no one stopped her, as though they couldn't see her either. Within minutes she'd left the indoor garden behind, stepping out in the cooler air of the corridor. Two guards nodded to her as she passed, and she inclined her head, wondering where Rasmus had gone.

On the floor ahead was an ivy leaf, and Sorrow went to it, spotting another a few metres away.

She followed the trail he'd left, tracking him through the discarded ivy leaves, deep into the royal palace, until she found a final leaf outside a door. She opened it without knocking, arriving in a small study, complete with a desk, a chair, shelves full of identically bound books. And Rasmus, standing in a patch of moonlight, his back to her.

He turned when she entered, but remained where he was as she closed the door behind her.

"This is foolish," she said again.

"We're fools," he agreed.

There was a moment, as long as a hummingbird's heartbeat, when it seemed they might resist temptation.

Then he was beside her, cupping her breast, his thumb grazing over her nipple. Need flashed through her body, and she ground against him drawing a moan from him.

He peeled the dress from her body and threw it somewhere behind him, and she tried to undress him, fumbling with the buttons on his frock coat. Frustration made her clumsy, and she was grateful when he took over, ripping the last few buttons away and shrugging the coat to the ground. His shirt followed suit and soon her breasts were pressed against his chest as his mouth sought her lips again. He found her tongue, coaxing it with his own, sucking it gently before he returned his attentions to her lips.

One hand slipped lower, and she pushed into the pressure, whimpering against his mouth. She reached for the waistband of his trousers then and began to tug them down, eager to touch him as he touched her.

He pulled away and the loss was unbearable, until he dropped to his knees to kiss a path along her inner thigh that made her tighten her grip in his hair, heat at her centre demanding more, insisting on it. He obeyed her unspoken command and lifted her easily on to the desk, his hand returning to between her thighs as his mouth met hers. She arched into him, gripping his shoulders so tightly she was scared she'd wound him as he stroked and caressed her, his fingers discovering her once again, her body delighted to welcome him back. Then he was covering her, fitting together as easily as they always had.

Her back and shoulders were stiff from being pressed into the hard wood of the desk, but the rest of her felt like liquid gold as she lay beside him, her head back in its old place on his chest, his arms around her as though they had no business being anywhere else. Neither had spoken since they'd separated, both remaining prone on the table. She didn't want to be the one to break the moment, though, and from the way his grip on her remained resolutely tight, she assumed he felt the same.

Finally he released her, and she immediately became aware of a sharp pain in her neck, forcing her to sit up.

"Ouch," she gasped, rubbing it, and then his hand was there, the pain fading away.

"You're good to me," she said.

He pulled her to him and kissed her forehead, her cheek, the tip of her nose, and each eyelid. Then he hopped down from the table, finding his trousers, and she watched as he pulled them up over his long thighs. He bent to pick up her dress, and she put it back on, before helping him find the buttons from his coat.

"Can I keep one?" she asked, without knowing why she wanted it, and he handed one over without comment.

When they'd tidied up, removing every trace of themselves from the room, they stood in silence, not quite able to meet each other's eyes. It had never been awkward between them before, but as the euphoria ebbed away, Sorrow realized that once again they'd been unutterably reckless. And once again, minutes after apologizing for her behaviour, she'd used Rasmus to drive out some of her own misery, used his touch to mend her—

She froze, as a terrible, unthinkable thought dawned on her...

How could she be so stupid? His touch removed her pain. Made her feel better... She craved him every time she felt sad, or lost, or scared...

She'd always thought it was just her physical pain he healed – after all, he hadn't been able to soothe away her grief after her grandmother died. But maybe that was a different kind of ache; maybe that was something nothing but time could heal. Whereas doubt and worry and fear – pain – they were all more tangible. All easier to explain. To heal. And her body knew it. Even as she'd tried to pull away from him, her body craved him, drove her to him whenever she was hurting, however she was hurting.

Like today.

Rasmus frowned. "Are you well?" he asked.

She nodded mutely, but it wasn't enough to convince him, and he reached for her, stopping dead as she recoiled.

How could she have been so blind?

Never again, she vowed silently. *I can't do this to him again. Or to myself.*

"Rasmus. . ." she began.

"It's all right." He spoke quickly. "I know. This was a goodbye, wasn't it?"

She nodded. "It has to be. This. . . This is wrong. Not because of laws, but because . . . I'm using you." There was a relief in saying it aloud, even as she hated herself for the truth of it. "Every time something goes wrong, it's you I run to. Not even you, but this. . . Being with you. I use it to fix me. I didn't know before now, I swear it. If I'd known I wouldn't have. . ."

He was silent for a moment. "I never minded," he said softly.

The floor beneath her seemed to shift at his words. He'd known. All along, he'd known. And he'd let her do it.

"So, if you did 'use me', which isn't how I'd phrase it, then

I consented," he continued. "In fact more than consented. Encouraged. I was willing to take you on whatever terms I could. It's not a great look for me, either."

Sorrow knew what he was trying to say, and do, but it didn't stop the shame that heated her skin.

"I'm sorry."

"Please don't be." He moved as if to stroke her hair, and then stopped, lowering his hand. "I don't regret a moment of it."

"I don't either. I never will."

"One day, we'll be able to be real friends," he said softly. "Not for a while, I think. But one day."

"I hope so," Sorrow whispered.

"I know so. I just need a few centuries to get over you first." He tried bravely to smile, and Sorrow nodded.

"Will you go back to the ball?" he asked.

"No," Sorrow said. "Will you?"

"No." He walked to the door and peered out. "It's clear, you're safe to go."

"Goodbye, Ras."

"Goodbye, Row," he said. His mouth curved gently, then he turned away from her.

Sorrow stayed where she was for a long moment, mastering herself, before she stepped into the hallway. The ball sounded as lively as it had when she'd left it, and she saw Luvian talking to Eirlys and the baron as she passed, all of them smiling.

Luvian spotted her and came after her, catching up to her in the main doorway of the keep.

"I thought you'd gone back to our rooms. I sent Irris after you."

"No. I went to get some air. I'm going back there now."

"The fireworks are about to start; don't you want to watch them?"

Sorrow shook her head. "I'd better find Irris."

"All right." Luvian nodded, his eyes sad. "I'll be back soon."

As the carriage pulled up outside the little palace, there was a whistling sound above her and she looked up, in time to see an explosion of colour across the sky, reds and greens cascading out, then fading. A split second later two more starbursts appeared, accompanied by echoing pops. She paused on the stairs and watched as the sky lit up, over and over, with coloured lights, the scent of smoke on the balmy summer air. For some reason they made her throat tight, her eyes prick with tears. When they finished, the final wisps of smoke drifting across the crescent moon, she turned and continued, feeling strangely bereft.

It was quiet inside the small palace, and she made her way straight to her rooms, only to find them empty. She must have missed Irris. She debated whether to go and find her – she knew she should; she'd hurt enough people for one day, without alienating Irris too. But all she wanted was a bath, and to sleep. Maybe a good night's rest would wipe away the despair that she couldn't quite keep down.

She sat on the side of the bath as it filled, the sound similar enough to the pool in the hall to make her flush at the memory of what had just happened. She stood abruptly and began to braid her hair, crossing to the mirror to pin it to her head, before slipping off her dress and pulling on a soft robe.

The main door to their set of rooms opened. "Irris?" she called.

When he didn't answer, she turned off the taps.

"Irris, is that—"

A giant hooded and masked figure appeared in the doorway.

The Sons of Rhannon.

32

The Tower

Sorrow backed away.

"Wrong," the man said, and Sorrow recognized his voice. He was the one who'd attacked her in Prekara. "Your friend is dead."

"No..." The world seemed to shift on its axis as horror roared through Sorrow. Not Irris...

"Don't worry, Miss Ventaxis, you'll see her very soon, I promise."

He began to move towards her, and Sorrow scanned the room for something, anything she could use as a weapon, all the while her mind chanting *no, no, no* at the thought of bright, brilliant Irris being dead. He was lying. It had to be a lie. She picked up a bar of soap and threw it at the man, but he dodged it easily, still advancing.

"Dain!" Sorrow screamed, praying the guard down in her library room would hear her. "Dain!"

"No one's coming."

She knew how to fight with a small sword, a foil and an épée, had been trained alongside Irris when they were children. She knew how to hit and punch and slap and kick. But when the man moved, vaulting over the bath in a fluid motion and grabbing her, moving far faster than she'd thought someone his size could, she realized none of the things she knew would help her. Not against someone who truly meant to harm her.

It didn't stop her from trying, though, thrashing in his grip, driving her head back until it connected with his face, causing him to groan and punch the side of her head. She saw stars then, falling limp for a moment, which was all it took for him to sink his hands into her hair and drag her back towards the full bath.

She barely had time to close her mouth before he pushed her head under the water, straddling her so she couldn't move. She beat his legs with her fists, tried to sink her nails into his calves, even as her lungs started to burn.

No. *No.*

Black spots appeared in her vision, bubbles streaming from her nose as her body demanded she release the air she was trying so desperately to hold, to take another breath. She tried once more to move, only for her attacker to push her head deeper into the water as she pounded the side of the bath uselessly. She opened her mouth and screamed at the hopelessness of it.

And then heard a shout, and the crushing pressure at her back and head was gone. She hauled herself out of the water, air flooding her lungs as she finally took a breath.

She collapsed, coughing, gasping, and looked up to see

Luvian facing the masked man with a broken bottle in his hand, edging towards him.

"You don't have the guts, Luvian," the man said to her advisor, as Sorrow retched, bent double on the floor.

"Try me." He feinted at the man, who dodged. As he did Luvian slashed for real, and the bottle tore the fabric on the masked man's arm. Blood welled from it.

"I didn't think you had it in you," the man said. Sorrow missed his next words as her stomach emptied on to the bathroom floor, catching only, ". . . be proud." When she looked up, wiping her mouth with a sleeve, both men had gone.

She pulled the robe around her where it had fallen loose, and moved to the door, only to scream hoarsely when she crashed into a figure.

Luvian wrapped his arms around her and held her.

"Are you all right?" His voice was muffled by her hair. "Sorrow?" He kept a soft grip on her arms and pushed her back so he could see her face. "He's gone. He ran. Come on," he said, guiding her out into the parlour, then into his bedroom.

He left her standing by the neatly made bed and peered under it. Then he went to his own bathroom and locked the door, opened his wardrobe and trunk, before pulling the curtains away from the windows.

"This room is clear," he said, reaching under his pillow and pulling out a wicked-looking dagger. "I need to go and alert the castle guards that there's an intruder. You stay in here, take this —" he pressed the dagger into her hand "— and lock the door behind me."

His eyes were bright, fixed on hers, and she gave a short nod.

"He killed Irris," she said, the words ashes in her mouth.

"Luvian, he killed..." She couldn't finish, disbelief stealing Irris's name from her. It wasn't true. It couldn't be.

Luvian swallowed. Then again. "Lock the door," he said finally. "I'll send Dain up to stand outside it. Don't open it until you hear my voice. Do you understand?"

Sorrow nodded, following him to the door and turning the key violently, before sinking to the ground. Her chest still felt tight, still ached, and she had a headache from where the man had hit her. She shuddered as she remembered the water rising up to meet her face, the feeling of submersion, the firm hand holding her there. And Irris... Irris... She gripped the dagger tighter, and waited, focusing on breathing, in and out.

Luvian was back within minutes, calling her name, and when she opened the door, her shaking fingers barely able to turn the key, he took the dagger from her and carefully led her to their small living room.

He sat her down as though she was a child, fussing with her robe, before pouring her a drink. The liquid was fiery, she didn't recognize the taste, and it burned its way down her throat, at the same time clearing some of the fog from her mind, and she realized something, frowning up at Luvian.

They spoke at the same time.

"It wasn't—"

"Do you—"

Before either could finish, five Rhyllians entered the room. And then Irris followed.

Sorrow burst into fresh tears. Irris ran straight to her and pulled her into her arms, both girls shaking and crying.

"I thought you were dead," Sorrow sobbed. "He said he'd killed you."

"No, no, not me," Irris said. "It wasn't me."

It took a moment to sink in.

"Who?" Sorrow pulled back. "Who did he kill?"

"I found Dain downstairs, in her room. It was Dain he killed," Luvian said.

"No. . ."

"I'm sorry," Luvian said.

Sorrow lowered her head to Irris's shoulder again, as her relief at Irris being all right curdled into guilt, then misery. Poor, poor Dain.

A man cleared his throat delicately, and Sorrow looked up at the Rhyllians, surprised to see the prince consort, Caspar, among them. She made to move to kneel, but he held up a hand.

"There's no need, Miss Ventaxis. Are you all right? Do you have the strength to answer some questions?"

She nodded, and Irris took her hand, sitting beside her as the prince consort continued.

"I'd like you to tell me what happened here tonight, as much as you can," Caspar said gently.

Sorrow took another sip of her drink, the warmth of the liqueur making false courage in her belly, then spoke, her voice surprisingly level. "I left the ball, and came straight to my room. Luvian said Irris had come here, but she wasn't here when I got back. I started to run a bath, and then I heard someone come in. I assumed it was Irris, but it wasn't."

"It was a masked man, Mr Fen said."

Sorrow nodded. "It was one of the Sons of Rhannon. I recognized his voice, he was the same one who attacked me in Prekara, when Mael was there. He said he'd killed Irris."

"And then he tried to drown you?"

Irris's grip on her hand tightened when she replied. "Yes.

Then I heard shouting, he let me go, and I could move again. I pulled myself out of the water and Luvian was there, with a bottle."

"A bottle?" Caspar turned to Luvian.

"When I came back, Sorrow's bedroom door was open and I could hear an odd thumping sound. I called out to her, and when she didn't reply, I went to look. I saw her being held under the water, and grabbed the first thing that came to hand, which was a bottle. I smashed the end off and went to her aid."

"And then what happened?"

"I fought, briefly, with her assailant, and I managed to slash his arm, then he ran. I followed but he was too fast. Then I brought Sorrow to my room, told her to lock the door, and came for you."

"He spoke to you," Sorrow said, and Luvian turned to her.

It's what she'd been about to say when the Rhyllians, and Irris, arrived. The man had spoken to Luvian and there had been a familiarity to it. As though he knew Luvian, and Luvian knew him. And there was the final thing he'd said . . . the thing she hadn't heard properly. Something something *be proud. . .*

If she hadn't been looking for a sign something was amiss, she would not have noticed the lightning flash of worry that flickered over Luvian's customarily calm face.

There was no sign of it when he spoke. "That's right." Luvian looked away from her, back to Caspar. "He told me I didn't have the guts, to which I replied, 'Try me,' and that's when I managed to cut him. Then he said, 'I didn't think you had it in you.'"

That was almost it. Almost. "'Luvian,'" Sorrow said. "He called you by your name."

"Yes," Luvian said, meeting her eyes steadily. "He would

have known who I am, of course. Almost everyone in Rhannon knows I'm your advisor." He turned again to Caspar. "I expect that's what he meant by saying I didn't have the guts. I hope he's learned now not to judge a book by its cover."

It was smooth. Plausible. Yet Sorrow didn't believe a word of it. If he knew who Luvian was from the campaign, then he'd know who Irris was too. He wouldn't mistake Dain for her. What had the man said while she was vomiting? She desperately tried to remember... Proud... Someone would be proud...?

"Do you need a doctor, Miss Ventaxis?" Caspar broke across her thoughts.

"No, I'm fine." She didn't want a doctor; she was too worried they might try to sedate her. She wanted to stay focused and alert. She wanted to remember.

Caspar stood. "I've summoned all of the guards to search the entire palace complex. With luck, we'll find your assailant."

Sorrow doubted it. If the man had managed to get into the supposedly impenetrable complex undetected, he would have got out the same way. Maybe scrambled over the roof... She gasped as she remembered something. Something she'd almost remembered once before.

"Wait," she said. She pressed her fingers to the sides of her head, as though it might help her recall. "Charon told me when he arrived that someone broke into the house in the North Marches where we'd been staying. They picked the lock on the balcony door to my room. And I don't think it was the first time," Sorrow said, as Irris inhaled sharply. "The night before the presentation I took a sleeping draught. I woke later – or dreamed I woke later – because I heard something on the roof, then at the doors of my balcony."

"Why didn't you tell me?" Irris began, but Caspar silenced her.

"Please go on," he said.

"It's all so blurry. I remember the chime of metal. I got out of bed and knocked a lamp over. It must have scared them away. I put the key back in the door, and then I must have fallen asleep. I'd forgotten it until now." Sorrow didn't miss the fact that Luvian had turned pale.

Irris nodded, gripping Sorrow's hand so tightly it hurt.

"I don't think we can rule out a possible connection," Casper said.

"What should we do now?" Luvian asked.

"That is up to you. If you'd prefer to leave at once, we'll make a carriage ready with haste. If you'd like to stay until morning, we'll move you to new rooms, and post guards outside your doors."

"I want to go. . ." She hesitated to say it.

"Home." Irris finished her sentence when she did not. "I'll take you home," she said softly, squeezing her hand again.

"I'll have a carriage ready to depart within the hour, and a contingent of guards to accompany you, all the way back to your home," Caspar reassured them. "And I'll have the body of the guard prepared to travel too."

"Her name was Dain. Dain Waters," Sorrow said. She remembered Dain's kind eyes, her soft voice. Her hopes. He didn't have to kill her. He could have left her. A small spark of anger lit in Sorrow then.

"Miss Waters will be accorded every respect," Caspar said. "I'll come back myself when the carriage is ready."

Sorrow nodded, lowering her head. Dain had died because of Sorrow. And Sorrow had liked her, despite her being from the Decorum Ward. She'd liked learning that Dain loved to read, that the taste of sugar made her eyes sparkle. That she was more than a brute. Sorrow had liked being wrong about her.

"We need to write to her mother. We'll tell her mother she can be proud of her," Irris said, patting Sorrow's hand.

Sorrow's head snapped up, her eyes on Luvian. Now she remembered what the man had said.

Mother would be proud.

Luvian shook his head, his eyes pleading, begging with her not to say anything.

"Miss Ventaxis?" Caspar said.

Sorrow tore her gaze away from Luvian and made a decision, praying it was the right one. Praying she was wrong. She didn't think she could stand to lose anything else that day.

"Forgive me," she said to the prince consort. "What did you say?"

"I'll leave guards outside for you," Caspar repeated, his eyes kind.

"I appreciate it."

"I'll go and tell my father we're leaving," Irris said to Sorrow. "Then I'll come straight back. Will you be all right?" Sorrow nodded.

Irris gave her hands one final squeeze as she followed the Rhyllians from the room.

She listened to their footsteps receding as she finished the last of her drink, borrowing strength from it. Though she didn't think Luvian would hurt her himself – he had saved her, and had ample opportunity to hurt her if he'd wanted to – she was glad to know there were guards within shouting distance if she needed them. She hoped she wouldn't. She hoped she was wrong.

Luvian barely waited for the door at the end of the corridor to close before he said, "Sorrow. . ."

"You know him, don't you? That Son of Rhannon. You know each other."

The fact he didn't immediately deny it damned him.

"He said, 'Mother would be proud'. Your mother."

"It's not what you think. . . It's not my life any more. I left it. . ." Luvian held up his hands.

"What life? Who are you? We looked you up. We investigated you and we found nothing."

"Sorrow, please trust me—"

"No! Stars, I wish people would stop saying that to me. Tell me who you are."

"I can't."

"Then tell me who he is. Tell me how you know the Sons of Rhannon."

"Sorrow, I can't. I'm begging you to trust me."

Sorrow looked at him. She had trusted him. With everything. Trusted him as much as she'd ever trusted Irris, and Rasmus, and Charon. And look where that had got her. Charon had lied to her for her whole life. She'd lied to herself about Rasmus, and she was lying to Irris now. It was all lies and all secrets and she'd had enough.

"Dain is dead," Sorrow said. "And you know who killed her. You're protecting them, working with them, for all I know."

"I'm not—"

"Shut up, Luvian. You're hiding the person who has now tried, at least four times, to kill me. One of the Sons of Rhannon. So, I'm asking you for the last time, who is it?"

Luvian shook his head, his mouth moving silently for a moment before he looked at her with large, pleading eyes.

"Fine. But remember, I gave you a chance to come clean. I gave you that chance and you refused it."

"Sorrow, don't..."

"Help!" she screamed. "Help me!"

Luvian turned, and ran.

The guards burst into the room a moment later, swords in their hands.

"What is it?"

"Didn't you stop him?" She stared at them.

"Who? Mr Fen?"

Sorrow covered her face with her hands.

"He told us to get to you," one of the men said. "We assumed he was going to fetch aid."

"He knows the man who attacked me," Sorrow said.

Without saying a word, one of the guards sprinted from the room, the other remaining with Sorrow.

She wasn't surprised when a body of guards returned, their leader telling her Luvian hadn't been found.

The journey back to Rhannon was long, but Charon wouldn't allow them to stop for longer than it took to change horses and use the bathroom.

"I want you where you're safe," he said. "Until Fen is caught, and we know who he is and what his connection is to the Sons of Rhannon."

She couldn't bring herself to argue, couldn't bring herself to do anything but slump in the corner of the carriage, pretending to sleep, all the while going over what had happened. She'd lost it all, she realized. Rasmus, Luvian. The possibility of a brother. Herself. As they moved through the North Marches she sat up, staring at every face they passed, looking for herself.

From the expression on Charon's face he knew what she was doing, and it wounded him, but Sorrow couldn't let that stop her. They headed to the port district of the East Marches, the seat of Arran Day, Charon's son and Irris's brother. They were to stay in the Days' ancestral home until the election.

Looking back, she realized all the clues were there that she should never have trusted Luvian as much as she had. His desperation for the job, writing to beg for an interview. The casual way he spoke of breaking into official places, the way he stole information and the painting. The way he never talked about himself, or his family, or his past.

And he'd stayed very quiet about his connection to the Sons of Rhannon. Dain was dead because of it.

Over and over she regretted screaming for the guards instead of trying to coax the truth from him. Now she knew nothing, and was a mere five weeks from an election she had no business even running for.

"We're here," Charon said as the gates to the Days' estate swung open.

And as they closed behind them, the iron ringing with finality, Sorrow gave in to the darkness that had been threatening to consume her.

PART THREE

All warfare is based on deception
Hence, when able to attack, we must seem unable;
When using our forces, we must seem inactive;
When we are near, we must make the
enemy believe we are far away;
When far away, we must make him
believe we are near.

—*Sun Tzu*, The Art of War

33

After the Storm

"Nothing," Irris said as she put down the letters that had arrived earlier that morning. "It's like he appeared from nowhere three years ago. How does no one know who this man is? It's impossible."

Irris had taken Luvian's treachery very personally, and had dedicated herself to uncovering who he really was. She wrote again and again to his tutors and classmates, the same people she'd asked for references when they were interviewing him. And they all said exactly what they'd said in the first place: that he was arrogant and undoubtedly cunning – admirable qualities in a politician, some might say – but he was an undeniably hard worker, and guaranteed to see a task through, come what may. While he wasn't considered unpopular, he hadn't had any friends at university, had remained on campus during breaks, joined no clubs, and kept to himself. The staff who worked in the student housing said his rooms were always neat and tidy, and he never returned drunk, or tried to sneak anyone into his bed. He was a model tenant, a model student. Too good to be true, many of them commented.

They had no idea...

"We don't even know what part of Rhannon he's from," Irris said. "If we did, we could go there and ask around. Maybe even offer some kind of incentive for information."

"If that was going to work, someone would have already come forward to claim the official reward," Sorrow said.

A statement had been released, saying Luvian was wanted in connection with the murder of a Decorum Ward commander by one of the Sons of Rhannon. Both the Rhannish and the Rhyllians had put up a significant amount of reward money, and Melisia had written to Sorrow directly to apologize for what had happened, offering any aid Sorrow might want in finding him.

But Sorrow was finding it harder and harder to care that he was still out there. Or about anything at all. The hollow feeling that had begun to consume her after Charon told her the truth about who she was had returned, and there was no sign of it fading or leaving. Save for the brief moments of respite when she'd been with Rasmus, it was there all the time, like a shadow, but inside her.

To avoid it she went to bed earlier, and slept later, sometimes managing as many as sixteen hours of blissful, ignorant sleep before Irris bullied her from her bed. When she did get up, all she did was lie on the fainting couch, staring at the ceiling, while Irris pored over the correspondence with as much rigour as Luvian had given to the reports of missing children. And every time Sorrow thought of those, she remembered who she was – or rather, wasn't – and the darkness inside her deepened.

Irris had given up trying to entice Sorrow to help her, after Sorrow said she was still recovering from the attack.

It was a lie, another one. All she had was lies.

She ached for Rasmus, for his touch, knowing it would take the pain away, however temporarily. And she hated herself for it, for wanting him, and for using him, and for being weak. For being like Harun.

The only other person who might have been able to chivvy, or more likely annoy, her out of the black hole she found herself in had been a lie too. And that's what hurt the most. For the first time in her life, she'd felt released from the curse of her name – if ambitious, bright, brilliant Luvian Fen thought she was something special, then maybe she was. His respect for her, his faith in her, gave her something she'd never had before, not from Rasmus, Charon, her grandmother, or even Irris. He hadn't known her his whole life, hadn't loved her or been her best friend. He was a stranger, and because of it his belief in her made her believe in herself.

But he must have had an agenda all along, she realized. Something more than launching his own career, or helping the people of Rhannon. Something so important to him it was worth trying to conceal the fact he knew who'd tried to kill her, and who'd killed Dain. He'd used her.

It had been easy to talk to Irris about losing Rasmus. But Sorrow couldn't stand to hear Luvian's name said aloud; every time Irris said it Sorrow felt ill, as misery and loss claimed her.

"We're plagued by imposters," Irris said, and Sorrow choked on thin air. "Mael, now Luvian. No wonder Luvian was so keen to be the one to look into Mael – he must have known all the tricks from his own dealings."

Sorrow hummed noncommittally.

"I don't suppose you want to do anything on finding out who Mael is?" Irris asked tentatively. "What about Luvian's lists? Or perhaps we could hire someone to find Beliss."

"No," Sorrow said forcefully. She'd lost the taste for proving Mael wasn't who he claimed to be since her own past had emerged. It didn't matter who he was; he wasn't her brother. She knew that for sure.

"Then what do you want to do?"

When Sorrow didn't reply, Irris picked up a stack of papers and began to go through them, turning each one over violently.

The reports that used to come to Luvian now came to Irris, who'd taken over running the tattered remains of Sorrow's campaign. Irris has issued a statement, saying Sorrow was taking a few days to recover from the attack, but then planned to return to campaigning. That was two weeks ago, and Sorrow hadn't so much as got dressed in that time, let alone done any work.

By contrast Mael had returned from Rhylla with a new-found zeal, vowing to find and arrest the Sons of Rhannon, to make them pay for Dain's murder and the attack on Sorrow. He wrote to her daily, and released a new statement almost as often. Irris read it out in the morning, while Sorrow ignored her breakfast and counted down the hours until she could go back to sleep.

"He's suggesting the Decorum Ward be converted into something called Peacekeepers," Irris had said that morning. "It sounds very much like your idea for Lawkeepers. Suspiciously so, don't you think?"

Sorrow had shrugged, and Irris had put her cup down with more force than she needed to.

She was getting irritated with her, Sorrow knew that. But again, the knowledge had no impact. It was a fact, like the sky was blue, the ocean was salt water, and the Humpback Bridge was deadly. Irris was disappointed in her. So what?

Outside a storm raged, and Sorrow watched it, transfixed by the aggression of it. Storms were common in Rhannon during the late summer, but she'd never seen any like those that ravaged the coastal district of the East Marches. They came without warning, lasting only minutes, but during that time it was hard to imagine the weather being any other way. The thunder boomed relentlessly; the rain poured down in thick sheets that obscured everything outside the windows. Sorrow liked them, liked that the lightning scorched her eyes, so when she closed them she could see the forks in red against her eyelids.

As the storm died away, a shadow appeared in the distance, eventually revealing itself to be a hawk, slightly sodden from the dregs of the rain. Irris rose to let it in, carrying it to a perch where it shook itself as she retrieved the scroll it carried. Irris waited until it was finished, before reaching into a bag hanging from the perch and tossing a dead mouse to the bird, her other hand already busy unfurling the letter.

"Shit," she said.

Irris wasn't given to swearing, and it was enough to rouse Sorrow from her inertia briefly.

"What?"

"Rhylla have appointed a new ambassador to Rhannon. It's Vespus."

Sorrow sat up. "Vespus? Vespus Corrigan?"

Irris nodded, and held the letter out to Sorrow.

She scanned it briefly and then read it aloud. "We are delighted to welcome Lord Vespus Corrigan, half-brother of the queen of Rhylla, back to his post of ambassador to Rhannon. Lord Corrigan looks forward to a long-lasting relationship with the new chancellor, building on the foundations of trust, respect and admiration that already exist." Sorrow paused. "Wow. They might as well come out and say he means Mael. Because it's clear this isn't about me. They've obviously decided I'm out of the running."

Irris remained silent.

"Don't you have anything to say about it?" Sorrow demanded.

Irris's eyes blazed for a moment, then cooled. "Row, you've spent the last two weeks lying exactly where you are right now, in your pyjamas. *You've* decided you're out of the running. They're simply saying it out loud. Maybe it's time someone did, so we can all move on."

"I. . ." Sorrow blinked at her. It wasn't the rallying comment she'd expected.

Irris offered a small smile. "I'm going to fetch tea. Do you want some?"

Sorrow nodded.

She looked again at the letter from Istevar. This was it, then. With three weeks until the election, Vespus was moving himself into position, establishing himself back in Rhannon. Once Mael was elected — and Sorrow understood that he probably would be, now — Vespus would already be there, waiting for him in Istevar. Whispering in his ear. And Mael would listen, at least at first, because Vespus had been like a father to him. Vespus was kind to him, when no one else had been.

She saw it all then, as though it was a game of Malice: where every piece would move to, and where it would be eliminated. Charon would be fired, Sorrow realized. Vespus wouldn't allow him to keep his role. Bayrum Mizil, Tuva Marchant, Arran Day ... they'd go too. Balthasar would go where the power was; he probably wouldn't even care that Vespus was Rhyllian as long as he kept his seat on the Jedenvat and the perks that went with it. Samad would be happy a man was in charge – the sexist values of the Astrians who bordered with the district of Asha had clearly rubbed off on him – and Kaspira... She didn't like Sorrow, but she did like her district, for all her grumbling about its crime-loving people. She'd likely go with the flow to keep her seat too.

There would be no one to oppose Vespus, save Mael. And while she believed Mael's intentions towards the Rhannish people, the Jedenvat under him would be made up of lackeys who Vespus would choose because he could buy their loyalty.

Once Vespus had got rid of Bayrum he could take the land he'd long wanted in the North Marches. Take the whole of Rhannon, turn it all into a farm if he chose to. Mael alone wouldn't be able to stop him, especially not against a Jedenvat Vespus had assembled. It would be easy for them to do what they'd done to Harun, and vote to depose him, leaving Vespus free to manoeuvre another puppet into place.

And now there was no one to stop him. It was too late.

Or was it? A cocky, traitorous voice whispered in the back of her mind. There were still three weeks until the election. If used correctly, there might be time to stop him. If an imposter was going to govern – surely it was better for it to be one who wasn't under Vespus's control? For her friends, and for her people. For her real family, who might still be out there. And for Dain, who'd wanted more. She could help them. Charon was right, she might never be able to go back, but she might be able to make their lives easier. Bring them some joy. She might be able to make something good out of the hideous situation she found herself in. She couldn't bring back the dead Ventaxis child, but she could take her place. She alone could stop Vespus's relentless march to the top of Rhannon. That was something, wasn't it?

For the first time since her night with Rasmus, the darkness inside her receded as a spark inside her heart took hold. They were her people. She was one of them.

She stood up as Irris returned with a tea tray.

Irris paused in the doorway, frowning, as though the changes inside Sorrow were already manifest on her face. "Sorrow?"

"You're off the hook. I did my own pep talk," Sorrow said.

Irris looked around the room as though she expected to see someone else there. "What do you mean?"

"You're right. Enough is enough. I have a job to do, and I know exactly where to start. I need to go out and meet the people. Forget what the Jedenvat said. I need to see where they live, and work. Get to know them, and what they need. What they want."

Irris walked to the table and put the tray down. "I'm glad you're feeling better, and I'm fine disobeying the Jedenvat, but ... is it a good idea, after what happened in Rhylla? If you're out in the open you're vulnerable. Maybe you could start by releasing some statements?"

"No. No more statements. No more bits of paper. Mael can do that, but I'm not. If I stay hidden away I'm as bad as

Harun," Sorrow countered. "I'm going out there. We're going out there."

"Let's write to my father," Irris said. "I'll make him see we have to. He can smooth things over with the Jedenvat."

"You do that," Sorrow said. "I'm going to take a bath. And put on some clothes."

Irris finally smiled. "Thank the Graces. I didn't know how to tell you, but you smell terrible."

Sorrow threw a pillow at her as she passed.

Charon sent a bird back that afternoon, and the haste of it made Sorrow's heart soar with hope until she saw the flicker of shock cross Irris's face.

"He said no?" Sorrow guessed.

"He says it's better for you to stay where you're safe."

Sorrow swallowed and looked away, tears pricking at her eyes. How could he deny her this?

"To hell with it." Irris screwed up the piece of paper and dropped it to the floor, kicking it to Sorrow. It bumped against her foot, and she looked over at her friend.

"What do you mean?"

"You're right. You need to get out there. It's the only way. Besides, you're eighteen. You're not a child. And neither am I. So let's do it."

Sorrow stared at her, trying to contain the hope that had flared once more. "Irris, it's one thing for me to rebel, but he's your father. . ."

"And he's wrong. This is your life, Row." She paused. "For Rhannon?"

"For Rhannon."

*

They spent the afternoon drawing up a list between them of all the places they could think of to meet the people: faculties at the universities, unions, guilds, schools and hospitals. Then they split the list, penning letter after letter to the heads and leaders, asking when would be a good time for Candidate Ventaxis to visit. They made sure never to say which candidate it was, relying on presumption to serve them.

And serve them it did.

The birds began to return the following morning, and kept coming. Invitations to address the law faculty at the Institute, the accounting faculty in Istevar, to visit the mason's guild, the physician's guild, and the miner's union right there in the east, based at the stone mine.

"Where do we start?" Sorrow asked. "One of the guilds? They're influential. Or the universities?"

"The miners," Irris said. "Start with the people. Write to them now. We can go this afternoon, at the shift changeover."

When the weather broke that afternoon and the storms paused, they took it as an excellent sign. Right up until the moment the guard stationed on the main door of the manse raised his spear as Sorrow and Irris approached.

"We need a coach," Sorrow said. "Now, please."

"I'm afraid I can't allow you to leave, Miss Ventaxis. I'm sorry." In his defence, the guard barring her way did look sorry, but Sorrow didn't care.

"Can't allow me?" She met his gaze with her own steady one. "Why not?"

"The vice chancellor's orders, miss. For your safety."

"So I'm a prisoner?"

"No, miss."

"If I'm not a prisoner, I can leave." Sorrow took another step and the guard raised his spear a little higher. "Get out of my—"

"Am I a prisoner too?" Irris moved forward, resting a hand on Sorrow's shoulder in warning.

"No one is a prisoner, Lady Day. Miss Ventaxis is being guarded for her own safety."

"And it's you who is charged with keeping her safe?" Irris said.

"That's right, my lady."

"Then you can come with us. Bring some friends. There's no point in arguing." She held up a finger to silence any protest the guard had been about to make. "Your job is to guard Miss Ventaxis, and so you will. Wherever she goes. And you know Miss Ventaxis is running for the chancellorship. I would have thought remaining on her good side might be a priority."

The guard swallowed.

"So I suggest you gather together four or five of your most trusted fellows, and meet us back here in ten minutes. I'll order a coach." Irris spoke with the authority of someone used to representing a district on the Jedenvat, of someone accustomed to being heard, and obeyed. The guard's resistance crumbled, and he nodded, turning on his heel and walking away. He looked back twice, and Sorrow didn't know if it was to check they were truly waiting, or because he was preparing to disobey, but in the end he disappeared around a corner. They waited in silence, and after ten minutes he returned with four other soldiers, all of whom seemed bewildered.

"Let me handle this," Irris said under her breath, and Sorrow gave a swift, discreet nod. "Excellent," Irris said firmly as the men approached, not giving them time to speak. "Now, because this visit is impromptu, and in the open, we don't anticipate any attempts to harm Miss Ventaxis, as no one knows where we're going; however, that doesn't mean you can relax. Two of you will sit in the coach with us, two of you will accompany the driver, and the last of you can sit on the roof."

"Where are we going?" the first soldier asked.

"To the mines. Miss Ventaxis is going to address the miners. We should be back here in good time for supper."

Irris turned on her heel and opened the door, and Sorrow quickly followed, leaving the men scrambling in their wake.

They arrived at the mines an hour later, the coach arriving into the grounds near the main building, Sorrow's stomach churning. She made for the door the moment the coach rolled to a halt, only for the soldier to bar her way, peering out of the window before he slipped through the door. A moment later he opened it, and nodded at her.

The courtyard was teeming with men, some covered in thick white dust from the mines, some clean before they started their shift, and they all turned as one to Sorrow as she stepped out of the coach. She faltered then, under their scrutiny, but most of them lost interest in her within seconds, and carried on with what they were doing.

"We need to find a foreman." Irris appeared beside her.

"And do what?"

"Ask if you can go down and see the mine."

Sorrow paused. "I thought I was going to do a speech to the union."

"Do you have a speech?"

Sorrow shook her head.

"Well, then."

384

"What am I supposed to do down there?"

"Watch. Learn. Talk. Be."

"Can I help you?" Sorrow didn't need to find a foreman; one had found her, and he didn't look too happy with his discovery. He drew himself up to his full height, bringing him eye level with Sorrow. "This facility isn't open to the public."

"Hello, I'm Sorrow Ventaxis." She held out a hand, and the man reluctantly shook it. "We wrote, saying we'd like to visit, and find out a little more about how I can help you and your men when I'm chancellor."

"We thought you were your brother," the foreman said bluntly.

"I hope you can see now that you were mistaken," Sorrow joked. The foreman didn't smile. "So," she continued. "What I'd really like to do is see the mine."

"*You* want to see the mine?"

"Yes," Sorrow lied. "I've spent my entire life in Rhannish buildings made of Rhannish bricks. I want to see where it comes from, and meet the men who raise it."

"I don't know if that's possible." The foreman scratched his ear, frowning. "We're not set up for visitors."

"I don't want a tour," Sorrow improvised. "I want to go down into the mine and see it in action. Maybe have a go myself."

"*You* want to—"

"I really do." Sorrow cut him off. "So, do I need any protective gear?"

A bark of something like laughter from behind her made her turn.

A man in dusty white overalls was watching her. "How fond are you of that get-up?" He nodded at her outfit.

"Not at all." Irris had told her to dress plainly and she had, in a pale grey tunic and trousers.

"It's cold down there," he said, looking at her bare arms.

"I'll be fine."

"Suit yourself. I'll take her down," he told the foreman. "I owe Yaris another cycle for last week. She can come with me, and I'll bring her back up after." The foreman considered it for a moment, and Sorrow could sense Irris getting ready to argue with him. But then he shrugged and walked away, leaving Sorrow, Irris, her soldiers and the miner, looking at each other.

"How long is a cycle?" Irris asked.

"Two and a quarter hours."

Irris looked at Sorrow, who shrugged. She could manage that, she was sure.

"Excellent," Sorrow said. "Ready when you are."

"Us too?" the soldier Sorrow had nominated as leader said, his worry evident in his creased forehead.

"One of you at least ought to," Sorrow said. Part of her wanted to force him to accompany her in revenge for barring her way earlier. She could tell, from the sweat on his upper lip, that the prospect of going underground frightened him. "Decide among yourselves." She fought her inner meanness.

"I don't mind. My father was a miner," one of them announced.

"Then let's go," the miner said. "I'm on the clock."

"What can I call you?" Sorrow said, falling into step with him as he walked away, the solider trailing after them.

"Mael," he said.

Sorrow blinked. "How old are you?"

"Eighteen. Same as you."

From both his appearance and his manner, Sorrow would

386

have guessed he was at least ten years older. To cover her surprise, she continued talking. "So you were named for him?"

"Me and half the mine." He paused. "They call me Braith. It's my surname. You can use it too. Mind your head," he warned her as they entered a tunnel.

The air was much cooler inside, and Sorrow regretted her bare arms. Braith led them down the tunnel, Sorrow turning sideways to counter the steepness of the incline, until they arrived at the bottom to a set of metal double doors. Sorrow was puzzled by what she would have sworn was birdsong coming from within, only to find, when Braith opened the door and urged her to enter, a shelf with a row of cages, each with a small yellow bird.

"Why do you have sun finches in here?" she asked.

"The air can be funny below. Sun finches are more sensitive to gases than we are. So we take birds down, and if they stop singing, or fall from their perches, we know it's time to go."

Sorrow didn't know if he was joking or not, until he reached up and took one of the cages.

"You can carry it, once you're kitted out." He put the cage down and crossed to a cupboard, pulling out a firm hat and a coat, passing them to her. He gave another hat to the soldier, and slipped one on to his own head.

"It won't save you if there's a cave-in, but some of the ceilings are low and it'll stop you getting a nasty bump," he explained as Sorrow pulled the coat on and placed the hat on her head.

She paused and exchanged a worried glance with the soldier. "Is there likely to be a cave-in?"

"Miss, it's not like the moonrise. It happens when it happens. If we knew, we wouldn't go down, would we? Right, grab your bird and let's get to the cage." He nodded at a second pair of doors, set back in the wall.

"The cage?" Sorrow asked.

"You'll see."

In the darkness of the room his teeth glowed ghostly white, and Sorrow shivered, knowing full well it wasn't because of the chill.

34

As Below, So Above

The cage was every bit as horrible as it sounded. Suspended on a thick chain, and operated by a team of four, it was designed to lower between thirty and fifty men at a time down to the underground reserves of the white stone mined for construction in Rhannon. Once, the stone had been closer to the surface, but demand sent the miners deeper into the bowels of Laethea for it, and it was there that Sorrow was to go to see them at work.

The cage wasn't meant to transport so few people at a time, and it swung precariously when Sorrow entered, forcing her to cling to the bars and the poor bird to go wild in its own cage, flapping its wings until yellow feathers showered the floor. Braith entered and slammed the door shut, frightening the bird again. He gave Sorrow a look as if to tell her to control it, then nodded to the operators. They each took hold of a large bar attached to a wheel, and slowly began to push. As they did, the cage jerkily descended, and Sorrow heard the soldier who was accompanying them whimper above the twittering of the bird. She didn't blame him. Even Braith looked uneasy, fiddling with the lamp he'd brought, his face watchful as they lowered.

Her treacherous mind turned to Luvian then, imagining him here. His pompadour hair flattened by the helmet, dust on his pristine suit. She could see the way his upper lip would curl, hear the sarcastic quip that would both amuse and infuriate her.

Or was that all part of the persona he'd worn to trick her? she reminded herself, stopping the smile in its tracks. For all she really knew of him, he was like the guard with her, born to a family of miners.

It couldn't have taken more than ten minutes, but to Sorrow it felt like for ever. She saw the layers of the rocks in the lamplight as they passed, the rainbow of colours in them, saw long-legged insects skittering over the surfaces away from the light, chased by pure white lizards that Braith told her gleefully had no eyes. Finally, the cage hit the ground, and Sorrow stumbled, banging her hip against the side as she tried to keep the bird in her arms. Braith pulled the door back, and all of them left the cage on shaking legs.

He led Sorrow and the soldier down a long tunnel lit at intervals by more lamps. Sorrow had expected it to be damp, but the air was clear, and clean, and the bird seemed happy enough, launching into song. She followed the miner towards the sound of metal against stone, and they entered a medium-sized cavern, where a group of twenty or so miners were busy hacking away at the glowing white rock in the walls. Five large columns of stone had been left, and Sorrow could see where a sixth was being formed by four large men carefully scraping at the rock there instead of hacking.

There were other birds down there too, dotted around in all the corners, and when Braith nodded to an empty one Sorrow carried the small cage over to a wooden crate and left the bird on it, its song mingling with that of the others.

She rejoined Braith and the soldier at a large drum full of pickaxes, taking one when it was offered and following him to a patch of wall where five other men were already working. They turned as one and looked Sorrow up and down. None of them looked impressed, and the largest of the men, towering a good foot over the next tallest, and thrice as wide as him too, went as far as to shake his head.

"Hello, I'm—"

"We know who you are," the giant of a man said, swinging his axe and loosening a large chunk of white rock, which fell to the ground. He picked it up and dropped it in the metal bin behind them with a decisive clang, before returning and swinging the axe once more. "We don't care."

Sorrow waited to see if anyone else would speak, her cheeks heating, but when they didn't she too began to hack at the rock.

Within five swings she realized she didn't have the physical strength to keep it up for long. Already her hands felt hot from gripping the wooden handle of the axe, her shoulders beginning to ache. As if he could sense her discomfort, Braith turned to her.

"You can stop, if you like. I mean, this is it. This is what we do. Work for two hours, then a fifteen-minute break. Then back to it. Four cycles per day."

"I can keep going." Sorrow swung the axe again and a small chunk fell loose. Pleased, she went to pick it up, but the man who'd dismissed her earlier spoke.

"Too small," he grunted, his own axe carving out a chunk three times the size of Sorrow's head, which he hefted easily on to his shoulder, then into the bin.

"How is it too small?"

"No good."

"Why not?"

The man paused, and wiped a layer of dusty sweat from his brow with a hand the size of a dinner plate. "Because I said not."

Sorrow met his gaze. "I don't accept that." She picked up her small piece of rock and took it to the bin, making sure to meet his eye as she dropped it in. It didn't make a sound, and her skin burned again as she waited for his response.

The man watched her, and the air between them became taut and brittle. The others around them had stilled, and the soldier moved closer to her, but the giant didn't pay him any more attention than he would a fly, his stony gaze fixed on her, his expression betraying no hint of his intentions.

Then he shrugged, and the tension vanished as he turned back to his work. Sorrow's heart was battering her ribs inside her chest, but all she did was take a deep breath and return to her part of the wall. She glanced at Braith and he gave her a brief nod of approval.

"How does the stone become homes and buildings?" Sorrow asked as she attacked the wall again.

"It's ground down, and mixed with a binding paste, then baked, to form bricks," Braith said, cutting out a medium-sized rock and carrying it to the bin. "The bricks are used for building."

"So size doesn't actually matter," Sorrow said as she swung again and loosed another small piece.

The giant who'd decided she was his enemy stopped mid-swing, driving the handle of his axe into the ground and leaning on the curved iron top of it. "What do you want, little girl? Why are you really here?"

Sorrow lowered her axe, and mimicked his stance. "Because I don't see how I can be the chancellor of a country if I don't know how it works. How it's built. Who does the building, and the mining. Because I saw the way my father governed, from a palace miles from here, a place he barely left, and I don't think it was right. In fact, I think everything my father did was wrong. And I think I can do better. To me, that means I have to start from the ground up. No – from beneath the ground up. I have to see what the foundations of Rhannon are built on. So I'm here to learn. You don't have to like it, but it's happening anyway."

She picked up her axe and swung it, carving out a decent-sized rock. Thanking the Graces for her fortune, she went to pick it up, only to find it was too heavy. Swearing under her breath, and aware she had an audience, she tried again, managing to haul it to her knees.

A large pair of hands took it from her, and carried it to the bin.

"Better," the big man said. "But I think you can still do more."

Sorrow accepted the challenge.

She sent the soldier back up with Braith when his overtime ended, but she stayed down there for another cycle, working beside the big man. When her arms grew too tired, she fetched water for the men from a table at the back of the room, passing it out and talking to them, asking about their families, their jobs, what they needed, what mattered to them.

A man named Wood lived in a village where they still pumped water from a well; all attempts at building pipes and reservoirs to supply fresh water from the river had been abandoned when Mael died.

Another, Salt, came from a family of celebrated violin makers, but the business had died, along with the family's fortunes, when Harun had banned music. Salt had become a miner because of it.

Tully Dearcross had watched his young wife bleed out while giving birth when a nurse was too frightened to save her because Cerena's life had ended thus.

Each story broke Sorrow's heart a little more, the small and terrible damages that had been inflicted on the people. But each story furthered her resolve to help them. To be the one to do so.

When they stopped for their next break she sat with them and accepted the bread and olives she was offered, spitting the stones into the same bowl on the floor, exhilarated when she finally got one in. It was only when the soldier returned, with a message from Irris saying they really should leave, that she said her goodbyes to a crowd that was much warmer than the one she'd first met, the giant even deigning to shake her hand between his massive ones. Whether that meant they'd vote for her, she wasn't sure. But they'd started to like her, she knew that. And she'd started to see ways she could help them. If she won.

They arrived back at the manse to three birds from Charon, all of them calling Sorrow reckless and stupid, every word reeking of rage that he'd been disobeyed. He chastised his daughter too, but the girls didn't care. While Sorrow had been down in the mine, Irris had been charming the mine's managers, and both of them felt positive for the first time since Sorrow had returned from Rhylla.

"Think we can woo the physician's guild tomorrow?" Sorrow said as the two girls ate their supper, both tearing meat from bones in their hunger.

"I think you'll have an honorary medical degree by the end of the day," Irris replied.

As the days passed, they entered the season of the Gathering Gala, and for the first time in eighteen years Rhannon would celebrate it. From what Sorrow had read, the Gathering was all about preparing for winter, harvesting the fields, readying the home for a change of season, and lighting fires to stave off the darkness. It was a time to put away the year gone by and look forward to the next. For Sorrow, this year, it had a touch of fate to it. A time to start anew.

Sorrow had never paid her respects to the Grace of Hearth and Plenty, nor had she painted a crown of laurels gold and worn it in her hair to mimic the natural turning of the leaves as they died, though she knew all the traditions from her books, and her grandmother (not her grandmother, she reminded herself). There was to be a large party to celebrate it, in Istevar. She, and Mael, were to go as guests.

She read in the morning circular that Mael was planning to host a small, pre-Gathering party of his own, no doubt at Vespus's insistence.

Sorrow, however, decided not to throw a party. She could have done as Mael had, and invited professors and local leaders to an exclusive event. Instead, she, Irris and their band of soldiers-cum-bodyguards toured Rhannon like a troupe of street players, celebrating the run-up to the harvesting festival with the people.

They never announced where they'd go, not wanting to tip the Sons of Rhannon off or give them time to plan, instead arriving with little fanfare, and never staying more than an hour or two. They darted across Rhannon, deciding where to go the night before: the South Marches one day, the West the next. Then south again to Asha, then skipping over Istevar to go to the far north.

They took every precaution, using unmarked carriages they hired on the day, never staying in a village or town they'd visited, never booking ahead or giving their real names. Sorrow and Irris shared rooms when they stayed overnight in inns, their soldiers sleeping on pallets outside the door, wedging a chair under the handle as an extra precaution. Windows were bolted, sometimes nailed shut, with Sorrow reimbursing the innkeeper the next morning. They kept knives under their pillows and Sorrow went nowhere alone; Irris even checked the bathroom before she used it, remaining outside to periodically ask if she was all right.

They became a well-oiled unit, visiting guilds and unions, farms, hospitals and schools across Rhannon, ignoring the occasional Sons of Rhannon graffiti they saw. The vigilantes didn't bother them, had fallen curiously quiet since they'd tried to kill her, apparently content with graffiti denouncing the Decorum Ward, and attacks on their buildings, their focus seemingly shifted away from her, and Mael, once more. In the dark moments that still sometimes plagued her she wondered if Luvian was responsible for it. Had he called his friends to heel? And was she supposed to be grateful for it?

She couldn't help wondering if he was keeping an eye on what she and Irris were doing, following the reports of her passage through Rhannon. And, worst of all, she wondered if he was proud of her. If he approved of what they were doing, if he thought it would help her win. But those thoughts were toxic and she raged at herself when she thought them, tearing through them in her head and throwing herself even harder at the next task, and the next thing to fix.

They sought out small villages that seemed to care very little who their chancellor was, as long as the wretched Decorum Ward would be a thing of the past and they'd largely be left alone. Sorrow promised them they would, and they seemed happy, but again, whether that would translate into votes was anyone's guess. They'd find out, soon enough.

As well as being the harvest festival, the Gathering traditionally marked the time the chancellor and his family moved back to Istevar from the Summer Palace, and it was on Sorrow's mind as she and Irris made their way to the Winter Palace, for the final celebration before the election. With a few days before the election, she was keenly aware that it might be the last time she ever went to the Winter Palace. She hadn't let herself think about what might happen if she lost, and what it might mean. Before she found out she wasn't a true Ventaxis, she'd assumed she'd continue living in Istevar anyway. But now she didn't know if she could. . . She shoved the thoughts aside as they turned on to the road approaching the Winter Palace, and looked out of the window.

Arran Day had written to his sister, mentioning there had been some renovations, but nothing could have prepared

Sorrow for the sight of her childhood home brought back to life.

Even from the outside, it looked completely different. The sweeping drive up to the white mansion was manicured, the trees trimmed into uniform sizes, the gravel freshly raked. The palace glowed in the late summer sun, the windows finally uncovered, reflecting the cloudless blue sky above them.

Sorrow was hesitant as she climbed the steps to the front door, where servants now dressed in soft green livery waited with wide smiles. She didn't know this place.

The staircase that dominated the main hall gleamed, the marble floor free of dust, the banisters polished to a mahogany shine. Everywhere was light, no shadowy corners; even the smell was different. The scent of her childhood home had always been burning oil, and sadness – she realized then sadness had a fragrance: mould, and dust. Neglect. But now it was gone. The palace smelled of lemons, and warm sunlit skin.

Grinning at each other, she and Irris began to explore, but were quickly hustled out of the ballroom, the chandeliers sparkling above them, by servants preparing for the Gathering. The formal dining room was also in a state of siege as staff readied it for the celebration, so instead they wandered into parts of the palace Sorrow hadn't visited since they were children, hiding away with Rasmus and snatching at tiny moments of joy. The winter breakfast room, made entirely of glass, looking out on to a now immaculately mown lawn. The games room, the green baize tables now uncovered and ready to be used. The ladies' parlour, where all the furniture had been re-covered in soft, buttery yellow velvet. Last time Sorrow had been in there, Rasmus had dared her to touch one of the old chairs, and the fabric had turned to dust under her fingers.

The piano in the music room played true when she ran her fingers down the keys; even the portraits of her ancestors in the walking gallery looked friendlier. It was as she'd imagined it, as she'd longed for it to be. A living palace.

The only place they didn't go was to the west wing, partly because it held nothing but miserable thoughts for Sorrow, but also as it was where Charon had informed them Mael would be housed. Both of them were staying overnight following the party.

Her old rooms were transformed too, the holey carpets and furniture replaced with bare floors covered in thick rugs, and new sofas and tables. Her mattress had been replaced too, and she enjoyed a few bounces on it before leaping off and throwing open her bedroom windows legally for the first time in her life.

Below her she could hear the preparations for the gala, and she leant out to watch the people bustling to and fro. A pair of swallows darted back and forth from their nest above her, leading Sorrow to believe they must have chicks in there, even this late in the year.

Because of the election, she had no official role at the Gathering, and was there as a guest only. So she took her time bathing, and choosing an outfit. Traditionally people dressed in the colours of nature, the golds and russets and oranges of the leaves, and Sorrow had chosen a burnt-orange dress in layers of crepe that fell to her ankles, paired with matching slippers.

She looked at the coronet of gold-painted leaves on her bed. Across the land, people would be fitting them to their heads, preparing for their own feasts with their family and friends...

Sorrow had an idea.

She left her rooms, coronet in hand, and ran down to Irris's door, knocking impatiently.

Irris answered the door, wearing a russet gown and a confused expression. "Yes?"

"I think we should skip the feast, and go into Istevar. I think we should take food with us, as a gift, and go door to door, offering our blessings."

"Sorrow, you can't. You're a guest here. This is the first Gathering in eighteen years."

"Exactly. A huge thing for everyone. I'm not saying all night, but a couple of hours, during the feast. We'll come back for the offerings to the Graces, and the party. Come on. One last push before the election. Think of the message it sends, that I left a huge, fancy feast to visit the people. . ."

Irris shook her head, and sighed. "There's never a middle ground with you, is there? Either you're adamant you can't or won't do something, or you're throwing yourself into it as though the world will end if you don't."

For a moment Sorrow faltered, before saying, "All part of my charm?"

Irris's lips twitched as she fought not to grin. "It's like you want my father to be angry with you."

"Nonsense. I simply want to be with my people. You go and get the guards. I'll write a note."

The palace kitchen servants had cheerfully loaded them up with fruits and pies and cheeses once the girls told them their plans, some even recommending houses to go to, where their friends and family lived. The guards, by now used to Sorrow and Irris's particular brand of strange requests, escorted the girls down into Istevar proper, not even questioning why they'd been asked to leave a feast to do so.

"Hello, I'm Sorrow Ventaxis, and this is Irris Day," Sorrow announced when the puzzled-looking citizens opened their doors. "We've come to wish you a fruitful Gathering, and offer you a gift, from our hearth to yours."

She held out the basket, and waited until they took something. Then she bid them farewell and moved on, leaving them standing in their doorways, watching after her.

After ten houses, people started to come out and follow her.

At the twelfth, a small, wizened old man stared at her, then walked back into his house. Sorrow and Irris exchanged puzzled looks, and the guards' hands casually drifted to their weapons, when he returned with a large lionfruit in his hands. He held the yellow, spiked fruit out to Sorrow, taking a bunch of grapes from the basket.

"Thank you," Sorrow said, surprised.

"Bless you," the man replied.

After that, not a single person took without giving something back, and when the guards finally urged the girls to return, warning them they'd miss the ceremony, fifty or so citizens walked behind them, waving and bursting into applause as Sorrow passed through the gates and turned to give a final wave.

"That went well," she beamed at Irris.

They arrived back in time for the ceremony, still bearing the basket of food they'd been given by the people, joining the procession of people trailing out of the palace and down into the grounds. As they all gathered in the grotto of the Grace of Hearth and Plenty, Charon spotted Sorrow and shot her the darkest look, not even attempting to hide his fury, but she was too happy to care. Happier still when Vespus, standing opposite her with Aphora, gave her a look to rival Charon's.

Mael, beside him, met her eyes, and his mouth moved as though he might smile, but at the last second he stopped himself and nodded. Something about the gesture sobered Sorrow, and guilt prickled at her. It wasn't his fault he was in this position, any more than she was to blame for hers. She offered a smile, feeling better when he returned it.

Then Vespus turned his gaze on Mael, and even Sorrow reeled from the venom in it. Vespus didn't appear to speak, but Mael's smile dropped at once, and he lowered his head. Sorrow had no time to ask Irris if she'd seen, as Charon moved his chair forward, and the ceremony began.

The Ventaxis family had never been devout, especially not in Sorrow's lifetime, so this was the first time she'd been to a traditional ceremony in honour of one. The icon of the genderless Grace of Hearth and Plenty was set into the west wall of the palace, guarding both the inside and out. It was the traditional placement for the Grace, and the crowd gathered beneath it, all of them with an offering in hand.

Charon placed a bowl of honey atop a plinth beneath the statue, then touched three fingers to his stomach before moving away. The rest of the Jedenvat followed.

Arran Day had become handsome since she'd last seen him two years ago, tall and statesmanlike, though still with the wicked twinkle to his dark eyes that Sorrow recognized from childhood. He was a full ten years older than her, and had gone away to university the year Rasmus had come to Rhannon. But it seemed he hadn't changed much, as he passed Sorrow and winked at her, before presenting a bushel of fresh silver fish from the east to the statue, and making the same gesture Charon had.

Tuva Marchant, too, grinned at Sorrow before she laid down her offering of dates and figs from the west, until every councillor had left something that represented their people's finest produce as an offering. Bayrum Mizil paused to kiss her cheek as he passed with bunches of grapes and a jug of wine. Samad and Balthasar ignored her, but to her surprise Kaspira gave her a curt nod.

Once the Jedenvat were finished, then went the other guests, one by one, adding their offerings to the Grace.

Across the country the scene would be the same – for the first time in eighteen years the temples would be filled with people celebrating the Gathering, thanking the Graces for a plentiful year, and hoping to bribe them into another one to come with gifts and offerings.

"Hello, stranger," a voice said, and Sorrow turned to find Arran Day had slipped in beside her.

He held out his arms for a hug, and Sorrow stepped into them. "Long time no see. You've grown up."

"People keep saying that as if it's unusual."

"You look well," he said, holding her at arm's length as he examined her. "Very chancellor-ish."

"Chancellor-ish isn't—" she began, only to fall abruptly silent when her heart pitched at the memory of Luvian telling her off for saying "scheme-ish". He would have loved this, she thought sadly. He would have been in his element.

"Row?" Arran was staring at her. "You OK?"

"Yes. Thank you. Sorry, I'm fine," she smiled sheepishly.

Arran laughed, and then greeted his sister.

"Father should be worried," he said. "You'd make a very good vice chancellor."

"You should be worried," Irris replied. "I made an excellent senator."

He laughed again, and then it was Sorrow and Irris's turn to make their offering. They stepped up together with the basket, touched their fingers to their stomachs, and accepted the glass of summer wine an attendant handed them afterwards.

"So . . . you two have had quite the tour of Rhannon these past three weeks," Arran said. "You've certainly rattled a lot of cages."

"Any in particular?" Irris asked, and Arran nodded to his left.

Vespus, Arta Boniface and Mael were standing talking. Or rather, Vespus and Arta were. Mael was silent beside them, staring at his wine, clearly ignoring them both.

"Rumour has it your opponent isn't thrilled with the counsel he's been receiving."

"Really?" It was the first Sorrow had heard of it.

"He blames Vespus for his strained relationship with you, so I'm told."

Mael looked over then, but when Sorrow smiled he looked at her blankly. Then he turned and walked away, heading towards the palace.

Vespus spoke, loud enough for Sorrow to hear. "Where are you going?"

"Away."

"Mael. . ."

But Mael ignored him, leaving Vespus glaring furiously after him.

Sorrow didn't stop to think. "I'll be back," she said, handing her glass to Irris.

"Sorrow. . ." Irris warned.

"Bathroom," Sorrow lied.

She weaved her way through the crowd, making excuses when people tried to waylay her, promising she'd find them later.

There was no sign of Mael in the foyer, and she wondered where he'd gone.

A door closed down the passageway and she moved towards it, passing through a reception parlour, and a smaller antechamber, until she reached the door to the library.

She knocked, and heard something inside fall, and footsteps. But no call to enter.

Too bad, she thought, and opened the door.

"Mael?" She stepped into the room, peering around. "Mael?"

A gloved hand closed over her mouth, as another pulled her flush against a body.

"Don't scream," Luvian Fen said in her ear.

35

The Thief's Return

Sorrow screamed.

The glove pressed over her mouth absorbed the sound, so she tried to pull free, wriggling and writhing in his grasp. How could this be happening again? Furious, she kicked him in the shin, causing him to yelp.

"Sorrow! Stop it. I'm not here to hurt you."

To hell with that, she decided. She planted her feet into the ground and shoved backwards, driving them both into the wall with a muted thud. Damn, she'd hoped to hit the door, hoped the noise would bring guards running. His grip loosened for a moment, then tightened, as he swung them around and pressed her into the wall, trapping her against it. She was surprised by his strength, realizing too late that his carefully tailored clothes hid lithe, disciplined muscle. The understanding needled her, another trick, and she jerked her head back, trying to headbutt him as she'd done to her last assailant.

She missed.

"Seriously, stop it," Luvian hissed in her ear. "Listen to me—"

She screamed into the glove again, tried to bite at it. She lifted her feet to stamp on his, making contact and wincing as he cursed loudly in her ear.

"Damn it, Sorrow, I found Beliss."

She went still in his grip.

"It's not a trick," he said quietly, still holding her tightly. "I've been in Rhylla searching for her. I found her. I found lots of things. I came here to tell you them. If I let you go, do you promise not to scream, or hit me?"

Sorrow paused, then nodded. If he'd wanted to really hurt her he could have done it already. He released her, and stepped back as she spun around to face him, hands raised in fists.

"Easy," he said. "I meant it. I'm not here for trouble."

She barely recognized him. He was wearing the pale green livery of the servants, hair shorn all over, scruff darkening his chin and upper lip. He wasn't wearing his glasses, and his eyes were slightly unfocused. He held up his own hands slowly to show her he wasn't armed.

Even so, Sorrow wasn't about to open her arms to him, metaphorically or otherwise. He was connected to the Sons of Rhannon, and they'd killed Dain, and almost killed her. "There's a soldier outside," she lied. "There are soldiers everywhere, so if you try anything. . ."

"I won't hurt you. I never would. I swear it."

She edged away from him, and he turned on the spot, tracking her path, though he made no attempt to follow her.

She moved behind a desk and picked up a letter opener with a bone handle, holding it up so he could see it. "Try anything and I'll use it. How did you get into the palace?"

He lowered his hands. "I stole a uniform from a man returning from his afternoon off, and came in through the main gates behind two others."

Sorrow made a note to have a word with Charon about the security. "Stole it from where?"

For the first time – ever, Sorrow realized – he looked contrite. "I might have had to hit someone. And tie him up. And leave him in an alley."

"Luvian!"

He had the nerve to smile. "I missed that. Sorry," he added hastily when she glared at him, one hand on her hip, her eyes narrowed. "He's fine," he assured her. "He'll be fine. Besides, I had very little choice. It's not like I could have made an appointment to see you. Most of Rhannon is on the hunt for me."

"What did you expect after what you did?"

He frowned, and his hand moved to his pocket. Sorrow gripped the letter opener tighter, but all Luvian did was pull his glasses out, sliding them on and blinking until he focused on her. "I didn't do anything. In fact, it's what I didn't do that's the problem. But let me tell you about Beliss first, that's more important." He paused, waiting for her to nod her agreement, before continuing.

"After I ran, I disappeared into Rhylla. I went to Beliss's house, like we planned. I . . . I thought if I could get her to admit Mael was an imposter, you'd forgive me."

"Did you get her to admit it?"

"She's dead."

Sorrow hadn't expected that. She leant on the desk, her mouth open. "Her too?"

"Quite," Luvian said. "That makes Corius, Gralys and Beliss. The only three people, besides Vespus, and Mael himself, who might possibly have proven it was a lie, are dead, all within the last few months. Coincidence, no?"

Sorrow shook her head. Of course it wasn't a coincidence. Vespus. He had to be behind it, tidying up loose ends, in case anyone went looking.

"So there's no one, save Vespus, who knows the truth? We can't prove it. He's got away with it."

"Yes... But I think I've answered another question. It concerns him. And I do have proof. Or at least, evidence that can't be ignored."

Sorrow raised her brows.

He took a step towards her, pausing when she brandished the letter opener in warning. Moving slowly, he crossed to one of the tall-backed chairs and sat on the arm. "I met some Rhyllians, in the woods, while I was trying to decide whether to come back to tell you about Beliss. Youngish nobles, on some kind of camping-cum-hunting trip. They either didn't know who I was, or didn't care, and to be honest, I didn't care either, so when they invited me to join them around their campfire, I did. We ate, and then someone got a bottle out. Starwater. And ... I tried it. I'm not proud," he said quickly. "But things were a bit bleak. You hated me; my glorious plan to win you back was in tatters. So I had some. And I promptly passed out, and woke up about four hours later to find I'd had a nosebleed in my sleep, and everyone else was unconscious too."

He reached into his pocket and took out a glass bottle, standing and crossing to the desk, placing it between them.

It was small, the base round, and there was a white powdery substance crusting the bottom, and marking a tideline around the long neck.

Her hand darted out for it, snatching it back. Careful not to look away from him, she pulled the cork from the top. The smell hit her at once, that acrid, sweet burn that caused pain to lance through her skull, making her eyes water. Lamentia.

She held the bottle at arm's length and he took it back, replacing the cork she'd dropped on to the desk. Her headache began to ebb, and she stared at Luvian.

"This was what the Starwater was in. I drank from this very bottle. But when I woke up, it looked like this." He held it up so she could see the white powder residue. "My guess would be that the alcohol in Starwater evaporates over time, when it's exposed to air, and this is what's left. It's Lamentia, isn't it?"

Sorrow nodded, unable to take her eyes from the bottle.

"Which means Vespus, as the only farmer of the Alvus tree, is the person behind Lamentia and introducing it to Rhannon. It can be no one else. He's behind Lamentia. Technically, he killed your father."

She'd forgotten about Lamentia since Harun had died. It seemed it had vanished from Rhannon. She blinked, his words ringing in her ears as her brain caught up with them. Vespus had given Harun Lamentia. Vespus had made him an addict. Vespus, Vespus, always Vespus, making the world into a circle so it didn't matter where you turned, there he was, always ahead, always following. Sorrow wasn't naive enough to pretend Harun was much of a father, or chancellor, before Lamentia, but after...

She'd been right, back at the Summer Palace. He'd brought

Mael back, and then killed Harun so he could move him into place.

Luvian was watching her with wide, hopeful eyes.

"How do I know you're telling the truth?" Sorrow looked up at him. "How can I trust you, after what happened? For all I know you've added Lamentia to some old bottle and you're saying it's Starwater to – wait—" She stopped as she remembered something. "Come with me," she said hurriedly. "Don't try anything stupid, just walk with me."

Luvian gulped, but nodded, putting the bottle back in his pocket as Sorrow palmed the letter opener, so the blade lay flat against her wrist.

Sorrow gave him a searching look and then made her way to the library door, opening it. Luvian followed her, back along the corridor, into the main hall, and up the staircase. He kept his head down, trying to keep up with Sorrow, who'd practically broken into a run.

"Walk in front of me," she ordered, and he did, listening to her whispered instructions of where to go.

She guided him into the east wing, along to her suite of rooms, through her parlour, her private dining room, and into her bedroom.

"Get over there." She pointed to a corner. "Stay there."

Reluctant to turn her back to him, she crossed to her travel case and dragged it around so she could still see him as she threw it open and began to ransack it.

Dresses she'd packed but had no plans to wear, laundry from their time travelling Rhannon that there had been no time to do, books, cosmetics, shoes, papers, all became an untidy mound on the floor as she tore through the trunk.

She pulled a small bag from the bottom, and Luvian

recognized it. It was the one she'd had with her the night she fought with Rasmus in Rhylla.

"I never unpacked," Sorrow said. "After we got back I just ... I left it. When we started visiting the towns, I threw what I needed in on top." She opened the bag and pulled out the flask of Starwater Rasmus had left with her. The contents were still liquid, protected by the darkness, and by the cork she hadn't removed, clear, oily-looking, when she held it up to the light. Sorrow carried it to her dressing table, taking the lid off a powder compact and pouring in enough to coat the bottom.

"We'll see what happens when it starts to evaporate," she said. "And in the meantime, you can tell me exactly who you are, who the man who tried to kill me was, and how you know the Sons of Rhannon."

"I don't want you to hate me," he said.

Sorrow said nothing, ignoring the flare of guilt as his face fell, reading from her silence that it might be too late for that. She didn't know how she felt about him. A little scared at that moment, and a lot betrayed. But hate? No. She didn't hate him.

"Just tell me," she said, though her voice softened a fraction. "We can deal with how I feel afterwards."

He nodded, his expression still crestfallen, as he sat on her bed without asking. "Well, to begin, my name is Luvian, but it's not Luvian Fen." He paused, taking a deep breath before he said, "It's Luvian Rathbone. And the man who tried to kill you is my brother, Arkady."

Sorrow stared at Luvian. Rathbone. The family in Prekara who gave Kaspira so much trouble. Who'd given all of Rhannon some trouble or other for at least the last century.

Her grandmother had told her tales of the Rathbones, from when she was a young woman. Stories of smuggling and black markets, knives in backs, and high-stakes gambling behind closed doors. How Andearly Rathbone had broken into a museum in the East Marches and, over the course of two years, had stolen over three million rals' worth of artwork from storage. At his trial he'd lamented the fact he wouldn't have been caught at all, had he not gone back to swap a portrait of a young woman for one his new wife had requested instead. He'd made the court laugh when he'd told them he didn't see the problem, given they were only taking up space in a warehouse, and that he'd installed a whole bunch of new gaslights in his home to best showcase them. The dowager had smiled faintly as she'd told the story, and Sorrow had suspected her grandmother had more than a small crush on Andearly Rathbone.

He'd said in Ceridog that his grandfather had been a lover of art. He hadn't lied about that, then.

But they weren't all charming rogues. Jeraphim Rathbone – who Sorrow realized must be Luvian's father – had been sentenced to his second term in prison six months ago, for almost beating to death two members of the Decorum Ward. Sorrow remembered because Kaspira had mentioned it at the first Jedenvat meeting Sorrow had attended, Meeren Vine waiting outside, calling for the blood of all the Rathbones. Sorrow had privately thought it was about time the Ward had a taste of their own medicine, but was wise enough to keep her mouth shut.

Sorrow shook her head. "*You're* a Rathbone?"

He looked a little cross. "Yes, all right. I know I don't fit the profile."

He really didn't. Nothing about her articulate, urbane advisor suggested it. The Rathbones were muscled brutes, by

413

all accounts, with a punch-now-ask-questions-later approach to problem-solving. No one could ever accuse Luvian, who was never happier than when verbally sparring, of being that. Thugs, liars, thieves, pickpockets and fences, an entire family of criminals, who, with Jeraphim indefinitely jailed, were headed by...

"Your mother is Beata Rathbone," Sorrow said. Rumour had it Jeraphim was not the one to administer the beatings, but had taken the fall for his wife, who wasn't born a Rathbone, but embraced her new name vigorously. The whispers Sorrow had heard from Irris were that Jeraphim offered to take the fall, for the respite a spell in prison would offer him from the formidable matriarch.

"Yes. That's Mummy."

"And your brothers are—"

"Lawton, Sumner, Arkady. Then me."

"Arkady tried to kill me?"

Luvian's cheeks darkened, and he nodded. "I expect it was him who broke into your room in the North Marches too."

Sorrow swallowed, her fists clenching, before she continued. "Were Lawton and Sumner with him that day in Prekara?"

"Sumner is in prison. Murder. But Lawton was probably there. He usually does what Arkady tells him to. Most people do; he's very, ah ... persuasive."

"Did you know they were going to be there?"

"No." His eyes locked on to hers. "If I had, I would have stopped them, or I would have stopped you from going out there. I swear to you. The first I knew of their being part of it was that night. And if I'd known they were going to try to hurt you, I would have reported them myself."

He didn't break eye contact with her at all while he spoke. He didn't fidget or shift or blink. There were no tells to say he was lying. But he was a Rathbone. Beata probably trained them to suppress their tells from birth.

"You didn't know they were part of the Sons of Rhannon?"

"We're not exactly on speaking terms right now," he said, pushing his glasses back up his nose.

"Why not?"

Luvian sighed. "My nickname, coined by my charming mother, is 'runt'. A bit because I'm the youngest, and the smallest, and probably the weakest, at least physically. You saw Arkady; there are mountains in Asha that aspire to be as big as him. He ought to have his own moon. And I've always been a bit – no, I'll be honest – a lot smarter than most of them. But not in a way that counted. So, as a last resort, my mother allowed me to apply for a scholarship, under her grandmother's maiden name. I was supposed to study law, so when one of my idiot siblings or cousins got caught in the act, I could get them off the hook. Doing my bit for the family. But in my second year I switched to politics and didn't tell them until I graduated. Then I applied for a job working for you. It didn't go down well. You being the enemy, and all."

"Is that why they came after me, more than Mael? Because of you?"

"Probably. But they'd have gone after him, eventually, once you'd been ... erm, eliminated." His cheeks darkened with embarrassment. "My family never liked your grandfather, or father. Reuben tried his best to crack down on them, and things got a lot harder for us – them – after the Decorum Ward were introduced. Father used to be able to grease the palms of the old police force to look away. But it didn't work with the

Decorum Ward. They wanted too much up front, then wanted a cut, wanted to be part of it. They wanted to run things, and didn't like being told no. Mother wouldn't stand for it. Father tried to smooth things over, but not Mother."

"So she, what? Convinced Arkady to form a gang of vigilantes to attack the Decorum Ward?"

"Knowing her – knowing them – yes. With Father imprisoned for attacking them, it seems likely. She'd want to retaliate. Not a lot of people would choose to ally with a Rathbone, even against the Decorum Ward. But the Sons of Rhannon ... a mysterious, anonymous group who fight the bullies... That's a little more appealing. And forming a secret society he can be the head of is a very Arkady thing to do." He looked for a moment as though he might spit on the floor, his lips pursing, his tongue running over his teeth beneath them.

"You don't much like your brother, do you?"

Luvian looked at her. "Let's say you're not the first person whose head he's held underwater."

"Wow," Sorrow said softly. "Sorry."

"Don't be. He was good enough to only ever do it in clean toilets."

It was supposed to be a joke, a classic Luvian quip, but it fell flat because of the way his shoulders hunched as he spoke. Sorrow didn't like it, it wasn't the Luvian she knew, and a new burst of anger at Arkady Rathbone surged through her, not only because he'd hurt her but because he'd hurt Luvian too.

"He loves me, in his own way," Luvian said softly, breaking into her thoughts. "If he didn't, he could have easily overpowered me in Rhylla. He didn't have to run. I think we all know it's a fight I wouldn't have won."

"They haven't bothered me since," Sorrow said. "I thought it was your doing."

Luvian shook his head. "They're probably waiting to see if I'm going to hand them in."

"But you're not?"

He swallowed. "Do you want me to?"

He was offering her the choice. If she said yes, he would. She could see that. Because he wanted her to trust him, because he felt guilty for what had happened.

"No," Sorrow said finally. "But if you could somehow ask them to stop trying to murder me, I'd like it."

"Done."

Sorrow closed her trunk and sat on it, looking at Luvian, who looked right back. He could be lying. He was bred to lie. And to cheat, and to trick. He'd probably learned to pick locks before he learned to pick his nose. She knew he had no problem committing crimes, despite distancing himself from his family. He'd broken into the registry in Rhannon, and he'd stolen Mael's portrait from the Summer Palace – despite only ever going there once for his interview.

"Why didn't you tell me on the night?" Sorrow asked. "When Arkady attacked me. Why didn't you say then who he was? Who you are?"

"Because I didn't want you to look at me the way you're looking at me now," he said. "I liked it when you looked at me like a person. A friend. I liked..." He fell silent and shook his head. "I thought if I could help you win, then it would mean something. It would prove I was more than my blood. And it's what you wanted too – to be more than just another Ventaxis. It felt like fate. Like I was supposed to do it. I didn't want my family messing things up. But they did anyway. They always do."

417

His words were so close to her thoughts about herself that she had to stop herself throwing her arms around him and telling him everything was fine. It was only remembering Dain that kept her from doing it. If he'd been honest from the start, Dain might still be alive. No matter how much Sorrow wanted to put the last few horrible weeks behind them, she couldn't keep from seeing Dain's hopeful expression as she'd offered her a new life. Dain had trusted her. And Luvian, and it had got her killed.

As though he could sense her thoughts, he stood slowly and walked over to her, kneeling in front of her.

"I shouldn't have lied to you. It's the thing I regret most in the world, and I will carry that guilt for ever. My only defence is that you wouldn't have hired me if you'd known who I was. But –" the ghost of a smile played at the corners of his mouth, and something inside Sorrow loosened at the sight of it "– you can't deny I was a good advisor. And great company." His expression became solemn once more. "I won't lie to you ever again. I won't keep anything from you. I'm on your side, until the end. No more secrets."

It was Sorrow's turn to look away, scared he was going to ask her to promise, and knowing if she did it would be a lie, because she had a secret, something much bigger than his confession. It was that knowledge – that she too was lying about who she was in the hopes it would help her change things for the better – that made answering his next question easy.

"Can you forgive me?" he asked, hope scored across his features.

She nodded, and his face broke into a wide, beaming smile that made her heart flutter as her own mouth curved.

He reached for her hands. "Thank you."

She squeezed them lightly, and then, strangely embarrassed by his sincerity, stood, returning to her dressing table.

The liquid had almost gone, only the smallest drop remaining. But crusting the glass was a powder, one that Sorrow knew without smelling it, though she did, flinching at the familiar pain in her head. Lamentia.

Luvian joined her, saying nothing as they both looked at the powder.

"You should tell Lord Day," Luvian said. "This is enough to arrest Vespus, at least. The drug that killed the chancellor is the by-product of something only Vespus Corrigan can create. And he had almost unlimited access to your father. It's enough."

Sorrow shook her head. She'd had a better idea. "I want to know for sure whether Mael is or isn't a Ventaxis. With everyone else dead, Vespus is the only person who can answer. So I'll use this knowledge against him. Unless he tells me the truth about Mael, I'll tell Charon. And Queen Melisia."

"It's not worth the gamble," Luvian said. "Take it from me. Tell Lord Day."

Sorrow looked down at the powder and ran her finger through it.

"No," she said. "Not yet."

36

Daughter of Rhannon

He didn't try to persuade her, though his disagreement was obvious in the set of his mouth.

"When?" was all he asked.

"After the address to the Jedenvat," Sorrow said.

It was the final part of the election. Usually the candidate would present their mandate to the Jedenvat at the beginning of the election period. But this year the public vote would be split between two candidates. And in the event of the public voting evenly for Sorrow and Mael, it would be down to the Jedenvat to make the deciding vote. So this year, it had been decided they'd present to the Jedenvat at the end, giving both Sorrow and Mael a final chance to bring them onside.

"Are you ready for it?" Luvian asked.

Sorrow nodded. She was. Irris had worked with her as they'd travelled between public engagements, until she'd created something she thought would appeal to all of the Jedenvat – even Samad and Balthasar. They'd want to feel their positions were safe under her, and she'd tailored her address to that end.

Whether she meant it was another matter.

"That's politics in a nutshell." Luvian nodded approvingly when she told him. "Meaning it at the time."

"What do we do about you?" she asked.

"I want to come back," he said instantly.

"How, though?" Sorrow said. "I told everyone you knew who my attacker was. If you came back you'd have to confess."

He nodded, the light dimming in his eyes. "I could lie."

"And say who?"

"Meeren Vine? You hate him, I hate him, my family hates him. Everyone wins."

"I would have recognized Vine," Sorrow reminded him. "And it would be too easily disproved."

"Oh. Yes." Luvian licked his upper lip as he nodded. "So, impossible, then."

Sorrow reached out and squeezed his hand. "We'll think of something."

He laced his fingers through hers. "You don't know how happy I am that there's a 'we' again." Then the sincerity turned wicked, his eyes glittering as he said, "And you are too, admit it. You missed me."

"I did no such thing."

He stepped closer. "Yes, you did, come on now. Life is more fun with me around. Say it. Say, 'I missed you, Luvian'."

"There is no way—"

"Say it. . ." He took another step, bringing their eyes level. "For me?"

"You're not going to shut up until I do, are you?"

He shook his head.

"Fine. I missed you."

His lips curved into a wicked grin and Sorrow laughed. His gaze dipped, resting on her mouth, and the mischief lighting his eyes faded, becoming something else.

"You should get back to your party," he said slowly, meeting her eyes once more. "It's been over an hour. You'll be missed."

He let go of her hand, and Sorrow's palm tingled at the loss.

"Yes, you're right," she said, filled with the urge to clear her throat. "What will you do?"

"No idea." He frowned. "I can't go home. I guess I'll hide out somewhere until we have a better plan. Fortunately for us, evading capture is in my blood." He paused. "Sometimes, at least. Let's hope I have better luck than my father and brother."

"Do you need anything? Money, or. . ."

Luvian shook his head and reached into the same pocket he'd pulled the bottle from, revealing a large gold pocket watch. "You hate Lord Balthasar, right?"

She laughed again, and his face contorted, moving between smile and frown.

"I should—" he began, but was cut off by the sound of a door banging. The outer door to the corridor.

Sorrow turned to Luvian in panic. "Hide," she hissed, throwing herself on to the bed. Luvian dived under it, and a moment later, when Irris and Arran Day, followed by a contingent of guards, flooded the room, Sorrow sat up, blinking and rubbing her eyes.

"I only meant to lie down for a moment," she said, thickening her voice.

The guards shook their heads and filed out, muttering to themselves, and Arran looked at his sister, who shrugged, before leaving too.

Irris waited, suspicion clouding her features, as Sorrow swung herself off the bed.

"What's going on?" Irris asked, once the door had closed behind them. "Why are you really up here?"

Sorrow crossed the room and picked up the make-up compact with Lamentia in. Silently she handed it to Irris, and watched as comprehension dawned on her friend's face.

"This is Lamentia. Why do you have this? Where did you get it?"

Luvian crawled out from under the bed. "Behold my redemption arc," he said.

Irris somehow managed not to scream, and Sorrow and Luvian explained, in rapid tandem, how he'd come to be there, and what he'd learned.

"You have to tell my father," Irris said immediately.

"That's what I said," Luvian agreed.

"No. Not yet. There's something going on between Mael and Vespus. That's who I was looking for when Luvian found me. I think maybe they've had a fight? But whatever it is, I don't want Vespus to know what we know while there's still time for him to fight back. I want him to think he's done it, and then I want to confront him. I don't want him to have time to plan, or run."

Irris nodded slowly. "That makes sense. In that case, perhaps wait until after the election?"

"Yes," Luvian said, his eyes lighting with a spark that Sorrow knew meant he was scheming. "That way, if you lose – not that you will – but if you do, you still have a way to discredit Mael, because of his connection with Vespus. You can still defeat them both. It's a back door. And I love a back door."

"Talking of which, shouldn't you be finding one?" Irris said. "We need to return to the party before someone else comes looking."

"You're right," Luvian said.

"So, after the election, we tell Charon about Vespus and Lamentia, and then confront Vespus?" Sorrow said.

"Agreed."

They left Luvian in Sorrow's rooms, returning to the party and mingling. Sorrow went out of her way to greet everyone, apologizing for her absence, summoning staff to supply drinks and canapés to the people she spoke to. She saw Luvian a little later, trying to sneak out, only to be furnished with a tray and sent into the crowd, and she tried to smother a smile, even as a frisson of alarm went through her. But no one recognized him, or even looked at him, hidden as he was by the camouflage of his servant's clothes.

She remained in the gardens until the last guest had left, waving as a local justice and her husband wandered tipsily towards the gates. Irris, Arran and even Charon had long since retired, and so Sorrow was alone, save for her guard as she returned to her suite.

She washed, and changed into her nightclothes, her childhood bed feeling unfamiliar now. As she lay on the pillow something rustled beneath her cheek, and she reached inside the pillowcase to find an unsigned note, telling her to watch for the "handsome moustachioed chap in red" at the Jedenvat presentation.

She smiled at the note, smiled into the dark. Luvian hadn't betrayed her. And he was back. Somehow, it meant the world to her.

Four days later, Sorrow waited inside an empty classroom in the University of Rhannon. Based in Istevar, the university was one of the oldest parts of Rhannon, established over seven centuries ago. It was Sorrow's first time there. The classroom was large, with wooden benches and desks set in a tiered semicircle around a small stage, where she now paced.

Irris had been sent to scan the crowd for Luvian, so Sorrow waited alone, save for four guards, two either side of the door, and two near the large windows at the rear of the room. Sorrow knew she was safe, given what Luvian had said about his brothers, but she was also keenly aware that this was the first time she'd be in public after the murder attempt, at a specific place and time. If Arkady and the Sons of Rhannon decided to attack her again, today would be a solid opportunity, albeit a difficult one.

There was a knock at the door, five taps, then two, then three, the code they'd developed to let the guards know not to swing freely when Irris returned.

She opened the door a moment later, and stepped into the room.

"Quite the crowd," Irris said.

"They're only here to see if I'm assassinated onstage," Sorrow muttered, sipping at the ginger tea Irris had given her earlier to calm her stomach.

"They're here because you invited them," Irris reminded her.

As well as the Jedenvat, the final presentation had – at Sorrow's request – been thrown open to the public. She argued that because the last one had been hijacked by the Sons of Rhannon, it was only fair they allowed at least some of the people to hear this one. Which was why Sorrow was pacing a room that smelled of old socks and ink, instead of in the Round Chamber of the Winter Palace.

"Anyone of note in the audience?"

Irris gave a small smile and Sorrow's heart lifted, but then a knock at the door sent her scrambling to her feet, upsetting the tea. Two of the guards moved to stand in front of Sorrow as the third opened the door.

A petite woman stood there, eyes wide as she took in the guards. "It's time."

The walk to the stage felt to Sorrow like a walk to the gallows, her heart ricocheting in her chest, a staccato beat that made her hot and then cold in turn. As she paused in the wings she closed her eyes, opening them again when a hand slipped into hers.

"Every single person in the crowd has been searched. There are palace guards in disguise, mixed in with the crowd, and obviously the Decorum Ward are out there," Irris said.

"Not Vine?"

"Not Vine. Everyone is from Dain's unit in Prekara. All of them trained by her."

It was a small comfort to Sorrow.

"I'll be right here," Irris said. She leant over and kissed her friend's cheek before adjusting the sapphire-blue tunic Sorrow wore over grey trousers. "And Luvian is front and centre."

"With a moustache?"

Irris smiled.

Sorrow took a deep breath and closed her eyes. She'd tried to tell herself that this wasn't that big of a deal, that the weeks travelling Rhannon and meeting with the people were more valuable, would have more of an impact on the election. But her body called her mind a liar.

Because this was where she had to prove she'd meant every word she'd said so far. Every promise she'd made, she had to reinforce. Every person she'd spoken to, this was where she'd show she'd listened. Here, in this ages-old institution, in front of a council of representatives, influencers, nobles and clerics, and citizens. Every word she said would be reported tomorrow morning across Rhannon. Every gesture, every pause. This was her best, and now only, chance to lay the ghost of Harun to rest and show that she could be the chancellor Rhannon needed. The only chancellor it needed. And she had no idea what Mael had up his sleeve.

Then someone was calling her name, and Mael's, the crowd was clapping, and she was walking onstage once more.

When she turned to acknowledge Mael, she gasped.

Four days previously, at the Gathering, he'd looked healthy and whole, if a little downcast. But the man who walked onstage now, grey-faced, shoulders rounded in, shadows beneath his eyes like bruises, looked as if he were suffering from a terrible illness. The applause died away as he reached the podium, and didn't wave, or look out at the crowd at all. What had happened to him?

Sorrow barely heard the announcer introduce her, and she tore her eyes away from Mael, and looked out into the crowd.

Luvian was sporting the most spectacular handlebar moustache she'd ever seen. It curled elaborately at the edges. He must have put it on after arriving; it was so clearly not natural there was no way the guards wouldn't have questioned it. He tipped her a wink, and she gave a surprised smile, looking out beyond him.

On a raised platform at the back, the Jedenvat sat, with Charon at the centre. Bayrum beamed at her, and Arran Day offered an indiscreet thumbs up. Balthasar scowled, and whispered something to Lord Samad, but it seemed the sand lord wasn't interested, as he waved him away. *Interesting*, Sorrow thought. Tuva Marchant gave her a firm nod. And Kaspira did the same. But before Sorrow could think about what it might mean, the announcer stopped speaking. It was Sorrow's turn.

"Good afternoon," she said, her voice echoing into the space. "My name is Sorrow Ventaxis and I'm here to tell you why you should vote for me tomorrow." She looked down at her paper, then out at the faces watching her raptly.

The speech she and Irris had written was detailed and concise, outlining every single promise she was making to the people. It was thorough and professional, laid out in the style that had been used by candidates for centuries. But it was bland and stuffy. Remote. It went against everything Sorrow had tried to achieve when she went out to meet the people.

"I'm eighteen years old," she said, ignoring the words on the page before her. "And I, like all of you, have spent the past eighteen years living in a country that knew nothing but grief and darkness. But I'm not like you. I grew up inside the walls of a palace; I didn't have to worry about food or money. I didn't have to raise my children not to smile, not to laugh. I didn't grow up fearing that the slightest wrong move might be interpreted as an insult, and fear I would be beaten for it. Whatever I thought I had suffered, you've suffered more. Hurt more. Lost more. And I can't undo that. I can't turn the clock back and right the wrongs Harun Ventaxis visited on you. Nor the ones his father did. In that, the Sons of Rhannon are right. The last century has seen Ventaxis after Ventaxis let you down." She paused. "Grind you down."

Across the room she saw Charon staring at her.

"I'm not like them," Sorrow continued. "I know it's an easy thing to say, as I stand up here, courting you. Trying to impress you because I want your vote. Why should you trust me? Why should you listen? You don't know me. But I want you to. And I want to know you. I've spent the past few weeks trying to meet you, trying to get to know you, and what you want. I know Arla Dove in Asha is frightened she'll die before she sees her great-grandson smile. I know Mael Braith in the East Marches can't imagine the sound of music. And I know a man who would have liked to be an artist, if Rhannon allowed the arts to flourish." She gave Luvian the briefest flicker of a glance at that, pleased when she saw him smiling up at her.

"I expect all of you have a story like theirs. Something lost to you. Opportunities you've missed, sacrifices you've made, seen loved ones make. You've all been asked to suffer so much. Today I was supposed to read out a list of things I plan to do for Rhannon, but I'm not going to. They're just words, and they mean nothing without actions. I want to be a chancellor of action. So here is my promise to you all: I plan to keep travelling Rhannon, to visit every district at least once every six months, more if needed, to speak to you. Not to my senators —" she nodded at the Jedenvat "— but directly with the people. I'm going to work with the Jedenvat to get to the heart of what you need, and figure out how we can raise the money for it without taxing you further. I want the museums to reopen, and the libraries. I want the universities to teach literature and philosophy and art and music again. I want to build relationships with the countries around us, and work with them to create more opportunities – things we haven't dreamed of yet: transport, tourism, science, medicine. And I'm going to listen to you and then decide what laws to change, or to make. I want Rhannon to be the country it should have always been. Because whatever else I am, first and foremost I'm the daughter of Rhannon."

She took a step back, and listened to the deafening silence that rang through the room, blood rushing in her ears as she took in the stunned faces below her. She'd gone too far.

She looked down at the paper, held in her trembling hand. Maybe it wasn't too late—

The room erupted into thunderous applause; the force of it jolted her bones.

Luvian's face was shining below her – she could already see the palms of his hands reddening from the force of his claps. On the platform Bayrum Mizil, Tuva Marchant and Arran Day had risen to their feet; Charon was sitting up tall in his chair, his hands raised over his head. Even Samad and Kaspira were clapping with more enthusiasm than Sorrow had expected. Balthasar alone remained still, but there was no surprise there.

Down in the audience the people clapped, on and on, guards and citizens daring to beam openly at each other. It was only when the announcer stepped forward that the cheers died away.

"Mael, would you like to present your plans to the people?"

He nodded absently, and looked down at the piece of paper in his hand. It was crumpled, gripped too tightly while Sorrow had been speaking, and she watched him smooth it out and scan the words. He opened his mouth once, twice, as though to speak, but no words came. Low murmurs rose from the crowd, the announcer cleared her throat, and Mael shook his head, before turning to Sorrow, his face expressionless.

"No," he said.

Then he turned, and walked off the stage.

Without stopping to think, Sorrow followed him, running to catch up as he tore through the corridors.

"Mael, wait!" she called.

He stopped so suddenly she almost crashed into him.

"Did you know that's the first time you've ever addressed me by my name?" He spoke without turning.

Sorrow faltered. "That can't be true."

"It is. Believe me, you notice these things."

There was an uncomfortable sensation in Sorrow's stomach. It was exactly as Harun had done to her. Calling her "daughter", never using her name.

She swallowed, trying to cover her sudden nervousness. "Is it? It's not as if we've had many chances to talk."

"We could have. I've tried to."

He began to walk away again, and Sorrow's unease grew.

"Are you. . . Are you all right?" she called after him.

He turned, and the expression on his face was so fierce, so twisted, that she took a step back.

"What happens to me, after you win?"

"What?" Sorrow was stunned. "Where has this come from?"

"Where do I go? I've been thinking about it, ever since the Gathering. The Winter Palace won't ever be my home, will it? You've made that very clear. You don't want me in your life. And Lord Vespus is done with me. He told me you're going to win. So, answer me. Where do I go?"

"He what?" Sorrow was stunned. "Mael. . ."

"Every time I have something it's taken away." He sounded like a little boy then, and something cracked inside Sorrow, shame spilling out of it. "I lost Beliss, and my home in Rhylla, and I thought it was all worth it, because I'd have a family here. Then my father died the day after – *the day after* –" he paused, pressing his palms to his eyes "– I met him. And Lord Vespus. . ." He paused, shaking his head. "And I have tried throughout all of this to build a relationship with you because I thought when it was over we. . ." He shocked Sorrow as he hit himself, one, two, three times in the face with the heel of his hand. "I thought I could come home. But it's like Lord Vespus says, I don't have a home. I'm nothing. I don't belong anywhere."

"Mael," Sorrow whispered, as her heart broke for him. And for herself. Because she realized then she'd behaved exactly as Harun had. All the fears of her bad blood stood manifest before her, broken by her. She was as bad as he was. "I'm so sorry. . ."

Footsteps behind made her turn, as Irris and Arta caught up with them.

When she looked back, Mael was gone, and Arta hurried after him.

"Come on, Sorrow." Irris took her by the arm and pulled her away. "Come on."

It Falls the Way it Leans

Sorrow didn't celebrate that night. Because the election was the following day, and the results would be announced in Istevar, they returned to the Winter Palace, but she declined Irris's suggestion that they order a lavish meal to her rooms, and instead she went straight to bed. The image of Mael's wretched, shattered expression wouldn't leave her; every time she blinked she could see it, the wildness there. The fear. Of being alone. Of having no one. Of being no one.

She'd done that to him. She, who knew better than anyone what it was like to mean so little to the people who were supposed to love you. But she hadn't done it alone. What had Vespus said to Mael to break him so completely?

How much of the misery all of Rhannon had suffered lay at Vespus's door?

It made her furious he was there, in the palace right now,

secure in his status as ambassador once more. Sleeping under her roof, in her country. *Not for long*, she thought viciously. At least, not outside of a jail cell. One more day. Then she could have her revenge.

A bird tapped her window and she got out of bed, opening it. The hawk remained still as she took the letter from the bag attached to its foot, and then vanished into the night.

She expected it to be from Luvian, congratulating her.

But it was from Vespus.

Come to my room, was all it said, signed with a neat V.

There were guards outside all of the wings, to prevent them from trying to get to each other. But she could use the passageway. And she wanted to. She wanted to lash out. She wanted to let Vespus know he wasn't as clever, or a sly, as he thought. That he didn't have all the aces.

She didn't stop to think, quickly dressing in a tunic and trousers, and turning her lamp on. Then she disappeared into her wardrobe, opened the passage and vanished into it.

Sorrow realized as the bureau moved she didn't know which room was Vespus's, but a hunch saw her knocking lightly at the door of Rasmus's old room.

When it swung open and his father stood there, smiling as though she'd pleased him, she knew she was right.

He held the door open for her and she entered.

"Hello, Sorrow," he said once the door had closed.

"What do you want?" Sorrow wouldn't be polite. Not to him. Not any more.

He said nothing, moving to sit at Rasmus's desk, where he'd obviously been before she arrived. There was a single candle on the table, beside a crystal flask full of clear liquid and two tumblers. Vespus's eyes glittered as he looked at her.

"Won't you have a seat?" he said, his Rhannish as perfect as ever. "Can I get you a drink?"

Sorrow eyed the flask. "If it's Starwater, no, thank you." She didn't bother to use the Rhyllian form. "I'm aware of the consequences of it."

"Are you now?" Vespus smiled silkily.

"I'm not here to play games, Lord Vespus. I'm tired of games. I have a long day ahead of me tomorrow. So let's please not waste either of our nights with wordplay and sport. What do you want?" She said each word slowly, deliberately, holding his gaze.

"I want to make a deal with you."

Sorrow laughed. "Are you joking?"

"Not in the least." He poured himself a little of the liquid and drank.

"All right. Why?" she asked.

"You know why. A little bird told me you know." He smirked. "Land, Sorrow. I want land in the north of Rhannon. Specifically the North Marches. The soil there is of exceptional quality, the light is good, the weather fair, but not too hot, and it's close to the river. Irrigation would be easy. In short, the conditions are perfect for raising Alvus trees. Even someone without my ability could, with the right amount of expertize, do it."

"So this is all because you want to be a farmer?"

"You said no sport, Sorrow." There was an edge to his voice. "Do you know anything about the Alvus tree?"

She wasn't sure if she was meant to answer, so said nothing until he looked at her pointedly, then recited, "The wood makes exceptional musical instruments." When his eyes flickered to the flask, she continued. "And if the sap is fermented, mixed with water, and then distilled, it creates a liquid called Starwater, which increases the effects of alcohol, at least in Rhyllians. In others, it's intoxicating in a less pleasant way." She didn't tell him she knew about Lamentia. Not yet. She'd play that card only once she'd seen his hand.

"Very good. Well done, Sorrow. Well done."

"I also know your half-sister hates it."

"Because she knows what it can do. What it can really do, not what my idiot son and idiot niece achieve when they lace their champagne with it."

Sorrow frowned. "What do you mean?"

"You were there, at the Naming. You saw the Blessers, feted, celebrated for their special gifts. And you know that not every Rhyllian is born with an ability. It's down to fate, or nature. Or the will of the stars, if the old fairy tale is to be believed. Either way, there's no predicting who will or won't have one. Some families have no one with an ability; in some everyone has one."

Sorrow nodded.

"Starwater heightens abilities," Vespus said, picking up the flask. "Taken by anyone who has one, it enhances the power of it fivefold. It's not the effect on other alcohol that makes Rasmus and Eirlys giddy. It's power. They're drunk on their own power."

Sorrow remembered the party in Rhylla, the mania in Rasmus's eyes and how it had scared her. She was scared now, she realized, as the magnitude of what Vespus was telling her sank in. Enhanced abilities. "How do you know?" she managed.

"How do you think?" Vespus looked at her.

"You've been testing on people?"

"Myself, first. Then others, when I realized what was

happening. The same thing every time. That's the true reason Melisia hates it. Why she's not fond of me any more. Because it would be a political disaster for her if it got out. A race of people who not only have gifts beyond what their neighbours have, but who have the power to amplify them. You know the tale of Adavere and Namyra? Imagine that power, already strong, magnified. Or Eirlys's power with ice?"

Sorrow saw exactly why it would be a problem. It would be tantamount to painting a target across the entire country; weaponizing the people would make Rhylla a potential threat to every land in Laethea. Every country would be forced to take action to get reassurances from them that they wouldn't use it. Astria and Nyrssea would be in uproar if they found out. They wouldn't settle for promises, or treaties. They'd want all sources of Starwater destroyed, perhaps even calling for the imprisonment of Rhyllians with abilities.

Unless they tried to harness them. Kidnapping them. Buying services from less scrupulous Rhyllians. Like Vespus.

Melisia had worked her whole life to bring peace to Rhylla, and had finally secured it, only for her own brother to discover a way to make it impossible for ever if word got out. And Vespus wanted to use Rhannon as the farm to make it happen.

Vespus waited for Sorrow to look back at him, her mouth an "O" as wave after wave of horror engulfed her, before he continued. "And there are other gifts as well. Gifts we don't talk about. Gifts Melisia keeps hidden away, because it doesn't suit her ideas of how Rhylla should be. She's nice when she needs to be, my half-sister, but I didn't get my determination from my father. Melisia has her fair share, she's capable of making tough decisions too, when she has to."

He paused, clearly waiting for Sorrow to ask what he

meant, but she couldn't, the air squeezed from her lungs, her terror a corset ever-tightening as his words and their meaning battered her.

When she remained silent, he gave a light shrug, and continued.

"As Rasmus can heal pain, there are those whose touch inflicts it. Rhyllians who can project visions into the mind. Imagine what that would mean, when amplified? My half-sister works so very hard to make sure the rest of Laethea doesn't see us as a threat. Why? We are a threat. Stronger, faster, gifted. And we could be more, thanks to the sap of the Alvus tree. A tree that only I can grow with any real success."

Sorrow finally saw then why the land was so valuable to him. Why he was willing to try for decades to get it. Why he couldn't and wouldn't ever stop. "If you have better land, you can grow more trees. Make more Starwater. Sell it."

"More than that, Sorrow. Power. For every person like Melisia who thinks it's an abomination, two others will want it. Fight for it. Fight for me to grow it for them. And that's only the start. No one knows the full extent of what the Alvus tree is capable of," Vespus said. "Or most plants, for that matter. Did you know all medicine comes from plants? All of it. Imagine how much there is to be discovered. What if Starwater is the secret to unlocking abilities in all Rhyllians? What if a daily dose of Starwater in a pregnant woman guarantees a child born with an ability? At present less than forty per cent of Rhyllians have one. Perhaps I could make that one hundred per cent."

Sorrow knew then that she'd made a mistake. She should have ignored Charon's warning when they first met Mael, and contacted the Rhyllian queen with her suspicions about

Vespus. Melisia obviously had concerns about her half-brother's ambitions all along, if Sorrow had only reached out...

She looked at the Rhyllian lord, the confident smile playing at his lips, and something else occurred to her.

"Why are you telling me this now?" Sorrow asked.

"Because you are going to give me the land I want after you win the election tomorrow."

He said it with such certainty that Sorrow caught herself about to nod before she managed to stop herself. "You have no way of knowing I'm going to win. Mael might."

"No, he won't. We both know that now. And even if, by some miracle, he did, he'd hand it to you. All he wants is for you to love and accept him. He seems to think I'm the reason you hate him, and that's why you have such a troubled relationship. He's made it very clear that if he were to win, I wouldn't be welcome here because of it. So I suppose it's lucky for me now that he's not going to."

"That still doesn't explain why you think I'd give you Rhannish land."

"Firstly, because I know about you and my son."

Sorrow's skin flamed as her innards turned to liquid.

"Don't bother denying it. I know." His eyes turned to the bed, his brows raised, and Sorrow's face burned brighter.

"He told you?" Sorrow said. There was no point in lying if that was the case.

"Stars, no. He'd sooner betray his entire country than harm you. No, he didn't tell me."

"Then how?"

Vespus took another sip of his drink. "You never did figure out who your spy was, did you?"

A shiver ran through her as some instinct woke inside her.

Something slippery and loose: a warning. She'd walked into the room believing she had the upper hand, but right then she wondered what other cards Vespus held, that he was so willing to show her the ones he had.

"Who was the spy?" She fought to keep her voice level.

"Not who. What." He looked at her. "Not even a guess?"

Sorrow shook her head.

"You remember Aphora? Her ability is an affinity with birds. She can summon them, ask them to do her bidding. It's not all that uncommon, as abilities go. I bet you didn't know the idea for training hawks as messengers originated in Rhylla, did you? Because of the ability. It sparked an idea. Except Aphora can *speak* to the birds. And they can speak to her. They can tell her everything they see, and hear. . ."

In her mind's eye Sorrow saw her outside the inn in Rhylla, the very first time she'd met her. How the hummingbirds that had so enchanted her had gathered around the Rhyllian woman, like moons orbiting a planet.

Sorrow had another flash of memory then – the night at the ball, when she and Rasmus had so recklessly kissed right there in the Great Hall in Adavaria. The birds that had flown above them, jewel colours flashing through the vines.

"In the Rhyllian queen's home. . . Shame on you both." Vespus read her thoughts on her face.

But she was too busy sifting back through the last few weeks to rise to it. Every time they'd had the windows open in the North Marches. In Ceridog, when someone had somehow seen them holding hands – the swallows darting outside. Birds. Birds everywhere.

In the ambassador's palace in the castle complex. The window was open; she remembered the smell of the roses. . .

Charon had closed it, but what had they said before? She couldn't remember.

Sorrow's heart was beating so hard her chest hurt. "You have no proof," Sorrow said. "The twittering of birds, and the word of a lackey."

"I don't need proof. The mere idea would be enough to damage you beyond repair. And Rasmus would be arrested. Melisia loves the boy but, as we've established, she'll put her dream of some fictional, utopian Rhylla before anything else." He paused to laugh. "You've rather reminded me of her, with your antics over this campaign. But, yes, she'd arrest him. It would kill her to, but she would do it rather than risk being seen to be making exceptions for her nephew. And even if no proof is found, he'd be ruined just by the gossip. No one would want him near them."

"He's your son. . ." Sorrow said.

"Ah, but not my only one. Come now, don't look so shocked. You met Xalys. I could easily legitimize one of my bastards. After all, Harun legitimized Mael. . ." He raised his brows.

Was that it? Was this the truth, finally? Sorrow made a guess.

"He's not Mael, is he? And you killed everyone who might have been able to prove it, prove that you've been raising him for this all his life, not just the last two years."

"Please. . . Beliss was an old woman. She was my nanny, you know. That should tell you something of her age. Gralys was an artist. Who knows what she did in her recreational time? And as for Corius . . . well. . . Accidents happen. I'm sure anyone can fall down the stairs and break their neck."

"I know he's not the real Mael Ventaxis," Sorrow snapped. "Stop playing games and tell the truth. Who is he?"

Vespus laughed. "And give up one of my great joys?

Hearing about your attempts to uncover his true identity has been quite the tonic, Sorrow. So, no, I'm not going to tell you, either way. Think of it as a little insurance for me. I'm the only person on Laethea who knows the truth. Should anything happen to me, it'll die with me. Could you live, not knowing?"

"I'm willing to find out," Sorrow snarled.

He laughed, and Sorrow's fury mounted.

"You'll slip up," she warned him. "Sooner or later."

"Your grandmother didn't." Vespus smirked. "And I'm not as bad a liar as Lord Day."

Sorrow froze.

Vespus leant forward. "Yes, I know. The girl who should have been Sorrow Ventaxis died before she ever took a breath. You really ought to close your windows a little more. It might be hard to prove you've been bedding my son, based on the twittering of birds and the word of a lackey, but if we dug up the First Lady's grave, I would think the bones of the baby buried in there with her would speak loudly enough for everyone. I'll dig her up myself if it comes to it."

38

Chancellor Ventaxis

In that moment Sorrow realized he'd do it all, and more, to win. That he'd been playing this game for so long the idea of losing was unthinkable. No matter the cost, he'd keep rolling the dice until his numbers came up.

"Don't look so downhearted, my dear," he said softly. "Say yes, and all of this will go away."

Sorrow turned to him, mouth slack with despair, hysteria rising inside her. This couldn't be happening, it *couldn't*...

"I will tell no one about you and my son. Or that you are not in any way eligible to run for this election. Or that Lord Day has spent the last thirteen years lying to the entire country and covering for the Dowager First Lady's crime. In return, when you win tomorrow, you will invite me to stay on as the ambassador. You will, in fact, insist upon it. And then, a few months later, perhaps I will uncover a plot by Bayrum Mizil to overthrow you, and you will reward me by giving me his lands. All of the North Marches."

"But the people. . ."

"Sorrow, do you imagine I give a shit about the Rhannish people?" Vespus said. "Have I not made it clear that I don't care how I get the land, as long as I get it? How it happens, you can decide, if it makes you happier. Make up a disease and quarantine it, offer the people a financial incentive to move. Close down the facilities – schools, hospitals, workplaces – so they have to move. I don't care."

Sorrow could only shake her head. She couldn't do it; she'd promised she'd make things better. . .

"Perhaps I could sweeten the deal. Throw in my son for you too. Have him return with me, and you could go back to your illicit nights."

Sorrow gagged.

"He wouldn't object," Vespus spat at her. "He'd sooner whore himself for you than do anything else. And you won't object once he touches you. . . Like father, like daughter, I expect."

Sorrow's blood boiled at his words, both ashamed and furious that he knew how close she'd come to being addicted to the pain relief Rasmus's touch offered. Now, she decided. Now it was time to play her only card. Now or never. It was all she had.

"I know you brought Lamentia to Rhannon," she said, fighting to keep her voice steady. "I know it's what happens when Starwater evaporates. I know it all."

"You do, do you? Tell me, how did I get Lamentia into the chancellor's hands, while I was in Rhylla, living a highly visible life at my half-sister's court, or on my farm?"

"You had an agent," Sorrow guessed.

Vespus rolled his eyes. "Obviously. Who? Come on, Sorrow... Who arrived in the Winter Palace mere months after I left, at exactly the same time Lamentia appeared... Another clue? Your family killed his, a long time ago, when they made their grab for power. If it wasn't for you Ventaxises, he might have been a prince, or a duke. One more ... he especially hates you, after you locked him away while his wife died."

Balthasar. Of course it was. He came from nowhere and won her father's favour almost overnight. With Lamentia. How had she not seen? How had Charon and her grandmother not seen?

"He's been waiting a long time for his revenge on your family."

Sorrow locked eyes with Vespus. "I'll reveal it. I'll say you made up this lie about me, about my grandmother, because I uncovered the truth about Lamentia. I'll force Balthasar to testify. Everyone will know it's your fault the last chancellor died."

"No one in their right mind is going to begrudge me that, Sorrow," Vespus sneered. "He was hated. Besides, in order for you to do that, you'd have to admit you knew about Lamentia all along. As did your grandmother. And the Jedenvat. You'd have to confess that you all conspired to cover up the chancellor's addiction, while the Decorum Ward ran amok and Rhannon crumbled. No one will care where it came from. Or how I managed it, despite being back in Rhylla. They'll be too busy burning your palaces to the ground and slaughtering the nobility. Again. It's already begun, hasn't it? The Sons of Rhannon... Well, they do say we're all doomed to keep reliving the past." His smile was slick. Victorious.

She had no choice. The realization was almost freeing, the band around her ribcage loosening. She couldn't beat him. Even if she fled, he could reveal what he knew and bring Rhannon to its knees. He'd find a way to get the land, one way or the other. He wouldn't stop. But she might be able to protect her people if she agreed to his terms. She'd be able to shield them a little, at least. And if she stuck close to him, watched him, waited. Bided her time as he had done, she'd find the chink in his armour.

"Well?"

She couldn't say it. Instead she nodded, a single, damning lowering of the head.

It was good enough for Vespus.

He held out his hand and she shook it.

"Until tomorrow, Chancellor Ventaxis."

She had no memory of getting back to her rooms. When Irris came to wake her the next morning she found Sorrow sitting on her bed, still wearing the clothes she'd worn the night before.

"Sorrow?" Irris rushed to her side. "What is it?"

But she couldn't tell her. Telling her would mean betraying Charon and revealing she wasn't Sorrow Ventaxis. Besides, what good would it do? Vespus had been plotting for twenty years, honing his scheme and moving the pieces where they needed to go. He'd sewn it all up so neatly that Sorrow, and Rhannon, were damned if she tried to retaliate. Retaliate *now*, she reminded herself. This wouldn't be for ever. She'd lure him in, wait until he was vulnerable and strike then. She'd learn from him.

Though even that seed of a plan wasn't enough to thaw the rime that had grown over her heart as she'd shaken his hand.

"Nerves," she ground out finally.

"You have no reason to be nervous. Today is your day. I know it."

Sorrow nodded, unable to speak.

She bathed, and dressed in the outfit Irris chose for her, a soft blue dress that fell to the floor, the same colour as the one she'd caught her grandmother holding up in front of the mirror all those years ago. She pulled a brush angrily through her hair, while Irris went to fetch the shoes that matched the dress.

Sorrow wished more than anything that Luvian was there. Perhaps she could confide in him... But no. He'd come to her because he wanted to be something other than what he was. He wanted something legitimate, and real. Something honest.

Words that could never be applied to Sorrow.

Sorrow threw the brush into the mirror, shattering it, causing Irris to run into the room.

"Sorrow? What happened?"

"It flew out of my hand," Sorrow replied in a monotone

Irris watched her for a moment, then moved to stand behind her. "Let me help you finish."

She brushed and painted Sorrow until she looked like a woman, not a hollowed-out doll. Then she left her, and Sorrow sank into a chair, staring into the distance.

The ballot had opened at six in the morning, and was due to close at midday. By six, the votes would all have been counted, and by nine in the evening the envelopes would have been delivered directly to the vice chancellor, and they'd know who the chancellor was. Sorrow stuck to her rooms, turning away the visitors who tried to see her: Bayrum, Tuva, Arran and even Charon. She sat on her bed, ignoring the frightened looks Irris kept giving her. There was nothing she could do, nothing anyone could do.

447

Unless she lost.

Vespus had convinced her she'd win; she hadn't even considered that she might not. She allowed that tiny possibility to unfurl, sifting through it. Again she wished she could speak to Irris; she was so much better at this than Sorrow was.

Think, she told herself. What would Vespus do if she lost? Would he still expose her, even though it would change nothing?

No, she decided. He'd want to hold on to the ace he held. Perhaps he'd try to use her to sway Mael instead. Could she flee then; would he allow it? He might. Exposing her would only weaken the Jedenvat, which would weaken Mael, and therefore him. That would be his very last resort; he'd only do it if he knew he'd lose, a kamikaze move to take them all down with him.

So if Mael won, she'd leave. Maybe Luvian would come with her; he didn't like his life in Rhannon any more than she did and he was still technically a wanted man.

"Sorrow? It's time," Irris said.

Sorrow looked up, bewildered. Time? But she'd only just sat down. . .

Irris herded her from the room and she saw the clock on the wall of her parlour. Half past eight. Had she eaten anything that day? She couldn't remember. She was like a shadow as she drifted behind Irris, as though if someone turned a light on her she'd be obliterated. The wood of the banister felt strange to the touch; her hand felt as though it was passing through it, and she had to concentrate on descending the stairs she'd known all her life.

The crowds outside the gates of the Winter Palace were five deep, the Decorum Ward fighting to keep them from climbing the gates. When they spotted Sorrow a great roar went up; she could hear them chanting her name, calling for the Graces to bless her.

It made her stomach turn.

Were her real parents out there, somewhere? Were they here today? Did they want her to win, the girl who had lived the day their daughter was taken?

"Sorrow," Irris murmured, urging her to where Charon and the Jedenvat were waiting on the steps of the Winter Palace.

The Jedenvat were dressed in formal robes – the first time Sorrow had ever seen them as such, out of their blacks. They looked fierce and proud, Bayrum in sapphire blue, Tuva in green, Arran in red, all of them smiling at Sorrow. Balthasar wore purple, and he smirked at Sorrow as she approached. Samad was in gold and he gave a curt nod; Kaspira in aquamarine also nodded, with a fraction more warmth.

Charon, dressed in a darker red than his son, his chair gleaming in the last of the sunlight, already held seven envelopes in his hands. The results. They would be opened live, in front of the crowd, and declared as they were opened. If there was an outright winner, if one of them had the majority of districts, the Jedenvat would have to do nothing but applaud. But if a district was tied, it would be down to the Jedenvat to decide. Sorrow and Mael would have to endure the entire process, winning and losing publicly.

There had never been a loser before.

Mael was already there, Arta beside him. Both men were dressed in blue, Arta whispering something to Mael, who seemed to be ignoring him. Sorrow tried to smile at Mael, but the muscles in her mouth wouldn't move and it wasn't as if he would have seen; he turned from her the moment he set eyes on her.

Sorrow looked away, searching the crowd for Luvian, but couldn't find him. Not as a servant, not as a moustachioed man. Not at all.

Someone handed her a glass and she drank the contents, barely tasting the summer wine. Irris frowned, and herded her to where Charon now sat with Mael at his right. Sorrow took up her spot on the left and waited.

"Are you ready?" Charon said in a low voice. Mael nodded stiffly, but Sorrow kept her eyes locked forward, looking beyond the crowd.

"Sorrow?"

"She's ready," Irris said.

Charon frowned, but began.

"People of Rhannon. You have cast your votes in this historic election. You have spoken and now will be heard. Without further ado, I have the results of the vote." He paused to open the first envelope, giving nothing away as he read it.

"The district of Istevar votes for Sorrow Ventaxis." His voice rang across the courtyard, and as it was picked up and carried, a great cheer rose up from outside once more. To Sorrow it felt like a knife to the heart.

Charon took another scroll.

"The district of the North Marches votes for Sorrow Ventaxis."

Again the rush of whispers as the news spread, and again a huge cry of joy.

Asha went to Mael, to no one's surprise, and Sorrow tried to meet his eyes to congratulate him. But he kept his gaze fixed on the horizon.

The East Marches went to Sorrow.

But then the tide turned.

"The district of the West Marches goes to Mael Ventaxis."

The hesitation was minor, but everyone close heard it, and Sorrow's head snapped up from where she'd lowered it. She turned to Irris, momentarily forgetting about Vespus. They'd thought the West Marches was a safe seat for her, Tuva had been one of Sorrow's staunchest supporters, and yet...

The tiniest spark of hope ignited in Sorrow at this unexpected development.

As expected, Balthasar's South Marches went to Mael.

It came down to Prekara. Kaspira had never truly liked Sorrow... And it was the home of the Rathbones. The birthplace of the Sons of Rhannon, and they despised her...

Over Charon's head she met Mael's eyes, and the two of them kept their gazes locked on each other as Charon reached for the final scroll.

"The district of Prekara goes to ... Sorrow Ventaxis."

The cheer was instant, deafening, and Irris hugged her tightly, holding her up as the Jedenvat all clapped and Charon beamed at her.

She'd won.

She'd lost.

From the corner of her eye she saw Mael walk away as people descended on her.

Bayrum Mizil had tears running down his face, beaming at her, as Tuva Marchant gripped her hand and thrust it skyward in victory. Arran Day was shouting something to her, his arm around his father's chair.

It was as though she was drowning on land; she couldn't move, couldn't breathe.

"She's in shock," she heard someone say.

Sorrow turned, looking for someone she knew, someone

she trusted, but there was still no sign of Luvian, and Irris had been borne away by those wishing to celebrate with them.

Then she saw him. Standing at the base of the steps, with ambassadors from Svarta, Skae and Meridea.

Vespus Corrigan looked up at her and smiled.

And Sorrow knew then, despite her attempts to tell herself she could fight back and that one day she'd defeat him, that the curse her mother had laid on her the day she was born had finally come to pass. To the people of Rhannon, and to the people she cared about.

Sorrow, for that is all she brings us.

The Ventaxis Dynasty

Former chancellor Reuben "Windsword" Ventaxis, *deceased*
Dowager First Lady, "Grandmama" *deceased*
Harun Ventaxis, chancellor of Rhannon
Cerena Ventaxis (née Mizil), former First Lady of Rhannon, *deceased*
Mael Ventaxis, *deceased*
Sorrow Ventaxis

The Jedenvat of Rhannon

Lord Charon Day, vice chancellor of Rhannon
Irris Day, acting senator for the East Marches
Arran Day, absent senator for the East Marches
Bayrum Mizil, senator for the North Marches
Tuva Marchant, senator for the West Marches
Kaspira Blue, senator for Prekara
Lord Eldon Samad, senator for Asha
Balthasar Lys, senator for the South Marches

The Rhyllians

Lord Vespus Corrigan, former ambassador to Rhannon, half-brother to Melisia
Rasmus Corrigan, attaché to Lincel, son of Vespus
Lincel, ambassador to Rhannon
Aphora, Lord Corrigan's lover
Melisia, queen of Rhylla
Caspar, consort of the queen of Rhylla
Eirlys, daughter of the queen of Rhylla
Baron Harcel Argus, friend to Eirlys

Others

Dain Waters, district commander of the Decorum Ward
Meeren Vine, captain of the Decorum Ward
Luvian Fen, political advisor
Arkady Rathbone, agitator

Acknowledgements

As ever, the first shout out is for my agent, Claire Wilson. I am a hideous person and she bears me with such generosity and grace. I don't deserve her, but the wonderful thing about brilliant people is their very existence encourages you to endeavour being worth them. I'll keep trying, Claire.

Thanks to Rosie Price and Miriam Tobin at RCW too.

Huge thanks to my trifecta of editors at Scholastic UK: Genevieve Herr, Jenny Glencross and Lauren Fortune. The world of *Sorrow* is so vast, and dense, and I wouldn't have been able to navigate it without your guidance. Extra thanks to Pete Matthews, for once again having to deal with when I try to out-copyedit him (I've literally just submitted my copy-edits, so I hope this massively public sucking-up takes the edge off a little...)

Playing the same old song for Jamie Gregory, in honour of ANOTHER exceptional cover. Five for five now. Thank you for always making my stories look beautiful.

Also thanks to Scholastic's finest: Lorraine Keating, Penelope Daukes, Roisin O'Shea and Olivia Horrox, for all of your hard work on getting my words out there into the world. Thanks to everyone behind the scenes who works so hard too. Thanks to my lovely author friends for the wine and the chats and the cry-laughing: Sara Barnard; Holly Bourne, CJ Daugherty; Katie and Kevin Webber-Tsang; Samantha Shannon; Alwyn Hamilton; Kiran Millwood-Hargrave; Anna James; Rainbow Rowell; Catherine Doyle; Moira Fowley-Doyle; Dave Rudden; and all of Team: Prosecco and Secrets. And also Team: Floored; Non Pratt; Lisa Williamson; Tanya Byrne; and Eleanor Wood. And to my new pal, Anna Day. I'm so lucky to know you all.

Always super special thanks to my best bro, Emilie Lyons. She's the Andy to my Paula, the Ricky Baker to my Uncle Hec.

Love to Sophie Reynolds; Lizzy Evans; Franziska Schmidt, and the whole Schmidt clan; Katja Rammer and the whole Rammer clan; Pam and Denis Lyons, and the Allports; Bevin Robinson; Hannah Dare; Neil Bird; Stine Stueland; Laura Hughes and Sara Scherbatsky; Asma Z; my brother Steven; Auntie Penny and family; Kelly; Tina and Craig; Billie; Auntie Cath, and Uncle Paul.

And thanks to you, if you're reading this. I don't know if this is the first book of mine you've read, but I sure hope it won't be the last.

Melinda Salisbury lives by the sea, somewhere in the south of England. As a child she genuinely thought Roald Dahl's *Matilda* was her biography, in part helped by her grandfather often mistakenly calling her Matilda, and the local library having a pretty cavalier attitude to the books she borrowed. Sadly she never manifested telekinetic powers. She likes to travel, and have adventures. She also likes medieval castles, non-medieval aquariums, Richard III, and all things Scandinavian.

She can be found on Twitter at **@MESalisbury**, though be warned, she tweets often.